The Magic Touch

Kelly Florentia

First published by Accent Press Ltd 2016

This edition published 2019

www.accentpress.co.uk

ISBN 9781786157225
eISBN 9781783757466

Printed and bound in Great Britain by Clays Ltd, Elcograf S.p.A

To Mum and Dad, with love.

Acknowledgements

Firstly, huge thanks to my husband Joe for his massive support and for being my number one beta reader; for listening to me droning on and on about my book, and for making me endless cups of coffee. Thanks also to my beautiful mum for her tireless reassurance and faith in me, and to my family and friends for their support and enthusiasm.

A heartfelt thanks to Margaret James for leading the way, for holding my hand, and for her endless help on my writing journey, and to Cat Camacho for seeing the sparkle.

And finally, many thanks to Katrin Lloyd, who has been an absolute pleasure to work with, and all the team at Accent Press for making the magic happen!

Chapter One

Things aren't always as they seem, are they? I mean, how often is an overheard comment misconstrued, a piece of hearsay taken completely out of context? And don't tell me you've never wanted to curl up and die the moment you realised you'd just fired off a text message or email to the wrong person. I'm still blushing from the last time I did that.

Mishaps and mix-ups happen all the time. And I've got to hold on to that thought, especially after yesterday morning.

I push the image to the deepest corners of my mind as I dial Caroline's number – she answers on the second ring.

'Emma! Hi, I was just about to call you. Literally, the phone was in my hand,' she squeals in her all-too-familiar cheery voice.

'Well, they don't call you psychic Caroline for nothing, do they?' I say, and we both laugh.

Caroline, my partner Harry's sister-in-law, is a professional palmist, and no, that's not the reason I'm ringing her. Honestly. No disrespect to her, but I'm not sure I believe in all that hyped-up psychic stuff. Don't get me wrong, Caroline is very good, very convincing. And she has given me some pretty accurate readings over the years, but as Harry keeps reminding me, she does know me well, and she's incredibly good at reading people. So no, I'm not after a reading. I'm just returning her call from yesterday morning.

'So, how're things?' Caroline asks.

'Great,' I say crisply. This is a complete lie. For one, I barely slept. How could I, with all those relentless thoughts tearing through my brain all night? I kept tossing and turning, my mind throwing thoughts back and forth like a ping pong ball at a finals tournament.

Staring into Harry's hostile back, I dozed off to the swishing sound of traffic and the delightful tweet-tweet of birds as dawn was breaking; only to be startled awake after what felt like five minutes, by a loud, annoying shrill. I reached out, clumsily searching for the alarm clock in a haze, eyes heavy, mouth dry. I stared at the clock until the numerals slowly came into focus – 7 a.m. I'd been asleep for two hours. I was alone. Harry had already gone without as much as a kiss goodbye.

'And you?' I ask politely. Caroline doesn't need asking twice, she's now gone into overdrive about her week's plans. I jam the phone between my shoulder and jaw, squat, pick up the laundry basket, and run up the stairs with it. The pain in my knee as I'm halfway up reminding me of yesterday's running injury.

In the bedroom, I grab the airer from behind the wicker chair. Perhaps I shouldn't grumble. I've got a nice home, a kind, hardworking partner. So we don't go out much and haven't had a holiday in over three years, but that's due to lack of finance, that's all. And Harry's heavy workload, of course; holding down two jobs is no mean feat.

Caroline is shrieking with laughter and I realise I've barely listened to a word she's said: something about a new app, clairvoyance, and a weekend away with Mas in Brighton.

'Emma, are you still there?' Caroline asks, clearly miffed.

'Yes,' I manage, 'it's just my knee. Go on, I'm listening.'

'Still aching from the dog action?' she giggles. This is true, but how the hell does she know? I was running along the pavement yesterday when a boisterous Labrador bounded towards me and jumped onto my chest, before thrusting its snout between my legs. In shock, I took a few hasty steps back and twisted my knee. 'I thought Harry sorted that out for you?' Caroline pauses, taking a sip of something. 'That's what he told me yesterday. Are you still in pain, then?' Ah, Harry filled her in while I was taking a shower. She and Harry have always got on well. I'd go as far as saying that I sometimes think she married the wrong brother.

'A bit, yes,' I explain, 'but it's starting to ease off. Harry thinks it might be an old injury.'

'You're so damned lucky, having a nurse on tap,' she groans. 'You really landed on your feet with Harry.' See what I mean? 'I know he hasn't got the business acumen that Mas has, but I'm sure he more than makes up for it in other areas.' She says the word 'areas' in a low, husky tone. I bet she's winking down the phone as well. Caroline always carries out gestures, even when you can't see her. 'Goodness, Emma, he's still *so* fit. Mas likes his moussakas and beer too much,' she sighs. 'Mind you, I'm one to talk. I almost broke the scales this morning.' She roars with laughter.

Caroline likes her food – especially the syrupy Greek desserts that Harry's mum often makes.

I glance at Harry's weights stacked against the wall. She's right about his fitness. At forty-five, he has the body and stamina of a man half his age. I'm sure a lot of it is down to all that cycling he does. But she's got the active sex life thing all wrong. I can't remember the last time we were intimate.

'I can't understand why you two still aren't married,' Caroline complains. 'How long has it been now? Seven, eight years?'

'Five,' I say, dryly. It'll actually be six in November, but I decide to spare her the details. I wish she'd give it a rest. In fact, I wish they all would. Why are people obsessed with me and Harry getting married, for goodness' sake?

'Well, anyway, we all think you're bloody mad. You could still have a baby if you get your skates on.'

'I don't think so, Caroline.' I laugh as I extend the clothes airer and lock it with my foot. 'I'll be taking the child up to bed on a stair lift.'

'Don't be so stupid. You're not even forty. Besides, lots of women have babies in their forties nowadays. Look at all those celebrities. And anyway, you're super fit with all that running you do; you'll sail through a pregnancy.'

'Caroline,' I wipe my forehead, feeling a trickle of sweat rolling down my lower back. Despite the rain, it's still twenty-seven degrees outside. But with September a week away I'm not complaining. We'll be back to shovelling snow off our drive before long. 'I know you mean well but...'

'You don't want to lose him, Emma,' she cuts in. My suspicious barometer goes from nought to a hundred in a matter of nanoseconds.

'What do you mean?' I can't hide the alarm in my voice.

There's a moment of silence, and then 'Oh God, Emma, I hope I haven't offended you.' I'm too stunned to answer. 'What I meant was... well... it's just that neither of you are getting any younger, are you?' I can almost feel the tension travelling down the phone.

'Has Harry said anything?' I ask accusingly. I know what this is about. It's because of what happened at their barbecue on Saturday.

'No!'

'Caroline!'

'OK, OK,' she says in the manner of a criminal being interrogated by the police. 'He just said something in passing, that's all,' she tuts, then sighs deeply. 'It's no biggie...'

'What did he say, Caroline?' My heart is rapidly picking up speed.

'Just that he felt hurt that you turned him down again, that's all.' I knew it. 'Em, he sounded quite upset.'

I take a deep breath and let out a long, loud sigh. Harry has asked me to marry him several times but I've never felt ready. Marriage is a big step, isn't it? People change when they get married, and I should know. I close my eyes briefly as a dark, thorny memory cuts through me.

And besides, with things being a bit stale between us lately, asking me to marry him in front of his entire family after we'd both consumed copious glasses of champagne (we were celebrating his nephew's place at Oxford) was neither romantic nor fitting.

'He told you that, did he?' I ask as I shake a wet shirt out furiously, phone jammed between my jaw and shoulder.

'Yes, when I called yesterday. We just got chatting while you were in the shower and I asked him if you'd said yes yet and... look, I'm sorry, Em. Forget it. Are we still on for tonight?' Caroline had suggested a girl's night out on Saturday and I'd agreed.

'Yeah, definitely.' I exhale loudly. I could do with a night out. 'I'm really looking forward to it, actually.'

'Great. Ola's up for it.' This is music to my ears. I haven't seen my lovely friend Ola since she got back from Marbella over a week ago. 'And Vicky said she might join us, too. You remember Vicky, don't you? The one with the young boy and twins?'

'Yes, vaguely,' I muse, hanging the last of Harry's vests onto the packed rail. 'She and her husband were at Mas' fiftieth, weren't they?'

'Yes!' she trills enthusiastically. Why do people do that; get all excited if you remember a minor detail about their lives? 'She hasn't had a night out in ages, either, so I asked her along. I didn't think you and Ola would mind.'

'No, that's fine, the more the merrier.' I stare out at the traffic swishing along in the rain, pulling my hair into a ponytail with one hand. My neck is damp, mainly from our heated conversation.

'And I'm really sorry about... you know...' Caroline falters, 'Bringing up marriage and everything. I know it's a sore point and it's really none of my business... so...'

'It's OK, Caroline,' I smile down the phone as I run down the stairs. 'I know you're only trying to help.' I wonder if I should confide my findings to her. I'm aching to tell someone, but I'm not sure I can trust Caroline. She may tell Mas, and that'll only make matters worse.

'He really is a great catch, though, Em.' Yes, he may be, but I'm not exactly a down and out, am I? 'I mean, don't get me wrong, I'm happy with Mas, but he's so different to Harry. Everyone says so. Harry's the brains and Mas is the brawn,' she laughs.

Actually, Harry's the brains *and* the brawn. Mas just got lucky when he took over his parents' restaurant. 'And he's always so bloody wrapped up in that business of his, he forgets I exist half the time. I keep telling him to slow down. He's at that dangerous age, you know.' True. Harry's always saying that most of the cardiac cases he sees are fifty-somethings who don't take care of themselves. Harry and I almost fainted when Mas announced that he was closing his restaurant for the night to celebrate his son's success. On a Saturday, too – his busiest night of the week. 'You'd think that after twenty years of marriage he'd remember our anniversary, wouldn't you?'

'Did he forget?' I fill the watering can at the sink, a yellow and blue novelty one in the shape of Cyprus, that Harry's mother bought me to remind me of her son's roots, even though he was born and bred in North-West London. 'He does work hard, doesn't he, Caroline? Probably got a lot on his mind.'

I never really got on with Mas. I can't stand his alpha male persona and he always complains that I'm outspoken, which I'm not. I just answer back, that's all, whereas everyone else seems to be in awe of him. He's never really liked me either, and makes no secret of it. He thinks that Harry's too good for a thirty-nine year old divorcee like me, and always makes snide remarks about my hair – blaming my flame-coloured tresses every time I confront or challenge him. My part-time job at the restaurant is purely for Harry's sake. As soon as I start bringing in my own money from my illustration business I'll never have to make a falafel again!

'Business is booming, isn't it?' I ask distractedly as I check my mobile for any messages. None. I toss it onto the worktop then sprinkle some water into the window box. 'Valentina and I had to make an extra batch of falafels last Thursday.' Valentina, Harry and Mas' auntie, is head chef at the restaurant and my boss. I'm the only other person who knows the secret recipe for her famous falafels. And I've been sworn to secrecy. 'It's our secret, Emma,' she said, pressing a finger to her lips. 'Don't tell a soul, not even Haritos or Marios.' She's also one of the few people who address Harry and Mas by their full Greek names.

'Yes, it's doing *really* well. Thank God,' Caroline says. 'How else could we put Andreas and Demi through university? And we are really grateful to you and Harry. I'd never have a holiday if it weren't for him. You know Mas doesn't trust anyone else.' Harry does the weekend shift just to make ends meet, but he also books time off work when Mas and Caroline go away. 'You both know that, don't you?' she says earnestly. 'I know Mas isn't very good with words.' He basically takes advantage of Harry's kind nature, often leaving him to run the restaurant while he goes off to run errands. But we're both grateful for our part-time jobs. We couldn't possibly survive without them. And Mas knows this only too well.

We end our conversation on the agreement that we'll meet outside The King's Head at 8.30.

I flick the kettle on and throw a teabag into a mug. That telephone call has got my mind ticking.

I lean against the kitchen sink, chin in hand, as the kettle starts to rumble. The exact spot where Harry and I stood cuddling yesterday after he'd spent forty-five minutes massaging and stretching the ligaments in my leg. Well, I say cuddling. I was actually all over him. I felt quite euphoric after I explained how I wasn't quite ready for marriage yet, because he seemed to take it in his stride, looked relieved even. I actually thought it must've been the drink talking at the barbecue.

'I know your family might not see it but I really do love you, Harry.' I said, stroking his face, '... and it's not a *no*, it's just a not now.'

8

I went on to explain how much he meant to me. I haven't told him that in, well, God knows how long. I said how grateful I was for all the sacrifices he was making to help me get my business off the ground. That I realised my freelance salary and two days at the restaurant didn't pay the bills. That I'd apply for a proper job somewhere if this extra work was too much for him. I didn't mind what kind of job it was, so long as it was full-time – anything, even stacking shelves in Tesco if need be. He laughed at my suggestion, tapping me lightly on the nose with his finger as if I were five years old, told me not to be so stupid, that he'd make sure I'd make it up to him when I became a famous artist.

I latched onto his back like an octopus, my arms tight around his trim, taught torso, feeling the leanness of his back and buttocks against my body as he filled the kettle at the sink. Then, taking in his familiar, comforting scent, I slid my fingers along the inside of his waistband, feeling the warmth of his skin. It was Sunday. I'd showered after my run. We could go back to bed, I thought. Rekindle the fire before it burns out completely.

'Emma,' he said softly, pulling my hand away, '... you know I'm on call.'

'I can't help it if you're so irresistible,' I said in a playful, disappointed tone. He looked over his shoulder at me then, a small, cheeky grin starting at his full lips, and I'm sure I saw a sweep of lust in his dark brown eyes, but then he turned his back on me and busied himself with the kettle. I knew in an instant that something wasn't right.

I held onto him as he moved around the kitchen, as if I was a ball and chain around his ankle. I wondered if I was. Did he see me as some heavy burden he yearned to be free of? Maybe that was the reason he was so aloof with me. Harry isn't the type of man who'd deliberately hurt anyone.

He'll just bottle things up, brush them under the carpet until they're forgotten. Or until I prise them out of him with twenty questions, which is what usually happens.

Of course, I know that Harry loves me. And he's the love of my life. My soulmate. But the question that was bursting to topple from my lips was whether he was still *in* love with me, whether he still found me attractive, desirable, sexy.

I'd been putting off asking him for weeks, afraid of what the answer might be.

Was he bored with me? Did he think our relationship was going nowhere? Was turning down his recent marriage proposal the last straw? Did that kill something inside him? Was that it? Did he think we wanted different things now? That our relationship had run its course? Or did he just not fancy me anymore?

I took a deep breath, ready to confront him, prepared to face the consequences head on. I opened my mouth to speak, but his mobile phone started to vibrate on the black granite worktop before merging with *Doctor Who*'s theme tune (he's a massive fan). He grabbed it urgently, saying that it might be important, might be the hospital. And the moment was gone.

Of course, that was yesterday morning before he ran out on call. Before he absentmindedly left his mobile phone on the coffee table. Before it rang with an unknown ID. Before I read the message that followed.

Chapter Two

I turn the key in the lock, Sainsbury's bags hanging heavily from my wrists as I shuffle into the hallway. It's just gone 5.00 so I've got a few hours before I need to get ready, but what to wear? Most of my going out clothes are in the ironing pile.

Harry's home. The music coming from upstairs drowns out the clank of the door as I press my back against it firmly. His bicycle is leaning against the wall, hogging the corridor. I frown at it as I work my way around the protruding front wheel, using the weight of the heavy bags as a balance. I drop the shopping bags onto the terracotta-tiled kitchen floor before shouting at the top of my lungs, 'I'm home.' I hate it when he leaves his bike in the hallway. I always manage to bash into it. Its usual home is the garden shed but I suspect he'll be using it tonight, which is odd because he's on earlies at the hospital this week.

The music fades. 'Up here,' he calls out cheerfully.

'OK,' I shout back. 'Do you want a cuppa?'

'Nah, I'm fine! Thanks!'

It's too hot for tea, anyway. I grab a glass and pour myself some water from the filter jug as the music resumes its previous thumping status. I finish my drink in two large gulps and then stare down at the tired, overfilled orange bags pooled by my feet. I didn't buy any chilled or frozen food – our freezer is jam-packed with leftovers from the restaurant – so unpacking can wait.

I grab Alistair's bag and force it into the bottom shelf of the fridge. Alistair just needed a few staples today; milk, bread, cheese, eggs, that sort of thing. But I popped in a packet of chocolate digestives as a treat. His pension won't stretch to goodies and I know how much he enjoys them, even though we are on a tight budget ourselves. I'll pop the bag next door to him on my way out later.

Upstairs, I find Harry in the hall in his boxer shorts ironing a shirt, Bazzi's 'Mine' blaring from his mobile phone on the docking station propped on the banister. He stops ironing, leans over, and switches it off before puckering his mouth at me. I smile. At least I know his mood has lifted. I move forward, my eyes not leaving his mobile as our lips meet. He tastes of mint. I avert my eyes to the bathroom and notice that the shower's been used. There are a few wet towels hanging over the edge of the bath and the sweet smell of lemon is slowly wafting its way to my nostrils.

'Going out?' I ask, rubbing my hand and trying to look nonchalant. The shopping bags were heavier than I thought and have left a deep ridge across my fingers.

'I'm working at the restaurant,' he replies cheerfully, throwing me a glance.

'What, on a Monday night?' I bite the inside of my lip, trying desperately to swallow the suspicion in my voice. He never works at the restaurant on a weekday, not when he's got a full shift at the hospital. And he *never* uses his special lemon shower gel for any old day – he saves that for dates with me. Or at least he used to when we actually had time for dates. That text message from yesterday, from that unknown ID, suddenly flashes behind my eyes and I can't help myself – thoughts of infidelity tear through my mind at top speed, each one chasing the other like a Formula 1 race car at the Grand Prix.

'Mas needs me to cover for him'

'On a weekday?' I protest. 'You've been on your feet for twelve hours.'

'It'll only be for a couple of hours,' he shrugs as he picks up the iron and shoots out a burst of steam onto the sleeve of the white cotton shirt. I notice immediately that it has his name embossed on the breast pocket in grey thread and the first letters of the restaurant name in large bold red beneath it – Meze at Sunset (an acronym of Mas's name, which he thought was very clever, and I suppose it is).

I raise an eyebrow. 'What's with the new shirts?' I peer over the ironing board. 'No one told me about a new uniform.'

'I only found out about them today. Mas breezed past the hospital for lunch and left one for me. It's only for floor staff, anyway.'

'Oh, I see.'

'Yeah, Demi's idea, she reckons it'll be good advertising.' I suppose Demi will be taking over the restaurant at some point. Mas can't go on forever, and her brother, Andreas, isn't at all interested in catering. Andreas is the academic one, more like Harry than his own father, yet at only seventeen Demi seems to have good business acumen. 'What do you think?' He holds it up against his toned, tanned chest. He caught the sun at Mas and Caroline's barbecue and it suits him. I gaze at his chiselled six-pack and strong shoulders.

'I suppose it'll make you all look smart.' I smile, nodding half-heartedly.

'Yeah, I guess so. It saves me having to wear my own gear, anyway.' He throws the shirt back onto the ironing board and runs the hot metal against it, this hiss of steam filling the already humid air with hot vapour mingles and mingling with the aroma seeping from the bathroom; it intensifies the smell of lemons, mint, and aftershave.

I frown, biting the edge of my nail as I glance at the phone again as if it's an evil entity containing information that's about to blow my world apart.

Despite the soft breeze coming in through the window I feel the heat on my face, the back of my neck. I might just jump in the shower now. Leave the unpacking in the kitchen until later.

'And you've got an early start in the morning,' I add as I kick off my shoes. 'Mas is a bloody slave driver. Why doesn't he just get Demi or Andreas to fill in for one night?' Obviously Caroline is no candidate as she'll be out with me.

'Come on, Em,' Harry says wearily. 'You know we owe him big time.' Mas lent us money when we bought our house three years ago. We were fifty grand short of the deposit. A hefty sum, I know. It was on a no interest, no strings, pay-back-when-you-can basis. They're a close-knit family and always have each other's back. But there are always strings attached, aren't there? 'We wanted a three-bedroom house with a garden, remember?' He's right. We could've bought a nice two-bedroom flat, and not had this huge mortgage and debt looming over us like a big, bruised, bulging cloud. But we were keen on a house with a little garden. I'm passionate about gardening and Harry's quite good at DIY.

'I imagine we'll be indebted to Mas and Caroline forever,' I grumble. 'We might as well have sold our souls to the devil.' I start unbuttoning my white linen blouse. I need to ask him about the text. It might be something. It might be nothing. There may be a perfectly good explanation for it – there probably is. But I need to know for certain. I wonder if now is a good time? I open my mouth to speak and...

'What are you doing?' He stops ironing and looks up at me, his thick eyebrows gathered worryingly, lining his forehead.

'I'm sweating buckets here, Harry.' I point towards the open window on the landing. 'In case you haven't noticed, it's boiling hot outside.' I glance over my shoulder into the bathroom. 'I was going to take a shower, if that's OK with you?' Clearly, he thought I had other ideas. His face muscles relax almost instantly.

'No... I...' he falters. Beads of sweat have formed at his greying hairline. He wipes it with the back of his arm. 'I just thought ...' He laughs nervously. This isn't like him. I know something's wrong. He's gone off me, I'm sure of it now. He's only sweating it out with me because we have financial obligations together. Oh God! He's met someone else younger and thinner, who'll marry him the moment he proposes, and who holds a full-time, well-paid job with maternity leave and can bear him six children.

'What? That I was after your body?' I snort. It's out now. I've said it. 'And what if I was?' I can't seem to stop myself. It's as if another entity has entered my body. 'We haven't had sex in ages.'

'I know.' He props the iron on its back then rubs his face with both hands, exhaling tiredly. 'Why's that?' He gives me a melancholy look.

'Well, you tell me, Harry.' I whip off my blouse, throw it over the bannister, then face him challengingly, arms outstretched like Lara Croft, ready for battle.

'We're always so tired, aren't we?' He picks up the iron again and I let out a little sigh of relief. At least he hasn't said that he wants to finish with me. Well, not yet anyway.

I shake my head in agreement. 'We should have a holiday,' he goes on. 'Get away from all this … this …'

'City madness,' I finish with a small smile. Perhaps he *is* tired. Maybe that's all it is. He does work hard, and I have got a bit of a colourful imagination. Ola has often said that with a mind as creative as mine I should been writing the books instead of designing the covers. 'That sounds like a good idea,' I say warmly. 'We should start saving. I could put a bit away each week. There are some brilliant deals on Groupon.'

'Yes, I suppose I could do a few extra hours at the restaurant.' I freeze as a zing of acid drops into my stomach. Extra hours at the restaurant? I thought he just said he was tired? I close my eyes and all I can see is *that* text message. I can't go on like this, questioning his every move. I need to ask him about the text. I brace myself, taking a lungful of steamy, lemon-infused air.

'Harry, I …'

'By the way, Ola called,' he interjects.

'Oh?' He's thrown me now. 'What did she say? Does she want me to call her back? Why didn't she call me on my mobile?' I fish it out of my pocket and see that I've two missed calls from Ola.

'She said she tried but you weren't picking up.'

'Oh,' I say, pressing the volume button. 'I had it on silent.'

He nods, smiling. 'And no need to call back, she just said she'll see you tonight. Something about a friend of a friend who's about to self-publish her novel and needs a good illustrator. Sounds promising, doesn't it? Money towards our holiday fund.' He looks up at me then, eyebrows raised, eyes bright, and we nod in enthusiastic unison. I do love him. I can't imagine my life without him in it. We need to fix this; I can't lose him.

16

The prospect of a proposed holiday and a new client has lifted my mood. I could do with the work; the last gig I had was over a month ago, and that was with Ola's help. Ola's a bookworm. Her Facebook friends consist of authors, reviewers, and avid readers, as well as some other friends and family, of course. The referrals always come in handy. I've had three so far.

'OK,' I say brightly. 'I'm sure she'll fill me in tonight.'

He smiles as he slides his freshly pressed shirt onto a hanger and props it onto the door. 'Do you need anything ironed before I put it away?'

I think for a moment, finger in mouth. I wanted to wear my blue flower print T-shirt, but didn't get round to pressing it earlier. 'Actually, yes, if you don't mind,' Our bare bodies touch briefly as I slip by him and make my way towards the second bedroom, to the pile of ironing on the armchair. As I shuffle through the laundry I hear his phone bleep with a message and my eyes widen. Silence. He's reading it. My heart picks up a little speed. I find the T-shirt and pull it out quickly.

'Can you press this for me, please?' I hand him the T-shirt just as he's replacing his phone back on the banister.

'Sure,' he grins, dropping his gaze fleetingly to my cream La Senza bra – a gift from him last Christmas with a matching pair of lacy knickers.

'Who was that text from?' I ask, curling my long fringe behind my ear, my breathing a little shallow.

'Mas.' He pulls my T-shirt over the body of the ironing board. 'Just to make sure I haven't forgotten about tonight.' I narrow my eyes. Why would he need reminding when Mas only told him about it this afternoon?

'Are you sure?'

He looks up at me with a puzzled expression. 'Yeah, I think so,' he says, a tinge of sarcasm in his tone.

'Or was it from someone else?'

'What?'

'The text message.' I nod at the phone.

'Yes, I know what you mean, Emma,' he says crisply.

'Well?' I demand. He doesn't answer. I lift the lid of the pine blanket box on the landing and pull out a fluffy blue bath towel. 'I hope you're not seeing another woman,' I laugh, trying to inject a little jest into my accusation.

'Yeah, right,' he huffs, shaking his head. 'Have you started on the booze already?'

I hug the towel to my chest, leaning against the coolness of the wall. 'Can I see the text, then?' I ask quickly, a hint of confrontation in my tone.

'Huh?' He stops ironing and looks at me. 'What's wrong with you, Emma? You've been edgy for days.'

'*I've* been edgy?' I lay the towel on the banister.

'Yes! You've been flouncing around with a face like thunder, giving me those looks.'

I take a sharp intake of breath. '*Me*?' He's clearly got this the wrong way round.

He starts ironing again, throwing my T-shirt around the ironing board as if it were a rag. I hope he doesn't burn it – I've only worn it a couple of times. 'Yes, Emma. You!'

'If you've nothing to hide then you'll let me see it.' I insist, puffing my bra-clad chest out.

I reach for the phone but he snatches it just before I do. 'Do I read your personal messages, hmm?' he asks, holding the phone above his head and out of my reach. I'm not short, but at six foot two he still has seven inches on me.

'Harry, I'm asking you, please,' I say tearfully. The fact that he doesn't want me to read it speaks volumes. 'Let me see it. Now.' Our eyes lock. 'I know it's from a woman. Don't deny it, Harry. I read the text she sent you yesterday.'

18

'You did what?' His voice almost breathless, his eyes darkening.

Chapter Three

I don't think I've ever sat in a pub on my own – a coffee shop, yes, a restaurant on the odd occasion after seeing a client, or when Harry's on lates and I can't be bothered to cook for one. But a pub? Never.

I take a quick look at my dodgy watch, giving it a bit of a shake. It's still running half an hour fast despite having changed the battery twice. It's only eight fifteen. I've been sitting on my own for half an hour and there's still another fifteen minutes to go until the others arrive.

I charged out of the house like a woman possessed, slamming the door so hard behind me that the entire house practically shook with my fury. I had to get out before one of us said something we may have regretted.

I hate rowing with Harry. And to be quite honest, during the last five years we've barely said a cross word to one another. But tonight was different. I've never seen him look so cross. And for what, because I read his text message?

I take a deep breath and stare around the pub, still reeling from our fight. I need to calm down, clear my head. It's quite busy for a Monday night; bustling, noisy. I wonder if we should've chosen a quieter venue, somewhere where we'd be able to hear ourselves think. I clear my dry throat to the dull, low beat of a rock song. I'm parched and tempted to buy a drink, but I don't like the idea of drinking alone. I drum my fingers on the table. There's only one thing for it.

I open my Ted Baker mock-croc black bag and locate my iPhone in the neat little compartment, inhaling the smell of new leather. Well, it is new. Practically – I've only used it twice. Harry bought it for my birthday last year. I told him not to spend a lot of money, that we couldn't afford it. But would he listen? No. I think it set him back about two-hundred quid. I zip the bag shut and place it next to me on the lime green, squishy bench where I can keep an eye on it.

I punch in my passcode as a whoosh of guilt weaves its way through me. He worked his butt off so I could have this leather luxury swinging from my wrist. Overtime at the hospital, extra hours at the restaurant. I love it, of course I do. But the trouble with giving me lovely, expensive gifts is that I hardly ever use them. I'm always afraid I might damage them.

I open Twitter and post several Tweets in succession.

Having a girl's night out in pub. Whoop whoop. #girlsjustwannahavefun.

Busy in King's Head for Monday night – thought there was a recession on?

Waiting for @caroline_33 and @olareynolds. Where are you?

Could murder a large glass of wine. NOW! #womancoulddieofthirstroundhere

I close Twitter as a roar of laughter from the depths of the pub fills my ears. I updated my Facebook status when I first got here –

Feeling happy (with a smiley emoji) *at King's Head Pub, Crouch End.*

I wonder if anyone has sent me any replies yet. Yes. I grin at my screen as if it's an old friend. There are four little red alerts on the corner of the icon, which I can't possibly leave for later.

The first one is from Ola –

What you doing there already?

I smile at that. I can't wait to see her, tell her all about what's been going on in my life while she's been sunning herself in Marbella. The second and third comments are 'Cheers' and 'Chin-Chin' from Facebook friends I've never met, but seem nice and friendly. I've got over 500 friends and my list is growing. I accept all of the friend requests I receive. I need to raise my profile as a freelance illustrator. Social networking has been a godsend. I've already had a couple of recommendations from satisfied customers. They've even shared the images of the book covers I designed for them on their timelines, and I've received great feedback too. Result!

I scroll down the page. My friend Reeva has just uploaded a video of herself doing a belly-dance at a Lebanese restaurant last night. I've just got to watch this. I tap on the screen and she starts shaking her booty. This girl has no shame. I laugh out loud, forgetting where I am, then look up quickly to check if anyone's looking. A man leaning against a deep red pillar gives me a wry grin and I feel my cheeks tingle. That's the trouble with being a redhead – every single emotion shows on my face, however small. I pull a little 'eeek' face at him then dip my head and start tapping at the screen.

I've got to leave Reeva a comment, this is just a classic. I type out –

Hey, good mover. At pub in Crouch End, come over!

I wish she'd join us, but I know she won't. She only lives on the other side of London, but it might as well be another continent.

Apart from Ola, Reeva is the only friend I'm in contact with from school. We lost touch somewhere along the way, but then she looked me up on Facebook. I was divorced by then and had changed my name back to King, and we haven't looked back since.

Oh, she's replied.

Ta, my lovely, but having dinner in town. Next week maybe?

I'm about to reply when I see a hand curl around the top of the chair opposite. I look up, finger still hovering over my iPhone. It's the man that was leaning against the pillar.

'Hello,' he smiles. 'Would you mind if I …?'

Oh God, I think I've pulled. I focus on two loud couples in the alcove nearby, clinking their glasses and laughing, then avert my attention back to him. 'Er, actually …' I cut in, screwing my face up apologetically, 'Sorry, but I'm waiting for some friends.'

'Erm …' He scratches his short beard, then looks around the pub as if searching for an answer in the crowd. He's young, much younger than me, by ten years at least, and very good looking. I don't defy the feeling of smugness that washes over me at being propositioned by such a young, hot guy. And particularly as my partner seems to have gone off me. I give him a reflex scan. He's wearing a

23

short-sleeved blue linen shirt that shows off his impressively strong forearms, and expensive-looking blue jeans held up by a worn leather brown belt. His tanned hand is still clutching the top of the chair, the other carrying a small Carphone Warehouse carrier bag.

'I was going to ask if I could borrow this chair? I'm just over there.' My eyes follow his hand to the small, round table next to mine. It has a pint of beer on it and a packet of cigarettes. A dwarf chair with a leather jacket draped haphazardly around it, almost touching the stripped floorboards, is half tucked beneath it. 'Just bought a new phone,' he explains, 'and wanted to open the box on a dry surface. The table's all sticky and grimy,' he scrunches his nose. 'Unless you're expecting a large group, that is?' He waves his big arm around expressively and I wonder if he's of Italian decent. He definitely has the striking, strong features. ''Cos if you are, I'll just ...'

It's a fair question. I'm sitting at a table for at least eight. I nabbed our favourite table – the one with the lime green sofa-style seating at the far end of the pub – the moment I arrived.

I feel like a complete idiot. I've gone red. I know I have. My face is boiling hot and despite the air-con being on full blast, my top feels like it's welding to my back.

'Oh God,' I say eventually, a gormless smile starting at my lips. I move forward, pulling my slightly damp T-shirt away from my skin. 'I'm so sorry.' I stand up, although not quite sure why, it's not as if I'm going to physically carry the chair to his table. 'Yes, yes,' I wave a hand, 'of course, take it.'

He grins, nods in gratitude, then spins the chair to the next table. How could I have been such a bloody fool? Of course he wouldn't want to chat me up. I gaze around the crowded pub. Not with all these twenty-something lovelies, who look like they've just stepped out of one of those glamorous online casino ads.

I swallow hard, regain my composure, and go back to Reeva's post, blinking back tears of humiliation to the loud babble closing in around me. I start tapping at the keypad, but I can't help listening to the crackling of bubble wrap as he unpacks his phone. I look up briefly and give him a quick smile.

'A funny text from your boyfriend?' he asks, pulling a shiny new phone out of the box. Boyfriend? Most people assume I'm married with kids.

'No, I'm just on Facebook,' I reply, waving the phone in my hand. I don't bother to tell him that my *boyfriend* is at home, probably still fuming after our row and possibly packing his bags to leave.

'Ah,' he pulls out some accessories and starts fiddling with the phone, 'I'm not into all that social networking stuff, but my ex-girlfriend used to live on Twitter.' Ex. Hmm, I see he managed to drop that in quite casually. But he doesn't fancy me. He can't. Why would he, when he can have the pick of any one of the women in here? And besides, I'm definitely not interested. I'm happy with Harry. We'll get through this blip. We'll sort it out, I'm sure. I don't want another man, and certainly not one as young and fit as this one.

'Oh, I see.' I scroll down my page lazily. 'I quite enjoy the interaction, but mostly I use it for work.'

'Yeah?' He frowns as a woman's hysterical laughter tears through the air. We both cringe as if her voice is a flying missile shooting over our heads. 'What do you do?'

'I'm an illustrator. Book covers, that sort of thing.'

He nods, impressed. 'I love books. Reading them, that is. Enjoy it?' He switches on his phone and the large, bright screen illuminates his flawless face.

'Yes, when I can get the work. I'm just starting out as a freelancer.' I glance quickly at the time on my iPhone. It's almost half eight – they should be here soon.

He narrows his eyes. 'Do you know what? I think I know you from somewhere.'

'Really? I come here quite often,' I offer.

'No, no, not from here.' He holds his chin.

'It must be off the telly, then.' I toss back my hair theatrically, staring up at the round, 70s-style glass lampshade. God, this pub could do with and update.

'You're on TV?' he squeals, clearly impressed.

I can't lie to the poor boy. 'No, I'm just kidding.' We both laugh for a few moments, his deep blue eyes twinkling mischievously.

'I've got it,' he says excitedly, clicking his fingers.

'Oh?'

'What school did you go to?' This man is insane if he thinks we were in the same school year.

'Not around here.' I unzip my bag and slip my phone back into its compartment. I'm not going to tell him how old I am, if that's what he's fishing for.

'Ah, I've got it,' he wriggles his fingers in the air quickly. 'You remind me of that actress. What's her name now?' He covers his mouth, narrowing his eyes.

'Angelina Jolie? Scarlett Johansson? Elisabetta Canalis?' I smooth down my hair in mock vanity.

'Nah, none of those.' I thought not. 'It's that ginger one.' He pulls an apologetic face, 'Eeeek, sorry, force of habit, hope you don't mind.' Mind? Why would I? I've had a lifetime of being called ginger nut, ginger minge, carrot head. You name it, I've been called it. 'Although I do love redheads.'

'Fiz from *Corrie*?' I suggest hopefully.

He inhales deeply, as if meditating, eyes closed. 'Julianne Moore!' He opens his eyes and points his finger at me, as if he's just answered the final question on *Eggheads*. I smile. I've been told this once or twice before. Only I'm nowhere near as beautiful. 'Only younger and fitter.' He takes a swig from his pint glass. A charmer, I see. But I'm too long in the tooth to fall for that line. 'Can I get you a drink or anything?' His accent is local, bordering Cockney, clearly a Londoner.

'No, my friends should be here soon.' I glance at the entrance. 'They're a bit late, but we'll be getting a bottle of something once they get here. Thanks, though.' I smile warmly.

'S'OK.' He takes another mouthful of beer as I look up at a couple of thirty-somethings who've just walked in. He's got one of those mod hairstyles and she's sporting a blonde beehive – obviously retro fans. They look at me and murmur something to each other. They probably want to sit at my big empty table. My companion's voice averts my attention. 'You wouldn't mind doing me a favour, would you?' he asks a little sheepishly.

'Depends what it is.' I fold my arms as the retro couple shuffle off to the bar.

'I've just got this.' He holds up his phone. 'Would you mind calling it so I can see if it works? You can hang up the moment it rings so you won't use up your minutes or anything.'

I shrug, 'Sure. What's the number?' He calls it out and I punch it in. It rings almost immediately and I end the call.

'Ta,' he says cheerfully. 'It's a replacement. The last one gave me so much trouble, kept cutting out and wiped all my contacts. At least I know this one's working.'

'Emma!' Ola has arrived. I stand up and we hug tightly for a few seconds. 'Why did you get here so early?'

'Because I missed you so much, obviously!'

She smiles and looks at the young man with the phone. 'And this is?'

'Marc.' He half stands, reaching out for her hand, very gentlemanly.

'Marc, hello. I'm Ola, Emma's other half.' She winks at me and his face drops. Ola lets out a loud belly laugh, hands on hips. 'Oh, relax, we're besties.' I grin at Ola roguishly.

He joins in the laughter, and says 'It's just that I very rarely get it wrong.' He gives me a flirty look over his pint glass and I look up at Ola quickly, my cheeks tingling. Ola raises her eyebrows. That girl is so sharp, she doesn't miss a thing.

'So, it's Emma, is it?'

'Sorry,' Ola says, sliding into the seat next to me and pulling her cross body bag over her head. 'Have you two just met?'

'Yeah,' Marc smiles. 'Emma kindly helped me set up my phone and I've been keeping her company until you arrived.' He takes another swig from his glass. 'You're late, by the way.' Ola pulls a face at him cheekily. She's such a flirt.

'Emma! Ahhh! Olaaaaa!' Caroline has arrived with Vicky. We're all standing up, hugging, kissing, all talking at the same time. Marc downs his pint and stands too, and as we continue to giggle and exchange preambles he gives me a little wave and a small smile as he slips away.

Chapter Four

'What?' Ola stares at me, mouth agape. 'Harry? An affair? Are you nuts?'

'Shhhh.' I grab her bare arm, glancing quickly in Caroline and Vicky's direction. 'Keep your voice down, will you?' Although I'm not quite sure why I just said that given that the place is heaving, and Caroline and Vicky are at least twenty feet away immersed in conversation at the bar.

'What did the text say exactly?' Ola says, concerned. 'Your hands are freezing, by the way.' I release my grip. Ola's looking nice and casual in a khaki vest and black skinny jeans.

'It said, "Thanks so much for the other night" with a kiss at the end.'

'Is that it?'

'What do you mean, *is that it*?' I hiss, glancing again at Caroline and Vicky, who are now leaning against the bar waiting to catch one of the flustered staff's attention. 'What more do you want? I said it was a text, not a sext.'

'Oh, for heaven's sake, Emma.' Ola throws her hands up. 'That could be from anyone. I thought you had hard evidence.' She smooths down her jeans and glances around the pub as my phone pings. I ignore it.

'This *is* evidence,' I retort. 'One text I might've been innocent, but two! I doubt very much the one that pinged through earlier was from Mas. I think Harry was lying to me.'

'Emma.' Ola looks at me silently for a while with a small, incredulous smile. 'So, did Harry say who the text was from?' She tilts her head to one side and bites on her lips, clearly humouring me. My phone pings again.

'A colleague, apparently.' I wave a hand, glancing out of the window at the Costa on the corner. 'Someone he helped out, they swapped shifts or something.'

'Man or woman?'

'Man.' My phone pings. 'So he says.'

'It's perfectly feasible, Emma.' Ola rests her elbow on the large wooden table, twisting her slender body towards me to another ping from my phone. 'I think you may have misconstrued the message. Are you still having trouble sleeping?' We both look up momentarily at two men who've just sat down at Marc's empty table with two pints of Guinness.

'Ola, I'm not imagining it. It was there in black and white.' White and green, actually, but you know what I mean. 'And what bloke puts a big kiss at the end of their texts, anyway?'

'John does.'

'Yes, to you! His wife.'

'Fair point.' She juts her lips thoughtfully, staring into Caroline's back, who is now chatting to a sweaty, distressed-looking barman. 'Adam always ends his texts with a kiss,' she muses.

'Adam's an old friend, that doesn't count. Anyway, I bet he doesn't put kisses at the end of his texts to his male colleagues.'

'Yes, but how do you know that this nurse didn't just accidentally put a kiss at the end of his message without thinking? I put a kiss at the end of a staff email last week.' She shakes her head, smiling. 'I've been the butt of their jokes all week,' she says to a sequence of pings from my phone. 'Emma, can you get that please, it's starting to get on my nerves now.'

I snatch the phone from my open handbag as if it's an annoying pest. Nine Facebook notifications. 'It's just Facebook,' I say scrolling through my newsfeed. 'I commented on a friend's post earlier, she won some kind of photography award and now she's bombarded with well wishes.'

'Oh, God, I hate it when that happens. I sometimes don't bother commenting to avoid all that harassment. Just unfollow the post. I always do.'

I switch my phone to silent, telling her that I'll do it later. 'Oh, I dunno, Ola.' I rub my eyes, forgetting I've got make-up on. 'It's all such a bloody mess.'

'What, like your face, you mean? You look like a little panda.' Ola searches inside her bag then pulls out a tissue. 'Lick,' she demands, pressing the tissue against my lips. I do as I'm told.

'I mean, the text, the marriage proposal,' I drone as she rubs a little harshly around my eyes with the tissue. 'Our dwindling sex life. Ouch.' I pull away, feeling my right eye tearing with pain.

'Sorry. If you'd keep still, I'm almost done.'

She dabs at the corner of my eye as I ramble on about our troubles. How suffocating it is living on a tiny budget every month. How we barely have time for each other these days. That I can't remember the last time we were intimate.

'Is that why you don't want to marry him?' She scrunches the tissue and puts it back into her handbag. 'Because of the sex blip?'

'No. Yes. Oh, I don't know.' My brain feels frazzled, I can't think straight. 'He was half-cut when he proposed at the barbecue, and he seemed to take it well the next day when I told him I wasn't ready. A bit relieved, actually.' I stare sadly into the distance. 'I think he just got caught up in the moment, what with all his family being there. Although according to Caroline he was quite hurt.'

'Because if it *is* the sex blip,' Ola goes on, ignoring the latter part of my reasoning, 'I wouldn't worry too much about it. It happens after years of being together. John and I sometimes go for weeks without sex.' She leans back into the squishy seat, folding her arms.

'What? But you're PE teachers,' I exclaim. Surely they must have bags of energy. I look at her toned arms and legs. 'You're fit,' I say, almost accusingly. Although Ola and I both wear a size twelve, she's far more toned than I am.

'So? That doesn't mean we're at it twenty-four seven, you know. We've got Ben to look after, and he's getting lots of homework now he's in year five, not to mention his after-school activities. Then there's Eric to walk twice a day. The house, our jobs. By the time we settle down in the evening we're bloody well knackered.' I give her a small, dubious nod, my right eyebrow raised. She has a point. 'I must say,' she goes on, 'the holiday did help.' She grins, gazing into space. I know that look and I do miss it, but I'm not sure Ola is getting this. It's not just the lack of intimacy that's worrying me. I feel as if we're drifting apart.

'So, how was the holiday? Apart from the great sex, that is?'

She breaks from her lustful reverie and looks at me. 'Really good, actually, except for John getting sunburn, as per. I did tell him to use the high factor I bought for Ben, but you know what men are like.' I nod in agreement. 'I spent most of the time hiding under an umbrella with my Kindle. He's still red now. He looks like a cooked lobster.' She bursts out laughing, and I can't help but laugh with her.

'Don't talk to me about sunburn. I learnt the hard way, remember?'

We giggle as we discuss a holiday in Ibiza years ago where I ended up with sunstroke. I even had to go into the sea wearing a T-shirt. I can still feel the pain now. 'Maybe that's what you two need,' she says, wiping away tears of mirth. 'A romantic weekend away somewhere – reignite the passion.' She nudges me with her arm playfully. 'Make up for all those lost weeks.'

'It's been a couple of months, Ola, not weeks. Besides, it's not just about the sex,' I protest. 'I'm not a sex maniac, you know.' She arches an eyebrow and I slap her lightly on the arm. 'It's just not like Harry, that's all.' I shake my head, staring at Vicky and Caroline fighting over the bill. 'I get that he's tired. We both are, for heaven's sake. I mean, I'm not up for it every night. I know I only do two days at the restaurant now, but I'm on my feet for ten hours each time. Then I've got the household chores, my book illustrations, building up my business. It's bloody exhausting.' Ola nods in agreement. 'It's just these last few weeks ... something's changed,' I go on. 'He's withdrawn, disinterested, preoccupied. I talk to him but his mind is somewhere else – or on someone else.' I run my finger along a long dent in the veneered table. 'And now these text messages. I mean, why was he so cagey over them? I just don't know what to think.' I look up at Ola. 'Something's not quite right. I'm sure he's seeing another woman.'

'Emma, if he's having an affair then why would he ask you to marry him?'

'Because he was drunk? Because he felt guilty?' I thrust my palm out for effect. 'Oh I don't know,' I sigh. 'I think that maybe Harry *does* want to settle down.' I rest my elbow on the table, chin in hand. 'And his parents constantly nagging him to set a wedding date doesn't help. They're old school, you know what they're like. They want us to have a lavish wedding with a religious ceremony and five-hundred guests. I did all that the first time around, there's no way I'd do it again. It was like a bloody circus.'

Ola nods thoughtfully. 'Harry's a decent guy, Emma.' She twirls a heart-shaped necklace between her purple manicured fingers. I blink as I try to focus on it. It's very pretty, silver and embedded with tiny diamantes. I haven't seen it before. John must've bought it for her in Marbella. 'He wouldn't cheat on you,' she insists, shaking her head defiantly. 'You've just slipped into complacency, that's all. Welcome to my world.'

'Hmm, maybe,' I say, rocking my head from side to side. 'Look, I'm not saying he's fallen in love with someone else or anything but something's changed in him. I think he's bored of me. Of *us*.' I shake my head. 'And he's started to take a lot more care of his looks – that's a sign, isn't it? I even caught him eyeing up that Just for Men colourant in Sainsbury's last week.' I hold my head in my hands. 'I can't go on like this, Ola.' I look up at her with teary eyes. 'What should I do?'

'Emma, listen to me, you've got a solid relationship with Harry. Stop winding yourself up, for God's sake. He might just be having one of those mid-life crisis thingies. If he said that the text was from a colleague then I believe him.' She pauses, letting go of her pendant. 'Maybe you should give him a chance. If marriage is so important to him ...' She hesitates, curling a strand of loose hair behind my ear. 'Would being Mrs Georgiades really be such a bad thing?'

'You know how I feel about marriage.' I push my hair off my face, holding it back for a few seconds in frustration. Ola, of all people, knows what I went through during my marriage to Carl.

'I know, honey, of course I do. But Harry's different. He's not like ...' She falters, her back stiffening against the seat. '*Him*, is he?' Ola can't even bear to say Carl's name. And who could blame her?

'I know, I know.' I exhale loudly, resting my elbows on the sticky wooden table. 'It's not that I don't want to. I just don't feel that now is the right time,' I say. But, deep down, I know that there may never be a right time for me; that I've been there, done that, and bought the T-shirt. But Harry's never been married and I know he craves that family unit. That seal. That union.

'Flipping hell,' Caroline says, putting a tray of four glasses and a bottle of red wine onto the table. 'Talk about a long queue, and they've only got two bar staff on.'

We're on our third bottle of merlot. I feel slightly giddy, but relaxed. Somehow Ola has managed to calm me, as always, helped me to see sense. Perhaps I did overreact over the text. It might well have been from a grateful colleague. I used to get them all the time when I was working at the advertising agency. I mustn't be so suspicious. If Harry says it's from another nurse then I believe him. Why on earth shouldn't I? What's wrong with me? I shake my head. I hope Harry isn't going to be too pissed off with me when I get home. I did go a bit overboard with the accusations. All that door slamming and stomping around in fury was enough to wake the dead. I take a sip of wine. I'll apologise when I get in, for accusing him of cheating and for reading his messages. Then we can put it all behind us and start planning that holiday. We need to make a few changes; get our relationship back on track. Spend more time together.

'Caroline tells me you're going out with her brother-in-law,' Vicky says, her soft voice breaking my thoughts. She's a good-looking girl – mid-thirties, slim, tanned, and confident.

'Yeah, Harry.' I smile as I take another sip from my glass, feeling a warm glow at the mention of his name on my lips.

'Must be lovely going out with Greek guy,' she says, smiling. 'His parents own some land in Cyprus, don't they? Just think, you might be able to build yourselves a holiday home out there one day. I love Cyprus. My parents-in-law actually own a house in Larnaca. They live there a few months of the year,' she nods, glass in hand, one leg crossed over the other. 'We just got back from visiting.' That explains the tan, then. 'Cyprus is a beautiful island, isn't it? Great food, friendly people.' She draws her legs in as a young couple rush past, giggling, hands all over each other.

'Yes, I hear it's gorgeous.'

'What, you haven't been?' She grabs my hand, astonished.

'No, not yet. We keep meaning to,' I say over the noisy group of young people who've been sitting at the next table for the last hour. I don't tell her that we can barely feed ourselves these days, let alone afford a holiday abroad. Yes, Harry's parents own some land in Cyprus, but they don't have a luxury home we can stay in rent-free. We'd have to cough up for a hotel. The flights alone would cost a fortune. 'Maybe next year,' I say loudly, holding my throat. If I'd known it'd be this rowdy tonight I'd have turned up with a megaphone. I've now developed a sore throat, having spent most part of the evening shouting like a manic football fan at a finals game.

'Hey, Emma,' cries Caroline. 'I was just telling Ola about my new psychic app. Download it, then wait a few weeks and give me a review.'

'Yeah, OK,' I yell over a blare of voices. 'What's it called?' The nearby group have started singing 'Happy Birthday' to a blushing student-looking girl.

'The Maaa ...' Caroline begins, just as the crowd scream out *'Dear Maddyyyyy ... Happy Birthday ... '*

'What?' I holler over the noise. I unzip my bag and fish for my phone so I can log it into my notes.

'The Mmm ... chhh.' Well, I missed most of that.

'What did she say?' I turn to Vicky. 'Did you catch it?'

'The Magic Touch,' Vicky shouts as the crowd starts clapping. 'Impressive, isn't it? Hope it's a success. She is very good. She did a reading for me a few weeks ago, said she could see sun, sea and a long journey. I told her there'd be no way we could afford a holiday. The next thing I knew, our in-laws surprised us with tickets to Cyprus.' She nods approvingly, then drains her glass. 'Though with three kids, a husband, and a flat, I haven't got time for entertainment apps.'

I log it into my phone and nod at Caroline. 'The Magic Touch,' I holler, and she gives me the thumbs up. 'I'll download it tomorrow.'

'OK.' Caroline raises her glass as the group of people settle down, some disappearing off to the bar and toilets. 'Thanks for that, Emma. If you just open it and touch the screen lightly, then let it read your fingertips. Once a day would be fab, if you can remember.'

'Sure thing, Caroline,' I grin. 'I'm looking forward to it.'

Harry's already in bed by the time I get home. He left the hall light on for me, bless him. I shower, remove my make-up, slap on my anti-wrinkle night cream, and slip into the cool sheets next to the love of my life. When I switch off my bedside light, I feel him reach for me in the darkness, his mouth close to my ear. 'I'm so sorry, babe,' he muffles into my hair. 'I didn't mean to shout at you.' He's kissing my ear. 'I hate it when we fight.'

I turn and face him as my eyes adjust to the darkness. I can see his profile now. The outline of his thick, wavy hair, his strong jaw line, his slightly curved nose.

'No, I'm the one who should be apologising.' I reach out and push my hand through his soft hair. 'I'm sorry I didn't believe you, Harry,' I kiss him lightly on the lips, 'and I'm sorry I read your texts.'

'No, no it's my fault,' he says gently, dropping soft kisses along my jawline. 'It's the stress of work.'

He's on top of me now, hard against my thigh. I close my eyes as he plants kisses along my collarbone, feeling the gentle scratch of his stubble against my skin. Then as he moves further down, a rush of excitement tears through me. I ache for him. I swiftly whip my camisole off, our mouths lock, and we kiss urgently. He tastes of peppermint, fresh and delicious. As he traces his soft lips along my neck, I run my hand up his firm bicep, tugging at his boxers. And then his phone bleeps with a text. My heart lurches in my chest. Who would send him a text this late? He ignores it, runs his hand slowly up my thigh, his mouth is on my breast, and then …

'Oh, Harry, stop it. I can't.' I push him away and he turns on his back, breathing heavily. 'I came on this evening.' And I did, suddenly, just before I went out. I think it was all that anger and stress that brought it on ten days early.

We both catch our breath, and he pulls me into his arms, and we lay together in the still of the night, silently staring into the darkness. I smile contently. He wants me. We're back on track. Then as I close my eyes, it suddenly dawns on me that in my haste to leave the house earlier this evening I left my tampons on the edge of the bath. But the packet was in the cupboard when I got home tonight. Harry knows I don't like having sex when I'm on.

It isn't long before he's softly snoring. I swear that man would be a hypnotist's dream. I whip back the duvet and slowly climb out of bed. I'm on my knees on his side of the bed, his phone in hand. I push the button and the screen illuminates. I slide my finger over 'unlock'. My hand shoots to my mouth as I stare at the screen in wide-eyed disbelief. He's put in a new bloody passcode.

Chapter Five

'Vav isn't a word.' Alistair peers at the board, eyebrows scrunched.

'Yes it is,' I protest, biting hard on the inside of my lip. I don't actually know the definition but I remember one of my friends using it on a *Words with Friends* move yesterday.

'What does it mean, then?' He looks at me over his rimless, oblong spectacles.

Lost for words I start shuffling the small tiles on my dark green tray, pressing my back against the high-back chair, the springs digging into my bottom.

'As in va va voom,' I say, trying desperately to stifle a laugh.

'Va va what?' He knots his thin, white eyebrows tighter. He looks rather sweet, bless him.

'Haven't you ever seen that Renault advert with that Arsenal player, what's his name? Henry Thoreau.'

'Thierry Henry.' Ninety-three years old and sharp as a pin. 'Henry Thoreau was an American poet. Get your facts right, Emma, and stop cheating.'

He opens the Oxford dictionary and starts trawling through the pages with a slender, slightly bent finger. He refuses to use a smartphone and thinks that a tablet is something you take when you're ill. And don't get me started on what he thinks of computers. He refused point blank to accept Harry's used laptop when Andreas gave us his old iMac. Well, I say old, but Andreas had only used it for about two years – so it was practically new, really. And it turned out to be a blessing – I was in desperate need for an iMac for my illustration business, and there's no way we could have afforded one otherwise. Mas' kids have all the latest gadgets, gismos, and upgrades. He spoils them like that.

'Well?' I ask, leaning forward for a better view. 'I'm right, aren't I?'

He slams the dictionary shut crossly. 'Hmm ...' He starts rearranging his letter tiles on his green tray. 'It's the sixth letter of the Hebrew alphabet,' he says begrudgingly, then looks up at me quickly, pointing his finger, '... not that you knew that.'

He's right. I've been rumbled.

We share a few moments of laughter. I only popped in to bring him his groceries and have ended up in a game of *Scrabble*. I ache to tell him about text-gate, but I don't think I could bear it if he thought badly of me. He's very fond of Harry. They sometimes play golf together or the odd game of *Short Tennis*. But, then again, Alistair is full of wisdom. I'm sure he'd put me on the right track. He'll know what to do. I haven't got a very good relationship with my own father, never have, not for want of trying. I idolised him as a child but I couldn't do right for wrong where he was concerned, no matter how hard I tried, I could never make him proud, and yet Alistair, without even trying, has filled that fatherly role these last three years that my own dad never could.

'I've got this friend,' I begin, swallowing hard and staring at my *Scrabble* tray.

'Oh yes?' He raises his eyebrows and examines the board, chin in hand, thoughtfully.

'She found a couple of text messages on her boyfriend's mobile that seem a bit ... well, odd.'

'Odd?'

'Yes, you know,' I wave a hand dismissively, '... suspicious.' I twist my lips to the side as I shuffle the tiles on my tray, giving him intermittent glances. I don't want to miss any facial responses.

'Suspicious how?' He looks up at me with a deadpan expression.

'She thinks it's from another woman.' I stare at him but he doesn't flinch.

We're silent for a few moments and then he says. 'I told you mobile phones are the work of the devil, Emma. But what does an old man like me know, eh?'

'Yes, well, anyway,' I say quickly, '... she's really worried now, thinks he's having an affair, because he's sort of gone off her a bit as well.'

'I see.' He takes a deep breath, diverting his eyes to the board. 'Which friend are we talking about here? The one who wants to bring her son to me for violin lessons?' Alistair's seen all my friends and relatives coming and going, but hasn't met any of them – apart from Mum, that is. We all had tea together on my birthday once.

'Dark, slim, about this tall?' I ask, raising my hand two inches above my head. Alistair nods. 'No, no, that's Ola. Anyway ...'

'Yes.' He leans back in his brown and orange retro chair. 'I remember her now. The one you sometimes go running with. Is she a model?'

I smile. A lot of people ask Ola that. She definitely has the credentials. 'No, she's a P.E. teacher. She looks a lot like Halle Berry, doesn't she?'

'Who?'

'You know, that actress.' He furrows his frayed white eyebrows, 'She played Catwoman. An agent in a Bond film.' Alistair looks bewildered. 'Oh, never mind. So, my friend ...'

'Not the small, plump one with the jolly voice?' He closes his eyes and clicks his fingers, 'What's her name now?' I frown at him, confused. He always gets my friends' names mixed up. 'Oh, you know the one I mean.' He clicks his fingers. 'That psychic one,' he says, unable to recall her name. 'Surely she'd know if her boyfriend was having an affair?' He laughs out loud. Alistair laughs at his own jokes, and I must admit he is very witty, often has me and Harry in stitches. But this, however, is no laughing matter. Not to me, anyway.

'No, Alistair. It's not Caroline. And she's not that sort of psychic. She's not a spiritual medium. She only reads palms.' He's unnerving me with all these questions. 'As I was saying ...'

'Which one is it, then?'

'Oh, for goodness' sake, Alistair, must you know her name?' I put my tray down onto the coffee table a little heavy-handedly. Two of the tiles slip off, hitting the blue and pink patterned carpet, which was probably laid in the year I was born.

'It's just that I could picture her then, and give you my honest opinion.'

'You've never seen her, Alistair. Reeva doesn't do house visits.' I bend down and pick up the tiles. Reeva will never know that I fibbed about her to Alistair.

'Oh righty-o,' he coughs, straightening the collar of his chequered blue, white, and red shirt. 'Reeva.'

'Yes, well, she spied on her boyfriend's phone,' I go on, 'by accident!' I add in quick defence.

'Reeva. Now what kind of a name is that?'

I hold on to the wooden armrests of the fabric chair and look at him in exasperation. 'Alistair, do you want to hear this story or not?'

'Sorry, love. You were saying she snooped on his text messages because she doesn't trust him, which already indicates that their relationship is weak.'

'Well, I wouldn't put it quite like that. She does trust him. It's just that ... well ... the phone was there and it chimed with a message while he was out, so she sort of looked.'

'As you do.' Alistair smiles, tongue in cheek. He's not taking this seriously.

I tell him the whole story and he nods, 'oohs', and 'ahhs' in all the right places. I then hit him with the latest development, the one that kept me up half the night. The passcode.

'So, why doesn't your friend just ask him about the passcode?'

'Because,' I say, almost squeezing the word through gritted teeth, 'because... he'll know she's been spying on his phone again after she promised she wouldn't. After she told him she believed it was a colleague.'

'I see.' Alistair winds one leg around the other, his pale brown trouser leg riding up to reveal a skinny, black-socked calf. He always does this when he's concentrating. He's so flexible. I'm sure that in another life he was a yoga guru.

'So, what do you think?'

'I think you should calm down and stop tapping your foot on my carpet. You'll wear it out if you're not careful.'

There are a few moments of silence as Alistair returns his attention to the *Scrabble* board and then I say, 'What are those plants doing in the hallway?' I slide to the edge of my chair and stretch my back. The run this morning was a bit full-on and I'm starting to feel it. Ten miles on an empty stomach wasn't such a good idea after all.

Alistair is concentrating hard on his next move, rubbing his finger along his thin, dry lips. He's competitive. We're neck and neck and I can see he's eager to beat me. He doesn't seem interested in my story about my imaginary friend. But why should he care about someone he doesn't even know? I shouldn't involve Alistair in all this, anyway. What can the poor man do for me?

I ache with sadness. I stand up and walk towards the window, leaving Alistair to sort out his next crucial move. I don't want to confront Harry about the passcode, not after waffling on all night about how sorry I was for reading his texts. How I trust him implicitly. How my outburst over him having an affair was a moment of madness brought on by PMT. He believed that because I came on that night. Quick thinking.

'Judith dropped the plants over yesterday afternoon on her visit,' he says finally. I sniff the air. She must've baked him a cake while she was here, too. I can still smell the aroma of butter and almonds infused with Alistair's signature scent – Aramis.

'She made some sort of apricot flan thingy. Help yourself to a slice if you want, it's on the kitchen worktop.' See, I was right.

Alistair has two daughters in their early sixties. Judith, the eldest, visits about once a fortnight and often cooks while she's here, but we don't see much of Sandra. I've never seen them together. Alistair said the sisters are estranged, something to do with a disagreement over their children years ago, which escalated.

'I suppose you'll want me to plant them for you.' I stare out of the window at the rain tapping against the pane.

'You're right. Only not today, love, because I'm playing *Short Tennis* in ....' He looks at his wrist watch, '... an hour and twenty-four minutes.' Every time he says "Short Tennis" I imagine a bunch of midgets on a tennis court with Alistair's six foot hunched frame looming over them like a giant.

'I've got an optician's appointment this afternoon, anyway,' I say, hands on hips. 'But I can pop round tomorrow if you'd like.' Alistair nods, then reaches over and places a long word across the board.

'There,' he says. 'That should do it. How many points is that?' He starts totting up the score in his head, his lips moving slightly.

'Aren't you too old to be playing tennis?' I say, tongue in cheek. 'I know it's indoors using a soft ball and all that, but still.'

He gives me a quick, sharp look. 'Don't you start. I already had Judith on my case yesterday. Mind you, those two probably can't wait for me to pop my clogs and inherit the house.' I'm sure his daughters aren't after their inheritance. Who'd swap such a lovely dad for cash? I know I wouldn't. Not in a million years. 'This home is all Olive and I managed, but it must be worth over six-hundred thousand pounds in today's market, surely?' He may very well be right. House prices in London have almost doubled since we bought ours three years ago.

I smile at him warmly. I know he misses his beloved Olive. I sometimes take him to the cemetery and wait while he lays down flowers, lights a tea light, and cleans her tombstone, all the while chatting to her about Judith and Sandra, the grandchildren that he hardly ever sees, his violin students, his column in *BBC Music Magazine*. Alistair is such a talented man.

'Right,' he stands up and shuffles over to the tall, marble oak sideboard, beautifully crafted with smooth, round edges and elegant lines, returning moments later with his violin. 'I'll play you a quick tune, help you relax a little. I've got a student coming this evening for a half hour lesson so I may as well brush up.'

'Shouldn't you upgrade that?' I nod at his violin.

'Shhhh.' He gives me one of his looks. 'This violin was my father's. It's of sentimental value and does the job perfectly well. That's all that matters.'

I lean against the wall and close my eyes as he starts to play. I love the sound of the violin; probably my favourite instrument.

'So,' he says, 'have you and Harry made up?'

I open my eyes quickly. 'What? What do you mean? Did Harry say something?'

'Walls have ears, my dear, walls have ears.' His thin arm moved smoothly over the violin, the old bow in his hand pressing expertly against the strings.

'Oh, I see.' I clear my throat. It didn't occur to me that Alistair could hear us effing and blinding through the walls last night. 'It was just a misunderstanding, that's all. We've sorted it.' I stare at my feet, 'I'm sorry I didn't bring your groceries in yesterday. I was out with Ola and Caroline and …'

'Oh, the *psychic* one? Tsk.' Alistair moves his fingers along the neck of his violin and plays the opening notes of Neil Diamond's 'Sweet Caroline'. He used to be professional and played in an orchestra for years. Since he retired he's been teaching, mostly mature students. I think he'd be lost without his music. It's the only thing that keeps him going.

'Alistair, each to their own, that's what you always say. Which reminds me,' I unzip my bag and pull out my phone. 'I've got to try out this new psychic app of hers.'

'A psychic app?' Alistair has stopped playing.

'An application for smartphones, app is just an abbreviation. They –'

'Yes, I know what an app is, Emma. I do have grandchildren, you know.' He pauses, eyebrows gathered. 'You don't believe in all the codswallop, do you?'

I shrug my shoulders. 'Some of them get things right.'

'Oh, that's just cold reading.' He waves his bow crossly. 'They just react to your body language, that's all. These people work on probability. The more common information they throw at you, the more chance of them getting something right.'

'Caroline's told me a couple of things that've come true,' I protest, albeit a little lamely.

'What, that you'll hear some bad news about someone?' I don't answer. 'What was it, a car accident? An illness? A burglary? Oh, don't tell me, it's coming to me ...' He presses his knuckles, bow in hand, against his head. 'An affair!'

I scratch my cheek nervously. It was actually about a theft. I hate it when he proves me wrong, which is more often than not. 'Yes, OK, Alistair,' I say a little crossly, 'she told me I'd hear about a theft and my mum's friend got mugged coming home from bingo. But she was right.' I insist, pointing my phone at him. 'It happened shortly after she did my reading.'

Alistair tuts, annoyed. 'That's just negative thinking, coincidence, and association. You draw on the negative energy around you, waiting for this bad news to land on your doorstep, then the moment you hear the word "theft", bang!' He runs the bow across his violin sharply and I jump. 'You think the psychic got it right.'

'Well,' I muse, 'maybe … I don't know.'

'Emma, please don't tell me you believe in all that rubbish. I had you down for a much smarter girl.'

'No, not really, but I like to think there's something after here, Alistair, don't you?' I scroll across my icons list.

'Nah, there's nothing. This is it.' He places his precious violin back in its battered case. I feel a sudden pang of sadness at what Alistair has just revealed. Thinking there's nothing more after this life at his age must be quite depressing.

'There might be, though, you don't know that. You might be pleasantly surprised.' I tap on The Magic Touch app. A crystal ball suspended in space fills the screen, stars twinkling around it. It is actually quite lovely; mystic and inviting.

'I'll tell you what,' he says, snapping his fingers. 'Let's make a pact. If there is, I'll let you know once I'm there.'

I close the app immediately. Finally, a flicker of hope about the paranormal. 'OK,' I say eagerly, 'whoever goes first, and it might be me…' He frowns, shakes his head, tells me not to be such a silly girl. 'Well, you don't know. But whoever goes first finds a medium and makes contact.'

'No!' he says firmly. 'No charlatans. I'll find a way of letting you know.'

'But how …'

'No,' he cuts in, 'you leave it to me.'

'OK, OK.' I smile lifting my hands up. 'You win.' But I hope that we won't have to face that day for many, many years.

'So, what about your friend and this elusive text of hers?' At last, he's showing an interest. But it's too late now.

'I'm sure she'll sort something out, Alistair, don't worry.' I pick up my bag.

'Well, my answer is on the *Scrabble* board if you need it.'

I knot my eyebrows tightly and walk towards the table. I study the board carefully. He used up all his letter tiles on the last move. I can see it now, it's against the E used in 'Energy'. BKDACODE.

'Hey,' I retort, spinning round to face him, 'that's not a word. It's gobbledygook.' He's trying to get me back for 'vav'.

'Look carefully, Emma, don't rush. Read it as you would one of your precious text messages.' He shakes his head disapprovingly. 'Young people have ruined the English language with acronyms and text speak.'

I stare at the word then it slowly starts to make sense. 'Break the code,' I whisper. Alistair nods.

'But how?'

'If you want to get to the bottom of this, it's the only way.'

'But I wouldn't know …'

'Come on, Emma,' he says, sliding his hand into his tweed jacket, 'you're a clever girl. Think of four numbers that Harry might use as a password, a birthday, an anniversary. You'll find it. I have every faith in you.'

The sly dog.

Chapter Six

Why is it that every pair of glasses that I try on make me look like my ex-school headmistress? I've been circling the stands laden with hundreds of glasses for the last forty-five minutes and I'm still none the wiser. Why do they have to have so many, anyway? It only makes choosing more difficult. I sigh deeply and the assistant gives me a small, sympathetic smile. I knew I needed to renew my prescription because for the last few months I've been struggling to apply my make-up in the magnifying mirror Harry fitted for me in the bathroom (I told you he's good at DIY). I slide on a pair of black tortoiseshell ones with orange lines along the arms.

'I see a lot of young people wearing these,' I muse, staring at my reflection through the finger-smeared lenses. 'They must be the height of fashion.'

'Yes, they're our latest range. They suit you, actually,' says the short, stocky assistant with a huge painted-on smile not too dissimilar to the Joker in *Batman*. 'The strong design gives you a trendy identity, and goes with the colour of your lovely hair,' she adds with a forced niceness that I pick up immediately. I get that from my mum – very little gets past us. Harry calls us Scott and Bailey.

I crinkle my nose disapprovingly and she hands me another pair from the clasp of her right hand. 'Oh, definitely these,' she enthuses. 'The round frames make you look smart. Very business-like.' She's gotta be kidding me, right? I look like my Aunt Muriel.

'I'm sorry,' I say, staring down at the half dozen *maybe* glasses in her left hand, and feeling a little sorry for her, 'I am fussy.' I start circling the stands again, ignoring the *maybe* selection she tried to thrust under my nose. I've been driving the poor woman mad since I got here.

'Oh, are you?' She pulls another pair from the rack that I've been eyeing. 'Is it Ramadan?'

'*Fussy*!' I say, clearing my throat, 'not fasting.' I'm beginning to wonder if she's actually paying any attention to me at all. She confirms this when her Joker smile finally fades and she hands me over to her colleague, a young Asian man with black, square glasses. Clearly she's had enough of me. And who could blame her?

An hour later, I'm still at the opticians, but at least I've decided on my frames. A rectangular, petite pair. I especially like the purple bar across the top and the rimless bottom makes them look less severe. Less like my Aunt Muriel.

Anyway, all the staff agreed that they suited me the most. Only one problem. They're BOSS Orange and cost £200. Harry won't be happy. Don't get me wrong, Harry has a very generous nature. Before we bought the house he'd often come home with lovely gifts for me and we'd eat out at nice restaurants a few times a week. But that was when we lived at the flat.

I smile as I recall the time Harry surprised me on my thirty-fifth birthday. I'd been working at the restaurant all day and was shattered. The only thing that kept me going was the thought of going home to a nice, hot bath and a home-cooked meal. I'm not big on celebrations so we'd planned to keep my birthday low-key. Harry had taken the day off work and was going to cook a romantic meal. He's a very good cook, by the way. All the family are. It must have something to do with growing up in the restaurant business surrounded by all that lovely Mediterranean food.

I arrived at our flat to find my suitcase packed and waiting for me at the door. Harry stood beside it holding a huge bouquet of pink and white roses.

'Happy birthday, my darling,' he said, thrusting them into my chest and planting a long, passionate kiss on my lips. I took the flowers from his arms, flustered, happy, and quivering with anticipation.

'What's all this?' I looked down at the packed suitcase by the door with glee.

'You didn't really think I'd let you get away without celebrating your birthday properly, did you?' He pulled out an envelope from the inside of his leather jacket. All sorts of destinations raced through my mind. A day trip to Paris – I'd always wanted to go there with him. A pamper day at a spa with sports facilities – we'd talked about doing that together, too.

I tore open the envelope with trembling hands and gasped. A weekend in Monte Carlo. I almost passed out with joy.

We had a weekend to remember. He'd booked us into The Hotel De Paris. It was exquisite, to say the least. If it wasn't for the fact that there was so much to do and see in Monaco we'd never have left our bedroom.

'What do you think?' the sales assistant asks, jolting me back to the present.

I bite the inside of my lip thoughtfully as I stare at the BOSS Orange glasses in my hand. They are very nice. I could put it on my MasterCard and economise on other things, like supermarket shopping. I could buy the Basics range from Sainsbury's, supermarket brand detergents and liquids, cut back on wine and snacks. I'm sure I've got a couple of hundred pounds left on my credit card. Harry said he'll go to the bank in his lunch hour today and sort my credit card payment. If that goes through today, I'll be fine. I wonder if he's had a chance to pay it yet.

My text to Harry is short and sweet:

At opticians. Glasses 200, only got 100 cash. Want to put on my CC. Have you paid bill yet? X

I'll give him ten minutes to reply. If he doesn't, then I'm back to square one.

I stare idly ahead at a lady trying on some frames. Unlike me, they all look good on her. She's got one of those classic, gorgeous faces, like Ola's: high cheekbones, smooth, satin skin, and dark, mysterious eyes. I could easily see her modelling most of these frames. And I bet she's not as fussy as I am either. She pulls her hair back into a ponytail and checks her reflection in the slim-line mirror. I look hopefully at my phone, willing Harry to text me back.

Every minute seems like five. I lean back in my seat, bored, then remember Caroline's psychic app. I opened it this morning at Alistair's, but then got side-tracked by his interest in the paranormal. It opens to the sound of howling wind. I look around quickly. A sales assistant and his client look up at me from the nearby booth. I lower the volume.

Right. What do I have to do? Touch the screen is what Caroline had said. I stare down at the italic greeting on the tiny screen – *Hello, Emma*. I had to put in my personal details, a prerequisite for added effect, I suppose. I follow the instructions and place three fingers over the blue imprints. A bar scrolls down the screen, scanning my fingertips to a scary gong sound. Who on earth designed this, Freddy Krueger? Oooh, the crystal ball is smoking over. I slide on my old glasses and read the prediction – *"A*

pleasant surprise from a stranger will open a new door."
Hmm ... I could do with some cheering up. I close the app just as a text buzzes through. Great. Harry didn't take long after all. I read the text –

Hi, Red. Remember me?

Red? Who the bloody hell is this? I quickly text back.

Sorry, no, who is this?

Within a few seconds, another text arrives –

Marc.

'Marc? Who the hell is Marc?'
'Pardon, madam?' A sales assistant is looming over me. Oh God, did I just say that out loud?
'I'm sorry,' I murmur, waving my phone in the air, he nods and dashes off, glad to greet a new customer and get away from the mad woman getting a psychic reading from an app.
I return my attention to the text. I haven't a clue who this is and I really haven't got time for wrong numbers. I close the text and look at my watch. I'm getting used to the half hour lapse. I've been here almost two hours now. I need to get home and make a start on my new work gig, a client I found on LinkedIn. Well, she found me, actually. Impressed by my profile and recommendations she asked to see a few of my covers, then hired me almost right away. She's already committed by paying a deposit and wants to see the 'roughs' by the end of the week. I look at my watch again, crossing one leg over the other as I'm now bursting for a pee.

Within seconds my phone buzzes again. Harry, oh, thank God. I look at the message from the unknown number with a sigh of exasperation.

We met in the pub last night.

What? Who is this lunatic? Then it dawns on me. It's the good-looking bloke from The King's Head. How the hell did he ... then I remember I called his number to test his phone. He must've logged it, the sneak. But what on earth does he want from me?

I feel a slight flutter in my stomach as I quickly text back, explaining that I do remember him, and how could I help? His reply is razor sharp asking me for a dinner date. Shit. I smile and shake my head as I text back.

Sorry. I'm with someone. Thanks tho.

I add a smiley face, just to be nice. I sit back in my chair, smiling at my phone and shaking my head. So he did fancy me after all. I glance at my phone again. No more texts. Good, he's got the message.

It isn't long before my phone starts vibrating in my hand. An incoming call. Please let it be Harry.

'Emma? It's your mother,' Mum says in a distressed tone.

'Hi, Mum.' I glance around the shop floor, lowering my voice. I hate having telephone conversations in public. 'Erm ... you OK? I can't talk for long, I'm at the opticians and I'm waiting for a call from Harry any moment now.'

'Oh, Emma,' she says tearfully, ignoring me. 'I crashed the car last night.'

'Mum!' I stand up quickly. A few customers on the shop floor look around at me sharply. The sales assistant at reception mouths 'Are you OK?' I nod.

'Mum, are you hurt?' I go on, pacing the blue tiled carpet, my heart racing. 'How did it happen, for Christ's sake? Was Mike with you?' Mike is Mum's second husband, a lovely, gentle man who takes great care of her. She calls him her soulmate and always says she wishes she'd met him before my father.

'I'm fine, I'm fine, and Mike's OK. He wasn't even in the car with me, sweetie. He insisted on getting out to read the restaurant menu so we could go elsewhere if it didn't suit his palate.' Her loud sigh is almost a growl. 'If he'd stayed put with me it mightn't have happened. He knows what my eyesight is like these days. And it was dark.' I let out a sigh of relief. Mike doesn't drive; never bothered to learn, said he's afraid of having an accident. 'I did it while trying to park the damned thing. You know I'm not good at parallel parking, Emma, but it was the only space available on the street. I didn't see the damned dwarf lampposts. They weren't there last week. Bloody council.'

'Calm down, Mum. At least you're not hurt. That's the main thing, isn't it?'

'Yes, I suppose.' She pauses. 'I wouldn't mind, but Mike had one of those parking bleepy things fitted onto the car for me last week. To help me park, he said. Only it's made things ten times worse.'

'Parking sensors?' I ask. I try not to laugh as I imagine my mum sitting in the car, jumping every time the bleeps go off.

'Yes, I think that's what Mike called them. The damned things go off when you're about two feet away from the kerb. How absurd is that?'

'Oh, I see. Maybe you should get them adjusted.' I sit back down, relieved that she and Mike are OK.

'No, no, they're working fine,' she says, sounding exasperated. 'They just get progressively faster as you get nearer to the object.' Mum isn't really a go-by-the-rules kind of person. She likes to make up her own as she goes along; trust her own judgements. There's no way she'd take any notice of bleeps getting louder – she would think she knows best. What the garage should do is fit the sensor with a voice that shouts 'Stop the fucking car! NOW!' as soon as she's in close proximity of another parked vehicle or lamppost. And preferably using a recording of her own voice. It's the only one she'll listen to.

'Mum, it's OK. It was an accident. Have you called the insurance company?'

'Mike's taking care of all that. When are you coming down, sweetie? I miss you. And how's that handsome man of yours? I hope he's treating you well.'

We talk for a few more minutes then I end the call, telling her that I love her and will pop up to Stratford-upon-Avon to see her shortly. It's always lovely to hear from Mum. She always manages to cheer me up, even when she calls with distressing news!

I glance at my watch for the hundredth time. It's been twelve minutes since I sent Harry that text. He hasn't replied. He's obviously too busy saving people's lives to bother with my designer frames. And they're way too expensive. We can't afford them. What was I thinking? I'll just hand them back to the assistant and choose something else.

As I get to my feet my phone buzzes with a message. I hope it isn't Marc again. He's very persistent, I'll give him that. Phew, it's Harry. Finally.

Buy them, baby. I've just paid it.

I smile, half pleased but half suspicious. They are an expensive buy that we can't afford. I wonder if it's his guilty conscience that's made him agree to this extravagant purchase. Unfaithful partners do things like that, don't they? Buy their unsuspecting wives or girlfriends expensive gifts in an effort to curb their guilt. I take a deep breath as I rummage through my bag for my purse. I'm overanalysing again. I've been here too long, I'm tired, hungry. He's said I can have them, so I will. All being well, I should get paid for the book gig before the credit card bill arrives. That's if I get my finger out and start working on it properly.

But then as I pull out my purse I picture the text I read on Sunday morning, the phone in my hand last night with the new passcode, Harry's voice telling me he has to cover for Mas on a Monday night. The scenes play out in my mind like a film trailer. I wince. I've got to find a way of making these ugly thoughts disappear. I think about Alistair's suggestion of breaking into Harry's phone and shake my head. Daft thing, couldn't he come up with a better idea than breaking Harry's passcode? It's just absurd, not to mention a violation. No, I couldn't do that to Harry... absolutely no way.

The assistant's voice breaks my reverie. 'So, that's two-hundred pounds, then, Miss King.' Oh, it's Miss King, now, is it? Gone is the dowdy Madam. I push my credit card into the handheld system and wait while it processes my payment. And at that moment another text comes through.

'Sorry,' I say, taking a step back. 'I've got to get this.'

Oh God. It's Marc again. Will this man not take no for an answer?

Just a drink? No strings. May have a client for u.
Sounds really interested. Call me so we can talk.

'I'm sorry, Miss King.' It's the assistant's voice again.
'Do you have an alternative card? This one's been
declined.' Oh bloody hell.

Chapter Seven

'Harry tell me your mama had car accident?' says Spiros, Harry's father, who's outstretched in his favourite armchair in front of the TV, beer in hand, feet up.

'Yes, that's right, last Monday,' I reply. I can't believe it's been almost a week since Mum rang me with the news. 'But she's OK, just a bit shaken, and there's minor damage on the wing of the car.' I swish the residue of the orange juice in my glass. 'It's at the garage now. They couldn't get a courtesy car off the insurance, though, so they're pretty much housebound.'

'Ah, bloody inshuriance. They all bastards,' Spiros says, then he suddenly leaps to the edge of his seat and covers his bald head with his hands. 'Noooooo! Oh my Goddd.' He shakes his head at the forty-seven inch LCD screen as I knock back the last dregs of orange juice. 'We bottom of league again now cos of that idiot.'

I chuckle. I love Spiros and Xenia's sweet English expressions with their cute Greek accents. 'Anyway,' he goes on, returning his attention to me. 'Tell that Michael to ring inshuriance and get a car for your mamma.'

'He has tried, Spiros, but their policy didn't include one, I'm afraid.'

Spiros rocks his head from side to side in disdain as he recites an anecdote about a claim he once made when the boys were very young. He explains how it took over six months to resolve. That he doesn't know how they'd have coped if it wasn't for his sister, Valentina, who did the school run for them and ferried them to and from the restaurant.

I smile as I listen intently to Spiros' story. Sunday lunch at Harry's parents' house has become quite a ritual, especially since his father's illness. They're a close-knit family. I get that, despite having never known it in my own family. My parents have been divorced for almost twenty-nine years. Mum and Mike moved to Stratford-upon-Avon shortly after they got married; they said they wanted a fresh start somewhere quieter, less smoggy. And with them both being avid theatre lovers (they met at an amateur dramatics class in East Finchley) Stratford seemed the ideal place. I miss her terribly but she loves it there, and who was I to stand in the way of her happiness? Anyway, it's only a two-hour drive and we're always nattering on the phone.

Dad lives alone in a council flat in Camden. He moved there after his second marriage crumbled, not surprising given his temper and love of Jack Daniel's. I haven't seen him in ages. I don't see my half-sister, Tessa, as much as I'd like to either. But that's more my fault, really. She does keep in touch, always suggesting we meet up, but I'm always too busy. I don't do it on purpose. Sometimes I wonder where all the time goes. She'll be giving birth to her second baby in a few weeks. I've got to see her before then. Besides, I bought Jamie, my gorgeous three-year-old nephew, a lovely leather jacket in the Gap sale. He'll grow out of it if I leave it any longer.

Tessa's always been Dad's favourite, anyway. He and I have never had a very good relationship. I couldn't do right for doing wrong where he was concerned. I could never please him, however hard I tried. But I always craved his approval, his love.

I remember when I was about thirteen, rushing home from school to show him my annual report card. I worked my butt off that year and got A's in every subject. I sat by his feet, staring at him with wide-eyed anticipation. When he finished reading he turned to me and said, 'You got an A minus for maths. Why's that? You need to work harder.'

Many of my parents' rows stemmed from me, with Dad always accusing Mum of wrapping me up in cotton wool and mollycoddling me. For some reason, I got under his skin. I had the same effect on Carl. I was beginning to think I would never have a good relationship with any man until Harry came along. I can't bear the thought of losing him. My eyes sting at the thought. For lack of a better distraction, I make my way towards the kitchen.

'Need any help in here?' I ask as I reach the kitchen door, dabbing a tear from my right eye before wrapping my black cardigan tightly around myself and walking inside. 'September seems to have brought the chill with it, hasn't it? I can't believe that it was thirty degrees only last week. Hay fever must still be pretty high, though,' I sniff.

'We're fine, I think, Em, aren't we, Mum?' Caroline stops peeling potatoes and nudges the small woman wearing an oversized apron at the stove. She mumbles incoherently, busily stirring something lovely smelling. Harry's mum won't let anyone near her AGA. She fusses over her family like a mother hen. But she's always warm and caring towards me and Caroline – and absolutely adores her grandchildren. I think she's a bit disappointed that Harry and I haven't produced another grandchild for her, particularly as Harry is her favourite.

'Emma, dahrli,' She looks at me briefly over her left shoulder, her large, round glasses resting on the bridge of her nose. 'Can you fix the table, pleeze?'

'Yes, of course I can, Xenia.' I could do with the distraction. My mind is like the Underground map these days, a bundle of thoughts, each one weaving into the other like a long plait.

I hover over Xenia, peeking over her shoulder. 'What meat is that? Smells divine.'

'Is pok,' she says, not looking at me, 'with wine and potato.'

'Oh, afelia?' I say brightly. That's one of my favourite dishes, pork in red wine with herbs and potatoes. 'Valentina and I made it last Thursday as a restaurant special.'

'That's all right. I know you like, Emma. Valentina telling me, she say you take picture and put on Twister. You good cook, Emma.' She glances at me approvingly, giving my arm a little squeeze. I have shown off a couple of our dishes on Twitter, got a few RTs for them too. 'But I makey biff and lum as well. Marios and Andreas no like pok. So, everyone happy.' A feast of pork, lamb, and beef. I will have to run twenty miles to burn off the calories tomorrow.

I start counting nine sets of cutlery.

'You OK, Emma?' Caroline asks, wiping her forehead with the back of her wrist, knife in hand, facing me. 'You look a bit … I dunno, down.'

'I'm fine, thanks. Had a bit of trouble getting off to sleep last night, that's all.' I look up at her briefly, clutching the cutlery in both hands. 'Your app is great, by the way.' I smile. 'Yesterday's prediction was, *"you'll get a big break at work with a little help from a friend"*. So, here's hoping for more referrals.' I look up to the ceiling, gathering my filled hands together as if in prayer.

'God will help, Emma,' Xenia calls out as she slices vegetables at the huge kitchen table. 'I always praying,' she pauses, pointing the large chef's knife in my direction. 'I light a candle for you and Harry this morning at church.'

'Thank you, Xenia. I hope so.'

'Ooooh, sounds promising,' Caroline says as she pulls her duck egg blue sweater over her head, complaining of an imminent hot flush. 'Any luck with the other predictions?' She throws her sweater over the chair next to Xenia.

I smile. 'No.' I wonder if I should mention the text Marc sent me about a referral while I was at the opticians. It would tie in nicely with yesterday's prediction to some degree. 'But it's good fun,' I add quickly, deciding against it. I mean, it's not as if I took up his offer, is it? I didn't reply to the message, nor did I bother calling him about it. I've got enough complications in my life right now – I really don't need any more.

'Yes, I know. It's just for entertainment, really. It's nothing like a live reading. But I do hope your business picks up.' She's not the only one. I can't tell you how embarrassing it was to have my credit card declined at the opticians. In the end I had to choose a cheaper pair. 'But if you need any extra shifts at the restaurant, just let me know. It's getting really busy again. I'm sure I can sort something out for you.' I thank her, but explain that two days a week is all I can manage if I want to make a go of it with my new business. 'OK,' she smiles, 'but the offer's always there. Harry told me you got head hunted on LinkedIn?' She throws a peeled potato into a yellow colander under a running tap in the sink.

'Well, I wouldn't quite call it that, but, yes, by a new writer who has self-publishing. I sent the proofs over to her on Friday, which she approved yesterday. I should have the job done by next week.'

'Oh, that's brilliant, Em. You're so talented.' Caroline turns the tap off then grabs a nearby tea towel. 'We'll have to find Valentina a new assistant before too long.' She dries her hands. 'Does it pay well?'

'It depends on what they want, to be honest. How detailed the illustration, how many hours I work on it, and whether they want changes after I send them the finished artwork. I'm charging her four-hundred pounds for this one. But it all seems pretty straightforward. She's not at all fussy. She just gave me a few pointers, then more or less left it to me. I hope she likes the finished product, that's all.'

'I'm sure she will,' she says, giving the washed potatoes a good shake in the colander while Xenia berates her for shaking too hard, saying she'll bruise them. 'You and Harry deserve a break. Such a lovely couple.' She throws me a warm smile, leaning into me with her arm gently. 'You are keeping a diary of the predictions, aren't you, Em?' she asks briskly. I tell her that I am as Xenia brushes past us, shouting something in Greek to her husband who's still perched in front of the TV in the living room watching Sky Sports. 'That's great.' She lowers the spuds into a pan of boiling water at the stove. 'I really appreciate your help on this one. Don't forget to review it in a few weeks.'

'I won't. I promise.'

'Muuuumm,' Demi charges into the kitchen, smelling and looking gorgeous, mobile phone in hand. 'I'm out of juice. Please tell me you brought my charger with you?'

'No, I didn't, Demi.' Caroline lowers the heat to simmer. 'It's still charging my phone at home. I'm sure there's something wrong with that handset. It keeps switching itself off when there's still about 40% battery left. '

'Oh, Mu-um, for God's sake. That's the last time I let you borrow it.'

'It isn't my fault,' Caroline protests, eyes widening with indignation, 'you should've said you wanted me to bring it.' Demi throws me a look of exasperation, her blue eyes darkening. Then she shakes her head, her four-inch silver earrings swinging against her unblemished skin. Unlike her brother Andreas, Demi has taken after her mum where looks are concerned. You'd never think she had a Greek gene in her body.

'You could borrow mine,' I offer. I always keep mine in my handbag as I'm constantly running low, what with being online most of the time. Demi's face surges with excitement. 'You've still got your iPhone, haven't you?' I add. Her face drops instantly.

'Upgraded to a Samsung Galaxy last month,' she holds up her handset languidly. 'Oh Muuummm! Why do you always have to ruin everything? I'm on level two-hundred and fifty-six on Candy Crush. I'm neck and neck with Andreas. He's gonna beat me now, thanks to you.' Competitive to the core, just like her father. 'Why don't you just buy a new charger for fu ...' Caroline fixes her with a warning look and she stops before the word 'fuck' slips from her bow-shaped lips. But only just, mind. 'Ohhhhaaa,' she growls, fists clenched, eyebrows gathered.

Caroline rolls her eyes at me whispering 'kids' and then, 'hormones.'

'I heard that, mother,' Demi says, shaking her head and smiling. 'And I think you'll find that you're the one with the hormonal problem, not me. That's why you keep forgetting everything. It's that flipping menopause. When's it gonna end?'

I close the cutlery drawer with my elbow as Caroline and I exchange a wry smile.

'Oi, don't be so bloody cheeky,' Caroline snaps. 'She's got her father's temper, you know.'

'Yeah, yeah, yeah, whatever.' Demi drones, folding her arms and leaning against the wooden worktop.

'Your Uncle Harry has the same phone,' I say. 'Why don't you ask him?'

'Has he brought his charger with him?' Her eyes flit around the kitchen, her long, blonde ponytail swishing each times she moves.

'I'm not sure, Demi,' I reply, clutching the knives in one hand and forks in the other. 'He does bring it sometimes if his phone is on low battery. Ask him.'

'Where is he?'

'Watching TV with your granddad and brother, isn't he?' I frown.

'They're in the garden,' Caroline calls out from the sink. 'Mas is having a sneaky fag.' She stares out of the window. I didn't think Mas had arrived yet. Caroline said he had some paperwork to do. 'Thinks he can sneak in from the side entrance and hide behind the shed without me seeing him, the rat.'

Demi and I peer over her shoulder, she clutching her mobile phone and I all the cutlery, inhaling an infusion of Caroline's spicy perfume and the aroma of kleftiko, which is resting in a pan on the cooling rack next to the sink. Harry is leaning against the shed, Mas semi-hiding behind him in a cloud of smoke. I wonder what they're talking about.

'I'll go and ask him.' Demi makes for the kitchen door.

'No, wait.' I hand her the cutlery. 'You finish laying the table. I'll go.' She snatches the knives and forks from my hand and disappears around the door, all the while ranting on about her mother's inadequacies.

I dodge the overgrown trees as I make my way towards the rear of the hundred-and-fifty-foot garden. They're so engrossed in conversation they don't see me approaching from behind the fig tree.

'Yes, but you know what she's like,' Harry sighs. 'What will I do if …'

'Just relax, Harry, yeah? It's going to be fine. Why do you worry so much?'

Harry's staring at his feet worriedly, hands on hips.

'Stop stressing, for fuck's sake.' Mas grabs Harry's shoulder firmly, reassuringly. 'It'll be fine. I promise. I'll look after you. OK?' Silence.

'OK.' Harry covers his brother's hand with his and nods.

'What will be fine?' I ask brightly, appearing from behind the fig tree like an apparition, arms folded.

Harry and Mas exchange a quick, sharp glance. 'Nothing, babe,' Harry takes a step towards me, his smile not quite reaching his eyes. 'It's just about work.' He pulls me into the warmth of his arms.

'Loves young dream,' Mas says with a good dollop of sarcasm as Harry wraps his arm around my shoulders and drops a kiss on my head.

'Really?' I raise my eyebrows quizzically, stiff in Harry's embrace. 'Only it sounded quite serious to me.'

'That's because you're a woman.' Mas stamps out his cigarette with the sole of his brown cowboy boot, blowing smoke from his mouth, his nose. I narrow my eyes at him. 'You women always misconstrue everything.' I look at him expectantly. He's not going to get away with it that easily and he knows it. 'Calm down, Emma, will you? We've got Environmental Health coming in next week, that's all.' He scratches his bristly cheek then pushes back his long, greying hair with one swoop of his large hand. 'They're always meticulous, you know that. Remember what happened the last time we had them round.' I do – he had to close the restaurant to carry out the repairs. We felt the ache in our pockets and that was only for a week.

Mas laughs, giving Harry a playful punch on the arm. 'Harry's got the heebie-jeebies over it, thinks they'll stitch us up.'

'Stitch you up how?' I chew the inside of my lip, my eyes not leaving Mas.

'Nit-pick.' Our eyes lock as he readjusts the collar of his denim jacket. 'Make us spend thousands on repairs.'

'And?' I ask confrontationally, wrapping my cardigan around me tightly, blocking out the cold wind that's been dancing on my bare chest. I knew I should've worn my sweater instead of this flimsy, drape-neck top. What was I thinking?

Harry, clearly sensing that we're about to lock horns, jumps in to diffuse the tension. 'If Mas has to lay off staff to cover costs we might lose our jobs, babe. And then where would we be? How would we pay the mortgage?' I twist my lips as my eyes flit between them. Losing our jobs at the restaurant doesn't bear thinking about. But they're lying. I'm sure of it.

'I've told him not to be so stupid,' Mas cuts in quickly, 'he won't lose his job, no matter what. Family comes first. Ain't that right, bro?' He pulls Harry from me and into his arms, and they hug like a scene from *The Godfather*. Then, before I can question them further, Demi appears at my side. Annoyed.

'Emma!?' I give her a puzzled look. 'The charger?'

I forgot all about that. 'Oh yes, sorry, Demi,' I lay a hand on her arm, 'we just got carried away.'

'Well?' She looks at Harry expectantly.

'Well what?'

'The charger? Did you bring it with you?'

As we walk towards the house, Mas engages me in conversation about the restaurant, boasting about how busy they are, how he's thinking of taking on more staff if Harry can't do the extra shifts, while Harry explains to a very disgruntled Demi that he left his charger at home.

'Oh, Dad, can you go and fetch my charger for me?'

'Sure, hun, but after lunch, yeah? I'm starving.' Mas reaches into his jacket pocket and pulls out his phone. 'Here, you can borrow mine for now, it's fully charged.'

'Noooo, Dad, your Motorola screen is way too small,' she retorts, making to walk off.

Harry snatches her by the arm. 'Here, Dem.' He unlocks his phone and my eyes twitch as Alistair's *Scrabble* move BKDACODE dances before my eyes. 'You can use mine.' He grins, handing Demi his handset.

I hadn't thought any more about breaking into Harry's phone since Alistair's brainwave last Tuesday. Particularly as Ola had managed to more or less convince me that updating your password is prudent, that everyone she knows does it at least once a year, including John, and that I should stop being so negative and suspicious all the time and concentrate on the positives in my relationship instead of trying to destroy it. But the conversation I just overheard between Mas and Harry has set my mind ticking like a time bomb.

'Oh, sick! Thanks, Uncle Harry. You're a lifesaver.' Harry puts his arm around her shoulders and she leans into him as Andreas appears at the door hollering that lunch is ready. I can't believe how quickly that boy has grown. Just a few years ago I was taking him to the cinema, and now here he is – a six-foot man with a forty-inch chest, dark curls sweeping his shoulders, and a long beard, which Caroline tells me he softens with conditioner.

We all shuffle inside to the ruckus of Mas grabbing a hold of Caroline and planting a loud, sloppy kiss on her lips, Demi gagging at the sight of them and shouting 'gross', and Andreas and Harry chatting enthusiastically

71

about Oxford. I follow behind them, arms folded, head down, wondering how long it will be before Demi tires of playing *Candy Crush* on Harry's unlocked phone?

Chapter Eight

I always vowed that I'd never succumb to smartphone games. They're for people who have too much time on their hands, nothing better to do, the Peter Pans of this world.

'You should try playing a game, it'll help you relax,' Harry had suggested, only last night as we sat in bed, him playing Bubble Drop and me watching rubbish late night TV, both of us shattered after a long, hectic day. 'Absolutely and categorically no bloody way,' I had replied, remote control in hand, flying through the channels.

Yet here I am, at the mercy of *Candy Crush*, addicted to the core. I'm already on level ten and I only downloaded it an hour ago.

Demi and I are slouched on the sofa in companionable silence, our fingers sliding over our phone screens to the soundtrack of the athletics coming from the television that no one is watching.

I stop for a moment, balancing the phone on my thigh as I slip out of my black cardigan. It's always so warm in Harry's parents' house, hence my decision to wear a short-sleeved top rather than a sweater this morning. Poor Caroline, she must be sweating buckets. No doubt they've got the heating on full blast as usual. Either that or this game is really getting to me. I reach behind the sofa and touch the radiator. 'Ouch.' My little yelp gives Demi a reflex frown.

'You OK, Em?'

'Yeah, I was just checking if the heating's come on.'

'It's boiling in here, isn't it?' She tugs at the collar of her long-sleeved, purple top, which has a print of a face that is half woman, half lion. 'Paps and Yiayia always have the heating on. It's cos they're oldies, I suppose, innit?'

'It is getting a bit nippy now, Demi. September's always a funny month.'

I wish we could have the heating on night and day. Our house is usually an ice box. Even in the winter we're careful, putting on layers of clothing instead of turning the thermometer up. God knows how we're going to cope this year with the imminent fuel price increases. I just can't understand how the government allows the energy companies to get away with it. People die from living in damp, cold housing each year, especially pensioners. I've heard some people say it's a question of whether to eat or keep warm this year.

'I'm not used to all this heat,' Demi says, her thumbs furiously sweeping over Harry's phone. Multi-tasking, admirable, she takes after her mum. 'Ours is usually on a constant low. Mum's always boiling, prancing around in a vest most of the time.'

'Menopause,' we both say in unison, then grin at each other.

I take a deep breath. 'Tell you what, Demi, I'm not looking forward to the menopause.'

'Ah, you've got ages yet.'

'I wish. I'm only ten years younger than your mum, you know.'

'Really?' Demi sounds astounded. 'She looks like she could be *your* mum.'

'Demi!'

'What?' She jerks her head up and fixes me with a long stare. 'She's twice the size of you, for a start.' Her eyes flit over my body. 'Where did you get those black skinny jeans from?'

I smooth my jeans down. 'I can't remember, they're old ... River Island, I think.'

'Ha! I bet they don't even make them in her size.'

'Demi! Of course they do. It's just not her style, that's all.'

'Emma, she's frumpy. She's let herself go. Most of her clothes are tents nowadays. Her fashion icon is that fat Greek singer who wears those weird kaftans.'

'What are you talking about?' Demi is starting to annoy me now. 'What Greek singer?'

'The one with that long hair and beard, name similar to mine.'

'What, Demis Roussos?' I say, my voice rising an octave.

'Yeah, that's him. My Yiayia's got his CD collection.' She reverts her attention to her phone again, completely unperturbed.

I shake my head. 'Oh, come off it, Demi, she's not as fat as he was.'

But Demi's like a dog with a bone. 'You know that banoffee pie she made?' I nod. It was delicious, but most of us were full after Xenia's banquet, so there was at least half a pie left. 'Well, she'll polish the leftovers off on her own by tomorrow.'

What is it with teenagers and their parents? Demi's got to stop criticising her mum. I wasn't like that with mine. I used to love spending time with my parents when I was her age – albeit individually because they'd divorced by then. 'Well, she builds up a healthy appetite running around after you lot.' I slap her leg playfully.

Demi looks at me with a deadpan expression. 'Emma, the only exercise she gets is when she's getting it on with my dad. They can't keep their hands off each other these days. He's always chasing her around the house, groping her at the sink. Urgh.' She shivers in disgust, as if her skin is crawling with cockroaches. 'She's overweight. End of.' She goes back to her game, eyes wide with annoyance.

'Maybe she's happy with her shape, Demi.' I hope Demi isn't being brainwashed by skinny girls on the catwalk. She barely touched her food at lunchtime, announcing, to everyone's astonishment, including her parents, that she was now a vegetarian and that there was nothing she could eat that didn't have meat in it, accusing us all of being racist.

'Don't be so stupid,' Andreas had said, cutting into a piece of lamb, 'animals aren't a race, they're a species, you doughnut.'

I look at Demi next to me on the sofa. 'Size zero isn't the way to go, you know. It's not...' I air quote with two fingers, '... normal.'

'Emma, she's bordering obesity.' She stops playing and looks at me, eyes full of concern.

'Well, I wouldn't go as far as that, Demi.'

'She's a size sixteen, for Christ's sake!'

'That's hardly –'

'She won't stop eating!' She cuts across me. 'And doesn't exercise. She needs to lose weight.' Her voice is suddenly quiet, delicate. 'It's dangerous at her age.' Her expression tugs at my heartstrings. She really does care about her mum. 'And I don't think she's happy with her shape. She won't stand in front of a full-length mirror.'

I didn't realise Caroline was having issues with her image; too wrapped up in my own life to even notice. Caroline's a good friend. How completely selfish of me.

'I'll have a word with her,' I promise. 'Maybe we can arrange to go on power walks or easy jogs. I can ask Ola to work out a healthy eating plan for us. One we can follow together.'

Demi says that's a brilliant idea and that a plan like that could even help with her menopausal symptoms. Satisfied, she leans in and gives me a small hug before returning to her game of *Candy Crush*.

I glance at Spiros sprawled on the armchair, his feet on the matching footstall in front of him, mouth agape, quietly snoring. He always falls asleep in front of the TV after lunch. He's a good dad. Harry and Mas are lucky to have such caring parents.

I remember when Harry first introduced me to them. It was at Meze at Sunset. They were working part-time for Mas. He didn't pay them or anything. They just did it to help their son and to have something to do.

I was nervous as hell when we got there; hands shaking, heart knocking wildly against my chest. I'd heard a lot about Harry's previous girlfriend from Mas. She was an Anglo-Greek Cypriot, like Harry, and they'd been together for seven-and-a-half years. Her name was Zafira, which I thought sounded very exotic, and she was from a wealthy background. Mas said she was a looker too, did a bit of modelling while she studied for her medical degree, and was an avid scuba diver. I had a lot to live up to. But I needn't have worried. Much to Mas's disappointment, Harry's folks welcomed me with open arms. Spiros confided in me later that he was secretly glad that Harry had split up with Zafira, that she and her family were a snooty lot from Nicosia, that they had Harry under their thumb. Caroline's appraisal was a bit more transparent.

'She was a bloody bitch, Emma,' she complained to me not long after we'd met. 'She got on with Mas like a house on fire because they had similar personalities, but I hated her. And I think the feeling was mutual. I'm so glad God sent you to Harry. An angel from heaven.'

Needless to say, I hit it off with Caroline from day one, and we've not looked back since.

I push my tortoiseshell spectacles back into position. I snapped them up in the sale at the opticians last Tuesday after my credit card was rejected. 'Where have the boys disappeared to?' I ask Demi as casually as I can, hoping they're not hiding behind the shed in the garden having secret chats again. 'They haven't gone out, have they?' Demi glances up with irritation at the sound of Caroline's laughter echoing from the kitchen. Xenia is teaching her Greek coffee cup reading, similar to tea leaf reading only with coffee. I suppose it'll add another string to her bow, although I'm not quite sure where she'll find clients that drink Greek coffee, not with it being such an acquired taste.

'Dad's gone to fetch my charger,' Demi replies. I glance at the phone in her hands. To my dismay, she hasn't let it out of her sight since Harry let her borrow it over two hours ago. 'And Yiayia sent Andreas and Uncle Harry to pick the last of the figs.' She pulls a face, 'Hate figs.'

'Oh, OK.' I sigh. 'Oh, damn.'

Demi looks up at me briefly, grinning. 'Level failed again?'

'Yes.' I say, indignantly, as my phone vibrates in my hand with a message. 'And I only had one more gel to clear.'

And just then, to my delight, she lays the phone down on the sofa next to me and my nose does an involuntary little twitch, like something out of *Bewitched*. I wonder if she's going to go somewhere, maybe into the kitchen to spend a little time with her mum and grandma. This could be the moment I've been waiting for. In a few seconds I could be reading Harry's text messages and checking his calls. But to my dismay she kicks off her shoes and stretches her legs onto the coffee table in front of her before picking the phone up again. 'Oooh, it's so annoying when you've got just the *one* gel,' she groans. 'Like, hello, are you trying to drive me insane?'

'I'm out of lives,' I complain, resting the phone on the armrest of the sofa.

'Do you want me to send you one?'

I frown at her as Xenia appears at the door. 'Another cub'o'tea, Emma?' She offers, rubbing her hands together.

'Oh, no, I'm fine, thanks, Xenia.' I pick up my empty teacup and saucer and hand it to her.

'You sure?' She says, taking the cup from my outstretched hand.

'Definitely.' I smile at her warmly.

She nods, then looks at her husband. 'Ah, he still asleep. Lazy.' She peers at the tiny coffee cup on the table. 'He didn't drink.' She rocks her head from side to side as she leans over and picks up the full cup. 'Is cold now,' she grumbles. 'No good. I make you nice cub' o' Greek coffee, then?'

I press my hand over my tummy gently. I shouldn't have had that large helping of banoffee pie straight after lunch. 'No, really. I'm full, thank you.'

'OK, dahrli.' Xenia looks at Demi, knocking her legs off the coffee table with her knee as she passes. 'Demitria, you want another cub'o'tea?'

'Yeah, OK, Yiayia.' Demi says, her eyes transfixed on the tiny screen, which she's now holding close to her face. 'Make it the Greek way, though, with those smelly twigs,' she calls out, as Xenia makes for the door. By this she means tea with cinnamon and cloves, which is quite aromatic, actually. We have it at home sometimes.

'Can you send me a *Candy Crush* life, then?' I ask Demi, as Spiros lets out a loud, sudden grunt, causing us both to jerk in our seats.

'Yeah.' She frowns at her sleeping granddad. 'Just send me a request and I'll fire one over to you.'

'Oh, OK.' I smile, picking up the phone. 'I wouldn't mind having another go.'

'Told you it was addictive, didn't I?' She chuckles. 'Now you can see why I was so pissed off with my mum.'

I send her the request, then sit back and retrieve the text message that buzzed through a few moments ago.

Hi Red. Having a good Sunday?

I can't believe it. It's that Marc from The King's Head pub again. I thought he'd got the message the other day when I didn't bother texting back. What a persistent man. I'm flattered that he finds me attractive but he knows I'm with someone, so I'm not quite sure why he keeps bombarding me with messages.

I text back –

Lunch with in-laws.

Good thinking about in-laws because it proves I'm either married or engaged.

He replies quickly –

Poor u. Dinner offer still on.

I shake my head as I text back. It seems like nothing will faze this man. I'm going to have to spell it out.

Sorry. Told u. With someone.

'Demi,' Caroline calls out as my phone vibrates with another message. 'Can you come here a moment, please? We need your expert opinion.'

Demi swears under her breath, ignoring her mother's request. The loving, caring daughter I saw moments ago is now replaced by the usual stroppy, whiny teenager. Caroline bends over backwards for her family - washing, cleaning, cooking, chauffeuring them to and fro. She's sacrificed everything for them. Her career as a primary school teacher dissolved the moment she gave birth to Andreas, choosing to be a stay-at-home mum, wanting to raise her children herself. Her kids and husband have always come first. They're her life. Yet they treat her like some sort of servant. It's a good job she's a tough cookie.

I go back to Marc's text –

Friends. I promise. Client is still keen. Wants to see ur work. It's a biggie too.

A biggie? I feel my antennae emerging. I could definitely do with the work and the exposure. Once I finish this job for the new novelist, I don't have anything else lined up. But meeting up with Marc, is that really a good idea? It's obvious he's got a bit of a crush on me.

Then, as if he could read my mind, his next text buzzes through –

Won't b just us. Client will attend too.

I almost leap off my seat with excitement. Brilliant. Perhaps he's a genuinely nice guy who just wants to help out, after all.

I text him back immediately, asking what sort of illustration she needs.

I gasp at his reply, causing Demi to give me one of her looks.

It's a book publisher. Prob lots.

Oh my God. If I could get in with a publisher I may get regular work. This could be my big break. The break that The Magic Touch predicted yesterday – *"You'll get a big break with a little help from a friend."*

I take a full, deep breath. I need to calm down and get everything into perspective. Caroline told me that the app was just for fun. I'm getting carried away. This client may hate my style. There are no guarantees. I bite the inside of my lip, regaining my equilibrium as Caroline screams at the top of her lungs 'Demi!'

'Oh, for God's sake.' Demi gets to her feet, tosses the phone onto her seat, and stomps off to the kitchen.

I stare at Harry's phone, eyes wide, as if it's a crystal ball containing the secrets to my future. I lick my dry lips, gazing at it longingly. In that phone lies my fate, for better or worse. It might make my life all rosy and dreamy, or it may blow my world up like an explosive. But either way, I have a right to know, don't I? I should read it. This is my golden opportunity. If I don't take it now it may never come again. As I reach for it, Spiros snorts loudly. I stand up, heart hammering, and lean forward on the sole of my shoe to get a good look at Spiros. He grunts and shuffles in his seat, still fast asleep. Demi, Caroline, and Xenia's voices echoing from the kitchen confirm they're engrossed in a heated debate about coffee stains and their meanings.

I slowly sit back down, my eyes not leaving Harry's phone as a rush of guilt washes over me like a big, angry wave in a torrential storm. I swallow hard. No, I shouldn't read Harry's messages. I promised I wouldn't and I don't want to break that promise. It would be an invasion of his privacy. A violation. I wouldn't like it if he started reading my messages, would I?

I take a deep breath as I re-read Marc's text, wondering if I should take up his offer. If it'll be the three of us then what harm could it do? I could potentially get lots of work out of this. Our lives could change. Harry and I could go on that holiday. We might even be able to pay Mas back some of the money we owe him. So what if Marc has a schoolboy crush on me? It's not as if I'll be on a date with him. He said it'll be the three of us. As I start to type out my reply a message chimes through on Harry's phone. Then another, and another.

His phone is suddenly in my trembling hand. I look at the screen as the messages pop through.

First message –

Sorry to disturb ur lunch. Are we still on?

Second message –

I know u said no messages till after 6.30 but I'm desperate. Can u get away?

I glance at the clock on the mantelpiece. 5.45.
Third message –

I need to see you. Ring me asap. Please!! ☹ XX

I almost cry out as my hand clamps over my mouth. My heart is beating so hard against my chest I'm surprised it hasn't given Spiros a migraine. I can't resist the opportunity. I slide the messages open and begin to text –

Sorry. Who is this? Phone crashed. Lost my contacts.

The reply is swift.

Isabella. You mad wine-o. Is this Harry's phone?

My eyes blur with tears. I feel as if someone has plunged their hand into my chest and wrenched out my heart. I can just about read the words that spring on to the screen –

Sorry. Wrong number.

And then I hear a voice. 'Emma?' I look up. Harry is standing in front of me, bowl of figs in hand, face ashen, jaw clenched. 'Can I have my phone back please?'

Chapter Nine

Our drive home is in stony-faced silence, punctured only by the hum of the blow heater and the tinkle of Magic 105.4 from the radio. I knew it. I knew there was someone else. I had that feeling deep down in the pit of my stomach, the one I had when Carl was having an affair. I knew about that too, long before Jan told me. I say affair but I really should be saying *affairs*.

Carl was unfaithful to me throughout our marriage. He even had someone on the go on our wedding day – a girl from admin called Stacey. Jan, his secretary at the time, let it slip over one of our morning coffee sessions several months later. 'But don't say you heard it from me,' she pleaded, desperate not to lose her job. I didn't believe her at the time. I just thought she was jealous, that she might've had the hots for Carl. Women threw themselves at him. Not because of his good looks – he was no stunner, nowhere near as handsome as Harry. It was more about his persona, his bravado. He had that air of confidence about him and the ability to make you feel like you were the only person in the room. And being a successful businessman always helped – he was always flashing the cash.

I got on well with Jan. We still keep in touch from time to time by email. Jan also confided that he even kept in contact with Stacey from admin during our honeymoon, which explained why he crept off onto the balcony to make his phone calls, fobbing me off with the usual business calls line and how he was unable to get good reception in our suite. And like a fool I fell for it. But Carl was nothing like Harry. He was such a smooth-talking, calculating man. I believed every word he told me in the early days.

I look at Harry now. His jaw is clenched, his temples throbbing. My heart aches, yet I feel completely numb. How could he do this to me? To *us*? Harry. Lovely, dependable, kind Harry. How? What went wrong? Why didn't I see the cracks?

I stare out of the widow as we whizz by houses and trees swishing in the rain. Some have lights on. Others look completely vacant. I wonder who lives inside those houses, what their lives are like.

I throw a glance at Harry. We're at the traffic lights, rain spitting on the windscreen, wipers swishing intermittently. I open my mouth to speak when Whitney Houston belts out 'I Will Always Love You' on the radio and I crumble.

Harry speaks first. He hates to see me cry, always has.

'It's not what you think,' he exhales loudly. His voice is solemn, firm.

I can barely speak through my tears.

'You promised me, Harry,' I gulp. 'You said you'd never cheat on me. Remember our deal?' We agreed when we first got together that if one of us wanted out then we'd talk about before running into someone else's arms.

He nods quickly. 'Of course I do, and I haven't broken that promise.'

'But you've lied to me,' I protest.

'No, I haven't.' He drums his fingers on the steering wheel, chewing the inside of his bottom lip. 'Well, technically I have but ...'

'You said it was a colleague,' I cry as the lights turn to amber.

'It is,' he insists, crunching the car into first gear.

'A man, you said.' Fresh tears flush my eyes, I can barely focus. 'A male nurse.'

'All right, all right. I'm sorry.' The indicator clangs loudly. 'It's a female colleague,' he admits as he takes a sharp corner.

'Don't lie any more to me, Harry.' I yank the sun visor down and stare at my reflection in the mirror. I look like a snotty-nosed monster. I wipe my wet, make-up stained cheeks hard with my fingers, making black horizontal lines across my face with the teary mascara as we fly over a road bump. I slam the sun visor shut. I can't bear to look at myself. I need to get home, take a shower, freshen up so I can think straight. 'You owe me the truth.' I close my eyes for a moment. 'If you've met someone else, if it's over between us, then just tell me straight,' I sniff. 'I'm a big girl. I can take it.'

He changes gear and puts his foot down on the accelerator. He stares ahead, wordless, soaring through the wet streets. His silence telling me that I'm right. It's over. He's leaving me for Isabella. My heart breaks a little more.

I feel slightly disorientated when he pulls up against the kerb. 'Why are you stopping?' I say, bewildered, dabbing at my nose with the back of my hand.

'What do you mean?' He looks at me as if I'm mad. 'We're home.'

'Oh.' I glance up at our lovely blue stained-glass door – our lovely home – the streetlamp light through the raindrops making the whole house glitter. I unlock my seatbelt. 'Oh yes ... I ...' I feel completely stupid. I bend down and pick my bag up from between my feet.

He turns the ignition off, then swivels towards me. His warm thumbs are caressing my sodden face. 'I'm so sorry, Emma.' My bag slips from my loose grip.

I shake my head, clamping my hands over my ears. I don't want to hear it. I don't want our relationship to end. I imagined spending the rest of my life with Harry, growing old with him. What am I going to do? I haven't got a Plan B.

'Come on, stop crying … let me explain.' We wrestle as he tries to pull my hands away from my ears. 'Emma, stop it. Listen. Will you … just. Please,' he yells, and I let go of his hands. 'I love you, you silly moo,' he says quietly, his soulful eyes searching mine. Yes, I'm sure he does, as one would love a sister, an aunt … or a pet dog. 'Isabella is more than a colleague, I admit.' Oh God, oh God, no! He's going to confess. I'm going to get the 'it's not you, it's me' speech. I can't bear it. I wish he'd just stop.

I look into his deep brown eyes. My beautiful man. Why did I let our relationship die? What have I done? If only I'd married him when he first asked me. This is all my fault. I got too complacent. I pushed him into the arms of another woman. Caroline was right to warn me. Obviously she knew something. Mas must've told her. That's what all that secret chatting was about in the garden earlier. It all makes sense now. Oh God, everyone knows. I'm a laughing stock.

'How long has it been going on?' I manage, blowing my nose loudly into a McDonalds serviette that I found stuffed in the back of the glove compartment.

'You make it sound like we're having an affair,' he says incredulously.

I give him a sharp look. 'Harry, are you having a laugh?' My tears have dried but I'm still completely broken. 'Credit me with a bit of dignity, will you?'

'We're not having an affair. I'd never do that to you, Emma, you know that.' OK, now I'm totally confused. What is he implying, that it was a one-night stand? That he was too weak to refuse her advances? That she's now clutching at straws, like some sort of bunny boiler, having an imaginary relationship with *my* man? 'Isabella is a good friend,' he goes on. 'She's been there for me, you know?' No, actually, I don't know, but I don't add fuel to the fire.

I stay silent. He rubs his tired eyes, then drops his head onto the steering wheel, defeated. And just at that moment my phone starts ringing. Shit. I ignore it. If it's important they can leave a voicemail. I interlace my fingers. They're cold. I rub them on my thighs as my phone starts ringing again.

'You'd better answer it. It might be urgent,' Harry sighs, looking up at me. 'It might be your mum or sister. Her baby's due soon, isn't it?'

I fish the blaring phone out of my handbag angrily. It's Marc. Oh, for goodness' sake, talk about bad timing. I press decline.

'How long have you known her?' I say icily, throwing the phone back into my open handbag on the floor between my legs. 'This Isabella. This *friend* that's been there for you? You've not mentioned her before.'

'Not long.' He tugs at his ear nervously. 'A few weeks, a month.'

'So, if you're not having an affair then what is it? A fling?'

He looks at me as if I'm insane. 'No! Have you not listened to a word I've said? We're not seeing each other. I don't fancy her, and she doesn't fancy me. We're just mates.'

'Mates?' I can't hide the disbelief in my voice. 'What, friends with benefits?'

'Don't be stupid, Emma.' He looks at me pointedly for a moment. 'She's half my age, for heaven's sake!' My heart sinks. A younger woman. I knew it. I hate her even more. 'Look, I shouldn't really be telling you this. I promised

Isabella, but I can't have you thinking the worst.' He pinches his top lip between his fingers thoughtfully, glancing out of the window as a motorbike races past us, tearing through the traffic. We watch as it swerves and sways into the distance. 'She's having trouble with her husband.' He drums his fingers on the steering wheel, not looking at me.

'What? She's married?' I say, aghast.

'Yes! To some bastard who's a bit rough with her.' I feel a moment of asphyxiation as Carl's face bounces into my mind. I try to swallow but my throat is dry.

'Oh come off it, Harry,' I manage after a few moments of clarity. Obviously this is just a ploy. He's trying to hit a nerve so that I can come round, but I'm not going to fall for that old trick. I lived with a philanderer for years. I know all the tricks and excuses. 'I wasn't born yesterday.' I look out of the window and spot Alistair's silhouette behind the nets. It's getting dark and he's drawing the curtains. I was meant to pop round this evening, have a game of *Scrabble* and a gin and tonic. But I'm in no mood for socialising now. I return my attention to Harry.

'Look, I'm telling you the truth,' he insists. 'She's just a good friend. You've got to believe me.' But that's the thing – I don't. And I don't have to believe anything, do I?

'Well, if that's the case. If all you are is *mates*,' I shout, 'then why didn't you just tell me that in the first place? Instead of making up all these lies about it being a male nurse.'

'Because I knew you'd react like this,' he yells.

'What?' I snort in disbelief. 'Are you saying that I'm jealous?'

'Well, aren't you?' He hits back. 'Why can't I have female friends? You've got male friends.'

'That's different,' I protest, blowing my nose. 'Most of them are clients, anyway. I *have to* wine and dine them. It's part of my job.' I take a deep breath of dense, humid air and my stomach turns. Our ranting has steamed up the windows. Any passer-by is going to think we're getting it on.

I rub the condensation off the window with my fingertips, leaving a zigzag pattern on the pane, and momentarily I'm transported to the back seat of my parents' BMW. I'm eight years old, drawing faces on the glass, playing noughts and crosses, then Dad's hand smacks across the back of my legs as I step out of the car, his loud, scary voice reprimanding me for smudging his windows. Mum screaming at him, telling him to leave me alone, that all children draw on steamed-up windows. Her arms around my trembling little body, ushering me gently into our cold, dark house. Dad silently following behind us, head bowed, sorry but always a little too late.

I open the window to let the glass clear, swallowing back another big, fat tear.

'What about that passcode? Why did you suddenly change the one on your phone?'

'Because it's safe?' He looks at me as if I'm five years old. 'You update yours, don't you?'

'I might do…' He's got me. I stall for time. 'How do you know, anyway? Have you been spying on me?'

'And how could I possibly do that? You and that phone are joined at the hip.'

'What?'

'You heard. You're addicted. Obsessed. Don't think I don't see you checking Facebook and Twitter in the middle of the night.'

I take a sharp intake of breath. 'I don't!' I do, actually. But only sometimes. When I can't sleep. Hardly at all.

'You're always on it, Emma. You can't leave it alone. You're obsessed. It's embarrassing sometimes, especially when we're with other people.'

'That is not true,' I protest. 'I only check my emails when we're socialising in case any work comes in.'

'Yeah, keep telling yourself that, Emma.' He shakes his head. 'I don't know how you can even concentrate on watching TV when you're giving a running commentary on Facebook.'

'I hardly ever do that on Facebook.'

'Well, Twitter, then.' He waves a hand in the air, annoyed. 'Same bloody thing. All crap, if you ask me.'

'You've got Facebook.'

He looks at me, amazed. 'I hardly ever use it. I only check it once a week.'

That's it, I've had enough.

'Stop trying to turn this around on me. You're the one who's suddenly put in a secret passcode.' He looks at me, deadpan. 'So, come on, how do you know I've updated *my* passcode?' I ask, trying to control the rising panic in my voice. I wonder if he's tried reading my text messages, too.

'You're unbelievable.' He shakes his head. 'I'm not like you, you know. I happen to trust you.'

'Yes, well I've got nothing to hide.' I cross my arms, staring ahead at a group of lads swaggering towards us, eating chips out of a paper bag, laughing, messing around. I shudder. The gap in the window has cleared the steam but the cold air seeping through is giving me a chill.

'Why wouldn't you trust me?' I say, shivering.

'I don't believe this.' He throws his hands up. 'Look, I'll take it off if it's bothering you so much.' He pulls out his phone from his jacket pocket and starts fiddling around with it. 'There. Happy now?'

'You didn't have to do that.' But I'm so glad he has because it's given me a bit of confidence.

We're silent for a few moments and then, 'I'm sorry, Emma. I know you're not happy about this, but I can't just stand by and let some monster push a woman around. She needs my help.' Silence. It's started to rain again, spitting on the car like tiny pins. The faint sound of an alarm whirs in the distance, merging with the shrill sound of a police siren.

'I see.'

'Good. Finally, we're getting somewhere.'

'A friend?'

'Yes, Emma,' he sighs loudly, 'a friend. Look, if you don't believe me then ask her yourself.' He thumbs over the screen of his phone.

'Oh, don't be ridiculous. Put your phone away.' I draw my lips in and bite on them softly to stop myself from accusing him of anything else. A young couple rush past us, the man holding his jacket over their heads, clearly in love. There was a time, not long ago, when we couldn't keep our hands off each other. What happened?

'You do understand, don't you?' He narrows his eyes, uncertainty in his voice.

I nod quickly, sniffing nervously. Of course I understand. A friend in need. A married woman. But it wouldn't be the first time he's rescued a victim and then fallen madly in love with her.

Chapter Ten

He said he loves me. That he doesn't want to leave me for another (much younger) woman. Why am I not full of joy? Relieved, even? Why does my mind keep flitting back to the texts she sent him over an hour ago? Those affectionate, imposing messages with 'I want you' silently weaved within the words, rising like a poisonous vapour, threatening to destroy my life. I pinch the bridge of my nose and close my eyes as a dull pain travels from my left temple and nestles over my eye.

'But why does it have to be *you* that runs to her rescue?' I ask, head down staring into my lap. 'Hasn't she got any family, friends?'

'Come on, Emma, you know how people don't want to get involved.'

There are a few moments of silence and then I say, 'She could go to the police.' I don't even know why I said that, and Harry doesn't credit me with an answer. 'What's he like, anyway?' I sniff. Carl wasn't very tall for a man – about my height, broad, and stocky. 'The big burly type or a weasel?'

'I don't know. I only saw him once, briefly, when he came to pick Izzy up. He didn't get out of the car and it was dark so I didn't really see him properly,' he says quietly, curling his hand around the steering wheel. 'But he's a bloke, isn't he?' His fist tightens around the wheel. 'And she's just a wee thing.' A wee thing? I feel a pang of jealousy at the affectionate tone in his voice.

I think about what Harry has said. Carl wasn't exactly a bodybuilder but he could certainly pack a punch. I'm being unreasonable and jealous, selfish, even. This woman is in trouble, and Harry could save her from a potential life of misery. I should let him get on with it, help her. If I'd had a knight in shining armour to help me in the early years I wouldn't have lost my good job, my dignity, my home. Besides, he's just promised me that there's nothing going on between them. Our relationship was built on trust and if that dies, we'll have nothing left.

'So, what does he do?' I press my hand over my mouth. 'Does he beat her up? Slap her?' I murmur through my ice cold fingers.

'No.'

'No?' I spin round in my chair and face him.

'Well, don't sound so disappointed,' Harry says, taken aback. 'He's a bully. He pushes her around, makes threats. That's how these abusers start. I see it day in day out in my job.' He's right about that, although Carl went straight for the kill with me, without any preambles. 'They've only been married a few months and already he's smashed up the crockery her grandmother gave them as a wedding gift.' He juts his lips out. 'She loved those plates.'

I close my eyes as thoughts of Carl dig their heels into the depths of my mind, demanding to be resurfaced.

We'd been married almost three weeks when he first attacked me. I barely knew him, to be honest. In fact, I don't even think I was truly in love with him. I just got carried away by the moment, each day slipping into the next like some kind of romantic Hollywood film. I accepted his extravagant marriage proposal on a gondola in Venice just months after I'd met him. A stupid mistake, I know. But I was intoxicated by the excitement of the beautiful city and my looming twenty-seventh birthday.

I was a bit of an idealist back in the day. I wanted the big, family house with a beautiful garden, two children (a boy and a girl, obviously), a dog, and a loving husband. And it all had to be done and dusted by the time I was thirty-two. Carl bought me a ring from *Le Gioie di Bortolo*, a smart jewellery shop selling beautiful vintage pieces. We came home all loved-up and engaged.

Mum and Ola were gobsmacked when I announced that Carl had booked a registry office wedding for two weeks' time. They warned me against it for all the obvious reasons, but also because they saw a controlling and manipulative side that I couldn't see through my rose-tinted glasses.

'Are you out of your mind, Emma?' Ola had screamed, hand on hip. 'You've only known him five minutes, and I don't like the way he is with you. You've changed.'

'Emma, please,' Mum had pleaded, 'he's not right for you. Don't make the same mistake I did. Please just give it another six months, at least, then if you still want to marry him, fine.'

I rubbished their concerns away. I was a strong, independent woman, earning a good salary as a graphic designer at a top London advertising agency. My career was going from strength to strength. I knew what I was doing. They just didn't know Carl well enough, that was all. Didn't realise how lucky I was landing someone as proactive and successful as him. I was sick of dating men who were in constant awe of me. I wanted a real man, someone who'd take control for once, look after me for a change. And Carl ticked all the boxes.

He slipped the diamond-encrusted, 18 carat gold wedding ring on my finger three days after my twenty-seventh birthday. Much to Ola's disappointment, Carl persuaded me to have his sister, Fran, as my maid of honour. His reasoning was that she'd done it twice before so knew the ropes, plus she was family and, unlike Ola, she was happy for us. He managed to wrangle one of the banquet rooms at The Dorchester Hotel at short notice, and I had my fairy tale wedding.

We had a champagne reception for our two-hundred guests with hot and cold canapés, followed by a five-course meal and more champagne. It was big, lavish, ostentatious. Halfway through the reception, Carl surprised me by assembling some of our family and close friends outside, then handed me the keys to my wedding gift – a brand spanking new Audi TTS Coupe in white. I can still hear the gasps, applauds and cheers from the crowd. I remember feeling like the luckiest woman on this planet.

We spent the next three weeks basking in the sun at a deluxe resort in the Maldives, all booked and paid for by Carl. I couldn't believe my luck. It was pure indulgence. I felt like I was living the dream. I had it all. A wonderful husband, a brilliant job, a great future. I had to pinch myself to make sure I wasn't dreaming.

On the last week of our honeymoon my fairy tale came to a sudden halt and I got to see the real Carl Clarke. We'd met another couple, Max and Cindy, also on their honeymoon. Coincidentally, they were Londoners too, but unlike us, they were childhood sweethearts. We'd shared a few drinks at the bar, had a laugh. Then on their last night, Carl suggested we all meet up in the evening for a farewell meal. I wasn't that keen to begin with, since we only had another three days to go, and I wanted to spend more quality time with my new husband before we headed back to our hectic, city lives.

'Come on, Emma,' he'd said, stroking my hair after we'd just made love for the second time that day. 'It'll be nice to spend some time with other people.'

The evening went quite well and I found myself enjoying their company. Carl was right, as always – it was nice to spend some time with other people. Max kept the champagne flowing all evening. We'd all had quite a lot to drink, so when Max pulled me up for a dance I didn't resist. Carl and Cindy followed behind us, laughing and joking. It was a great evening. One of the best we'd had.

Back at our suite, I threw my arms around his neck and told him how much I loved him, how I'd enjoyed every moment of this holiday, and was looking forward to my future as Mrs Clarke.

His lips brushed mine but then he suddenly pulled away and pushed me back so hard that I landed on my back. I was horrified. What was happening? Was he having some kind of seizure?

'Carl? What the hell is wrong with you?' I stared up at him in horror.

'Don't play the victim. You were all over him,' he spat, his face red with fury.

'What?' I scrambled to my feet.

'I saw the two of you rubbing against each other like something out of *Dirty Dancing*.'

'Carl, what are you talking about? We were dancing, that's all.'

'No,' he shook his head, his grey eyes shone with fury. 'It was more than that. You wanted to fuck him,' he barked through gritted teeth, fists clenched. 'I know your sort, business women. You like variety.'

I couldn't believe what I was hearing.

'Carl, for goodness' sake, I'm your wife. I don't want anyone else!'

'Don't you bloody lie to me, you bitch,' he screamed, his face inches from mine. 'I saw you, the way you were bumping and grinding your body against his, your hands all over him like a fucking octopus.'

'Don't be so bloody ridiculous,' I retorted, getting to my feet and pushing him back. I'd had enough of Carl's stupidity for one night. I'd never seen him have more than two drinks up until now. Obviously, he wasn't a good drunk. 'You're drunk. Sleep it off. I'm going for a shower.'

Then, as I turned to walk away, he grabbed me by the hair and brought me to my knees. He then yanked me up by the arm, bending it behind me. I fought as he dragged me towards the bathroom. His hand hit the back of my neck like a vacuum. I held onto the doorframe, trying to get out of his grip but he was too strong. My hands slid off the doorframe and he forced me into the bathroom, kicking and screaming. My face hovered over the toilet bowl. 'Oh God,' I panted, panic bursting in my chest. 'Carl, please.' I felt the bile rising in my throat.

'Apologise,' he screamed, foaming at the mouth. 'Or I swear I'll flush your head down this fucking toilet.'

I'd never been so terrified in all my life. 'But I haven't done anything wrong. Carl, please … I …' He shoved my head into the bowl, one hand on the flush. 'OK, OK. I'm sorry.' I yelled.

'Say you won't ever, *ever* humiliate me like that in public again.'

'But, Carl, I …'

'Say it!'

'I promise,' I wept.

'Louder, I can't hear you.'

'I'm sorry,' I cried, my voice thick with tears. 'I promise.'

He let go, chest heaving, took a few uneven steps back, then wiped the sweat off his forehead with the back of his arm before staggering back into the bedroom, leaving me a weeping heap on the floor.

I woke the next morning with a sore head. Every part of me ached, especially my soul. He'd forced me to sleep on the floor, saying I was a whore and deserved to be punished. My bubble had burst. The dream was over.

'Good morning, beautiful.' Carl was on his knees, bright-eyed, clean shaven, holding a breakfast tray on his lap.

'Carl …' I croaked, trying to focus. My throat felt like sandpaper, my head was throbbing. 'What …'

He put the tray down and pulled me up gently. He held me as I limped to the bed, my left arm and shoulder numb.

'Here,' he said, feeding me orange juice, which I gulped down thirstily. 'Too much champagne last night, methinks.' How could he possibly joke about last night's events? Was he insane? Had I married a psychopath?

'Carl, what happened to you? I didn't recognise you last night.'

'What do you mean?' He picked up the tray and placed it onto my lap, then explained each item on the plate in detail, including where the eggs and bacon were sourced from.

'I mean …' I began.

'I thought we could go on a trip,' he cut in, drawing up the blinds and flooding the room with hot sunshine. A trip? Was he completely mad?

'Carl, about last night …'

He closed his eyes and for a moment he looked contrite, but then he suddenly snapped back into his jolly mode, spun round on his heel, and started opening drawers and cupboard doors, assembling clothes.

'There's a boat trip at twelve. We could just make it if you get a wiggle on. Then I thought we could go into town, do a bit of shopping, stop off for some lunch and …'

'Carl, you hurt me,' I cut in softly. He stopped dead in his tracks. 'You do remember, don't you?'

He was silent for a while, and then I got the horrible notion that he was about to turn into The Incredible Hulk again. 'Emma.' I recoiled as he rushed towards me. 'Oh God, oh God. Please don't be afraid of me. I won't hurt you. I promise.' He was on his knees, kissing my hands repeatedly as if I was the Pope. 'I'm so sorry. I'm a lousy drunk. I don't usually drink that much. It was that Max's fault, he kept topping up my glass all night. I haven't been like that in twelve years. Please tell me you'll forgive me.'

I shook my head. I knew I'd made a mistake marrying him right then. Mum and Ola were right. I could end it now, I thought. Get out while it was still early. 'Carl, I'm sorry but last night I saw a different side to you and I don't think …'

Then he started crying, begging me to forgive him. 'Please, Emma. I love you. I don't know what came over me. It's because I love you so much and seeing you with another man was hard.'

'What?' I said in disbelief.

'No, what I mean is,' he grabbed my hands but I snatched them away. 'I know you were only having a friendly dance,' he went on, looking hurt, 'but … but … the drink mashed up my brain and … Look, I should've told you this before but, well, I'm on prescription drugs.'

'Drugs?'

'Don't look so worried. It's nothing serious. Just something to help me relax, you know?' I looked down at his hands, clasped together tightly in his lap, his knuckles white. 'I'm such a stupid fuck.' He dropped his head in his hands and started to weep again. Big, fat tears fell onto his cream linen trousers. 'I promise you, I'll never, *ever* hurt you again. Ever.' He put his hand on his chest. 'I swear on my mother's life. Just please don't leave me. I'd die without you.' I looked at him, and pity crawled through my veins as he cried and cried like a lost little boy. If it was mixing drink and drugs that turned him into a monster then perhaps he deserved another chance, right?

'OK, OK, stop crying,' I said, rubbing his shoulder and sighing loudly. 'Let's put it behind us and start again.'

That was the beginning of five years of hell.

I look round at Harry.

'She's frightened, Emma.' His voice is solemn, concerned.

I sweep my hand through my hair. 'OK, let's just go inside and talk about this.' I open the passenger door and dangle one leg onto the wet pavement, but then I hear the engine running. 'What are you doing?'

'I won't be long.'

'What?'

'Look, she wants to move in with her parents for a while, have some time to think. I said I'd give her a lift, she's got some heavy stuff.'

'Harry, you can't just drop everything and run to her every time she calls. She could take a cab, for goodness' sake. You've got a wi ...' The word dies on my lips.

'But that's just it, Emma. I haven't got a wife, have I? Because you don't want to marry me.' I swing my legs back into the car and close the door, hard, and I'm sure I see Alistair's curtains twitch. 'Is that what all this is about?' I ask, crossly.

'Of course it isn't.'

'Because if it is, then ...'

'Then what? You'll say yes?' He snorts, a twinge of sarcasm in his voice. Not like Harry at all. This must be Isabella's influence. Clearly she's already started to work her magic on him.

'Harry, we've been through this before. I mean, what's the rush? It's not as if we've got children to worry about or anything, is it?'

He looks at me incredulously. 'Now you're talking crap.'

'I'm just saying ...'

'Emma, you don't know what you're saying,' he cuts across me. 'People don't only get married for children, you know. They do it because they love each other. To be a family. A unit. For commitment.'

I can't believe what I'm hearing. 'Yes, I know but, I ...'

'Oh, stop it, Emma. We all know the reason you don't want to marry me. You don't think I'm good enough for you. A two-bit NHS nurse.'

I'm mortified. 'Harry! That's not true and you know it.'

'Isn't it? Just stop blaming Carl, will you?' He looks at me and our eyes lock. 'I'm not Carl. I'll never be Carl. I don't know what your problem is. Why you won't marry me.'

I feel as if I've been hit by a bulldozer. Where is this coming from? 'Please, Harry, don't go. Come inside, we need to talk. Sort this out. You can see her tomorrow.'

'See,' he slaps his hand onto the dashboard in disbelief. 'You can't even discuss it, can you?'

My hand flies to my chest. 'Harry ...'

'I'm sorry, Emma,' he cuts in, his eyes on the road ahead. 'I gave Izzy my word. I can't let her down.'

'Fine, you win.' I shake my head as I step out of the car.

'We'll talk when I get home.' He leans over and looks up at me. 'I'll be an hour, tops. I promise.'

Chapter Eleven

An hour, tops, he said. I stare at the clock on the sideboard as the second hand thunders towards the twelfth numeral. It's eleven o'clock. It's official. He's two hours late. I storm into the kitchen, furious, wrench the fridge door open, and pour myself another large glass of wine. Surely he's dropped this Isabella off by now. What on earth are they doing? I shuffle back into the lounge, sipping from my glass.

I take another sip, and then another, feeling the cool, zesty liquid sliding down my throat. Its stimulating effects making me heady, light. She's doing the right thing, this Isabella. She's only been married to him a few months, that's what Harry said. She's a brave girl. I take another gulp. Get out while it's early, before routine sinks its ugly teeth into your world and starts sprouting roots in your soul. I sit heavily on the sofa, lean my head back, and close my eyes as my mind spirals into my past like a spinning roulette ball.

I couldn't count the times I'd forgiven Carl for his jealous outbursts and affairs over the years. I even left him on two occasions. The first time was after he'd grabbed me by the throat and pinned me against the wall. I gasped and spluttered, unable to breathe, but he wouldn't let go. He clenched his teeth, his eyes full of hate as he squeezed and squeezed. My life flashed before me like a film trailer. I thought it was the end.

I remember trying to concentrate on the rain lashing against the windowpane, just so that I wouldn't lose consciousness. I thought I was going to die. He eventually let go when a neighbour started banging on our front door, asking if everything was all right. I staggered to the kitchen, coughing and wheezing. Then, while he got rid of the neighbour at the door, I locked myself in our bedroom, leaving him to sort out his mess.

Later, when he'd collapsed onto the oversized leather sofa in a drunken stupor, I tiptoed out of the bedroom, made sure he was asleep, threw a few things into a holdall, and ran out of the flat as fast as my legs could carry me. I arrived on my dad's doorstep cold, frightened, and drenched from head to toe. I didn't have much money and he was only a bus ride away.

Unfortunately, my dad wasn't too pleased to see me. He was a bit in awe of Carl by this time, a little frightened of him, even. Needless to say he wasn't very supportive, told me to go back to my husband, to sort it out and to stop dragging other people into it. He was also quick to remind me that he, Mum, and everyone else had told me not to rush into this marriage. I'd made my bed and now I had to lie in it.

Susan, his then wife, was more sympathetic. She made me a cup of tea and gave me a warm towel to dry myself off. I stood in their tiny kitchen, mopping up my wet hair with an fraying orange bath towel while they discussed, quite loudly, my imminent future in the next room.

Susan persuaded him to let me stay. They only had a two-bedroom flat, but as fate would have it, Tessa was in France with some uni friends, so I slept in her room. I promised Dad that I'd be out of their hair in a couple of days, that I'd ring Mum in the morning and go to Stratford-upon-Avon. All I needed was my train fare and the rest of my stuff, and he agreed, albeit reluctantly, to let me stay.

But the very next morning, as I lay asleep in Tessa's bed, curled up on my side like a foetus, he secretly called Carl. And before I knew it, Carl was driving me home.
When I walked out on Carl it really shook him up, and there was a brief lull in his violent disposition, but it didn't last long.

The second time I left him I took refuge with Ola and John. But it wasn't long before he was hammering his fists on their front door. Ola stood up to him, bless her, told him to leave me alone, that she'd call the police. I stood at the top of the stairs shaking like a leaf, listening intently, hoping Ola's threats would make him back off. But then when I heard him threatening her, I knew I had to go with him.

Ola begged me not to go, pleaded with me to leave him, said she'd risk any repercussions, urged me to call the police. She even offered me refuge in her home for as long as I needed. But I had to go, you see. I had no choice. They didn't know what he was like. What he was capable of. Carl didn't get to where he was by selling used cars independently. He knew people. He was dangerous.

Life more or less went back to how it was. We had good days, we had bad, but most of the time I was covered in bruises. Then, quite unexpectedly, I discovered I was pregnant and everything changed. Carl was overcome with joy. It was as if a lightbulb had been switched on, illuminating his world. He couldn't do enough for me. He became the man I fell in love with once again. I had hope. I could see a light at the end of the tunnel. So, against all the odds, I decided to give him one final chance. I'd lost everything by now. My job, my friends, my self-esteem.

This baby was all I had left. And I wanted him or her to have a proper family. A mum and a dad.

True to his word, Carl gave up the booze and didn't lay a finger on me after I announced I was carrying his baby. We started trawling through the estate agents, looking for a new place to live. 'A fresh start', Carl had said, 'that's what we need.' Living in a luxury, open-plan apartment was great if you were single or a power couple, as we once were, but not the best place to bring up a child.

I was almost three months pregnant when I first met Harry. We'd viewed several properties before seeing his garden flat in Chalk Farm on that Saturday afternoon, and we didn't like any of them. I was beginning to lose hope. I was even starting to think that staying put in our Hampstead penthouse might be the best option.

I remember Harry being late and Carl getting agitated. Then, just as we were about to give up and leave, Harry came charging down the path on his bicycle. He leant it against the bay window, his face red and flustered as his black cat, that'd been waiting outside the entire twenty minutes with us, meowed and twirled around his legs. He apologised profusely for being late and introduced himself as Mr Georgiades as he pushed the key in the lock. We followed him inside silently, his black cat rushing in before us.

As Harry showed us around his spacious, three-bedroom flat, cat in tow, he told us that he was moving in with his girlfriend in Winchmore Hill, where he'd also be closer to his parents. He wasn't in a chain and, if we were interested, a sale would be swift.

'It's got a nice garden,' Harry said, as the cat climbed onto the sofa beside him. 'With a lovely terrace. I only had it done a couple of years ago.'

'Do you share the garden with upstairs?' Carl asked, giving a fleeting look at the cat as it sauntered towards me. Carl hated animals; said he was allergic to them. All of them.

'No,' Harry said as his cat pushed its head under my hand. 'It belongs to this flat.' He smiled, his eyes flitting from me to the cat. I could tell that he was a sensitive soul.

'What're they like?' Carl asked, rolling his eyes towards the ceiling.

'They're a nice couple, actually, very friendly.'

'A couple of busybodies, then,' Carl groaned, looking out into the garden.

'No, no, on the contrary, they're very quiet.' Harry joined Carl at the window. 'I hardly see them, to be honest. They're a professional couple. Away a lot of the time.'

I looked over Carl's shoulder into the garden. It was square and neat, minimalistic, with a nice vibrant lawn and an apple tree tucked at the bottom left hand corner. A couple of terracotta pots brightened up the sandstone patio. My heart lifted. I'd always wanted a garden of my own, and I knew I could do a lot with the landscape.

'How long have you had this lovely creature for?' I asked, as the cat purred under my caress.

'What do you mean?' Harry furrowed his brows, hands in pockets.

I gestured at the black feline. 'Your cat, how long have you had it?'

'It's not mine,' Harry said, surprised.

'Oh. Whose is it, then?'

'I dunno,' he said, bewildered. 'I thought it was yours.' At the revelation of this mix-up we both exploded into a fit of giggles.

'Who'd bring a cat with them on a viewing?' I could barely speak from laughter.

'I know. I thought it was a bit strange, but I didn't want to say anything,' Harry said, laughing with me. 'Some people are really attached to their pets, aren't they?'

But next to me, Carl had become stiff, tense. I looked at him, his face deadpan, and my blood ran cold. I gulped, the laughter dying in my throat in an instant.

'So, are you interested?' Harry folded his arms and puffed out his chest, clearly sensing the tension between Carl and me.

'I love it,' I began, glancing at Carl carefully. 'It's just what –'

'We'll let you know,' Carl snapped, cutting right across me, his voice as bitter as his glare. 'Won't we, Emma?' He shoved his hands into his trouser pockets angrily. 'We've got lots of other places to see.'

On the way home he took to the road like a maniac, driving through red lights, taking sharp corners, and flying over road bumps, all the while screaming at me for flirting with the vendor. He called me a slag, a whore, called our baby a bastard, demanded a paternity test. He blamed me for his excessive drinking, said it was my fault that he had no friends, that I'd made him a laughing stock.

Later that evening, Carl broke a chair over my body and left me for dead. Ingrid from next door, who'd heard the commotion, called the police. They had to break down the door to get in.

I woke to a familiar face hovering over me.

'Emma?' The man's voice was soft. I squinted at him through a haze until his face slowly came into focus.

'Mr Georgiades?' I croaked. And for a few moments, I felt disorientated. I thought we were back in Harry's flat, that I'd fainted or something.

'You've been hurt but you're going to be fine.'

I tried to speak but my chest felt tight. The pain in my limbs was agonising. I had two broken ribs and a fractured collarbone.

'Where am I?' I said, trying to sit up.

'Shhhh,' Harry soothed. That's when I noticed he was in blue scrubs and that there was another nurse beside him. I was in a hospital bed. A drip in my arm.

'My baby?' The words scraped along my lips in a whisper.

'Take it easy, Mrs Clarke,' the other nurse said softly, trying to hold me down.

'I've lost it, haven't I?' I was breathless, exhausted, looking into Harry's dark eyes and almost losing myself in them. He nodded, wordless, and my heart broke into a thousand pieces.

That was the end of the line for me and Carl. I'd had enough of being his punch bag. He'd killed my baby. I could never forgive him for that.

Harry persuaded me to press charges and said he'd support me all the way. I got an injunction on Carl then had him locked up for GBH. He was out of my life for good. The last I'd heard from Jan was that he'd emigrated to Spain shortly after he got out of prison, wanted a fresh start, she'd said.

With the help of Ola, Tessa, my mum, and Harry, I slowly resurfaced, clawing back my life inch by inch. One day at a time. Once I'd regained some of my confidence, Harry got me a part-time job as a waitress at Mas and Caroline's restaurant. I lived alone in a one-bedroom flat above a charity shop in Finchley. It was small but the rent was cheap and I was safe. Harry and I didn't get together as a couple until he split up with his girlfriend two years later. I've not looked back since. Until now.

I'm on my third glass of wine when my phone starts ringing. It's got to be Harry. Who else would call me in the middle of the night? I jump to my feet, spilling some of the wine onto my red pyjama bottoms. Shit. Where the hell is it? I follow the sound, taking two steps at a time, but as I reach the top of the stairs it stops ringing. Great.

I wipe my wet fingers on my pyjamas then scramble around in my bag for my phone in the hope that he's at least left me a voicemail. An hour, tops, he said. What on earth can they be doing for three hours? Of course, there is the possibility that they're tucked up in bed in some cheap hotel. My stomach clenches. Then my phone starts ringing again.

I stare at the incoming call. It's Marc. I hesitate for a moment but fuelled with the warmth of alcohol and my vision of Harry in bed with some young, buxom nurse, I answer it.

'Red?'

The roar of a car engine sends me rushing back down the stairs, phone clutched to my ear. 'Hi, Marc.'

'You OK? You sound … breathless.'

'Yes, yes, I'm fine.' I yank back the curtains in the living room as Harry pulls into the drive.

'Oh. Right. Erm … you didn't answer my texts and I just wanted to know if you were interested in meeting up with the publisher. She's really keen and wants to see some of your work. I mean, you can say no if you want and I'll tell her to find someone else.'

'Oh yes, the client.' I listen out for the jangle of the front door.

'I mean, I hope you don't think I'm harassing you or anything, but it's a good gig, you know?'

'Yes. Just give me a moment to think.' A publisher. A long contract. Regular work.

Harry walks into the living room. 'Sorry I'm so late, babe. It took a bit longer than I thought and ...' When he sees me holding the phone to my ear he mouths, 'Sorry'.

'That your fella?' Marc asks.

'Yes, you were saying?' I go on, giving Harry a fleeting look. 'We could meet up to discuss your requirements. What time would suit you best?'

'Ah, you can't talk, huh?' Marc laughs. 'Is he the jealous type?'

'I'm available anytime.' I give Harry a forced smile, hand on hip.

'Who is it?' Harry whispers, poking his finger at his wristwatch.

'A client,' I mouth back, shaking my head and shrugging my shoulders.

'Oooh, you're available anytime, are you?' Marc chuckles. 'I see.'

Harry drops onto the sofa, tilts his head back, and closes his eyes.

'Friday, then,' I say firmly, as he rambles on about it being four days away and couldn't I meet up tomorrow? 'Yes, I know Café Rouge in Highgate. OK, great. Look forward to meeting you. See you on Friday at 5 o'clock, then.'

I end the call and exhale loudly, shaking my head. 'I can't believe these clients. They've got no sense of time at all. No considerations for ... Harry?' I fold my arms as I lean forward on the ball of my foot and nudge Harry's calf with my knee. He's bloody well fallen asleep. Typical. I wanted the post-mortem, damn it. Then just as I'm about to walk away I spot a red mark on his neck. I take a sharp intake of breath. It's a love bite!

'Harry,' I shake him awake. 'Harry. Wake up.'

'What?' He opens his eyes sleepily.

'What's that on your neck?'

'What?' His fingers brush his neck languidly.

'You've got a red mark,' I snap, 'What is it?'

'I don't know,' he says grouchily, closing his eyes, 'must've been from shaving this morning.'

And I'm supposed to believe that, am I? It wasn't there before he went out.

'Harry,' I give his arm a shake. 'Harry, wake up. We need to talk … Harry!' He frowns, groans, then lets out a low snore. Great!

I switch off the TV, leaving Harry asleep on the sofa. I'm not very happy about this new friendship with Isabella. Something doesn't feel right. I mean, if she's genuinely a victim, like I was, then I want him to help her, of course I do. But there's a niggling feeling inside me, a little voice in my head telling me all is not as it seems.

As I make my way up to bed, glass of water in one hand, mobile in the other, I'm suddenly overwhelmed by a rush of excitement at meeting Marc and his publisher friend on Friday. I could do with a bit of light-hearted fun. Cheering up, even.

Today's prediction on The Magic Touch was: "*Let go of negativity and let your hair down for a change. Life is short.*" I'm warming to this app by the day.

Chapter Twelve

Caroline is completely taken aback when I call her the next morning to apologise for leaving so abruptly yesterday, and to ask her, as subtly as I possibly can, if she knows anything about Harry and Isabella's friendship.

'No!' The shrill of her voice tears into my delicate head. 'Harry hasn't mentioned anyone called Isabella to me. You know I'd have told you if he had. Who is she? What does she do?' I picture her, hand on hip, eyebrows drawn together in disdain. I know she's telling me the truth, as much as she loves Harry she wouldn't protect him under these circumstances. Caroline's very moral. A girl's girl. 'What sort of friendship are we talking about here? Do you want me to have a word? Is everything OK, Emma? You sound dreadful.'

'No, no, I'm fine. I just overdid it a bit with the wine last night.'

I fell into bed exhausted last night, and lay still like a corpse, arms by my sides. I was asleep before the backlight on my phone went off. I woke to the rumble of the shower, followed by the whir of a toothbrush. Harry's side of the bed hadn't been slept in. I was still in a daze when he dropped a kiss on my forehead before heading off to work, with no mention of last night. As if it didn't happen at all.

'It's just that Mas and Harry were talking in the garden yesterday and I just thought … oh, never mind.' I hold my head. 'It's just my imagination running wild again.' I throw two paracetamol into my mouth and wash them down with a glug of water.

'Oh, I see.' Caroline sounds concerned.

'Don't worry about it, Caroline. I just thought I'd ask you on the off chance. I know Harry thinks a lot of you. I thought he might've spoken to you about Isabella and her problems.' I rub the back of my neck, expecting Caroline to say something, but she's quiet. 'We had a bit of an argument yesterday afternoon,' I go on, filling in the silence, 'while you lot were in the kitchen reading coffee cups. I found a few text messages on his phone from this new nurse and ... well, I just got the wrong end of the stick, that's all.'

I wish I hadn't said anything now. If Mas gets wind of this it'll become the next topic of conversation at the dinner table – he thrives on belittling Harry in front of the rest of the family, especially if he can get at me. Harry always says that he's just messing around, that I'm an easy wind-up. But many a true word is spoken in jest.

It's not that I hate Mas or anything. I just find him incredibly irritating. Sometimes, when he's in an exceptionally good mood, he can be very nice, charming even. And I look at him and think, deep down there's a good person in there fighting to get out, if only you'd stop batting him down with your rod of insecurity. What a shame.

I pour the rest of the water down the sink, then flick the kettle on as yesterday's events play out in my mind. Harry hovering over me with a bowl of fresh figs, asking for his phone back, telling me off for reading his texts again. Me leaping to my feet in anger, shoving the phone under his nose and demanding to know who Isabella is, accusing him of sleeping with another woman. Spiros jumping out of his skin at the sound of my voice, holding onto the armrests of his chair for dear life, bewildered as Harry and I scowled at each other.

'Oh, I see,' Caroline says finally. 'That explains your sudden departure. I thought I heard raised voices but Harry told us you felt unwell. We were all worried, Em.'

Well, I was unwell, theoretically. I felt sick to the stomach. 'I was going to call you but Mas told me I should let you rest.'

'Yeaaah.' I cringe, gathering the lapels of my dressing gown close to my chest. 'I'm sorry about that. I meant to say goodbye.' I flounced out of the house like a hormonal teenager. I couldn't bear it. I needed to get some air.

'So, tell me more about this nurse. What's making you feel threatened?' Caroline asks to the clatter of crockery and pans. She's probably loading or unloading the dishwasher in her state of the art kitchen, which is the size of our lounge.

'Because she keeps texting him all the time. Apparently, she's got a husband that pushes her around or something.' Caroline isn't going to let me get away without an explanation. I pinch the bridge of my nose, feeling the pain sear across my forehead. 'He spent three hours helping her move to her parents' last night.'

'Where to? Edinburgh?'

'Exactly.' I'm so glad that Caroline is my sister-in-law. Well, pseudo sister-in-law.

'I'm sure he's telling you the truth, Emma. You know what he's like. A knight in shining armour.' Yes, I know that. I haven't forgotten that he rescued me. 'Harry isn't the type to play around, is he?' Maybe not, but how long will he be able to resist the advances of a young, hot nurse? Especially with things being a bit stale at home.

'*Is* there a type?' I ask rhetorically, then before she can respond I add, as cautiously as I can, 'Mas didn't tell you what they were whispering about in the garden yesterday, did he?'

There are a few moments of silence and then she says, 'No, but then you know what those two are like. Thick as bloody thieves.' I can almost feel her rolling her eyes. 'Mas,' she calls out. Oh, God, I didn't think he was in. Why isn't he at the restaurant, for goodness' sake? They'll be opening for lunch in about an hour.

'Hasn't he gone to work today?' I croak nervously, then clear my throat. 'Or is he having a sneaky day off?'

'We're seeing our solicitor this morning. We need to sort out a Will. I know, I know, morbid, but it's got to be done. That's probably what they were discussing yesterday afternoon. Mas said he needed to run through a few details with Harry. Oh good God,' she says suddenly, 'Will you look at the state of that? You'd better shower and shave before we leave.'

'Yes, boss,' Mas calls out. I glance at the clock on the sideboard. It's almost 10.30. Ola's introducing me to a new client during her lunch break today, so I'd better get a wiggle on.

I rinse out my mug as Caroline tells me that Mas didn't get home until 3 a.m. last night: there was a fault with the alarm at the restaurant which kept making it go off all night, which is why, she explains, he looks like a complete car crash.

'Mas,' she yells, 'before you disappear into the loo for half an hour,' I twist my mouth in disdain, what an awful image, 'did you know about Harry and this new bird at work? This nurse friend? Bella or whatever her name is.' I hear a bit of mumbling, then, 'What do you mean you're not your brother's keeper? You two are joined at the hip. Ouch, get away from me, your beard is pinching.' Caroline giggles, then says, 'I'm sorry, Emma, sex on the brain, that man.'

'Well, at least he still fancies you.' Oh God, did I just say that out loud?

She laughs. 'I should hope so. I suppose you and Harry still can't keep your hands off each other. It's all right for some. You wait until you get to my age.' She pauses, waiting for me to agree. 'Emma?'

'Yes, yes,' I lie, 'the passion is still burning.' I decide against telling her about our dwindling sex life. I can't risk her telling Mas. Caroline is lovely but she's not very good at keeping secrets from him.

When Harry and I first got together I let it slip that we had a marathon sex session over the weekend, and the next thing I knew I was getting funny looks and sly remarks from Mas. Then two weeks later at their New Year's Eve party, fuelled with bourbon and high on the excitement of the festivities, he decided to announce it to a room full of people. I stared at Mas, mouth agape, feeling my face turning scarlet. I think I stayed that colour for the remainder of the evening.

'I just meant that after all these years together,' I go on, 'you know ... doesn't it all get a bit ... stale?'

'Well, actually, now that you mention it,' she whispers. 'Hang on a minute, Emma, I'm just going into the conservatory.' My curiosity antenna starts to emerge. This should be interesting. I fill the cafetière with boiling water. There are a few moments of silence and then, 'Oh bloody hell, Mas. Jesus! Have you got Louis Armstrong in there?'

I laugh. 'What's wrong. Caroline?'

'Men, that's what. If they're not burping and snoring, they're farting the house down. My God, I think I'm going to be sick.' I hear Mas' voice mumbling in the background. 'No, it's not natural, not the way you do it. Don't forget to open the window when you've finished. And make sure you use plenty of air freshener. What? Of course it's in there. It's in the cupboard under the sink. Jesus Christ, do I have to do everything?' There's a thud and then, 'It's OK. I'm in the conservatory now, he can't hear us. As I was saying,' she says conspiratorially. 'I've been trying to liven up our sex life. This menopause is a flipping marriage wrecker, it's killing my libido. I bought this book a few weeks ago. It was recommended on one of those breakfast programmes. They had the author on, some sex therapist who was promoting it. It's called *Pulling Back the Passion*, have you heard of it?'

'No, I haven't.' I pour myself a cup of coffee and start stirring. 'Sounds interesting, though. What's it about?'

'It's about reigniting your sex life.' My eyes widen with interest. 'Did you know that statistically only forty per cent of couples have sex three or four times a week?'

'No way!' I'm intrigued. I want to find out more. 'What about the other sixty per cent?'

'Twenty per cent rarely or never do it.' I stir faster. If I don't get a grip there'll be no coffee left in my cup to drink. 'And the rest only manage it once or twice a week.' She pauses but I stay silent. 'Anyway,' she goes on excitedly, 'as we fall into the sloping category I thought I'd try to add some, you know, oomph into it. Spark things up a bit.'

'And?' I take a sip of coffee too quickly, scolding my lips. Maybe I could learn a thing or two here.

'Well, I took some of the advice and it's blooming well backfired on me.'

She goes on to say how the information is explained in easy to digest bullet points, and that one of the tips was to talk to your partner after sex, tell him you love him and what you enjoyed about your love making etc.; that it's supposed to give him confidence, make you more

120

desirable, and boost your sex life. 'The thing is, Em, I've been faking it for years. I couldn't think of anything I really enjoyed, so I made something up.'

I start to giggle quietly. 'Go on.'

'I told him that I liked him licking my ear.' Eww. I'm not so sure I want to hear this now. 'Only, I don't really, of course,' she adds quickly.

'And?'

'Well, he keeps doing it now and I'm starting to hate it – dread it, in fact. I feel as if I've been submerged in water, do you know what I mean? Urgh. And if that wasn't enough, he now wants sex morning, noon, and night. I can't go on like this. I've had cystitis twice!'

'But the advice given in the book worked, right?' I stare out of the patio doors. Graham, Alistair's son-in-law, whom Alistair refers to as Bart Simpson in private, is wandering around his garden, shears in hand, in a pair of knee-length shorts and lumberjack shirt. I frown. I was supposed to prune his garden and replant the pots Judith bought for him; we discussed it just the other day.

'Worked?' Caroline's voice averts me from the window. 'I don't think they've worked, love. They've only made matters worse, if you ask me. I should sue that flipping sex therapist.'

'Oh, Caroline.' I'm laughing now and she's laughing with me. She always cheers me up. Caroline is such a people person. She's wasted being a housewife. I really do hope that this new psychic venture takes off for her.

'Anyway, going back to what you were asking,' Caroline says, her laughter slowly diminishing. 'Mas said he's no idea about Harry and this Isabella woman. But if he's lying I'll get it out of him. I always do. He's a rubbish liar.'

I'm in the garden, coffee in hand. I really ought to be getting ready for my meeting with Ola but I saw Graham's square, large head bobbing up and down over the fence a moment ago, followed swiftly by Alistair's curved frame, and I wanted a word.

I lean over the fence. Graham is on his knees planting and Alistair is looming over him, shovel in one hand and garden fork in the other. It looks very much like a scene out of a murder-mystery drama.

'Good morning, Alistair,' I call out. At the sound of my voice he spins round stiffly, releases his grip on the gardening tools, and hurries over, leaving Graham to converse with himself.

'I wanted a word with you,' he says a little breathlessly.

'Oh, that sounds ominous.' I take a sip of lukewarm coffee.

'That twat,' he throws a hand over his shoulder, 'hasn't a clue what he's doing with those plants. Are we still on for you doing a bit of gardening this week?'

'Yeah, course,' I say. 'I did tell you that I'd plant them for you.'

'Yes, well, Judith sent him round, didn't she, make sure their inheritance is well cared for.'

'Oh, Alistair, I'm sure that's not ...'

'Shush,' he says crossly, 'I know what I'm talking about. Now,' he curls his fingers over the fence, 'did you sort out that text message business with Harry?' I tell him that I have. I don't want Alistair worrying. 'And what about that idiotic psychic app? I hope you've deleted it.'

'Oh, Alistair, don't be mean. It's just for entertainment.' I fish my phone out of my dressing gown pocket and fire up The Magic Touch. 'Look, it's just a bit of fun, that's all.' I press my fingers over the screen and moments later it pings with today's prediction.

'Well?'

I twist my lips in disdain as I read out the prediction. *"You need to get some rest, and your appearance will take a turn for the better."* It's not that funny, Alistair.'

'I told you it was nonsense.'

'I don't look that bad, do I?' I gaze at my reflection in the patio window and run a hand over my unruly tresses.

'Of course you don't. You look as lovely as ever, my dear.'

'Dad!' Graham calls out. 'What are you doing up there? I'm doing you a favour here, you know.' Goodness, no wonder Alistair calls him a patronising twit.

'See!' Alistair whispers as Graham gives me a small nod and a twitch of a smile. 'Blithering idiot has only just realised I'm not there.'

'Come on, then,' Graham calls out irritably. I open my mouth to speak, to tell Graham to shove it, to leave the plants, that I'll do them for him later. But Alistair, sensing my tension, squeezes my hand over the fence to silence me, and the words catch in my throat. 'It's almost eleven,' Graham goes on. 'I've got a golf lesson in twenty minutes. Where do you want these?'

'Oh God,' I screech. 'Is that the time?' I run a hand through my dry mane. I'm meeting Ola and the potential client in under an hour. I can't meet a new client looking like a cave woman. I'll have to at least run the straighteners through my hair before I leave.

'Coming,' Alistair calls out. He rolls his eyes in exasperation, then looks at me pointedly. 'When can you fit me in for gardening?' He presses his long, slender finger to his dry lips. 'I'm playing *Short Tennis* tomorrow, then bowls on Wednesday. Thursday suit you?'

'I'm working at the restaurant Wednesday and Thursday this week.'

'Friday, then? Say about four o'clock. I've got students in all morning.'

'OK, Friday it is.' I make for the door and then it dawns on me that I'm seeing Marc from the pub and his publisher friend on Friday at five. 'Alistair,' I call out. 'Let's make that Saturday instead. I'm seeing a client on Friday afternoon. I'll call in when I get back to let you know what time.'

'Right you are, Emma,' he calls out, 'I'll see you on Friday evening, then.' And then, with his back to me, he raises his arm high in the air and leaves me with his signature Charleston wave.

Chapter Thirteen

'I didn't have you down as a lightweight,' Marc says over his beer glass once we get the preambles out of the way. He lives in Highgate, in a two-bedroom flat around the corner. Very nice. He looks every inch a city stockbroker in his smooth, single-breasted navy-blue suit. I bet the bar he's wearing across his floral tie is 18 carat gold, too. And that sun-kissed skin tells me he's just got back from lazing around on some lounger by the sea. He also revealed very quickly that he's single and has no intention of walking down the aisle, in case I was interested, which, of course, I'm definitely not.

'What?' I ask, looking up at him from the depths of the red velvet sofa seat.

He nods at my white coffee cup. 'Are you sure you don't want anything stronger?'

'Oh, I see. No.' I smile up at him, sliding my finger through the ceramic handle. 'I like to keep a clear head when I'm discussing business.' I look at my watch. 'What time did your friend say she was meeting us?'

He smiles and leans forward, elbows resting on the square table. I'm in very close proximity to his stylish, neatly-trimmed beard, a shade darker than his light brown hair. I wonder if it's bristly or if he, like Andreas, moisturises it. 'Shall I let you in on a secret?' He grins, revealing a set of perfect white teeth.

I nod, frowning as I draw the cup to my lips. 'Sure, if you must.' He drops his gaze to my lips fleetingly, then fixes me with a stare only a feline could perfect.

'There isn't a client.' I almost choke on my coffee. I bloody well knew it. I feel instantly deflated. It took me ages to prepare my portfolio this evening. And I had to lug it around on two buses. 'So, you may as well have that drink after all.' He leans back in his chair confidently, his eyes not leaving mine.

I run a hand over my face, suddenly aware of Eurovision-style French music in the background, the hiss of the coffee machine, the chatter from nearby diners.

'Oh, come on.' I feel his hand over mine. 'Give a guy a break for trying.' I pull my hand away and curl it into a loose fist. He twists his lips, looks away, clearly disgruntled. I glance around me, miffed. An elderly man at an adjoining table, who's just asked the waiter for a glass of water, turns towards me rigidly and gives me a small smile. Marc takes a swig of beer. The silence between us is painful. I want to leave.

'I told you I'm with someone, Marc,' I say quietly, looking into my coffee cup. I'm flattered, I can't deny that, but I'm not interested in anyone else. Even if Harry is.

It's been four days since he helped Isabella move and we haven't spoken about her since. We've barely spoken at all.

'Is this how you're going to be now?' He'd said, rubbing the red sore on his neck, which on closer inspection, was an abrasion. 'I told you she's just a friend, now can we please drop it? I've had a long day and I need a coffee. Do you want one?'

I wrap my hands around my coffee cup. 'Look, Marc.' I'm not happy that I've been lured here under false pretences but I don't want to make a scene. 'I'll finish this coffee and then I have to go.'

'Oh, no, come on, don't be like that.' His voice is desperate, pleading.

'Marc, I can't be on a date with you. You know that.'

'Yes, of course I do. But why can't we just be friends? We get on, don't we?' I stay silent, feeling the heat from the cup tingling my fingers. 'Come on, you're here now.'

I suck in my lips, fold my arms, and shake my head in disbelief.

'Can I see a smile?' He points his finger at me cheekily. God, he looks so young. His face barely has a crease in it. 'I can, can't I? There it is.' He touches a waitress lightly on the arm as she's passing by. 'Can you get us a bottle of wine, please?' He looks at me, his hand still on the waitress's arm. 'Emma? What's your poison – red, white?' I open my mouth to protest but he's too quick. 'No, let me guess.' He narrows his deep blue eyes, rubbing his bristly chin. The waitress and I exchange a knowing smile. 'Get us a bottle of champagne, will you?' A man after my own heart. I absolutely adore champagne.

We've been talking nonstop for the last two-and-a-half hours over a delicious two-course meal. Hand on heart, I'm having fun. I'm enjoying myself. Anyone would think we've been friends for life. I can't actually believe how much we've got in common. We've seen so many of the same films, read the same books, have similar taste in music. He even runs three times a week. We get on to the subject of technology and his new phone, which he calls 'kismet' because it brought us together. I don't think I know anyone who has a pet name for his phone.

'What is it?' I lean forward on my elbows, glass in hand. 'A Hawaii?'

'Huawei?' he asks, laughing, and I nod. 'Nah.' He buffs the phone screen on the sleeve of his white cotton shirt. I'd never do that to my iPhone – I wouldn't want to scratch the screen. 'I'm a Samsung Galaxy man.'

'Oh, I see.' I scramble in my bag for my phone. 'Nothing like the iPhone,' I say challengingly. We dispute the advantages and disadvantages of Apple and Android, in particular the apps.

'Look at how fast this loads,' I say, opening The Magic Touch. I may as well read my prediction while I'm at it. I haven't had time to do it today. It'll be a bit of advertising for Caroline, too. Hopefully, he'll be impressed enough to download it, spread the word. A young, hot guy like him must have lots of girlfriends and contacts. 'This is a brilliant little app. You might want to download it.'

I tap the screen a few times and wait for it to load today's prediction to the soundtrack of abrupt laughter and the clatter of plates. He leans in, curious, our shoulders touching. I can feel the warmth of his proximity, the aroma of his spicy cologne. I look up at him and for a moment our eyes meet, but we're saved by the loud gong of The Magic Touch prediction.

"You will hear of a death."

'Blimey.' Marc's eyes widen as he leans back in his chair. 'Are you sure about this app?' He takes a swig of champagne. 'Is your friend a witch or something?'

I gasp, phone still in hand, staring at the screen as the words slowly disintegrate in a ball of fire. 'It's not usually this brutal,' I say, stunned. I shudder as I reach for my glass and remember my gran's anecdote about someone walking over your grave when you spontaneously shiver. I know it's just a fun app but it's shaken me a bit. I hastily regain my equilibrium and try to laugh it off. 'You should download it, you know, it's free for the first month and –'

'No way,' he cuts in. 'I've got enough problems of my own. I don't need some app giving me bad news every day.' He takes another sip from his almost empty glass, fear etched on his face.

'Oh, you're such a girl,' I joke, tossing my hair back. 'It's only a bit of fun. It isn't real, you know,' I say, a little unconvincingly, slipping the phone back into my open handbag.

We're on our second bottle of champagne (his treat for stringing me along about the bogus client) when we start discussing holidays. Naturally, he's well-travelled, having seen most of Europe, and he's even been to the Far East. 'I've seen a bit of America, too,' he says matter-of-factly, fiddling with the small dessert menu the waitress handed to us moments ago. 'But most of my trips there were for business. Except for a stag do in Las Vegas,' he grins, glances up at me, and starts spinning the menu on the table.

I raise an eyebrow, chin in one hand, champagne flute in the other. 'What happens in Vegas stays in Vegas?'

His lips curl into a wicked grin, fingers spinning the menu. 'Something like that.' The menu flies off the table and lands by the seat of a rowdy family. A dark-haired waitress stops, picks it up, asks us if we'd like to order dessert. We decline. I don't think I could eat another thing.

'I've only ever been to Italy and Spain,' I muse. 'Oh, and the Maldives.' I take a sip of champagne, watching the dark-haired waitress work the floor like a catwalk model. 'Oh, no, no,' I point my finger at him as my long fringe falls into my face. 'I've been to Monaco, too. Harry took me there for my thirrrrr ...' I'm tipsy but I'm not hammered. He laughs as he reaches out for my hair, telling me that age is just a number, that he's dated women far older than me.

'What do you mean?' I joke, quickly tucking my fringe behind my ear, blocking his hand. 'I'm only twenty-one.' He finds this hilarious, knocks his head back, and roars with laughter. I glance at the shell-style wall lights as a young, blonde waitress with sunken features dashes past our table, calling out 'Maria.'

'So how old are *you*, then?' I say, licking my dry lips. No doubt the lipstick that I applied before I left the house has vanished. A trip to the ladies is definitely in order before we leave.

'Twenty-four.' He gives me a tight grin, his head slightly inclined as if to say 'I know you're not going to be impressed'. And he's absolutely right. 'Almost.'

'You're twenty-three!' I almost choke on a gulp of air, grabbing the table in shock and it shakes. He catches his champagne glass before it topples over. Quick reflexes. Impressive.

'What?' He protests, leaning forward and biting on his thumbnail. 'You're not that much older.'

'Yeah, I am.' I grab my flute and knock back the last dregs from my glass, then look at my watch. 'And I've also got a boyhub who should be home shortly.' This is a lie. Harry works Friday nights at the restaurant. He won't be home before midnight, but I can't stay with this man all evening. I shouldn't even be here in the first place. I ought to have left the moment he told me that there was no client.

'Boyhub?' He furrows his brows, creating several lines across his taut skin.

'You know,' I pick my bag up, 'boyfriend/husband?' I have actually just made this word up. But I couldn't think of a more fitting phrase for 'a boyfriend who is like a husband in all but paper.'

'Haven't heard that turn of phrase before.' He pours more champagne into my glass, all the while eyeing me curiously. 'Did you just make it up?'

Clearly there are no flies on him. I don't answer. I just grin at him. Our eyes lock for a moment. I break the stare, look at my watch, and push my chair back. 'Marc, it's been great. Thank you for dinner,' I take one last swig from my glass, 'and for the lovely champagne but I'm going to have to make a move.'

'Already?' He reaches over and grabs my wrist. I flinch and draw my hand back quickly. 'Sorry, Emma.' His eyes flit from my face to my wrist then back again. 'Did I hurt you? I just wanted to look at your watch, that's all. I never wear a watch. That's why I'm always late.'

I'm silent for a few moments. He looks at me worriedly. 'No, it's OK. I'm sorry,' I say. I'm really starting to feel the effects of the champagne.

I stretch my arm towards him and he reads the time on my watch. 8.30. 'It's nine, by the way.' I give him a small smile as I twist my long fringe between my fingers and tuck it behind my ear. 'My watch is slow, I keep meaning to buy a new one, but …'

'Have you tried changing the battery?'

'Yes, several times. I think it's just had it.'

He lets go of my wrist, presses his hands on the table, then looks at me curiously for a few moments before saying quietly, 'I'll get the bill then, shall I?'

I get to my feet. 'I'll ask for it on my way to the ladies',' I offer, and he nods, in a bit of a fidgety way, as if he's put his foot in it.

In the dimly-lit toilets, I peer at my reflection in the mirror as I wash my hands under the running tap. I shouldn't have drawn my arm back so sharply. He's going to think I'm

131

some kind of weirdo. Poor kid. How was he supposed to know that Carl used to squeeze my wrists under the table when we were in public? I'll apologise when I go back out. Tell him that I'd just had a bit too much to drink, and was feeling a bit dizzy. I'm sure he'll be fine about it.

I move my hands under the hand dryer, but as I'm strapped for time, abandon the dryer, grab some loo roll from one of the cubicles, and mummify my hand with toilet tissue.

I think about Harry as I ride my foot over the bin pedal, wondering if I should tell him about tonight; about Marc and how he strung me along about a client, that I think he might fancy me a bit.

I apply a sweep of lip-gloss, then fish around in my bag for my Oyster card to the backdrop of a flushing loo. I thought we'd just be having a coffee this afternoon instead of a champagne dinner. I'll have to put something towards the bill, of course. I can't expect Marc to foot the entire thing. That'll be more like a date, and I don't want that. I'll let him pay for the champagne, of course, that was his treat. But I'll pay for my share of the food. However, this does mean that I'll have to get a bus home instead of a taxi, as planned.

I pull out my leather card wallet, a birthday gift from Harry last year, as I reciprocate a smile to a middle-aged woman in the mirror washing her hands at the small basin. And just at that moment my phone bleeps with a text message. It's from Harry. He's finishing a bit early, says he has a tension headache. He's on his way home and wants to know if I've eaten or if he should bring me something from the restaurant. My heart melts. He's always so considerate. I text him back immediately, saying that my meeting extended and I've eaten.

Moments later, another text pings through –

OK. C u at home. We need to talk.

We need to talk? That sounds ominous. Perhaps I should be worried, but the champagne has numbed my worry gene, which isn't a bad thing.

I feel a trickle of guilt as I shoulder my bag, the weight of my portfolio digging the strap into my skin. I'm regretting dinner with Marc. I don't know why I stuck around after he told me it'd be just the two of us. I'm in a relationship. I love Harry. I hold the toilet door open for a young woman as I pass through, and she smiles, thanks me. Is Isabella as young and as gorgeous, I wonder?

By the time I return from the toilets, Marc has gone. Oh no, please don't tell me that he's stitched me up with the bill. I start fumbling around in my bag, looking for my purse, my eyes flitting around the restaurant like a lost dog tied to the railings outside M&S, searching for its master each time the automatic doors slide open. Shit. I've only got twenty quid on me. The champagne alone was £37 a bottle. My heart starts pounding. Oh God, oh God, what have I done? He might be some sort of gigolo who gets off on freebies. How could I have been so bloody stupid? The waitress is approaching me, a small white plate with a bill in her hand. 'I'm sorry.' I say desperately. 'Did you see where my friend went?'

'Yes, madam, he left a few moments ago.' My heart plunges. Oh bloody hell!

Chapter Fourteen

Marc lifts one finger in the air when he sees me, then slides his hand into his trouser pocket, the other holding the phone close to his ear. He's pacing up and down the pavement. He seems irritated, as if he can't get a word in. He looks at me, rolls his eyes, then mimes 'I'm sorry.'

I fold my arms, feeling the chilly evening air snap against my bare calves. I should've worn a jacket instead of this flimsy cardigan over my blue and pink floral dress. Harry and I call it my business suit. I always wear it when I'm seeing a new client. They're both old but the cardigan is pure silk. Harry bought it for me in the sale a few Christmases ago from Karen Millen. Harry. I wonder if he's feeling any better. I'll make him a mint tea with honey when I get in. That usually helps.

I pinch my top lip between my fingers as I stare down at my three-inch sling back navy stilettos. I wonder what Harry wants to talk to me about? Us, hopefully, and how we can get back on track. That's the thing about texting. You can't get the tone right, which is why I always end mine with emojis or kisses. Harry can't be bothered with all of that stuff. His messages are usually quite stark, so I never know what he's thinking.

Marc is strutting confidently towards me, ending the call, narrowly avoiding a collision with two young women who glance back at him approvingly. I smile as they giggle at each other, and for a moment I imagine him on a catwalk dressed in weird and wonderful creations in dark Ray Bans and tousled hair...

'Sorry about that, Emma.' He slips his phone into the inside of his jacket. 'I couldn't hear anything in there.' He rubs his hands together. 'It's getting a bit nippy, isn't it?'

'It's OK,' I smile, feeling guilty for thinking that he'd run off and left me with the bill. *Of course* he'd paid before leaving the restaurant – why was I always so quick to jump to the worst case scenario? 'Here.' I open my purse and hand him a twenty pound note.

He looks at the money as if it's a hand grenade. 'What's this?'

'Look, I know it's not much but ...'

'No, no, Emma.' He closes his hand over mine, crumpling the note in my palm. 'Put your money away. I told you, dinner was on me.'

I try to force it into his hand. 'At least take this for my share of the food bill.'

He backs away, hands outstretched in front. But I won't have it. I have to pay my way. I try to force the money into his pockets and, to the amusement of a couple dining by the restaurant window, we end up doing a bit of a fighty dance on the pavement.

'Please, Emma.' He tries to grab me as he tilts his body from side to side. 'Don't,' he giggles, 'I'm ticklish.' He grabs my hands and pulls me close, my arms against his chest, money clenched in fist. 'You can buy me a drink another time,' he insists, letting go of my hands.

I agree, but only out of politeness, a throwaway remark. As I tuck the crumpled twenty pound note back into my purse, I take a few hasty steps back and catch my stiletto heel in between a gap in the pavement. I try to wriggle it free but it won't budge. I wriggle harder and feel it snap beneath my foot. My knee gives. Marc rushes forward, grabbing me with one hand as he hails a black taxi with the other.

'Where to, folks?'

'Cockfosters please, mate, via …' he pauses, still holding me up, 'Emma, where do you live? I'll drop ya.'

I pull out of his embrace feeling dishevelled, yanking my broken heel from the pavement with absolutely zero grace. 'It's OK, Marc. I've got my Oyster.' I start limping towards the zebra crossing.

'Hey, come back. Don't be stupid. You can't walk with a broken heel.' He's next to me, sighing loudly. 'Look, I've got to see this client, anyway.' He waves the phone as if the client is inside it. 'It'll be no bother at all.'

We're in the back of the black cab. His arm is stretched across the back of the seat. He smells clean and fresh, as if he's just stepped out of a shower. I sneak a peek at him as he stares ahead. He has the chiselled features and strong jawline of a model. I wonder if he's done any modelling. I hold onto the side bar as the taxi flies over a bump on the narrow Southwood Lane, trying my utmost not to fall into his lap.

'Sodding road bumps,' he groans, bouncing around on the seat. He gives me a sideward glance. 'All they do is cause havoc.'

'I thought the Mayor was supposed to get rid of them all?' Five or six jingles chime from my bag in succession. Marc glances at it. 'It's OK,' I wave a hand dismissively. 'It's a WhatsApp message. Probably Harry's niece wanting me to send her a *Candy Crush* life. You were saying?'

'Yes, well, these politicians promise us a lot of things before they're elected, don't they?' He says, and I nod in agreement. 'They're all the bloody same. All they really care about is lining their own pockets.'

I continue nodding to everything he says, like a nodding dog. I felt alright in the sanctuary of the restaurant surrounded by other people, enveloped in the hum of French music, but sitting here alone with him in the taxi has unnerved me.

'So, have you always been an illustrator?' He asks as we approach Muswell Hill Road. Not long to go now, thank God. Then, before I can answer, he adds, 'Do you realise that we discussed everything tonight over dinner apart from work?' He laughs. 'Yet that's the reason why we met up in the first place.' I don't miss the twinkle in his eyes.

He's attractive. But I don't want to go there. Even if I were single, I still wouldn't go out with him. He's way too young, too flirty, too up himself. Besides, young and gorgeous as he is, he isn't as sexy as Harry. Hasn't an ounce of his charisma or style.

'In answer to your question,' I say, tugging at my dress which is riding dangerously close to my knickers. His eyes flit to my thighs and I feel my cheeks burn. 'Yes, I have always been an illustrator.' He nods, eyes fixed on mine, spurring me to go on. 'I worked for an ad agency in town for several years. Then as a waitress after that, before being promoted to the kitchen. I'm a sous-chef now, but only twice a week, just until my freelance illustration business picks up.' I'm not going to tell him about the in-between years. The years where I was so consumed by fear and panic, I could barely leave my home, let alone hold down a responsible job.

He gives me that Hollywood smile. 'Not just a pretty face, then.' He simply can't help himself, can he? 'What about your old man, what does he do?'

'Old man?' Why on earth does he want to know about my father? Creepy.

'Your manfriend, your bloke ... you know, your boyhub or whatever you like to call him?'

'Oh, Harry!' I laugh. In all these years, no one's ever referred to him as that. He sits up in his seat, straightens his jacket.

'Harry?' I hear a little click as he stretches his neck from side to side, 'Is that his name?' No, I just randomly shouted out the first name that came into my head. Of course it's his name, I want to say. But I don't know him well enough to interject with any sarcasm, however tempting. And besides, he has just paid for an expensive meal.

'Harry works for the NHS.'

He raises his eyebrows, impressed, as we rock over the bumps of Muswell Hill Road. 'Really?' he says, scratching his cheek. 'I knew you'd be with someone clever, like a doctor. You've got that superior look about you.' I frown at him. 'But in a good way,' he adds quickly, as the taxi driver swerves the cab around a cyclist before shouting at him through the half open window. Harry always groans about irate, selfish drivers. He's had a few near misses himself. But the trouble with London is that there aren't enough cycle lanes. Where are the cyclists supposed to go? They're not allowed on the pavement, drivers shove them off the roads. I fear for Harry's life each time he takes to the road on his bike, despite the fact that he's an exceptional cyclist. If his parents had been more supportive, he'd have been a professional by now, competing in races. But they dissuaded him, told him it wasn't a 'proper' job.

'He's a nurse, actually,' I say to Marc, turning in my seat to see if the cyclist is OK. I suppress a giggle as he lets go of the handle bar and makes a V sign at the driver.

'Ah,' Marc says, as if he's put his foot in it.

I spin back quickly, miffed. 'I'm very proud of him, actually,' I protest. 'Nurses work long hours, you know. And the care and support they give to their patients and their families is incredible. They're life savers. They actually save lives. Every day!' I fold my arms, shaking my head incredulously.

'Whoa, whoa.' He stretches his arm out. 'I wasn't being flippant.'

'No, I know you weren't.' I glance out of the window as we swerve around Muswell Hill roundabout. 'I'm sorry, I'm a bit tired.' It's been a long day. I need to get home, get out of these clothes and into my jimjams. 'It's just that they don't get the recognition they deserve, that's all.'

'Hey,' he says, touching my arm. 'You don't need to apologise or justify yourself to me. I'm sorry.' There are a few moments of silence and then, 'You're quite protective, aren't you? What star sign are you?'

'Scorpio.'

'Ooohoho.' He shakes his hand back and forth and whistles. 'That explains a lot, then.'

'What do you mean?' I slap him playfully on the arm.

'Put it this way, I wouldn't want to cross you.'

'Yes, well you'd better behave yourself, then,' I tease.

'So, is it true what they say about Scorpios?'

'Haha … Don't believe everything you hear about us.' I feel my cheeks tingling. 'We're loyal, determined, intuitive.'

'Vindictive, secretive.' He pauses, leans into me, and whispers. 'Suspicious.'

I clear my throat, pulling my cardigan around me. 'You seem to know a lot about star signs.' I catch the driver's eye in the rear-view mirror and he grins at me knowingly. 'What sign are you, then, Marc?'

'Cancer,' he sighs, staring ahead. 'But I don't know that much about the zodiac, to be honest.' He rubs his palms up and down his thighs. 'I just went out with a Scorpio girl once. She was into all that kind of ...' he falters, 'stuff.'

We're at the traffic lights on Colney Hatch Lane, the indicator clangs loudly. Not long to go. 'What about you?' I ask, 'Have you always been a stockbroker?'

He nods. 'But I had odd jobs in between. I've worked as a barman, a waiter ...' He stretches his long legs in front of him, crosses them, then folds his arms. His tan leather brogues look new. 'I had a stint as a model for a while.' *I knew it!*

'What happened?' I ask as we turn into Alexandra Park Road, minutes away from my lovely, cosy home.

He shakes his head, scrunching his nose. 'I just did it for some extra cash.'

'Was this pre-beard?' I don't know why I just said that.

His hand flies to his face. 'What?'

'Oh God, I'm sorry.' I shuffle nervously in my seat. 'I wasn't being rude or anything. It's just ... you've got such nice skin and you're hiding it away behind all that hair.' I give a little laugh that comes out like a muffled squeak.

He grins, smoothing down his beard. 'Yes, it was BB,' he jokes. 'Before beard.'

I sniff nervously, crossing my arms. 'Did you enjoy it?' I wave a hand, 'the modelling, I mean, not *not* having a beard.'

He juts his bottom lip out. 'It was all right, I s'pose,' he says nonchalantly. 'Easy money. I love what I do now. The sheer excitement of knowing you can make some serious cash is ...' I can still hear Marc's voice but I'm not listening any more. All I can see are the blue flashing lights outside my house as we approach.

'Pull over,' I bark at the driver, almost toppling out of my seat. 'I live just here.' There's an ambulance parked outside our house, a small crowd of people, paramedics. What's going on? I'm on the edge of my seat, my hand on the door latch. I yank it up and down madly. It won't open. I feel panic searing through me, my heart thrashing against my ribcage, quickly, violently. I've got to get out. I rattle the door lever again. 'Open the bloody door!' I cry.

'Emma, what's wrong?' Marc looks horrified. He's leaning forward, telling the taxi driver to let me out, and to wait, that he still needs to get to Cockfosters.

'No. I'm not.' I press my hand against the window as I stare wildly at the scene. 'Oh God. What's happened?' I crane my neck, trying to get a better view. A body is being carried on a stretcher by two burly paramedics. 'Oh my God, oh my God,' I cry in a little strained voice. I grab my bag and whip my shoes off to the clank of the security locks disengaging.

We're standing on the pavement. 'Emma,' Marc says, looking shaken, 'do you want me to come with you?'

'No,' I say firmly, raising my hand as if to back him off. 'I've got to go.' And with this, I hastily step off the kerb. The tarmac is gritty and cold beneath my bare feet but I don't care.

A car blasts its horn as it whooshes past and the driver swears at me behind his steering wheel, his face twisted in fury. I take a step back, my hair flying in the wind, wisps of it sticking to my lip-gloss. I look frantically from left to right with mounting terror. Cars are soaring up and down the road at top speed, their headlights dazzling, wheels screaming in my ears. I can't get across. Why won't someone stop and let me pass? Oh God. What's happening? 'Please, stop,' I shout. 'I need to get across.'

I turn around at the roar of the taxi taking off. Marc is looking at me worriedly through the rear window as it soars into the distance. I manage to get half way across the road, and that's when I see it. Harry's bicycle sprawled on the pavement, wheels twisted.

Oh God, no. Please no. Horns blast, lights flash. 'Harry!' I cry as a car screeches to a halt in front of me.

Chapter Fifteen

I collapse into Harry's arms behind the ambulance. He holds me tightly as I blub into his heaving chest, feeling his heart thrash against my face.

'I thought ...' I squeak, 'I thought ... that ... it was *you*.' I fall to pieces as the last word slips through my wobbling lips, almost collapsing to my knees. Hot tears are sliding down my face without mercy, without respite. Harry pulls me up gently. I wipe my snotty nose with my sleeve. My cardigan is ruined. I'll need to send it for a dry clean now.

'Shhhh,' Harry strokes my hair. 'I'm OK,' he kisses the top of my head, 'come on, stop crying.'

I look up at him through a blur of tears. 'I thought I'd lost you ... I thought that ...'

'Well, you haven't. I'm OK. Look at me.' He lets go of me and stretches his arms out by his sides. 'I'm fine. See? Stop worrying.' He wipes my tears with his thumb. 'Stop crying.' Harry's eyes keep flitting from me to the ambulance, his face etched with concern. The paramedics are rushing around us. One of them calls out to Harry that they're ready to go. Everything feels surreal, as if I'm caught in a tangle of bewilderment and absence.

'Come on,' Harry says. 'Let's get you inside.' My tears are drying but I feel sodden and congested. I glance at the ambulance, and one of the paramedics offers me a small smile, which I manage to reciprocate as I wipe my nose with my sleeve again, and in that moment I have a bolt of clarity. Harry's OK, but someone else is on that stretcher, someone's been badly hurt. A spit of acid dances in my stomach. 'Who've they bundled in there?' I ask urgently. The paramedic looks at me gravely, wordless, then glances at Harry, asks if he's going with them.

Harry nods, 'Just give me a minute, mate.' He puts a protective arm around me and shepherds me towards our house 'Just go inside … I'll call you when …'

I tear out of Harry's embrace as a second bout of terror washes over me. He snatches my arm, pulls me back. 'Don't go in there, wait …' I break out of Harry's grasp. I'm at the ambulance door watching as paramedics hover over Alistair's body. I cover my mouth with my hands and keel over as fresh tears flood my eyes.

I can't believe that Alistair is dead. Perhaps I should've been expecting it. He is – was – ninety-three-years-old. I wanted him to live forever, rattling around in the house next door, ordering me around, playing me tunes on his battered violin, beating me at *Scrabble*.

'I didn't even get to say goodbye,' I say to Harry as we sit opposite each other, two mugs of untouched tea, which must now be stone cold, on the table in front of us. 'I was supposed to do some gardening for him tomorrow.' I close my eyes briefly. 'I said I'd call in this evening to confirm. I didn't think the …' I falter, '… meeting would go on for so long.' I study my nails. 'I can't believe I'll never see him again.'

'I tried to save him, Emma. I did everything I could before the ambulance arrived – CPR, chest compressions.' He squeezes his lips between his fingers, his dark eyes full of remorse. 'When I got home he was at our front door, holding his chest.'

'Outside our house?' My hand flies to my chest. I feel as if I've fallen into a pit of darkness. Alistair was looking for me. He wanted my help. And where was I? Out flirting with some guy, massaging my ego.

'I jumped off my bicycle and threw it against the pavement when I saw him bent over.' That explains the warped wheel and broken spokes. That bike is Harry's pride and joy. Andreas gave it to him recently when he upgraded his. It's a *Specialized* and worth at least five-hundred quid. 'He collapsed into my arms, Emma. I called the emergency services right away.' He covers his face with his hands. 'If I was here just ten minutes earlier,' he says irritably, wringing his hands. 'I could have done more... acted faster.' He pushes his hands through his hair and holds it at the top of his head, closing his eyes. 'If I'd taken a different route back from the restaurant and avoided the traffic at Camden; if I didn't serve that last customer, I'd have been home.' He opens his eyes and looks at me pointedly. 'Alistair might still be alive,' he finishes.

We both glance out of the window as a gang of teenagers chase past, screaming obscenities at each other.

'Did he say anything?' I ask solemnly, as their voices fade into an inaudible echo.

'No, Emma. I'm sorry.'

I stare into my mug of cold tea with a heavy heart, suddenly aware of the swishing of traffic outside. 'Do you think he was in a lot of pain?' I manage with a small voice.

Harry takes my hand across the table. 'I don't think so, babe. It was all very quick. He died before we got to the hospital. His face looked relaxed.' He leans back in his chair, rubbing the back of his neck. 'Happy, even.'

'It won't be the same around here without him.' I take a lungful of air, my hands flat on the table.

'I know.'

'He was my friend.' I look up at Harry through a mist of tears. 'You know I don't make friends easily.' I've always found it difficult, even when I was little. I remember coming home from school in floods of tears once because Bridget, my best and only friend, was off sick and I had to spend breaks on my own.

'The other girls don't want me, Mummy,' I cried into her chest. 'They call me a ginger nut.'

'Shhh, baby. It's their loss,' she said soothingly. 'You've got to learn that not everyone is going to like you. You can't please everyone. Always remember that, yes? So, just dust yourself down and move on.'

I never cried again when Bridget was off sick, and I've carried Mum's advice with me throughout my life. It's what got me through university, then straight into a top advertising agency in London.

Harry's voice breaks into my thoughts. 'And he was very lucky to have had such a good, loyal friend like you, Emma.' The landline starts ringing as he reaches for my hand. 'You were more like a daughter to him. He always told me that. He loved you.' He squeezes my hand reassuringly, then scrapes his chair back. 'Hello, Mum.'

I take a sip of cold tea and think about what Harry has just said as he takes his mum's call in the kitchen. A smile spreads across my face as I cup my hands around my cold mug. Alistair and I did have some great times together. I'm so glad I made him happy, made a little difference to his life.

'Mum wants a quick word.' Harry's back at the table; hand over the mouthpiece. 'Wants to offer her condolences.' I nod and he hands me the phone.

'Hi, Xenia,' I manage, clearing my throat.

'Ah, Emma mou, am so sorry about your friend.'

'Thank you, Xenia. I appreciate that.'

'His heart attack. Harry said he dead in the amboula.'

'Yes, that's right, he died in the ambulance. But he wasn't alone, Harry was with him.'

'That's ohright,' Xenia affirms. 'Harry said to me he wanna save him but was traffic coming home. There was an axidah on Oxo Street that's why he come home late.' Harry didn't mention an accident on Oxford Street to me. I frown and look at him but he's on the sofa with his phone, hands flying over the screen. 'A bus hit man on bike. You tell Harry to stop that bloody bike, Emma. He listen to you.' Ah, so that's why he didn't tell me. We talk a little more about how short and fickle life is, then end the call.

'I need to get some sleep,' Harry says as I slot the phone back into its cradle. 'See if I can shake off this damned headache.' He runs a hand over his face.

I ask him if he's taken any medication and he says he has. 'But they're not working.' He rubs his temples. 'I just need to sleep it off. I've had a tough day. I'm tired.'

I nod. He has had a very long day. Poor Harry.

'How did you get on with the publishing client, by the way, any luck?'

I suck my lips in, my back to him. I want to tell him about Marc. But what am I supposed to say? That I met a young guy in a pub and agreed to go out with him? That he tricked me into thinking he'd set up a big gig for me and I fell for it? That instead of being pissed off and angry that he'd wasted my time, I cosied up to a champagne dinner with him? I can't tell him, not after what's just happened. And not after accusing him of being unfaithful. It's going to sound wrong, vindictive. 'She said she'll let me know,' I lie, gathering the mugs from the table, 'but she liked my work.' I glance at him over my shoulder.

'Well, that sounds promising.' He gets to his feet.

'Yes,' I give him a tight smile, guilt trickling through my veins. I know I haven't done anything wrong as such, but as I've been nagging and arguing with him over his friendship with Isabella I feel like a complete hypocrite. I hate lying to Harry. But it seems that these days it's all we do to each another. 'Harry,' I call out just as he reaches the door. 'What was it that you wanted to talk to me about?'

'What do you mean?' He holds onto the door frame, a puzzled expression on his tired, pale face.

'You said in the text earlier that we need to talk.'

He shakes his head, waving a hand. 'Ah, it was nothing important.'

'But you said …' I press on.

He hesitates, licking his dry lips. 'It's just our rotas at the restaurant. Mas is making a few changes. That's all. We'll talk about it in the morning.'

I nod, swallowing hard. Alistair is dead and we're planning our work timetable. 'I'll be up in a minute. I'll just run these under the tap.'

I stare out of the kitchen window and into the darkness. Alistair's garden is floodlit. A cat or a fox must be wandering around through the lawn. I want to go out and shoo it away. Alistair always complained about them weeing and pooing on his plants. What right have they got to be in his garden now? As I place the mugs onto the drying rack, my phone chimes with a text message on the worktop. It's from Marc.

Hope everything is OK?

I chew my nail to the backdrop of Harry stomping around upstairs. That's sweet of Marc to be concerned. I text him back, explaining briefly what happened. He did seem shaken. I owe him that at least.

He fires back right away –

Sorry 4 ur loss. Hope ur OK.

I will b. Thank you. ☺

I enjoyed tonight. Thanks :D

I hesitate before I reply.

Me 2.

I did have a nice time and I'm not going to see him again, so what harm could it do?

Gr8. Know it's cliché but if there's anything I can do. Call me. X

I smile sadly at the screen before slipping my phone into my pocket. Alistair's garden lights have gone off. I'll check for debris in the morning.

Upstairs, I climb into bed next to Harry, aching with grief. Where is Alistair now? I can't bear to think of him alone in some hospital morgue. As I pull the covers over me, Harry's phone buzzes with a new message. I shut my eyes tightly and cover my head under the duvet. I'm not going to check it. No way. I promised myself, and Harry for that matter, that I wouldn't sneak around checking his messages anymore. I trust him implicitly. I snuggle close to him, contently, and he grunts. And I won't check his internet history anymore either. I had to check his history for porn because I read somewhere that that's one of the signs that your partner is going off you. Thankfully, all I found on Harry's history was cycling sites, *Doctor Who* events, news reports, and Google searches for various dog breeds and rescue centres, which I did find a bit puzzling.

I turn on my back as the darkness closes in around me and focus on the tiny red power light on the TV, which I somehow find safe, comforting. I'm not going to get out of bed and check that message because I trust him. I turn on my side, spooning him. I lay my head between his shoulder blades. He groans for a moment, adjusting to the intrusion of my touch, then settles down. I close my eyes tightly. I need to sleep. I've got a tough few days ahead of me – coming to terms with Alistair's death and finishing off some work. I need to ring my sister back; find out how she's getting on with her pregnancy. I break away from Harry and he turns onto his back, snoring lightly.

I close my eyes again taking deep, full, yoga breaths. My hand over my tummy. One, two, three, breathe in. One, two, three, breathe out. One, two, three, breathe in, one, two, three … Dog breeds. I breathe out. What was that all about? One, two, three, breathe in. I hope he doesn't turn up with a rescue dog. I'm not good with dogs. I'm more of a cat person. One, two, three, breathe out. Harry knows that. Even when I visit Mum they have to put Macy, their Rottweiler, in the kitchen. And then it dawns on me. What if the dog's not for us? Oh God, I hope he's not buying Isabella a puppy! I whip the sheets back and swing my legs round.

Harry stirs as I creep around to his side of the bed and I stop dead in my tracks like an intruder. I stare down at him until he starts snoring again. His phone illuminates as I press the home button. Aha, he kept his word – no passcode. Brilliant.

I read the text.

Sorry about before. Can you forgive me? Hope ur feeling better. C u on Mon. We'll talk then X.

Oh, bloody hell. My heart sinks like a stone descending quickly into the depths of a murky river. Sorry about before? What's that supposed to mean? Did they have some kind of fall out at work? Is that why he got one of his tension headaches? And why does she always text him in the middle of the night? Why can't she just leave him alone?

My eyes sting with tears of anger as I make my way back to my side of the bed, the mattress already cold as I climb under the duvet. I can't possibly sleep now. I turn on my bedside light, grab my phone, and start opening apps.

After a few status updates on Facebook, several Tweets, and a quick scroll through Instagram, I resign myself to the fact that all my cyber friends are either out or asleep. Then, as I'm about to turn out the light, I remember the morbid prediction The Magic Touch gave me this evening. *"You will hear of a death."* Which actually did come true. Completely by fluke, of course. I look at my alarm clock. The Magic Touch is fixed for a one-day reading. It's gone midnight so I'm allowed another go. I fire up the app, place my fingers over the pads on the screen, and wait.

Moments later my prediction appears within a hazy ball.

"Don't misconstrue a message, and beware gifts from a stranger."

Oooh, a double predication today, how lucky am I? I snort incredulously as I switch off the bedside light. I can see how people become addicted to this sort of thing. How easy it is to get sucked in. Caroline's app is free for thirty days, but then you need to pay a monthly fee of a pound or something to keep getting the predictions. Or coincidences,

I should say, because that's what they really are. You subconsciously link the predictions to things that happen to you in your daily life, i.e., the message I just read. That's what Alistair said, and he was right.

My head hits the pillow and I stare into the semi-darkness, half the ceiling illuminated by the light of my phone. I think about Alistair's family. How devastated they must be. I can't believe I won't ever see him again. Why does everything always seem so much worse at night?

I look over at Harry sleeping soundly and thank God that he's still here. I trace my finger along his shoulder. I'm not going to let another woman take him from me. I'm not. I know he still cares about me. He proved that tonight.

Harry turns on his back and mumbles something incoherent. I look at the digital alarm clock. 12.45. I turn on my back, sighing loudly. My feet are frozen. I can never sleep when my feet are cold. I stretch my legs out, brushing my feet onto Harry's warm calves. He flinches, snorts, then turns on his right. I turn to my left into a foetal position. A huge, cold gap divides us. I don't need a stupid app to tell me what to do. Harry and I need to spend more time together, that's all. We need to become lovers again. A bit of intimacy, that's what we need. There's nothing a night of great sex can't fix!

Chapter Sixteen

We're both panting, exhilarated, grinning at each other like a couple of teenagers.

'That was bloody fantastic, Emma.'

'I know,' I pant, trying to catch my breath. 'It was brilliant, wasn't it?'

'We really should do this more often, you know.'

'Tell me about it,' I grin. Sweat pours off our hot faces as our chests heave in synchronisation.

'How did we do for time?'

I look at my watch as my heartbeat slowly regains its natural rhythm. 'Twenty-seven minutes and sixteen seconds.'

'Woo hoo.' Ola jumps up and down on the spot. 'That's a PB for us, isn't it?'

'Yeah, I think it is.' I manage, catching my breath. 'It was twenty-seven, twenty-five last time, wasn't it?' I push my hair off my damp face with my forearm. 'But that was over a month ago.'

Ola nods, her breathing becoming steady. She pulls the cap off her water bottle, takes a large glug, then hands it to me. 'Come on, Em, let's do a power walk around the park to cool down.' I nod, wordless, wiping my mouth with the back of my hand as I hand the bottle back to her. Very undignified, I know, but runners really don't care what they look like.

Three giggling children dash past us, followed by their mother who looks like she hasn't slept in a week. Trent

Park, a stone's throw from where Ola lives, is always busy on a Saturday.

I don't know how I managed to keep up with Ola today, let alone shave nine seconds off our 5k run. I wasn't keen when I read her text this morning suggesting we meet for a run, given that I'm bereaved and tired, but Harry thought the fresh air would do me good. And he was right.

'So,' Ola says as we take large strides along the path. 'Do you know when the funeral is?'

'No,' I sniff, 'not yet. But it'll probably be sometime next week, I'd imagine. His daughters are taking care of all that stuff. Harry called them with the news last night.' Ola puts an arm around my shoulders and gives me a little squeeze. 'Although, I would've liked to have been involved in Alistair's send off, even in a small way.'

'Why don't you ask his family if you could read a poem or a psalm?'

'Yes.' Our arms swing by our sides in synchronisation, like soldiers on a military parade. A young couple walking hand in hand towards us step out of the way. 'That might be a good idea. I'll ask Harry to suggest it to Judith.' I stop marching. Ola spins round and looks at me, concerned. 'I didn't even get to say goodbye, Ola. I still had lots to do in his garden. He wanted me to plant a camellia tree. We were going to go to Crewe's Hill next week to pick one out.' I cup my hands over my mouth and nose and hot tears flood my eyes.

'Oh, baby.' Ola pulls me into her arms and gives me a hug. 'Why don't we sit down for a bit, hey?' She gestures at a nearby bench.

Ola takes another swig from her water bottle, then hands it to me. I really ought to bring my own but I can't be arsed to carry it around with me.

'I mean, I know he was old, but he was my friend. I loved him. He was like a dad to me.'

Ola nods. Her warm, brown eyes full of compassion. 'But he did have a good run, honey, didn't he? And at least his departure was quick and painless. My dad suffered for six months before he died. Towards the end he didn't even know who we were.' She glances at me quickly, taking the water bottle from my extended hand. I don't know what to say. Ola and her father were very close. 'Because of all the drugs, you know? If it wasn't for those nurses at the hospice ...' she trails off, clearly upset. I give her a moment. 'They were just extraordinary. We couldn't thank them enough.' She takes a long, deep breath. 'I'm going to take part in the *Stand Up to Cancer* campaign next month. Try and raise some cash for the charity.'

I wipe my sweaty face with the edge of my luminous pink top. It's a warm day for September. 'That's a great idea, Ola. Harry and I will sponsor you. It won't be much, though.' I reach over and give her arm a light squeeze as she stares doe-eyed at a father lifting his little girl onto his shoulders. The little girl grabs his head with one hand, fingers in his mouth stretching his face, as she secures her blue bike helmet with her free hand.

I never had that with my dad. He wasn't at all tactile. I'd be lucky if I got a hug at Christmas. My dad was a strict parent; he had rules that had to be obeyed or else. There were certainly no trips to the park or fairground. Mum took me on her own sometimes on her day off.

The little girl is bouncing on her father's shoulders now, squealing with excitement. Ola and I look at each other and smile. One day that little girl will think back on this day with a glow of warmth in her heart. I couldn't wait to grow up, not because I wanted to wear make-up and high heels but so that I could get away from my controlling father. I was secretly delighted when Mum divorced him. I was free, a weight had been lifted. Until I met Carl, that is.

'Will you be going to see him at the parlour?' Ola's voice breaks into my thoughts. 'You could say goodbye then.'

'Parlour?'

'Yes, you know. The funeral parlour.'

'Oh, I see. I didn't think of that.' We're silent for a few moments as I digest Ola's suggestion. Then I turn to her, 'I haven't seen a dead person before. Do you think it'll freak me out?'

'Depends.' Ola muses, crossing one leg over the other. 'I didn't go to see my dad. In fact none of us went, except his brother. Cancer is a cruel disease. I wanted to remember him as he was. But I did go to see my auntie when she died last year, and that kind of gave me some peace. Closure, if you like.' I nod thoughtfully as a fly lands on my leg.

I twang my Lycra-clad thigh and it buzzes off. 'I'll think about it, see what Harry thinks.'

'How're things between you two, anyway?'

I shrug my shoulders. 'One moment, I think everything is fine, and the next ...' I pause. 'He just seems to be blowing hot and cold with me. I mean, he's still caring and everything, was really supportive last night, but ... oh, I dunno.' I take a deep breath and stretch my back. 'Sometimes he just makes me feel invisible. He just doesn't seem to have time for *us* anymore.'

'Has something else happened?' She touches my elbow, her eyebrows knotting. She knows me so well.

I lick my salty lips. 'Isabella sent him another midnight text.' Ola and I draw our legs in as two boys thunder past us on skateboards, cheering loudly. 'It's not that I mind him having female friends, but not ones that text him in the middle of the night. Not ones that demand so much of his time. That's just not right. I mean, don't get me wrong, I do understand that she's having a rough time of it, but, honestly, how much can Harry really do? He's got enough on his plate as it is. I think it's all stressing him out.' I shake my head. 'He's not the same man.'

'So, he's still adamant about being her superhero, then?' Ola has hit the nail on the head.

'Yes! And I think she's got *other* ideas. If nothing's happened yet then it's only a matter of time.'

Ola nods thoughtfully. 'At least he took the passcode off his phone, I suppose. That proves he's got nothing to hide. What did the text say this time?'

I tell her about Isabella's text, then about the one that Harry sent me while I was at Café Rouge, saying we needed to talk. 'But then we got caught up in the turmoil of Alistair's heart attack,' I say bending down and pulling out a feather that's tangled in the lace of my battered Asics. I discard the long feather and sit up straight in my seat.

'What were you doing at Café Rouge?' Ola stands up, grabs a hold of her ankle, then stretches her leg back up to her behind. A man with a black and white Cocker Spaniel glances at her pert bottom as he walks past. The dog stops, sniffs at Ola's blue shorts, then drops its nose onto her top-of-the-range luminous yellow *Nike Air* running shoes, which cost a cool one-hundred-and-eighty quid.

'He can probably smell Eric.' Ola smiles at the creepy looking man. 'My Cockapoo.'

The creepy man nods a little too eagerly at Ola. His thinning white hair falls onto his red face, revealing a bald patch in the centre of his head.

'Come on, George,' he pushes his hair back with one swoop and gives George a low whistle and the Cocker Spaniel shuffles off, his long, floppy ears swinging from side to side.

'So, come on, you were saying?' Ola glances at me.

'I was with Marc,' I reply finally as the creepy man and George hobble off into the distance. 'You remember him, don't you?'

'What, that hot guy from the pub?' Ola's eyes widen. Ah, so she does remember him. I nod. 'He went out with you?'

'Don't sound so surprised.'

'I didn't mean it like that, you pleb.' She swaps legs. 'What were you doing out with him?'

I explain how he lured me to Café Rouge under false pretences, but then seemed so nice that I didn't have the heart to reject his dinner invitation.

'Well, I hope you're not seeing him again, Emma.' There's a warning tone in Ola's voice, similar to the one she used when she told me I was insane to marry Carl.

'I'm seeing him tonight, actually.' I pull off my hair tie and secure it between my teeth.

Marc called this morning to see if I was alright. OK, I know I said I wasn't going to see him again but he can be very persuasive, and Harry rejecting me just half an hour before didn't help. I reached out for him in bed, running my hand along the inside of his thigh. 'Oh, shit,' he yelled irritably, whipping back the sheets. 'Is that the bloody time? Why didn't you wake me?' Then, before I could answer, he had one leg in his jeans.

'Emma!' Ola looks horrified, plonking herself back onto the bench. 'Talk about pot calling the kettle black. How old is he, fifteen?'

'Almost twenty-four.' I sweep my hair back and secure it tightly. 'Anyway, we're just mates.'

'That's my exact point.' Ola sits back down heavily. 'Only moments ago you were complaining about Harry and this … this …'

'Isabella.' I begrudgingly remind her.

'This Isabella woman and this friendship,' she bursts out, 'and here you are telling me you're about to do the same thing. It isn't going to solve anything, you know.'

'This is different,' I insist, staring ahead.

'Different how, exactly?'

'I'm going out for a friendly drink with him. I'm not going round to his house or anything. I'm not involved in his domestic life.'

'So, you don't find him attractive, then?' she asks accusingly. 'I mean, come on, he's sexy.'

'Yes, he's good looking, I admit but ...'

'See.' She points her finger at me.

We fall silent. The traffic hisses in the background, birds tweet-tweet in the trees.

'You've got it all wrong,' I say, staring into my lap. 'Marc and I are just two friends going out for a drink. He's like a kid brother, he makes me laugh.'

'Oh, so it's *Marc and I* now, is it?'

'Ola, please.' I lift my palm up. 'You're twisting things.'

'Emma, look, whatever Harry's up to, and I'm pretty sure it's not what you think, you going out with another man isn't going to solve anything, is it?'

I hold my head in my hands. 'I know, I know. But nothing's going to happen between me and Marc! It's just a bit of harmless fun, for God's sake.'

'Hmmm,' Ola murmurs, unconvinced. 'Well, he fancies you, Em. I could see that from the start.' She gives me a look that says 'Don't even think about lying to me. I know you inside out.'

OK, I know Marc has some kind of *Mrs Robinson* crush on me. Of course, I can't admit this to Ola. It'll only add fuel to the fire.

'I know it's not what you want to hear,' she goes on, touching my forearm lightly.

'It's just going to be a one-off drink, that's all,' I say, meaning it, 'to say thanks for dinner last night.'

'I don't think you should go, Em,' Ola says softly. 'I think you should call him, make up some excuse.'

'I can't now.' I gaze at a couple with their toddler in the distance, feeling Ola's eyes on me. 'I've promised. Besides, I don't want to be on my own tonight, not after what happened.' I pat my lips lightly, nervously.

There's a brief moment of silence. 'I know.' She puckers her lips thoughtfully, drumming her long, slim fingers on her knee. 'I'd ask you round but we're driving to Bath tonight. It's John's parents' anniversary.'

'Yes, I remember you saying.' Ola mentioned it last week when we met for lunch.

'Look.' She cups her hand over mine. 'I understand that you think it's just a friendly drink, but I think he's got other ideas. You don't want to lead him on.'

'I'm not,' I say, a little too loudly, as a young Asian couple lay out a picnic blanket under a tree in front of us. 'Why would he be interested in me when he can have his pick of young, beautiful women?' Silence. 'Oh, don't look at me like that, Ola.' A wasp starts buzzing around my ear. I wave it away. 'He's just a nice guy who enjoys my company. We've got so much in common, you wouldn't believe.' I stare pensively ahead. 'He must be an old soul.'

She shakes her head at me, incredulously.

'What else am I supposed to do, Ola?' Sit at home on my own all night grieving and winding myself up about Harry and Isabella?' The couple look up at us and murmur something to each other. I bet they think we're having a row. 'Harry won't be back until at least midnight.' I lower my voice. 'Saturday nights are always busy.'

'If this is about Harry, why don't you just go and talk to Isabella at the hospital? I can come with you, if you like.'

I look at her as if she's just told me to strip naked and dance around the park. 'No bloody way. I'm not a bunny boiler.'

'Well, invite her round for dinner, then.' I gnaw my thumbnail silently. I suppose it mightn't be a bad idea – what's that cliché? Keep your friends close but your enemies closer. 'Just to put your mind at rest, that's all.'

'No, I can't.' I shake my head. 'It'll seem as if I don't trust him with her. And this thing with Marc,' I wave a hand, not looking at her, 'I promise you it'll be a one-off.'

'Emma, for goodness' sake.' She twists in her seat, facing me. 'This'll be your second date. He'll be buying you flowers soon and sending you love texts.'

'Date?' I say incredulously, annoyance smothering my throat. 'Don't be so stupid. He knows I'm living with someone. And, anyway,' I go on, rubbing my hands up and down my thighs nervously, 'Harry spends most of his free time with Isabella nowadays, so why can't I have a bit of fun, hmm? It's nice to be complimented. He makes me feel attractive, what's wrong with that? I'm enjoying the attention.' There. I've finally admitted it. 'Well, say something.' The wasp is back, buzzing manically around my head. I shoo it off but it's relentless. 'Oh, bloody hell.' I jump to my feet, waving my arms in the air.

'Just be careful, that's all.' Ola stands up, waves her hand gently at the wasp, and it whizzes off as if responding to her magic touch. 'Two wrongs don't make a right.'

Chapter Seventeen

I want to make one thing perfectly clear. Drinks with Marc is purely on a friendship basis. A payback for last night's elaborate meal. That's all. I am not, as Ola suggested this morning as I was getting into my car after our run, considering Marc as a Plan B in the event that it all goes pear-shaped with Harry. The idea is completely absurd. He's sixteen years my junior, for a start. Plus, I'm really not that calculating.

Ola just got a bit carried away, that's all. She can be a little hot-headed at times, especially when she's stressed. She probably had a barney with John before she came out and was letting off steam. They always have a bit of a domestic before they visit his parents in Bath. It's a sort of ritual.

'I saw this today.' Marc reaches into his jacket pocket as the taxi stops at a set of lights on Camden High Street. 'And thought of you.' He hands me small gift-wrapped box.

'What is it?' I look at the box in his hand as if it's a venomous spider as The Magic Touch prediction jumps to the forefront of my mind. "*Beware gifts from a stranger*".

'Open it and you'll find out.' He grins. 'I don't want to spoil the surprise.' He jiggles the box at me as I stare at him blankly. He looks different somehow – fresher, younger, more toned. Can your biceps expand overnight? 'Well, take it.'

I take a deep breath. Oh God. Ola warned me something like this might happen. Perhaps she was right, after all. Why don't I ever listen to a word she says? She's always flipping right. But it might just be a joke gift, mightn't it? Something silly, like a packet of fruit gums. I told him last night that I get all nostalgic whenever I see them on a newsagent's rack. Or maybe it's a booby trap. Yes, that's it! I bet the box will explode the moment I open it. He did confess to being a bit of a practical joker and had me in stitches yesterday evening with anecdotes of his clever pranks.

I tentatively take the box from his hand as if it might bite; the taxi pulls away suddenly from the traffic lights and I slide from my seat.

'Steady.' His grip on my upper arm is firm, strong, which is just as well as I almost hit the floor. I'm not sure if it's my imagination but he does seem to be sitting a little closer to me now. I can feel the warmth of his skin on my cheek, smell the strong scent of his musky cologne. I swallow hard as I start tugging at the expensive-looking gold paper. A whiff of tobacco pinches my nostrils. He must've had a cigarette while he was waiting for me outside my house with the taxi. He leans back in his seat, and thank God for that. His close proximity was suffocating.

I glance at him furtively as he stares into the distance, swaying to the motion of the taxi. He definitely looks different. I bet he had an afternoon snooze under a sun bed. His teeth look whiter and his blue eyes are all twinkly and bright. 'You OK?' he says, his eyebrows gathered in confusion. 'You're shaking.'

'Yes, yes, I'm fine,' I say, curling my hair behind my ear and glancing at him nervously. 'You look different.'

Whoever wrapped this gift box has done a bloody good job. I can't seem to get an edge on the damned thing.

Marc scratches his chin. I look at him in horror as I manage to unpick a corner of the box and tear it off loudly. 'The beard ...' I mutter, giving him a feeble smile. 'It's gone.' A little nervous cackle slips from my lips. 'I hope it wasn't something I said.'

'Nah.' He runs a hand over his chin and neck. 'Boss wants us all clean-shaven for an important meeting in Munich next week. He's doing my bloody head in, to be honest. Anyone would think he was my old man.' Phew. I feel my muscles relax as he takes the torn paper from my hand, scrunches it into a ball, and pops it into his jacket pocket. I open the box and stare down at the item in disbelief. I want to cry.

'What? Don't you like it? Because if you don't I can change it or ...'

'Marc.' My hand shoots to my neck, which I'm sure is now covered in red blotches: it always happens to me when I'm anxious or overwhelmed. 'I don't know what to say ... I ...'

He takes the box from my hand, gently disengages the watch from the curved velvet holder, and secures it between his little finger and palm. I stare at his manicured hands, which put mine to shame; digging and weeding has a lot to answer for.

'I remember you saying last night that your watch was running slow.' He takes my wrist and starts undoing the strap of my old watch while I look on like a dumbfounded two-year-old. 'This one will go with your bag.' He gesticulates at my black bag pressed against my thigh. 'It's got the same mock-croc design on the leather strap. There. Fits beautifully.' He gazes into my eyes like a love-struck teenager. And suddenly, the box slips off the seat, hits the

164

floor, and the moment is broken. Thank goodness, because for a moment there I thought he was going to kiss me. I try to gather my thoughts as he scrambles on the floor trying to grab the box which is sliding around the cab, all the while yelling at the driver to close his window, that there's a draft back here.

A cold shiver ripples through me as I stare at the watch on my wrist, stunned. 'Marc,' I gulp. 'I wasn't dropping hints when I said I needed a new one.'

'Yeah.' He picks the box up and settles back into his seat, his face red and flustered. 'I know but …'

'I can't accept it.' I start unbuckling the strap hurriedly as Marc looks on, mortified. I suppose he's not used to rejection. But there's no way I can keep it.

'You don't like it, do you? Shit, shit.' He slaps his thigh, and the taxi driver glances at us briefly in his rear view mirror. 'I knew I should've bought you the one with the silver bracelet instead of listening to the advice of that numpty salesman.' He rubs his clean-shaven chin petulantly.

'Advice? Salesman?' I croak, imagining Marc hovering over a brightly lit display unit in Selfridges discussing my requirements with a young, fashionable salesman in a sharp suit and square-rimmed spectacles.

'Yeah, he asked me how old my friend was and I said about thirty.' He looks at me, eyes narrowed, hand rocking back and forth; charming and generous, great attributes but they're wasted on me. 'That's about right, isn't it?' I give him a twitch of a smile but stay silent. 'He told me this one was more within your age range, but I thought the other was more your style, you know? Classy. But I can see that this one does look a bit masculine now, what with the large, blue face. But then I thought the black strap might go with your bag. Oh, never mind. If you don't want it … give it here.' He throws his arms up in exasperation.

I remove the watch and hand it back to him wordlessly. He seems to be taking it quite well; better than expected. At least he's taken it back without an argument. I can't ask for more than that, can I? A gift being refused is quite gut-wrenching. I should know. I gave up buying my dad gifts years ago.

'I'll return it on Monday; swap it for the other one.' Oh God, no. I close my eyes briefly.

'Marc,' I clear my throat. 'I don't want a replacement. I want you to take it back and get a refund.'

He looks stunned, his eyes wide, eyebrows furrowed. 'You said you like Ted Baker stuff,' he says, almost accusingly.

'That's just the point. I can't accept an expensive gift like this. Or any gift, for that matter. I barely know you.'

'Why not?' He looks genuinely surprised. 'I can afford it.'

Ola's words of warning bounce around in my mind like a basketball. She was right. I shouldn't have come tonight. It was a stupid decision. What was I bloody well thinking? Clearly, Marc does want more than friendship. How could I have been so naive? Isabella-gate and grieving, that's how. They've clouded my judgement. Oh God, I hope he doesn't think that I've been leading him on. I start to feel a little panicky.

'Marc,' I say, looking at him pointedly. 'You do realise that we're just mates, don't you? I mean, I am with someone, you know that.'

'Yeah, course I do.' He shuffles in his seat, adjusting his jacket. 'I just wanted to cheer you up a bit, that's all. You've had a tough week, losing your friend and that.'

166

There's an awkward, painful silence as the taxi thunders along Hampstead Road. Marc stares out of the window, squeezing his bottom lip between his thumb and index finger thoughtfully. I gaze out at the buildings, elbow on the armrest, fingers lightly tapping my lips, wondering what on earth I've let myself in for. OK, so if he has acknowledged that I'm in a relationship, that we're just friends, then what's with the grand gesture? Then it dawns on me. I bet he was hoping to get his leg over tonight. That I was some lonely, frustrated, middle-aged housewife in need of a quick shag. The gift is just a ploy to get me in the mood, woo me, make me feel special. I bet he's booked a room in a swanky Mayfair hotel. My heart picks up speed.

'Marc, I …'

'Look, Emma …'

We've both spoken at once. 'No, you first,' he says, waving a hand languidly.

I swallow hard as we whizz along Euston Road. 'Marc, I hope you don't think I've been leading you on or anything, and I'm really sorry if I've given you the wrong impression, but I am very happy with Harry.'

'Are you?' He arches an eyebrow. Our eyes lock. 'Only the way you were talking about him last night … I thought … well, what I mean is, he sounds like he takes you for granted, that's all. A woman like you deserves more.'

I frown thoughtfully, trying to recall yesterday's conversation. I may have indicated, after several glasses of champagne, that Harry was a bit complacent of late, and that, like many couples who've lived together for a long time, we don't spend enough quality time together. But that was all. 'No, I think you must've misunderstood,' I say, and shake my head vigorously. 'When I said he hasn't got much time for me, I meant that he works very long hours, and isn't home much. We're a solid couple, Marc. We've been together for five years. We've a home together, history.' I pause as the words swim in my head. 'I hope I haven't given you the wrong idea,' I add softly.

'No.' He drops his head, placing his hands firmly on his knees as my phone starts ringing in my bag. 'You haven't.' He stares at his black leather Chelsea boots. 'I don't think that at all.'

'Because if I have …' I fish in my handbag for my phone, my eyes not leaving him.

'Emma, stop,' he cuts in, placing a hand on my arm. 'You haven't done anything wrong. I get it. You only want friendship, and that's fine.' He tilts his head back on the headrest and exhales loudly. 'Obviously, I find you very attractive.' He glances at me and I feel a little glow pinching my skin. 'And if you were single, I'd definitely want to go out with you. But I'm happy being friends. I just love spending time with you.' He grins. 'Honestly.' He places a hand on his chest. 'Cross my heart.'

'Good,' I say, satisfied, as I pull my phone out of my bag. It's Tessa, my half-sister. She rarely rings me after 9 p.m. I frown at the screen. She can't have gone into labour already, she's got weeks yet. I chew the inside of my lip. It's probably something trivial, like when we should meet up next. Her birthday's coming up soon. I'll give her a call back later. First I need to make sure that Marc understands the situation completely. I reject the call and return my attention to him. 'About the wristwatch, I …'

'It was a stupid, stupid thing to do,' he interjects before I can finish. 'I'm so sorry, Emma.' He holds up his hands. 'I can see that now. It's just that, well, a hundred-and-seventy quid is nothing to me. I buy my friends gifts all the time. That's just the way I am.' He is very generous, he proved that last night. I look at his sad little face, which is now also covered in red botches, another thing we've got in common, and my heart softens.

'Yes, Marc,' I say as gently as I can, 'I appreciate that you like treating your friends, but we've only just met. We're not close friends, are we?'

He curves his lips. 'I feel like I've known you for years, though.' I know what he means, but I don't want to encourage him by agreeing. I stay silent. 'I've offended you, haven't I?' He scrunches his nose as my phone starts ringing and throbbing against my leg.

'No, of course you haven't.' I reject Tessa's call and turn my phone to silent. 'I just want to be clear, that's all.' The poor boy looks as if he's about to cry. 'And we are now, aren't we?'

He closes his eyes. I draw my lips in and bite down on them gently, narrowing my eyes, willing him to agree. 'Crystal clear,' he says opening his eyes and looking at me pointedly. 'I promise,' he presses his hands together as if in prayer, 'that I don't want anything more from you than friendship. You have my word.'

I let out a little sigh of relief, lean back in my seat, and nudge him on the arm. 'I'm too old for you, anyway.' I stare ahead, a smug smile on my lips. I will never tire of being told I look youthful.

He crinkles his nose. 'Yeah, you are a bit.' The smile dies on my lips in an instant. Cheeky sod. 'But just out of interest. If you *were* single, would you?'

'Marc!'

'No, no, I don't mean have sex with me.' Thank goodness for that. 'I mean, would you go out with me?'

'Yes, well I'm not single am I?'

'But if you were?'

'I can't answer that question because I don't know how I'd feel about you if I were single. I mean, you are only twelve years old,' I joke.

'No, come on, seriously. Please, just humour me. Will you?'

'Maybe.' I give him a sideward glance and he smiles contently. 'But only if you were at least fifteen years older.' I jab him lightly on the arm with my elbow. 'Just take the watch back and get a refund.' He nods, putting the box back into the inside pocket of his soft leather jacket.

'And drinks are on you tonight.' He points his finger at me, grinning. 'It's your shout, remember?'

I nod, then look at my watch. 'Are we almost there?' My watch says it's almost nine-thirty, which means it's almost nine. 'I'll only be able to stay for a couple of drinks. I need to be home by the time Harry finishes work, OK?'

'Don't worry.' He gives my hand a light squeeze. 'I'll have you home by midnight, Cinderella.' I grin back at him, feeling a rush of adrenaline sweeping through me. I haven't had a night out in town in ages.

Chapter Eighteen

The music is still pounding in my ears as I unsteadily push the key in the lock of my front door. I haven't had so much fun in years. Who'd have thought that a quiet drink would've turned into a hell raising event?

Initially, I got away with a cheap round of cocktails at a glitzy bar in Soho where all the staff knew Marc by name. Drinks were on a buy one get one free offer. Result. I had two Porn Stars, not literally, of course – a delicious concoction of passion fruit, vodka and prosecco, which went down smoothly, and a bit too quickly, to be honest. Within the hour my second glass was empty. But then instead of coming home like I was supposed to, like I'd planned, I let Marc and the effects of the Porn Star cocktails persuade me to go on for one more drink at the Met Bar. Then one thing led to another and we ended up in a cocktail bar crawl via a nightclub. I know, a woman pushing forty out on the razz, go me.

I almost stumble over Harry's bike as I fly through the door. I stagger around the narrow hallway like a fly that's just been blitzed by insect repellent. I really shouldn't have had that limoncello nightcap at The Bar at The Dorchester. I did tell Marc not to order one for me, but by the time I returned from the loo he was sipping his, and mine was waiting for on the table in all its lovely yellowness.

I feel around in the darkness for the light switch, flick it on, and take a sharp inward breath. 'Oh, bloody hell,' I cry. 'You scared the shit out of me. Why are you sitting in the dark?' Harry's at the kitchen table, *Doctor Who* mug in front of him, squinting at the sudden brightness.

'Where've you been?' He asks coolly, glancing at the clock above the door.

I kick my stilettos off and rub my right foot. I feel as if I've been walking on nails – I'm not used to wearing heels. And I haven't hit the dance floor in years.

'I told you, I was seeing a potential client.' I open the cabinet, grab a glass, and fill it with water from the jug. 'Anyway, why are you still up, isn't it way past your bedtime?' I narrow my eyes at the clock, which is swaying against the wall in my double vision. 'It must be gone midnight by now, surely.'

Harry looks at me with a deadpan expression. 'It's almost four in the morning,' he says sternly.

'What?' I exclaim. 'It can't be.' I go to look at my watch, then remember I'm wearing Marc's Ted Baker gift, and cover it clandestinely with my sleeve.

'You forgot your portfolio.' Harry nods towards the lounge. 'It's still on the dining table.'

'Oh, yes.' I let out a little nervy laugh as my fringe falls onto my face. 'I did. But I didn't need it, really. I gave the client my blog address. I uploaded all my recent images of past work and testimonials on there the other day.' God, when did I get so good at lying? I gulp the glass of water down in one go.

'So, how did it go?'

'How did what go?' I pour more water into my glass as I contemplate dissolving a sachet of Dioralyte into it. I am seriously dehydrated.

'The meeting with the *potential* client,' he says crisply. Why is Harry looking at me like that? I haven't done anything wrong. 'Any luck?'

'Er ... I'm not sure yet.' I take another gulp of water, securing my long, wild fringe behind my ear. 'He said he'll let me know after he's seen the samples. But I'm not holding my breath. I think he found my rates a bit high, to be honest,' I say, trying desperately to control my slurring tongue.

'He?'

I've had enough of being interrogated. 'Yes, Harry, *he*.' I slam the glass down onto the table and lean toward him. 'A man! Have you got a problem with that?'

He winces at the tone of my voice, then pushes his tongue against the inside of his cheek. He always does this when I'm getting on his nerves but doesn't want a row. As if he's trying to seal his words inside his mouth.

'I see,' he says finally, pressing the palms of his hands firmly on the table. 'You were out all night. With a man. A man who probably won't be hiring you because he found your fees too high. Yet it took you, what?' He glances at the large clock again. 'A mere seven hours to come to that conclusion?' I don't answer. Instead I start faffing about with the crockery on the drying rack.

'Well?'

'Well what?' I snap. 'Yes, Harry. I was out all night with a man enjoying myself. Satisfied?'

'Where were you until now?' He folds his arms. 'You said it was only going to be a half hour meeting.' His dismissal of what I've just confessed fills me with rage. I want him to care that I was with a male client, to be jealous, feel threatened.

'Why? What do you care?' I feel him watching me as I drain the glass. 'What?' I huff. 'Don't tell me you're actually *jealous*?' I wipe my mouth with the back of my sleeve, narrowly avoiding the disclosure of the Ted Baker watch.

173

He rubs his stubbly chin, exhaling loudly. 'Should I be?' Finally, a reaction.

I'm not sure if it's the drink that takes over my vocal cords, but the next thing I know I hear myself shouting, 'Yes, Harry, maybe you should be. After all, you haven't touched me in months.'

He looks at me, aghast, for a few moments. A piercing sound of a screaming fox rips through the silence.

'What?' He asks finally, his face creased with confusion.

'You know what I mean.' I yank the fridge door open and pull out a carton of orange juice. I need to top up my vitamin C levels, Ola's tip after one too many.

'No, I don't, actually,' he says crossly, scraping back his chair. 'Enlighten me, why don't you? It takes two to tango, you know, but do you hear me complaining?'

'What's that supposed to mean?'

'It means you're just as lax as I am, that's what!'

'You don't fancy me anymore, you never say romantic things. You don't WANT me,' I yell back in retaliation.

'What are you talking about? Is it my fault if you don't like having sex when you're on? Is it my fault that you're always snoring by the time I come up to bed?'

I breathe in sharply. 'I don't snore,' I object, shaking the carton furiously. 'You knew I had my period that night, don't deny it.'

'Huh?' He's gets to his feet and I notice he's wearing his stripy blue and grey pyjama bottoms beneath his V-neck black sweater. He always sleeps topless. He must've gone to bed then woken up. I wonder why?

'You put my tampons away. Remember?' I open a drawer, close it, then start rearranging the mugs on the drainer manically. I don't know what I'm doing. I can't think straight. I grab a glass and half fill it with juice.

Harry's looking at me as if I'm mad. 'You've really lost the plot now, Emma.'

'*I've* lost the plot?' I take a mouthful of juice and notice that my hand is shaking. 'You're the one who's shagging a mystery woman.'

His eyes darken. We glare at each other in agonising silence to the backdrop of the clock ticking away, louder and louder in my ears like an imminent explosive.

He takes a deep breath in, pushing his tongue to the side of his mouth, eyebrows knotted.

'I'm going to ignore that, Emma,' he says calmly, as if I'm someone who's lost my mind, 'because I know you're upset about Alistair.' He pauses, licks his dry lips, hands on hips. 'And you've obviously had too much to drink.'

'I'm not drunk,' I burst out. I am a bit tipsy but can hold my drink quite well.

He snorts, gathering his eyebrows incredulously, then leans towards me. 'You stink of booze, Emma.'

'What about Isabella?' I demand, changing the subject. 'I saw that text she sent you last night,' I point my finger at him. 'Why is she sending you messages at midnight like an insatiable lover if there's nothing going on?'

'I thought we agreed you weren't going to read my messages again.'

'Yeah, well …' I take a gulp of juice, then swish the residue in my glass.

'Look, I told you,' he says indignantly, 'we're just friends. Why can't you trust me like I trust you?'

'Yeah, friends for now maybe,' I yell, my heart banging in my chest. 'But how long is that going to last, hmm? How long before you jump into bed with her? Hell, who am I kidding? You've probably done that already.' Bile rises in my chest and the room spins. I think I'm going to be sick. I steady myself against the sink, waiting for the feeling to subside.

'I can't talk to you when you're like this.' He heads for the door.

'Where are you going? You can't just walk away in the middle of a row.'

'To the loo,' he shouts over his shoulder. 'If that's alright with you?' The toilet door slams and I wince.

I try to gather my thoughts. Oh, God, this wasn't meant to happen. I wanted to come home and flop into bed, not have a screaming match with Harry. I push my trembling hands through my unruly hair, catching the strap of the Ted Baker watch in my tresses. I remove it hurriedly and slip it into my pocket. Marc strapped it around my wrist after we got off the dance floor at The Cuckoo Club. A prize, he said, for learning how to do The Floss, which his friend Cindy the barmaid, a twenty-something 1950s retro girl, taught me during her break. She was also keen to teach me to slut drop, but I wasn't going to stoop to that level. I wasn't that pissed. And yes, I was the oldest one on the dance floor but who cares? I accepted the watch in the heat of the moment as we collapsed in a fit of giggles onto a squidgy sofa seat. I shouldn't have. I should've stuck to my guns. I'm going to have to return it, of course.

Harry's taking an awfully long time in the toilet. What the hell is he doing in there? I tap on the door. 'Harry, you OK?'

'Yes,' he snaps. 'Can't I even have a pee in peace?'

'I only asked, keep your hair on,' I mutter as I shuffle into the lounge. I can't believe I left my portfolio behind. I pick it up and leaf through it idly.

I find Harry in the kitchen pulling the yellow blind up, telling me he thought he heard a noise. I peek over his shoulder as Alistair's floodlights come on. 'Probably those damned foxes again,' I complain and walk away. 'Er …'

'What?' Harry spins round.

'What did you do with my juice?'

'I didn't do anything with it.'

I stare at the worktop, hands on hips. 'I left it here.' My eyes trail around the kitchen, finger in mouth. And then I spot it, upturned in the sink drainer. 'There was a bit left in that, why did you chuck it away?' I ask accusingly.

'I didn't touch it,' Harry protests in a high pitched voice.

'What do you mean you didn't touch it? I left it here and now it's there,' I point at the glass angrily.

'Well, maybe you rinsed it yourself?'

'No way,' I insist. 'I definitely left it on this worktop.' I stroke the smooth granite. 'You must've poured it down the sink. You're always throwing my things away. You should get a job with Stelios on that hoarding programme on Channel 4. They'd love you.'

Harry shakes his head, staring at his feet. 'Emma, it's four thirty in the morning. I'm not going to stand here and argue with you over a sodding glass of orange juice. You're hammered, I'm tired.' He brushes past me.

'Huh,' I snort, 'walk away, why don't you?' I say to his back. 'Don't worry about …' And at that moment the kettle suddenly roars into action and the words die on my tongue.

'Harry.'

He stops in the hallway, turns around, clearly irritated. 'What is it, Emma? I'm knackered.'

'The … the … kettle.' I point a limp finger at the rumbling kettle, staring at the water bubbling away through the water gauge. 'It's come on.'

Harry tuts, exasperated. 'So?'

'What do you mean, *so*?' I hiss. 'It's boiling.'

177

'Yes, well, isn't that what kettles are supposed to do?' His voice is cold, sharp. 'Boil water?'

'I mean it came on on its own.' I push the white plastic lever up and the blue illumination goes off. 'I didn't touch it, Harry,' I say quietly, hand on my chest. 'I swear.'

He walks back into the kitchen and flicks the switch on and off in quick succession. 'Seems all right to me. Are you sure you didn't switch it on by accident?'

'What, from five feet away?'

He glances at me, lips curved downwards, shaking his head in confusion. 'It must've got caught when I made a cup of coffee just before you got in.'

'Harry, that was over forty minutes ago. And you need to press it down firmly.' I stare at it. 'There's no way it could've caught on anything.' I clamp my hand over my mouth. 'You don't think it's …'

'What?'

My chest tightens as a feeling of dread washes over me. Alistair said he'd find a way of getting in touch. Is this it? The kettle, the glass of orange juice, the lights coming on in his garden. 'Alistair …' I murmur. I look at Harry intently, willing him to disagree with me.

'A ghost?' He asks, and I nod silently. 'You really are pissed, Emma, aren't you? First the disappearing glass, now the ghostly kettle. What did you have to drink, for heaven's sake?' I feel my muscles relax. He's right. I'm being stupid, paranoid.

'Just a couple of cocktails,' I lie.

'Well, they must've been lethal if they're causing this.'

I circle the kettle with trepidation as if it's a living, breathing entity. Maybe I did overdo it tonight. I'm not used to drinking cocktails, well, not so many of them, anyway. 'Do you think?' I say. Then a bolt of acid hits the pit of my stomach. Oh God, I hope Marc didn't spike my drink with ecstasy or anything. I wouldn't put it past him. I close my eyes briefly, taking a deep breath. Of course he didn't spike my drink – what the hell am I thinking? He's a bit of a rogue but he's not a psycho. 'Oh no,' I blurt. 'I hope it doesn't keep coming on while we're asleep. It might burn the house down.' I cover my mouth with my hand, heart pounding wildly.

'It's just an electrical fault,' Harry says reassuringly, his face softening. 'I'll check it tomorrow.' He pulls the plug out of the socket. 'There, happy now?' I nod quickly. 'I'll see you upstairs, then.' He heads towards the door.

'Harry,' I rush behind him. 'Wait.'

He stops, hand on the bannister, tongue pressed against the side of his mouth. 'What now?'

'What were you doing up?' I pull my sleeve over my hand like a six-year-old about to be reprimanded.

There are a few moments of silence.

'Your sister called this evening. Several times, in fact,' he says quietly with a little, sharp sigh. 'She said you weren't answering your mobile.'

Oh yes, I rejected Tessa's call in the cab. I was meant to ring her back, but after a couple of cocktails Marc and I started taking selfies and before I knew it my battery had drained. 'My battery ran out of juice,' I offer lamely.

'Yeah, I figured, what with you never being off it. Anyway, she said she sent you texts and DM'd you on Facebook. She even put a Tweet out in case any of your mates knew where you were.'

'Facebook?' I say looking pensively at my bag containing my mobile phone. 'Tweet alert?' Why would she do that?

'And she called again about an hour ago.' He sits heavily on the step, hands dangling over his knees.

'What, in the middle of the night?' I ask, crouching down beside him, suddenly sober. 'What did she want? Oh God, please don't tell me something's happened to the baby.' Anxiety fizzes in my stomach.

Harry shakes his head. 'No, no, the baby's fine. Tessa's fine.' Phew.

'Well, what is it?'

'Look, Emma, I think you need to sober up.' He gets to his feet. 'Come on.' His hand curls around my wrist. 'I'll make you a coffee and we can talk.'

'Harry, please.' I snatch my hand away from his light grip. 'Just tell me, will you?' My eyes search his. 'Spit it out, for heaven's sake, you're scaring me now.'

He looks at me carefully, biting down on his upper lip, hands loosely on hips. 'I've been up half the night waiting for you to come home, to tell you the news but now ...' He lifts his arm up then lets it drop by his side. 'I don't know if you're in a fit state to –'

'Right, 'I interject crossly. 'If you won't tell me what's going on, then I'll drive round to Tessa's and ask her myself.' I snatch my bag off the floor and start fishing inside it for my car keys. 'Don't think I won't do it.' I point the bag at him as if it's a loaded gun.

'Don't be so stupid, you're way over the limit. Emma, stop it.' He tries to grab the bag from my hands but I won't let go. We both tug at it like fighting dogs. 'OK, OK. I'll tell you.' I stop the search and look at him expectantly, cheeks burning, hair in my face. 'It's your dad. He's been taken ill. He collapsed yesterday evening.' My face freezes. 'They had to call the emergency services.' Our eyes lock. We're both still clutching my bag tightly. 'She wants you to call her first thing in the morning,' he says softly. 'It's serious.'

Chapter Nineteen

'Oh, bloody hell, Emma,' Caroline exclaims. 'When did you find out?'

'Three days ago,' I sigh. Tessa called again on Sunday morning, before I even had a chance to get out of bed, desperate to share the burden of Dad's illness, to find out if I'd be willing to help. Of course, Dad's illness has put everything into perspective. Harry and I haven't spoken about my drunken night out or Isabella-gate since. The news has knocked us for six.

'What are you going to do?' Caroline's voice breaks into my thoughts. We're sitting in the family room at Milford and Sons funeral parlour, waiting for them to get Alistair ready for 'viewing'. I've come to say goodbye, and Caroline kindly agreed to come with me.

'I don't know,' I suck my lips in. 'I don't hear from my dad in years and now he wants my flipping kidney.' Tessa was a complete wreck, she blubbed down the phone most of the time, barely able to string a coherent sentence together. You'd never believe she was a medical professional, the way she was going on. 'Mind you,' I say to a stunned-looking Caroline. 'I didn't even know he had Type 2 diabetes, let alone renal disease. Anyway, I've been sworn to secrecy. I've promised Tessa I won't say anything to Dad. Well, not just yet. And, obviously, as I've lost contact with him it's not likely to happen anyway, is it?' I shake my head in disbelief. 'Even at a time like this he's shutting me out. He and Tessa have always been close,' I groan. 'Even though I'm a lot more like him.' I twirl a strand of red hair around my finger and stare into the distance, pensively. 'I mean, he's *my* dad too, you know, despite everything.'

'Emma, sweetheart.' Caroline places a warm hand over mine. 'You and him aren't exactly close. I mean, it's a giant risk. A big ask. Think of the health implications.' I stare at Caroline. She looks a bit odd today. I wonder if she's changed her hair colour.

'Yes, I know.' I say eventually, glancing around at the photos of coffins and floral tributes adorning the magnolia walls. 'But I can't just let him die, can I?'

'What about your sister the dentist?' She pulls her handbag close to her tummy and tucks her legs under her chair. 'Can't she give him one of hers?' She says, as if a kidney is a spare car tyre. 'She must be used to operations, given her line of work.'

'It doesn't make you immune to fear,' I say. 'Anyway, Tessa said she'll get tested once she's had the baby. But even if she's a match she can't offer it to him right away. I don't think she'll be in a fit state for months. Maybe even a year.' I dab at my eye with my knuckle, sadness piercing every fibre in my body. 'It might be too late by then.'

'Oh, sweetie,' Caroline says sympathetically. We fall silent for a moment. 'Can't he go on dialysis?' She pulls out a packet of wine gums, pops one into her mouth, and extends the tube to me.

'My dad?' I shake my head and she slips the sweets back into her cardigan pocket. 'On a machine three times a week for four hours at a time? I don't think so. I think he'd rather die. Besides, it's no long-term cure, is it?'

Caroline nods thoughtfully, chewing on her sweet. 'It is a big op, Emma. All sorts of things can go wrong.' I know she's right, but she isn't helping. 'You really do need to think this through properly.'

'I know, I know,' I exhale loudly, rubbing my forehead. 'That's what Harry said. And your app said something similar.'

'The Magic Touch?' Caroline wriggles in her seat with glee. 'Really? What'd it say?' She nudges me on the arm, chewing faster, eyes bright.

'Quite a lot of random things that have actually come true, or at least made a lot of sense. I'm really, really impressed.'

'Such as?'

I give her a quick rundown of the predictions I've been having, then tell her about the one I had on the day of Tessa's phone call:

"A family tie brings with it a burden too heavy to carry. Let sleeping dogs lie."

'You're joking,' she exclaims a little too loudly, her puffy face now a shade of scarlet.

'No, I'm not. But since Sunday it's gone a bit bonkers.'

'Bonkers?'

'Hmm …' I nod, studying her face. She must've had a facial. 'It's been saying things like:

"Oooh, what bliss."

"I'll be there if you need me."

"I'm fine, stop being an idiot."

"Get a move on, I can't hang around here forever."

'Just stuff like that. Weird, don't you think? I think it must've clashed with another app or something.'

'Hmm, sounds like it.' Caroline looks around the relatives' room, tugging at the collar of her purple tunic. 'It's probably a bug that needs fixing. Try uninstalling it and downloading it again.' She stands up, whips off her long black cardigan, and pushes a hand through her golden

183

bob. 'It's so hot in here, isn't it?' She fans herself with her hand.

I actually feel OK in my khaki parka jacket. She must be having another one of her hot flushes. Our journey here consisted of the air-con going on and off at thirty-second intervals, with the passenger window going up and down, up and down like a yoyo, our hair flying in the wind. We arrived looking like a couple of witches who had just stepped off our broomsticks.

The trill of my phone makes me jump. Oh God, I hope it's not Marc again. I rang him after I spoke to Tessa last Sunday, told him I'd a family crisis and I could meet him quickly to return the watch but that would be all.

'Don't be stupid, Emma,' he said. I could hear him taking a long drag on his cigarette. 'Family comes first. Forget about the watch. I told you, it's a gift. Keep it.'

'No, Marc, I couldn't possibly. I'll return it to you as soon as all this is over.'

'Sure, take your time,' he said, taking another lungful of smoke. 'Hope everything goes well. You take care of yourself.'

I ended the call, grateful that he was so understanding, then hid the watch at the back of my knicker drawer. However, since that call he's sent me several text messages, pleading with me to meet up, and won't seem to take no for an answer.

I look at my phone with trepidation. Phew, it's Ola with a three-page text wanting to know some more Greek phrases. I turn to Caroline, who's now picking wine gums from between her teeth. 'Do you know how to say "would you like to take a siesta" in Greek? Ola wants to know.' I wave the phone at her. 'There's a young student teacher that's got her boyfriend's folks over and she wants to learn a few phrases, impress him, and them, obviously. I've told her all the ones that I know.'

A few moments later, I press send. 'Thanks, Caroline, you're so good at Greek, better than I'll ever be.' I gaze at her. She definitely looks different.

'What?'

'Caroline, have you been on a sunbed or something?'

'No, I haven't. Why?'

I point at her face. 'Your face, it looks … I dunno … Are you trying out a new cream again?'

She leans down, her voice drops to a whisper. 'Botox.'

'Botox?' I exclaim.

'Shhhh …' Her eyes widen but her face is stiff. 'And a few fillers. I had them done this morning. Do I look awful?' She touches her puffy cheek then stares around the room wildly. 'Is there a mirror here?'

I gawp at her for a few moments. 'Well, no, not awful but …' Her hands fly to her face. Oh God, I hope I haven't offended her. I pull her hands away and look into her teary blue eyes. 'You look fine, Caroline, don't worry. It's just that you don't need it, do you? You look younger than I do, for heaven's sake.' And she does. I can't think what possessed her to mess about with her lovely face. She's a good-looking woman, everyone says so.

She folds her cardigan over her forearm and sits back down. 'I didn't expect it to turn out like this. I thought it'd be more subtle. Mas'll go spare when he sees me.' She shakes her head. 'And when he finds out how much it cost!'

'Don't worry, you look fine. I'm sure it'll wear off a bit by the time you get home.' I look at her shiny face. She doesn't look convinced. 'It's the funeral next Tuesday,' I offer, changing the subject.

'Oh, really?' She snatches a leaflet from the round table in front of us, and starts fanning her rosy cheeks furiously. 'Do you want me to come with you?' She asks as the words "What to do when someone dies" sweep in and out of my vision in large, bold letters. I gulp as images of my body on an operating table spill into my mind, followed in quick succession by my own funeral.

'No, it's fine.' I place a hand on her arm affectionately and she stops fanning. 'Harry's booked time off work. Compassionate leave. He wouldn't want to miss Alistair's funeral.'

A strong, heady scent wafts towards us as the funeral advisor bustles into the room wearing a grey pinstripe suit over a cream blouse – she's in her mid-thirties with long, silky brown hair, large eyes, and a wiry frame.

'Miss King? Hello, I'm Susie.' She extends a hand. 'I'll be assisting you today.' Her hand feels limp and small in mine. 'Alistair is ready for viewing now.' She presses her hands together joyfully, as if we're about to see the unveiling of a royal portrait. 'If you'd like to follow me, please.' Despite her business attire, she has a saintly persona; a zen-like goddess in a suit.

We scramble to our feet. Caroline pushes her arm into her cardigan as we trot behind Susie. Her stilettos click quickly against the parquet floor as she strides along the narrow corridor, throwing the occasional glance over her shoulder.

'You don't have to go in if you feel queasy, Em.' Caroline extends her hand reassuringly as we reach the Chapel of Rest. I nod, feeling my throat tighten. I hope I'll be OK. I've never seen a corpse before, but I can't let Alistair go without saying a proper goodbye. My heart thumps in my chest, its rhythm reaching my throat and stomach. Oh God, I can't feel my legs.

'Are you OK?' Susie asks gently, sensing my tension. I nod quickly, taking shallow breaths like a woman about to give birth. The sooner I get this over with the better.

'She's scared shitless,' Caroline pipes up, stepping in front of me like a shield. Thank you, Caroline, you've made me feel ten times worse. 'I think I should go in first. I'm psychic, you see. I'm used to these sorts of things.'

'Oh, really?' Susie inclines her head, impressed. 'Can you feel anything here?'

'A bit,' Caroline shivers, glancing around her. 'Although I am a palmist, so I don't see people who've passed but I do get strange feelings sometimes. Right, let's do this.' She straightens her cardigan, glancing at me over her shoulder. 'You just stand here by the door, Emma, and I'll let you know when to come in.'

'Ready?' Susie asks with a warm smile, twisting the door handle. We both nod. I take another deep breath, then square my shoulders. Come on, Emma, you can do this.

The door flies open. We're a few steps in. Alistair's casket is propped up in the middle of the small room beneath a glaring spotlight, as if he's part of some historic exhibition. My eyes widen as I peek at him in the casket, his head resting against white padded fabric. Then just as I take another small step forward a loud, shrill scream tears through the room.

'Caroline!' I look at her aghast. She's gone pale. She must be having another hot flush or something. 'Are you OK?'

Susie, startled by Caroline's outburst, straightens her jacket and regains her composure. 'Goodness, you're more frightened than she is,' she says with a little laugh.

Caroline is rooted to the spot, eyes wide, nostrils flaring, face tight with Botox. She looks at me desperately, then at

Susie, a trembling finger pointing at Alistair.
'He's … he's …'

Susie reaches out, placing a hand on my arm, then tells
me that Caroline is clearly upset, that she'll escort her to
the relatives' area while I say my goodbyes. 'He's alive,'
Caroline squeaks, as if she's just inhaled helium gas.

'Caroline?' I glance at Susie worriedly. 'What's going
on, Susie?'

'It's just a bit difficult for some people,' Susie whispers
glancing at Caroline as if she's a special needs patient.
'That's all.' She touches Caroline's back gently. 'Were
they very close?' She turns her lips downwards in an
exaggerated fashion, and for a moment she reminds me of
the sad face emoticon.

'She'd never met him,' I reply, astonished. 'Caroline,
are you OK?' I ease Susie out of the way and take Caroline
firmly by the shoulders. 'Do you need some air?'

'But …' Her bottom lip is juddering.

'What is it? Are you hot?' I touch her sweaty forehead.
'She's freezing cold!'

'It's just the shock of seeing a corpse.' Susie reaches out
for Caroline. 'Come on, lovely, let's get some fresh air.'

'I don't need fresh air.' Caroline shrugs her off.
'What's the matter with you two?' She glares at us. 'He's
sitting right there.' She grabs my arm tightly with both
hands. 'Can't you see him? He's still alive.'

I look at her searchingly as she digs her nails into my
forearm. 'Caroline,' I say with a shaky voice. 'He's in the
coffin. He's dead.'

'Em … Emm … I can't …' She lets go of my arm and
presses her chest, taking quick, shallow breaths.

'Oh God, what is it, Caroline?' Jesus, I hope she's not
having a heart attack.

'I can't … I can't …' And with this she keels over, missing the casket by millimetres.

'Quick.' Susie falls to her knees, checks her pulse. 'She's breathing.' She gives Caroline several slaps on her puffy cheeks. 'Caroline? Can you hear me? Caroline?'

I'm on my knees. 'Oh God,' I say urgently. My heart is beating like a drum roll. 'Call an ambulance,' I scream at a clearly shaken Susie. She nods, rocking back on the balls of her feet.

'My phone's in reception. Is there anything wrong with her?' She asks, her face ashen.

'What do you think?' I snap.

'No, I mean an ongoing illness. Is she diabetic or anything?'

'No. I don't think so,' I say, feeling a surge of panic. 'Oh, wait,' I add quickly. 'She is menopausal. She's been having all the symptoms. Racing heart, hot flushes, loss of concentration,' I jabber. 'Jesus, can you die of that?' I empty the contents of my bag onto the gold carpet and go on a manic iPhone search. 'Siri will know,' I pant, hysteria flooding my brain. I speak into my phone. 'Can you die from the menopause?'

Within seconds my iPhone beeps. 'I'm afraid I don't know the answer to that, Emma.' Oh bloody hell. Why can't he ever answer any of my personal questions?

'Oh, for goodness' sake.' Susie pushes me out of the way, tossing back her shiny brown hair. 'Of course you can't die from the menopause. Help me lift her onto that chair.' Well, that's just rude. It didn't take long for the zen-like goddess to transform into Godzilla. OK, in retrospect it was a stupid thing to say, but I'm panicking, what does she expect?

'OK, OK, I'm sorry,' I say grabbing a hold of Caroline's other arm and hoisting her onto the chair. 'I'm not thinking straight. It's just that Caroline's been complaining of … oh wait,' I cry, 'She did say she had Botox this morning, you don't think that …' I trail off at the faint sound of Caroline's voice.

'Where am I?' Caroline half opens her eyes. Thank you, Lord. 'Mas?'

'Caroline? Are you OK, honey? It's Emma.' I hover over her like an apparition. 'We're at the funeral parlour. Can you hear me? You had a little faint. You're going to be OK. Speak to me, Caroline … Caroline?'

'It's OK, she's coming round.' Susie gets to her feet and brushes herself down. 'She just had a panic attack from the shock. We've seen it many times before. I'll go get her some water. Just keep her seated, will you?'

Ten minutes later, we're standing over Alistair's casket. Susie slipped away once the commotion was over, saying she'd give us a few moments alone with Alistair. Personally, I think she took us for a couple of nutters and couldn't wait to get away. It was that glint of terror in her eyes as she carefully backed out of the room that gave it away.

I take a step forward and notice immediately that Alistair has his hands crossed over his tummy. He actually looks like something out of Madame Tussauds. They've dressed him in his favourite blue suit, white shirt, and blue tie. His thin, white hair has been gelled back and parted to the left. They got that wrong. Alistair always wore his parting to the right. His lips, usually purple-blue, are now ruby red and I swear I see a hint of a smile on his face.

'He doesn't look real, does he?' I whisper.

'He looks like he's had a spray tan.' Caroline muses, glass in hand, mascara smeared all over her tight face. 'Or was he always that colour?'

'Of course not, he's usually quite pale.' I inch closer. 'He's not there, I can see it now. It's just his shell.'

'It's the formaldehyde,' Caroline says, taking a sip of water. 'The embalmer did a good job on him.' She tilts her head.

'The what?' I rub my neck. 'God, my mouth is so dry.'

'It's a chemical they use to preserve the body.' She hands me her glass and I take a few sips. 'Stop it from rotting.'

'Oh, I see. He does look a bit puffed out,' I hand her the glass. 'His cheeks, I mean.'

'What, a bit like mine?' She jokes, and suddenly she jumps, losing her grip on the glass. 'Did you feel that?' She shrieks. I watch in horror as the glass hits the floor. 'That whoosh of air?' She says, following my eyes to the glass. 'Oh, leave it, at least it didn't break.'

I look around the room as I retrieve the glass from the small puddle on the immaculate carpet, which now looks like a dog has weed on it. 'Shit, Caroline, we've caused so much havoc. They're going to chuck us out.'

'Oh, it's only a bit of water. It'll dry up in a mo. Arghh ... did you feel that? Just then as you stood back up?' She sniffs the air. 'And what's that smell? Is it Aramis? My dad still wears that.'

'No. I didn't feel a breeze,' I say, unable to mask the exasperation in my voice. There aren't any windows in here, Caroline,' I put the empty glass on the chair. 'I can't see how any wind could get in. And they probably spritzed him with Aramis, it was his favourite aftershave. Although I can't smell anything.'

'Oh, Christ on a bike,' she says, fastening her hands over her mouth. 'He's back.'

Oh no, she's having another turn. 'Who's back, Caroline?' She's really starting to freak me out. It must be those Chinese herbs her acupuncturist prescribed for the menopause. Harry told me that Mas has been complaining about her sudden mood swings and irritability since she's been on them. And how she keeps misplacing things then accuses Mas of moving her stuff. Well, he can add hallucinations to that list of side effects.

'Alistair,' she says calmly. 'He's over there.' She points to the corner of the room. 'A translucent version of what's in that coffin but with a glowing outline.' She makes a shape in the air with her finger. 'Oooh, he's saying hello.' She waves at a blank magnolia wall.

'Caroline, I think we should leave.' I glance around frantically. 'Are you feeling faint again?'

'No, I'm fine,' she says cheerily, waving a hand. 'What? Tell her what? A map? What kind of map?'

Oh my God. Caroline is having a conversation with a blank wall. She's completely lost the plot. 'Caroline,' I murmur, unable to hide the dread in my voice. 'Let's get you home then we can ring Harry, ask him to call round on his way home. Make sure you're OK, yeah? That the Botox hasn't harmed you in any way. '

'What, sweetie?' Caroline says, ignoring me. She twists towards the door. 'No, we can't come with you *now*, for heaven's sake. God, was he always this bossy?' Caroline rolls her eyes and tuts. 'He wants us to go with him somewhere. What, love? Slow down. I can't understand what you're saying,' she says to the door. 'Did he have a speech impediment, Emma?'

'No,' I say worriedly. 'He was quite eloquent, actually. Look, Caroline, I think we should go. I've said my goodbyes. Come on.'

'He's saying something about a hostel? Does that mean anything?' I shake my head. 'I can't catch everything he's saying, the words are cutting out. Like a bad telephone line, do you know what I mean? A motel? Oh, a *hotel*.' She looks at me with glee. 'He wants us to follow him to some hotel, reckons it's dead important. No pun intended. Ha.'

I chew my bottom lip. Surely she can't be for real. I look at her carefully. But there's no way Alistair would stoop this low. He hated mediums and he made a point of telling me that we weren't to use one. No, Caroline is hallucinating. It's the Botox and the Chinese herbs – not a good mix, obviously. I've got to get her home and call Harry.

'Come on.' Her hand feels cold and clammy in mine. 'We're leaving.' I look at Alistair. 'Goodbye, my lovely friend. Sleep tight.' I blow him a kiss, then wrench the door open. 'Come on, Caroline. I've got to get home. I've some emails from clients to catch up with.'

'Alright, alright, hold your horses. It's not my fault he popped in for a chat, is it? My goodness, Emma, you can be so domineering at times.'

I bustle her out of the room. 'Let's go, Caroline.'

'Emma,' she says joyfully as I frogmarch her along the corridor. 'I can see dead people.' Oh God, help us. What have I done?

Chapter Twenty

I don't know what to wear. Should I wear black, as Valentina suggested yesterday as we stood side by side in the sweltering kitchen rolling meatballs in readiness for deep frying? Or just a dark colour? Maybe something bright? I didn't think to ask Judith when she called with the funeral details last week. It's too late now.

I run a hand along the clothes rail. Maybe my Mango blue and white patterned dress, which I bought several years ago but have only worn once. That's quite smart. I yank it off the hanger and quickly slip into it. It still fits, that's a good start.

I tiptoe in front of the full-length wardrobe mirror to see how it'll look once I've got my heels on. It is a bit short. I rush around the bedroom, tugging at the hem as if that'll magically lengthen it to just above the knee. If anyone walked in now they'd think we'd been raided by burglars. I trample over the sea of clothes lining the floor and dash to the window in the second bedroom, hoping to catch a glimpse of arriving mourners. My mother warned me that I'd end up being a curtain twitcher myself one day, whenever I berated her for spying on the neighbours, but I didn't believe her.

A shiny red Mini Cooper with white horizontal stripes has just pulled up outside our house, I can just about see the silhouette of a couple sitting in the front seats. Across the road a middle-aged woman in black jeans and a black and white patterned blouse is crossing the street, dragging a little girl by the hand. She must be a mourner. The thud of the car door reverts my attention back to the couple in the Mini. He's sliding an arm into his dark blue jacket. She's still in the car, pressing her lips together and staring into the mirror of the sun visor. She's checking out her teeth now for smudges, no doubt. Oooh, she's just got out. Result. She's wearing a floral, navy blue dress with killer heels.

I sigh with relief at the jangle of the front door. 'I'm home.' Harry's voice in the distance.

I charge down the stairs to greet him. He puckers his lips and reaches for me over his bike, hands still firmly on the handlebars.

'Do I look OK?' I stand back self-consciously, straightening my dress, tugging at my hair. 'Or is this dress too short? I should've worn my black one, don't you think? I'll nip up and change.' I turn on my heel.

'No, it's fine. Stop fussing. You look great.'

'Oh God, Harry. I know I'm making a fuss but I want to look good for Alistair. I mean, I know he won't physically be there but ...'

'I know you do, Emma. And you look fine, honestly. Alistair would be proud if he could see how much effort you were making for his send-off.'

'But what about my hair?' I comb my fingers through it, looking at my reflection in the hallway mirror. 'It's way too short, isn't it?' Gino, my hairdresser, turned into Edward Scissorhands yesterday afternoon, chopping off at least three inches more than I'd asked him to.

'Your hair looks fine,' Harry says reassuringly.

'Do you think?' I take a step back, examining my new shoulder-length bob. 'Oh my God.' I stare at my reflection in horror as Harry pushes his bike into the hall.

'What?' He asks over his shoulder.

'One side is flipping longer than the other, that's what. Hell, what has Gino done to me? Alistair would've been mortified.' Alistair was a perfectionist – things had to be just so, and he'd spot an imperfection immediately.

Harry leans his bike against the white wall, releasing the kickstand with his right foot with a clank. I only cleaned those encaustic floor tiles this morning, and he's already marked them with grime from the wheels of his bike. He's standing behind me groping my hair as if he's Nicky Clarke. 'It's all good, Em, stop worrying.'

'No,' I say, panic sluicing through me. 'Look.' I pull it all forward and comb it down with my fingers.

He stands back and looks at it methodically. 'Oh, yeah, I can see it now, about an inch on the right.' Oh God. Now it's confirmed, I feel even worse.

My stomach twists. 'What am I going to do?' I don't know what's wrong with me today, I seem to be on constant 'worry' mode.

Harry looks genuinely concerned. 'Come on.' He makes for the door. 'I'll run you back to Gino's in the car. Get him to fix it for you.'

'I haven't got time to go back,' I hiss, stamping my feet like a two-year old.

'Emma.' Harry stretches his hand out. 'Didn't he show you your hair in the mirror before you left? Even my barber does that,' he says, his tone denoting. 'Are you a complete idiot?'

'Yes, but I didn't get a proper look, did I? He just kept yanking the mirror up and down behind my head quickly. I couldn't see. Ooohwwa.' I pull at the shorter side, hoping a tuft of hair might magically make an appearance from behind my neck, praying I've made a mistake. But no chance. It now looks worse than ever. 'I can't say goodbye to Alistair looking like this.'

'It doesn't really show, Emma. Don't —'

'Oh God, Harry. Stop trying to make me feel better,' I cry. 'It's not working. I've got to do something.'

I take the stairs two at a time, burst into the bathroom, grab my comb and a pair of scissors, and thunder back down the stairs. 'Cut it for me,' I demand breathlessly, handing him the scissors and comb.

Harry looks horrified. 'What? I can't. I …'

'Come on, Harry. We'll be late.' I shove the comb and scissors against his chest. 'Just comb it at the back and cut off the longer side. You can do this. You're used to casualties.'

'I'm a nurse,' he snaps, 'not a flipping hairdresser.'

'Harry! Don't be such a wuss. Please. You know how much today means to me. I've got to look my best.'

He grimaces as he takes the items from my trembling hand.

Harry drops his car keys onto the dining room table with a clang as I kick off my shoes. He looks tired. His skin is dry, his eyes puffy and dark. He really does need a break. We both do. 'I'm so glad that's over with,' he says, collapsing onto the sofa and grabbing the remote control. 'I was dreading today.'

'Yeah, me too.' I flop into the seat next to him, exhausted. 'It was a lovely service, though, wasn't it?'

'Yes, it was, and a great turnout, too.' He switches the TV on. 'I didn't think Alistair had that many friends, to be honest. He barely had any visitors except for Judith.'

I nod. 'A lot of his students turned up to say goodbye,' I point out, stretching my legs onto the coffee table while Harry starts flicking through the channels. 'I was a bit disappointed that we couldn't go up to the coffin at the end to say goodbye.'

'Yeah, family only, they said. But we were like family to Alistair, weren't we? He often told me you were like a third daughter.'

'I did want to go up there, you know.' I swallow back a tear that's tugging at the back of my throat. 'I almost did but then I thought … well, I didn't want to offend anyone.'

Harry settles on a re-run of *Poirot* then leans back, putting his arm around me. I snuggle into the warmth of his familiar embrace. We haven't done this in months. If there is a positive to a negative, a ying to a yang, then the funeral and my dad's illness have somehow drawn us closer together. 'And all those grandchildren,' he goes on, 'with their tributes. It was all very touching. Although I did think one or two of them overdid it…' He glances at me, scrunching his nose. 'Especially that grandson who sang a rendition of *Seasons in The Sun*.'

I snort. 'Yeah, he was a bit over the top. Isn't he the one who works in theatre?'

'Yes, I think so, a wannabe singer, at least that's what Alistair always said. I wouldn't mind but he belted it out like he was flipping Pavarotti. And did you see the way he stood there waiting for the congregation to applaud him? I've never seen anyone sing at a funeral before. Our Orthodox ones are like a Greek tragedy. It's a case of who can cry the loudest. I swear the wailing is synchronised.'

Despite my sadness, he's made me laugh. 'Stop it.' I nudge him in the ribs as the phone trills in the background. 'They're not that bad.' I reach for the phone. It's Ola. The moment she hears my voice, she launches into a rant about the "siesta" translation I texted her last Wednesday for her colleague – the student teacher with the Greek boyfriend whose parents were staying over. I can barely get a word in.

'The girl was in floods of tears, Emma. We had to send her home. Her boyfriend's parents were outraged.'

'But …'

'If you weren't sure about the translation, you only had to say.'

'Ola, the translation was correct. I'm certain. Caroline's fluent in Greek. I …'

'What did you text me, Emma?' I visualise her, hand on hip, shaking her head. Ola really ought to apply for the position of headmistress at her school.

'I can't remember, I …' I stammer as I quickly retrieve the text. 'Oh, here it is.' I pass my mobile to Harry. 'Doesn't this mean "Would you like to have a nap?"'

Harry frowns as he reads the text, then his lips start twitching. 'No, this means "Would you like to be shagged?"'

My hand shoots to my mouth. 'Well?' Ola asks. I stare wide-eyed at Harry who is now convulsing with laughter.

'You're joking,' I murmur through my fingers, 'but Caroline translated it as I typed …I …'

'Thelis na KIMITHIS, is would you like to sleep. Thelis na GAMITHIS, is would you like to be shagged.'

I feel my face go red. Oh my God. 'Oh, Ola, I'm so, so sorry. I must've misheard. I mean, you must admit, they do sound similar, don't they?'

'Only they're not, are they, Emma?' She says sternly. 'In fact, they're very different.'

'I know, I'm sorry,' I gulp. 'Is the girl OK? You caught me at a bad moment, Ola. I was at the funeral parlour. I wasn't myself. I wasn't concentrating.'

I babble on with excuses until Ola calms down and eventually sees the funny side of it. I've always had the knack of winning her over. We end the call on the agreement to meet up on Saturday morning at Alexandra Park for a hill run. Phew.

Harry pulls me back into his arms and I snuggle up to him, feeling like I've come home. 'Only you could make a mistake like that,' he laughs.

'I know. Poor girl. Hope she sorts it out with her boyfriend.'

'I'm sure he'll see the funny side. I would.'

'Yes, but not everyone is as generous as you are.' I touch his lips lightly and he kisses my fingertips. 'Thanks for sorting my hair out, by the way.' Harry did a great job. 'You're a life saver.'

''S'alright.' He presses his chin over my head. 'I'll cut your hair for you from now on, save you a few quid.'

I look up at him. 'Yeah, right.' We both laugh. 'I've missed this.' I stare contently at the muted TV.

'So have I.' He rubs my shoulder with his thumb tenderly, my face on his chest. 'I'm just so sorry ...' He trails off as his phone bleeps with a text message. He rummages in his trouser pocket for it.

I pull away and fold my arms. 'Is it her?' My voice is cold, drained.

'Yes,' he says quietly, and I feel like a guillotine has sliced between us. Why does she always have to spoil everything? She's like a bloody thorn in my side. 'Just wants to know how it went.' He sits up in his seat, sighing heavily into his hands. 'Emma, as I was saying ...' He drops his hands to his knees. He looks worried. Irritated. 'Look, I'm sorry ...'

'Sorry?' I don't let him finish. I feel my anxiety tightening my chest. I swallow hard, my muscles tense. 'For what?' I gulp, curling my hands into a loose fist. Oh God. He's going to confess. Tell me he's been having an affair. I can sense it. That's why he's been so kind to me these last few days, to soften the blow. I bet he's been planning on telling me for days but was waiting until after the funeral. Typical Harry. He'd never kick someone when they were down. I take a lungful of air. I've imagined this moment for weeks, rehearsed it, played it back over and over again in my mind, but now that it's here I'm not sure I want to hear it. I don't think I'm ready.

'I'm sorry for being such a miserable dick lately, that's for what.' I release a slow sigh of relief feeling like a deflating rubber ring. 'It's just the overload of work. And now all this stuff with Isabella … well, it's just dragged everything up …' He wrings his hands nervously.

'Of how we first met?' I drop my gaze to the floor, my hands limp in my lap.

'Yes.' He glances at me briefly. 'But maybe you were right. I shouldn't have got so involved with her.' At last, the words I've been dying to hear for weeks. Hooray. Fifteen-Love. 'Her problems seem to be getting worse, out of control.' He pushes his hand through his thick, greying hair. 'I think I misjudged her. She's so mixed up. I don't think she knows what she wants. I don't think I can help her, Emma.' He wipes his face with his hands as if trying to wash away a heavy burden. 'I should've listened to you.' Thirty-Love. I stay silent. 'I'm going to back off.' Forty-Love. 'I don't want anything more than a working relationship from now on. A coffee in the canteen, maybe, but that's all. She'll have to start sorting out her own problems. I'll tell her on Monday.' Game, set, and match. I do a silent whoop. He twists round and faces me. 'I'm just so tired, Emma.' I cup a hand over his cheek. His bristles feel rough against my skin. 'What's happened to us?' he asks softly. 'We used to be so close, told each other everything.'

'I know,' I gulp. 'We got too complacent, I think, too wrapped up in our own little worlds.'

He grabs my hands and holds them tightly. 'I want us to try harder, save our relationship. Go back to how we used to be.'

'Harry, you don't know how happy that makes me feel.' I close my eyes briefly, savouring the moment of pure relief. 'I thought you'd gone off me. I ...'

'Gone off you? Are you mad?' He looks at me searchingly for a few moments, then leans forward and kisses me. Soft, playful bites to begin with, then he rolls on top of me. His tongue parts my lips and we kiss wildly. His hand slides up my thigh, pushing my dress to my hips. My heart starts to race. I ache with desire. His mouth is on my neck, my collarbone, and then back on my lips again, kissing me madly, hungrily. He pulls his sweater over his head as I reach for his trouser belt, and then my phone starts ringing.

'Leave it,' I say, pulling him down. Our mouths lock. I tug at his zip, feeling him hard against my wrist. The ringing stops and then starts again almost immediately.

We pull apart, chests heaving. 'You'd better get it,' he pants. 'It might be work, or Tessa with an update on your dad.'

I straighten up in my seat. Push my wild, crazy hair off my face, then reach down for my handbag.

'Alistair's funeral has made me see how short life is, Em.' Harry pushes his head through his sweater as he gets to his feet, and I feel a wave of disappointment. Our make up loving didn't last long. 'I want us to get back on track. And if work keeps coming in from your book jacket business.' He crosses his fingers. 'We can talk about giving up our jobs at the restaurant.' My heart stops. Chuck in his job with Mas? Surely I misheard. 'Spend more time together. That's all I want.' I don't question his rash suggestion. It mightn't be a bad idea. Since Ola introduced me to her novelist friend, business has picked up nicely. It's amazing what word of mouth can do in my line of work. 'No more secrets. No more Isabella.' He straightens his navy sweater. 'And no more wild nights out with clients for you, missus.' I feel my face tingle as I stare into the darkness of my cluttered handbag, a rush of guilt sluicing through me.

'That sounds like a plan,' I say. My phone stops ringing the moment I find it. Typical. A text message blares through within seconds.

'We'll get a takeaway tonight, yeah?' he says eagerly, and I agree as I retrieve the message. 'We got any wine in the fridge?'

'No, I finished the half bottle the other night.' I stare at my phone. It's Marc.

'OK, I'll just pop out for a bottle. Actually, let's push the boat out and get a bottle of Prosecco. We'll have a nice night in. We need to talk, Em, about us, what you're going to do about your dad, our future, and the changes we need to make.' I can hear him clattering around, the scrape of his car keys as he grabs them off the table, the swish of his leather jacket as he slips into it. 'You listening, Em? Who rang? Was it work? Any luck? I bet they loved your book design. You're so bloody talented, and once ...'

I can hear Harry talking but his voice is now a muffled sound of babble in my ears. My eyes are transfixed on Marc's text.

You can't just switch me on and off like a light bulb. I want my watch back.

'Em, you OK?' Harry smiles. 'Who's the text from?' He makes to read it but I close it down quickly.

'It's just Reeva.' Our agreement for no more lies didn't last long, did it? 'She wants to meet up.' I look up at him, blink a few times, a weak smile twitching at my lips. 'Prosecco and a takeaway sounds great.' I paint on a smile and feign enthusiasm. 'I'll set the table. Don't be long.'

Chapter Twenty-One

The moment the front door slams I start texting Marc urgently, thumbs flying all over the place.

Sorry didn't reply to last few texts. Mad busy. Funeral. Work, etc.. Thought u said 2 take my time re; watch. But yes, will give back. Next week OK?

I chew my thumbnail as I anxiously await his reply. Sure enough, within moments it buzzes through.

Sorry, no can do. Need it back today.

Shit. Shit. Shit!! I thrust a hand through my hair. Why did I put a question mark at the end of that text? I should've just made a statement. I look briefly at the window as if I've got a bionic eye that will see Harry approaching from around the corner. I've got to sort this out before he gets back. What's wrong with the stupid sod? One minute he's telling me to keep the watch and the next he wants it back urgently.

OK, I've got to calm down and focus. Deep breaths. I sit on the sofa and close my eyes. One, two, three, breathe in, four, five, six, breathe out, and again. Right. I'm going to have to lie to Marc, stall him. Tell him I'm away or something. There's no way I'm going to meet up with him today. Not when Harry and I are back on track. And I'm working at the restaurant tomorrow. My new rota is

Tuesdays and Thursdays. I can meet him briefly on Friday, but will he hold on for another forty-eight hours? Sodding bloody watch!

I text back hurriedly.

Can't do today. At funeral all day. Busy all week. Fri OK?

I press send and immediately regret ending it with a question mark. Again. Ugh.

I wait, drumming my fingers on the armchair, my heart beating, my mouth dry. Nothing. Perhaps he's finally got the message. I did tell him I didn't want the damned watch in the first place. It's not my fault that he forced it upon me while I was half cut, then got tetchy because I didn't reply to his texts right away. I get to my feet, agitated, flushed. I need a drink. As I head for the kitchen the doorbell rings. Harry's shadow is at the front door. He must've forgotten his keys. My hand is on the latch as Marc's text message pings onto the screen.

You sure about that?

I narrow my eyes, my heart in my mouth. What's that supposed to mean? Is he suggesting that I'm lying? I yank the door open, my eyes fixed on Marc's intimidating text. I look up. He's standing in front of me. One hand on the door frame, the other in his trouser pocket. I stare at him in wide-eyed horror.

'What the hell are you doing here?' I hiss, gazing around him wildly.

'Well, that's not a very warm welcome, is it?'

'What do you want? I told you I'd give you the watch back on Friday.'

'I didn't have you down as being rude, Emma,' he says wryly, peeking over my shoulder. 'Aren't you going to invite me in? I'd love to see your beloved garden.' He glances behind him. 'Nice mosaic footpath you've got going on there.' He then lets out a slow whistle as he strokes the inside pane of the door. 'Wow, call me old-fashioned but I love stained glass. Is this all original?'

I grab him by the sleeve, looking this way and that like I'm about to harbour a criminal before ushering him inside.

'Blimey, you're eager.' He shuffles into the hallway as I slam the door and lean my back against it. His strong aftershave floods the corridor.

'Marc.' I run my tongue over my dry lips, feeling the remnants of this morning's plum lipstick. 'You can't stay.' I raise my hands as if warning him off. 'Harry's due home any moment now.'

'You've had your hair cut. Nice.' He studies my hair, ignoring what I've just said. 'Mind you,' he presses his index finger against his lips thoughtfully, 'I did prefer it long.' As he reaches for my hair, I knock his hand away. 'Oooh, feisty.' There's a flash of lust in his eyes. 'I like it.'

'Did you not listen to a word I just said?' I bark. 'Harry's on his way home. Now. And if he finds you here, he'll … he'll …' I scratch my head nervously.

'So? We've got nothing to hide. It'll be nice to meet him.' His smile doesn't quite reach his eyes. 'I can tell him what fun we had the other night. What a good sport you were.' He brushes my cheek with his finger. 'He does know about me, right?'

I back away from him. He looks weird. I wonder if he's been drinking or taking drugs. Fear starts creeping into every fibre of my body. I read in a magazine recently that most victims know who their attacker is.

'Marc ...' I gulp, taking a step back. 'Look, I don't know what you want from me.'

'Coffee would be nice.' He raises his eyebrows. 'Got any chocolate digestives?' I narrow my eyes. 'Oh, relax, Emma, I'm not going to hurt you, for heaven's sake.' I look at him with trepidation. 'I promise.'

I let out a little sigh of relief. OK, maybe I'm overreacting. He's obviously got an unhealthy fixation on me but I'm sure he's not a rapist. Still, I can't cosy down to coffee and biscuits with him. Not when I lied to Harry about him being a client, and certainly not now he's morphed into Glenn Close in *Fatal Attraction*.

'I want you to leave.' I tug at the collar of my dress, suddenly feeling hot, and notice that I'm shaking. 'Now.' His presence is asphyxiating. I've got to get him out of the house before he sucks all the oxygen out of the room. 'I promise I'll give you the watch back later,' I falter. 'This evening.'

He wanders idly into the lounge, hands in pockets, as if I haven't spoken. I rush behind him urgently, anxiety swishing around in my stomach. 'Did you hear what I said?' I say, a hint of hysteria in my voice.

He's sitting on the sofa. On the exact spot where Harry and I were about to make wild, passionate love just moments ago. 'Nice gaff.' He stares around the room. 'I love all that coving around the ceiling. And I like your curtains. John Lewis? Women of your age love their stuff, don't they?

'Look, Marc, please. I'd give you the watch back now but ...' I wring my hands, throwing a glance at the window worriedly. 'It's just that I'm not sure where it is.' But he carries on talking over me, babbling on about how impressive our 52inch TV is, that it's the pièce de résistance of the room – is it another John Lewis purchase?

Does it support screen mirroring, is it 4K? I feel the fear rising in my throat. Clearly, he's a man on a mission. It doesn't look like he's going to leave without his precious watch. 'Look ... just ... just ... stay there, will you? I'll find your watch. Don't move.'

I take the stairs two at a time. In my bedroom I stare around the room like a woman possessed, trying to retrace my steps on Sunday before last. I remember putting it in a safe place, somewhere where Harry wouldn't find it. Of course I now have no notion of where that safe place is. I start opening drawers and emptying the contents onto the floor. Scarf drawer, no. Sock drawer, no. Bra and tights drawer, no. I stand back, one hand on my hip the other rubbing my chin vigorously. Where the bloody hell is it? Then it suddenly hits me. I hid it at the back of my knicker drawer.

I root around in the drawer, my hands like an octopus. And then I have it in the palm of my hand. I gawp at it as if it's a precious stone. 'Thank you, Lord.' Relief swirls through me as I pound down the stairs and fly into the lounge, 'I've found it,' I say excitedly, watch in hand, sweat trickling down my back, my forehead. I stare around the empty room.

'Marc?' I shout. Has he left? Did the thought of Harry's imminent arrival give him the jitters? Ha, I feel my muscles relax. I knew he wouldn't see it through. Bloody wimp.

'In here,' a voice calls from the kitchen, and my heart sinks.

My eyes flit between him and the two *Doctor Who* mugs on the counter. What on earth is he doing? Is he some kind of nutter? This kind of stuff doesn't happen in real life. You only see it in films, read about it on the internet. A rattle at the front door startles me. I look around quickly at the shadowy figure behind the stained glass panel, my heart pounding. A leaflet drops through the letterbox.

'Where do you keep your coffee?' Marc says blithely, throwing a glance in my direction as he fills the kettle at the sink. Jesus Christ. This can't be happening.

I march up to him, grab the kettle from his hand, and shove him out of the way.

'Hey, steady on.' He stumbles against the stove.

'Here's your watch.' I press it hard against his chest. 'Now jog on.' I point at the front door. 'We've had a tough day. Harry will be back any minute and the last thing I want him to see is a strange man making himself a cup of coffee in his kitchen.'

He looks at the watch against his duck egg blue shirt, then at me, a wry smile starting at his lips.

'Nah, you can have it,' he says, pushing me away.

'What? But you said …'

'I've changed my mind. Keep it. It suits you.'

He truly is insane. 'I don't want it. Just take it and go!'

'Oooooh, Emma's got a temper. It's true what they say about redheads.'

'Marc, please.' My patience is running thin. What on earth have I got myself into? 'I don't know what you want from me but I'm with Harry. I made that perfectly clear from the start and you said you understood. I'm sorry if you thought otherwise, but that's really not my fault, is it?'

As he opens his mouth to speak there's a clatter at the front door. 'Home!' Harry's jolly voice echoes in my ears. I stare at Harry in the hallway like a deer caught in headlights, and for one brief moment I think of opening the back door and kicking Marc down the five steps that lead onto the patio. 'The off-licence was closed.' He drapes his jacket over the bannister. I think I'm going to faint. 'Had to go to the deli by the library.' He's strutting towards me, all smiles, bottle in hand, unaware that Marc is in front of me leaning against the cooker.

I look at Marc, our eyes lock, and then out of nowhere he pushes me against the fridge and presses his mouth onto mine, forcing my lips apart with his tongue, one hand squeezing my breast.

'What the ...?' Harry slams the bottle down onto the worktop, yanks him off me, and pushes him over the sink. I feel my limbs shaking as I watch Marc's red face pressed against the gleaming tap.

I stagger around, gasping, the taste of his cigarette breathe making me heave. I steady myself against the doorframe until I regain my balance.

'Hey, take it easy, mate.' Marc's strangled voice fills my ears.

I look up. Harry has him in a lock. He can't move. I knew I'd see his Aikido skills one day, but wasn't quite expecting them to be under these circumstances.

'I'm not your fucking mate. Quick, Emma, call the police,' Harry yells at me over his shoulder. 'How did he get in?' Then before I can answer he says, 'I told you not to open the door to bogus gas readers, didn't I?'

'Tell him, Emma,' Marc squeaks through squashed cheeks. 'Please. I can't breathe.'

Harry looks around at me sharply, his eyes full of horror. 'You know him?'

'He's ... he's ...' I rub my clammy hands together. 'A friend. Sort of ...'

Harry's eyes flit quickly from me to Marc. 'A friend?' Harry loosens his grip and Marc tries to wriggle free. 'You were snogging his face off, Emma.' He spins Marc round and pins him against the worktop, his duck egg blue shirt a mass in Harry's big hand. Their faces are almost touching.

'No, I wasn't,' I insist. 'He forced himself on me. He's been hounding me for weeks. He's got some sort of ...' I struggle to find the right word, '... crush on me or something.'

Marc's mouth twists into a sinister grin. 'We shagged on Saturday night,' he whispers into Harry's face. 'Someone had to give her one.'

As Harry draws his arm back, curling his hand into a tight fist, I lunge forward and pull him away. 'He's not worth it,' I cry as Marc wriggles free.

Harry looks me through betrayed eyes.

'Harry, I don't know what he's talking about,' I plead. 'I didn't sleep with him. I promise you. He's mad.'

We stare at each other in silence. Marc is shuffling around, panting. The wall clock is ticking away in the background like a time bomb. I move forward with trepidation, placing a hand on Harry's arm. 'Harry, I...' He shrugs me off furiously.

'I knew something happened that Saturday night,' he says darkly, pointing at me. 'You came home at four in the morning. Pissed.' He glowers at me. I don't think I've ever seen him this angry.

Marc dusts himself down, straightens his jacket, then puts a hand through his messed up hair. 'We had sex on Saturday night at The Dorcester. Several times, in fact. She's got great stamina for a woman her age. Must be all that running she does, eh?' He licks his lips, still panting from the scuffle. I can't believe he's said that. It's a complete lie, obviously, but I'm too stunned to speak. It's as if my lips have been sealed together with Super Glue.

'Well?' Harry glares at me.

'No, he's lying. I swear I ...'

'I've got photos of us in the bar on my phone if you don't believe me,' Marc cuts across me.

Oh my God, why is he doing this to me? If he thinks that these bunny boiling tactics are going to make me leave Harry and sail off into the sunset with him, he's completely mad.

He reaches into his inside pocket as the horror of the moment we took selfies in the hotel bar bounces into my mind. We took one smiling into the camera, and then again because I had my eyes closed, then another closer one cheek to cheek, giggling, happy, tipsy. 'She's a great lay, by the way.' And with this, Harry grabs a hold of Marc by the lapels of his tailored suit and drags him into the corridor.

Images of Carl swim before me. I want to be sick. I swallow back the bile as I chase after them.

'Harry, stop it,' I cry hysterically. 'Please. Let him go.' I try to prize him off but I haven't got the strength. 'Nothing happened. I swear,' I scream. 'Marc, please tell him the truth.'

At the mention of Marc's name, Harry stops dead in his tracks. 'Marc?' He gasps, taking a step back, chest heaving. 'I knew I'd seen your face before.' He narrows his eyes, a finger in Marc's face. 'Marc Quinn.' His eyes fill with tears of rage and his lips tighten. 'You fucking bastard.'

And with this they start to scuffle. I can't control them. They're on the floor rolling around on my precious vintage tiles, punching, kicking.

Harry is older but he's stronger, faster. It isn't long before he has Marc face down in a lock, blood trickling down his chin.

'I want you out of my house, Quinn. Now.' How the hell does Harry know him? My mind is about to explode. My heart is pounding furiously against my ribcage as hot tears stream down my face.

'OK, OK, man.' Marc struggles to breathe. 'I'll go. Just let me go, will you?'

'Harry, for heaven's sake,' I plead, pulling at his sweater, tears blurring my vision.

Harry twists round, looks at me, eyes shining with adrenaline, then releases his grip. Both men are on their feet, chests heaving, arms outstretched like two alpha male gorillas sizing each other up.

Marc rolls his tongue over his bleeding lip. 'You had it coming, man,' he says, wiping his mouth with the back of his sleeve. Blood. On his expensive suit. It might not come out, not even in a dry clean.

'What are you talking about?' I manage in a little, bewildered voice. 'What's going on? How do you two know each other?' Has Harry been following me? Could Ola have warned him? She made it clear she wasn't supporting this new friendship of mine from the onset.

'This.' Marc points at Harry, glaring at him in disgust. 'Your precious boyfriend has been screwing my wife for weeks.'

'Your wife?' Marc's married? None of this is making any sense. I feel rigid, frozen to the core. I can't take it all in. It's all happening too fast. 'Harry,' I quiver. 'What's he talking about?'

'How the hell should I know?' Harry stares at his feet, exhaling loudly.

'How the hell should I know?' Marc mimics Harry in a silly voice as he circles me. 'He and my wife are lovers,' he whispers, his lips almost touching my cheek. 'They're having an affair. Screwing. Fucking. Comprendo?'

'No,' Harry says, shaking his head vigorously, fists clenched by his side. 'You're wrong.'

'Don't you lie to me,' Marc hollers in a theatrical tone, pointing at Harry. 'I've seen the two of you together.'

'Harry? What does he mean?'

'And now we're even.' Marc spits.

I see the fury rising in Harry's eyes immediately and I leap in front of him. 'Enough!' I scream at the top of my voice, arms outstretched between them like a referee. We all fall silent. 'Will someone please tell me what the hell is going on?'

Then in a flash, in a single moment of clarity, the penny drops.

'Oh my God,' I say quietly, covering my mouth. 'Isabella.'

Chapter Twenty-Two

Harry looks at me gravely beneath tight, furrowed brows. 'It's not what you think,' he says, glancing at Marc briefly.

I'm staring at Harry, mouth agape. I can't speak. I feel like my tongue has been injected with local anaesthetic. A multitude of thoughts race through my mind, each one demanding priority.

'I'm done here.' Marc's voice shakes me out of my stupor. 'You stay away from Isabella,' he warns, pointing his finger at Harry.

'Oh my God,' I manage in a weepy voice. I cover my mouth as a dark dread tears through me like a ferocious tsunami to the shrilling sound of the landline. I'm silent for a few moments. The ringing pounds in my ears as I try to gather my thoughts. Isabella is Marc's wife. The very woman whom I've feared has been trying to steal my partner. 'So, it's true.' The words slip through my trembling fingers. 'I was right all along.' The phone stops ringing. There are a few moments of respite before it starts again. The annoying loud, shrill is almost too painful to bear. I answer it on the third ring.

It's Xenia, asking how the funeral went, was there a big turnout, did I wear black, was there enough food at the wake? God, this is all I need.

'We didn't go to the wake, Xenia.' I'm back in the corridor. Both men are frowning at their mobile phones. Typical. I bet Isabella's phone is having a meltdown. 'We came straight home,' I go on.

216

'Oh no,' Xenia groans, 'I come bring you Kolokasi. Me and Valentina made just now at the restorah.'

'No, please, don't,' I say a little abruptly. The last thing I want is Harry's mother in the mix. 'We're fine.'

She's quiet for a few moments. All I can hear is the sound of her breathing, the rattle of pans, Valentina and Mas' voices speaking in Greek. I hope I haven't offended her. 'Ah, OK, love,' she says finally, 'But you must eat. At lease make a nice sandouwidge with the halloumi I bring you from Cyprus, yes?'

'Yes, I'll make us a couple of sandwiches, Xenia, don't worry. Would you like to speak to Harry?' I look at Harry. He stops texting and frowns at me.

'Bleeeease,' Xenia says warmly.

'It's your mum.' I hold out the phone but he shakes his head.

'Tell her I'll call her back later.' He pushes his mobile into his pocket as I end the call with parting platitudes.

I chuck the phone onto the stairs then start pacing the narrow hallway, wringing my hands, a mass of thoughts marching around in my head, stamping their feet for my attention. How long have they been sleeping together? Is it serious? Are they still at it? But no, he told me on the sofa not long ago that he wants to back off – was that because her husband had found out? Has she given Harry the boot? Am I his Plan B? I swallow hard. What's going to happen now? Am I going to die alone, an old spinster surrounded by cats? Do I even want him now he's been with her? Perhaps Marc has done me a favour. Oh my goodness. Marc. What on earth is that all about? Have I been some sort of lackey? My stomach twists.

'Stop playing me, Emma,' Harry's voice, dark with anger. 'Don't try turning this around on me. You're the wrongdoer here. You're the one that has been at it with

217

him.' Marc looks up briefly from his mobile phone, then slips it into his pocket.

'No,' I say firmly, but he's not listening.

'You knew about Isabella,' he yells. 'And about our … our …' he struggles with his words, 'friendship, and how I was trying to protect her from this monster.' He curls his lips in repulsion.

'Protect her? I'm the one who needs protecting. She's a bloody alley cat. You should see the scratches on my chest.'

'So, come on,' Harry says, ignoring Marc. 'What's all this about? Tit for tat? Oh wait, let me guess. You bumped into each other outside the hospital while you were both spying on us, exchanged notes over coffee, then fell head over heels,' he air quotes, 'in love.'

'Us?' I whisper, his unwitting confession flooring me. 'So you admit it?' I look at Marc. He's standing still, arms folded, watching the show. 'AT LAST.' I throw my hands up in the air. 'I've been vindicated. Hallelujah. I'm not losing my marbles after all. I'm not imagining everything.' Anger rips through me like a typhoon. I've been lied to and manipulated by both of these men. 'And the BAFTA for stupidity goes tooooo, drum roll … Emma King.'

'Calm down, Emma,' Harry says, pushing his hair off his red, sweaty face, 'this isn't helping. I –'

'Don't tell me what to do!' I scream. 'All this time you've been making me think that I'm some mad, obsessed, jealous freak. When all along …' I turn to Marc. 'And you, you fucking little shit. You should get a bloody Oscar for your performance.' I'm so angry that I barely notice the tears of fury streaming down my cheeks until I feel them sliding into the groove of my lips, taste their saltiness in my mouth. I wipe my snotty nose on my sleeve, storm into the kitchen, tear off a piece of kitchen towel from the rail, and stomp back into the ring, ready for round two.

'I've done *nothing* wrong, Emma,' Harry says, his voice now calmer. 'Don't listen to his bullshit. His marriage problems have got nothing to do with me.' Still denying it despite everything. Unbelievable. I sniff, dabbing at my nose with the hard paper towel.

Marc reaches inside his jacket pocket, then pulls out a piece of paper, all the while gazing at Harry dubiously. 'You might want to see this.' He shoves the paper under my nose, his eyes not leaving Harry. The words are a blur. I can just about make out the words 'Hotel Invoice' at the top of the page.

'What's this?' I sniffle in a nasal, congested voice. I give my nose a final wipe before discarding the kitchen towel up my sleeve.

He slaps the paper with the back of his hand. 'It's a hotel receipt paid for by none other than your very own male version of Florence Nightingale.' He takes a step back and starts reading. 'Guest name: Mr Georgiades. Date: Monday, 26th of August. Arrival time: 8 p.m. Departure time: 10.15 p.m. Accommodation: Double bedroom. Ring any bells?' His trump card. My legs wobble.

'Where did you get this?' Harry leaps in front of Marc, trying to snatch the receipt but Marc is too quick.

'I found it in Isabella's handbag.' He twists his arm behind him quickly, out of Harry's reach. 'Stuffed in the zip compartment. As if I wouldn't look there.' He raises an eyebrow. 'She really underestimates me, that girl.'

The two men glare at each other. I look at the scrunched receipt in Marc's tight fist, then at Harry.

'Harry?' I collapse into a squat on the floor, head in my hands as my mind rewinds, tracing events like a scene out of *Columbo*. Monday the 26th of August. That was just over three weeks ago. I'd come home from Sainsbury's and Harry was getting ready to do an unexpected shift at the restaurant. My hand fastens over my mouth as fresh tears swell in my eyes. 'Oh God, no.'

Harry swings his hands out as if he's discarding a piece of rubbish. 'I don't have to listen to this.'

There's a crunch as Harry takes a step. He's broken the phone. Marc seizes the opportunity, snatching him by the sweater as he stumbles over the handset. He swings him round and straddles him, one hand holding him down by the throat, the other scrunching the paper into a ball in his fist. 'You fucking wanker,' he cries, forcing the paper between Harry's tight lips, tears streaming down his face. 'She's my wife!' he wails, saliva foaming at his mouth. 'You've got to pay, man. You've got to pay.'

'Marc, get off him!' I jump to my feet and grab him in a bear hug. 'He's going to choke. Stop!'

He throws his arm back, knocking me to the floor. 'You stay out of this, Emma. This has got nothing to do with you.'

Harry spits out bits of torn paper, raises his knees, and kicks him back hard, throwing him against the front door, then without as much as a glance in my direction he takes the steps two at a time.

Marc is on his feet, chest heaving, his cut face full of rage. He wipes his angry tears with the back of his hands then reaches for the door latch.

'Wait,' I demand rushing behind him. 'I'm not finished with you yet.'

As Harry stomps around upstairs, floorboards creaking, doors slamming, Marc tells me how he suspected Isabella was seeing someone else weeks ago. That she'd become cold, withdrawn, refused him – blamed it on the night shift.

Where had I heard that before? But his suspicions grew when she started taking on extra overtime. He spied on her mobile phone to see what he could find, explains how she thought she was being clever by deleting her text messages but forgot to delete her call logs.

'I questioned her about it,' he says, 'and she told me Harry was the work mate she introduced me to one night when I picked her up.' That's right, I remember Harry telling me he had seen Isabella's husband once. 'Said he was having a domestic, needed a friendly ear, you know.' So, they agreed on the same alibi. Priceless. 'She told me the geezer was old enough to be her dad, married with grown-up kids, and I believed her.' He lets out an exaggerated, throaty laugh. 'But that's not true, is it?'

I stare at him in stunned silence, gathering my cardigan at my chest with my cold hands as if he's about to steal it from my back. 'And then?' I ask quietly.

'Well, I left it at that,' he replies, 'but then she started having the odd night out with friends – friends I'd never heard of, friends I couldn't trace.' He rubs his face, then leans his back against the wall as I catch a glimpse of my reflection in the large hallway mirror. A female version of Beetlejuice stares back at me and I wince.

'What did you do?' I ask, smoothing my wild hair down.

'I started searching her internet history. Her Twitter and Facebook, her Instagram,' he waves a hand. 'She's obsessed with social networking sites. I searched her friends list and found Harry Georgiades' face smiling back at me. Bingo,' he snorts. 'I hung around outside the hospital. And sure enough, I saw them leave together, her arm through his, laughing, joking as they headed to the pub around the corner.' He pauses, clearly distressed.

'Go on,' I say, folding my arms, suddenly feeling very cold.

'She'd come home stinking of booze, then tell me she'd been to see her mum, that they'd had a glass of wine,' he says, each word tearing my world apart. 'But then I thought, OK, she knows I'm a jealous guy, maybe she lied because she didn't want to wind me up, you know?' He pinches the bridge of his nose. 'I mean, work mates go for after-work drinks, don't they? That doesn't mean anything, right?' I nod, wordless. 'And it's plausible that he had problems. I mean, he does look stressed with those bags under his eyes and that.'

I feel a pang of resentment. Harry doesn't look that bad. 'Do you hurt her?' I ask quietly.

Marc looks up at me quickly. 'What do you mean?'

'I mean … like … you know,' I throw a hand out nervously, 'hit her …'

'I'm not a wife beater, if that's what you're asking.' He stands up straight, hands on hips, eyebrows furrowed in disdain, and for a brief moment I see Carl's face morphing with his. I take a step back, feeling slightly unsettled. This is all too much for me.

'It's just that …' I falter.

'Don't get me wrong. We fight. Big time. A few things have flown across the room, yeah.' I close my eyes as I slip into a dark reverie. Carl clearing all the items off the fireplace with his arm in one fell swoop, broken glass all over the floor. His hands around my throat. The crunch of his knuckles against my nose, the taste of blood in my mouth. His stocky frame looming over me, chair held high up above his head, then darkness. 'But she's a volatile chick.' Marc's voice again. I open my eyes. 'Gives as good as she gets, you know.' He grins, his anger dissipating, as if he's proud of her feisty disposition.

'Oh, I see ...' I clear my throat. 'Go on,' I urge, hand on my neck. I need to glean as much information as possible if I'm to make any sense of this fiasco.

'Anyway, I tried to convince myself that it was all in my head.' He jabs his right temple, his anger returning. 'She's always saying I'm controlling, possessive. And who could blame me? She's a bloody stunner. I paid for those boobs. Why should someone else have the pleasure of them?' I twitch. That's a detail I could've done without. 'And then I found this.' He lifts his hand languidly, as if it's made of lead, the receipt in tatters in his limp fist.

I swallow hard. 'So, how did I come into all of this?'

'You got caught in the crossfire,' he says, an inkling of guilt in his voice. 'I just wanted to destroy her lover's relationship like he's destroyed mine.' He covers his face with his hands, wedding band glinting in the sunlight streaming through the stained glass window. I'm quite surprised I didn't notice any marks on his finger when we met. Very unlike me, but then I had no reason to doubt him. 'She's left me, you know,' he says quietly, looking at me through the gaps between his fingers. 'It's over.' Am I supposed to feel sorry for him? I don't think so.

'But how did you know where to find me?' I ask, bewildered. 'I met you that night in the pub, how did you ...'

'I'm following you on Facebook.' He sweeps a hand over his face, exhaling loudly. 'I found your name under Harry's relationship status, then sent you a friend request under a pseudonym, and you took the bait.' He cocks his head sideways, shrugging, as if to say it's not my fault that you were so stupid. 'Luckily, when you updated your status saying you were at The King's Head I happened to be in the area,' he sighs loudly. 'Look, I didn't plan on leading you on. I was going to tell you about them, about the affair, but then when you told me you were in a happy relationship …' he tails off.

I hold my head in my hands. 'You bloody bastard,' I say through gritted teeth. Everything starts falling into place. 'That's how you knew so much about me.'

He twists his mouth, biting the inside of his bottom lip. I can't believe this. I can't believe I've been such a complete fool.

He takes a step forward, pushing my hair off my face. 'I'm sorry, Emma. I didn't think we'd hit it off.' He lifts my chin up gently with his hand. 'I really did mean all those things I said to you, you know. I think you're really fit and I don't mind the age gap if you …'

'Are you out of your fucking mind?' I scream, slapping his hand off my face. 'Get out.' I push him with all my strength and he staggers back. 'Go on! I want you out of my house.'

'Oh, come on, Emma. Don't let them win. What've you got to lose now?' This man is a complete head case. 'Just think; something good might come out of all this.' I stare at him in disbelief as Harry thunders down the stairs, overnight bag in hand.

'I hope you'll be very happy together.' Harry says coldly. Then I realise that Marc's hand is resting on my waist. I push him away furiously.

'Harry, what are you doing?' I rush behind him. 'Where are you going? Wait. I want to know what's going on. I want an explanation.'

'Leave me the hell alone, the pair of you.' He nudges me off then lifts his bike up with one hand. 'Get out of my way.'

'Harry, we need to talk. Harry!' As he wrenches the front door open, a gust of wind hurls into our faces, bringing with it the golden, dry leaves off Alistair's path.

'Woah,' Marc shields his face with his hand. 'What's going on out there? Met Office said warm, dry weather today.'

'You can't leave *me*!' I scream into Harry's hostile back, 'You're the one who's having the bloody affair!' I pull wisps of hair out of my mouth. 'I hate you! You bastard!'

I'm on the doorstep shouting and screaming as he jumps onto his bike. A teenage girl looks at me as if I'm mad as she scurries past. An old couple across the road with an aging dog stop and stare, nudge each other, and point before slowly shuffling off. Marc's arm slides around my shoulders as Harry disappears into the distance. I shrug him off furiously. This is entirely his bloody fault. I close my eyes, defeated, as the warm autumnal wind suddenly dies, taking with it a chunk of my heart.

Chapter Twenty-Three

'I still can't believe what's happened.' Caroline leans back in her chair, shaking her head, then opens the menu, her Prada cats-eye glasses perched on her nose.

'Me neither.' Ola gives my hand a gentle squeeze. 'I thought you two were solid. Soulmates, you know. Is there any chance you can sort it out?' I shake my head. Harry hasn't bothered to get in touch since he left with an overnight bag stuffed with smalls and T-shirts. Not a single text or phone call in forty-eight hours. If Caroline hadn't told me he'd moved back in with his parents, I'd be none the wiser. How could he be so cold after all we've been through together?

I give Ola a strained smile. We're at Café Martinez in Highgate, one of our favourite girly haunts. When it's warm we sit outside and do a bit of celeb spotting, gazing over Pond Square, nudging each other and giggling if we spot someone famous. But not tonight. Tonight the mood is sombre.

I wasn't intending on venturing out of my self-imposed prison. The girls persuaded me – no, demanded – that we meet up for a bite to eat, insisting that moping around the house in my dressing gown all day, drinking coffee, isn't going to get me anywhere. I know they're right, but it doesn't lessen the raw, gnawing ache that twists in my stomach each time I think about what has happened. In two days my world has been ripped apart. All my plans, dreams, aspirations. Gone.

'I mean, Harry's such a genuine guy,' Caroline says, scanning the menu. 'Who'd have thought it?' Bless her, but she isn't helping. 'Sometimes it's the quiet ones you've got to watch, isn't it?'

'Has Mas said anything?' I croak. I start fiddling around with the cutlery neatly wrapped inside a napkin. Ola pushes an open menu under my nose, telling me that I look pale, that I must eat to keep my strength up.

Caroline stops reading and gazes at me over her spectacles. 'Only that he doesn't want to get involved.' She leans in, almost tipping over my half-filled wine glass with her elbow. 'I'm sorry, sweetie. You know what those two are like. He'll never run him down, no matter what. Thick as bloody thieves,' she says, returning her attention to the menu.

'I bet he's blaming me for all this,' I groan. I can just hear Mas telling Harry that he's better off without me. That he'd told him I'd let him down from the start. 'But Harry does know that Marc was lying about us having sex that night, right? Marc promised me he'd set the record straight, even if it meant ringing Harry himself.'

Wracked with remorse, Marc called me several times the next day. I declined all his calls to begin with, so he proceeded to bombard me with text messages instead. That boy is tenacious, I'll give him that. When I finally picked up, all I could hear was the gabble of his distraught voice apologising repeatedly for his abhorrent behaviour for what he'd done to me. He said that he had barely slept, kept having night terrors, hearing voices, seeing images at the foot of his bed telling him to own up and tell the truth or he'd be damned forever. He reckoned it was his subconscious because deep down he's a decent guy – his words, not mine. It's a pity guilt doesn't have this magical

227

effect on everyone, isn't it? The world would be a much better place if it did. I look at Caroline. 'Well?'

Caroline shrugs, stroking the edge of the round ceramic table with her finger. 'I'm not sure, Emma. Mas didn't mention anything about a phone call from Marc.'

'So I'm still the bad guy, right?'

'Sweetie, you did go out on a date with Marc, though, didn't you?' Ahh, clearly Mas has got to her, as per. Don't get me wrong, Caroline is a tough cookie, but Mas has this hold over her. He controls her like a puppet sometimes. 'And how old is he, twelve?'

'Caroline!' Ola shrieks, giving her a daggered look.

'Sorry, Ola,' Caroline says indignantly, then looks at me. 'But if it's that kid you were talking to at the pub that night, he looked like he wasn't even shaving yet.'

'He's almost twenty-four,' I grunt, staring around at the diners. 'And it wasn't a date. Well, not as far as I was concerned, anyway.'

'Still young enough to be your son...' I bite my lips swallowing back my fury, and for a moment I imagine her as a ventriloquist doll, sitting on Mas' knee with his arm shoved up her arse. 'What were you thinking?' she finishes softly.

'She's not a bloody cougar, Caroline.' Ola widens her dark eyes. 'If that's what you're implying.'

'No, that's not what I'm implying, Ola, thank you very much. What I mean is men of that age only want one thing, don't they?' She picks up her menu again.

'Caroline!' Ola exclaims, widening her eyes and leaning forward as if she's about to punch her on the nose.

Caroline, clearly exasperated by Ola's interjections, gives her a look then turns to me, pressing the menu against her ample chest. 'Emma, sweet pea ...' She pauses for a moment, licking her lips. I can see she's struggling to find the right words. 'What I'm trying to say is that we all make mistakes, and it's not a crime to …' Oh I see, she doesn't bloody believe me. She thinks I slept with Marc.

'It's OK, Caroline,' I cut across her, holding my hands up. 'I know I messed up by going out with Marc. And yes, Ola, I should've listened to you.' I shake my head, swallowing back a huge tear that's crawling up my throat. I can't cry. Not again. Not here. 'But I swear nothing happened between us. I'd been drinking, yes, but not enough to have sex and not know about it. I didn't even kiss him, for crying out loud.' Although he did try to snog my face off on our taxi ride home, but I don't think they need to know that. 'Harry's the one who's been cheating. Why am I being blamed?' I tap hard at my chest with my fingers. 'I'm the victim here. I even got to see the hotel receipt where they were shagging all evening.' OK, I didn't see it with my own eyes but Marc read it all out to me and Harry didn't deny it.

Caroline chews the inside of her lip. 'I know,' she says quietly. 'Look, I do believe you, Emma. I'm sorry. I can't believe he's done this to you. Bloody men. Rotten, the lot of them.' Finally, the old Caroline is back. 'Do you think he's having a midlife crisis or something? Men of that age get a bit funny, don't they? Mas went out and bought himself a BMW when he was in his forties, do you remember that?'

I nod, smiling. It was a sleek, black, two-seater convertible. He didn't have it for long. Caroline made him take it back within a week. 'But Harry's not like that,' I protest. 'He doesn't have a problem with aging. In fact he loves celebrating birthdays, tells me we're lucky to be alive. It's probably got something to do with his job, seeing so many young people die.' I stare ahead forlornly as black uniformed waiters whizz around the floor in their tiny black aprons.

'Have you tried getting in touch with him, Em?' Ola asks gently. 'Just to find out what he's thinking? If he's with *her*?'

'No, he's not seeing her anymore,' Caroline interjects, tucking her chair in, and smiling up at a young blonde diner, making room for her and her partner to sit at the table behind ours.

I look at Caroline, stunned. 'So you *do* know.'

'Look,' Caroline sighs in exasperation, 'I promised Mas I wouldn't take sides, Emma, but ... well, yes, they've spoken. But Mas said it's over between them. That it was just a silly affair.' She waves a hand.

I close my eyes. I feel like I've just swallowed a golf ball. 'I can't believe Harry sacrificed everything for a quick shag.' I grab my glass and down the wine in one. Ola and Caroline exchange glances but say nothing.

'All the more reason to call him, Emma, see where ...'

'Ola, he's had an affair,' I snap, a little too loudly, causing the blonde girl to glance round. I lower my voice. 'I'm not calling anyone.'

'Don't you even want to know why? Just for closure if nothing else?'

'No, I'm fine. I don't need closure,' I huff, folding my arms. The blonde girl throws me a sympathetic smile as she reaches across the table for her bloke's hand.

'Look,' Ola closes her eyes briefly. 'Please make sure this is what you want, Emma. Just because he's had an affair doesn't mean it's the end of your relationship. She's only known him five minutes. You've got history together.'

'She's right,' Caroline says softly, her face suddenly serious, 'a lot of people get through affairs. If you still love him ...'

I don't answer. I can't even bear thinking about Harry with another woman, let alone fight for him.

'Do you want him back?' Ola's voice is heavy, concerned.

'No, I bloody well don't,' I complain, anger digging its heels into my heart. 'Not after where he's been.' Ola and Caroline exchange another glance. I wish they'd stop doing that. I am here, you know. 'And can you believe he had the cheek to deny it until the very last moment?' I add incredulously, shaking my head. 'And to think I believed him when he told me he was too exhausted for sex.'

'No sex?' Caroline exclaims. An older couple at the next table look round. I widen my eyes at Caroline as I incline my head towards them in a quick, sharp motion. Her voice drops to a whisper. 'For how long?'

'Oh, I dunno.' I wave a hand. I know I've said too much but I don't care. I'm angry. 'Long enough.'

'I suppose you and Mas are at it like rabbits,' Ola chuckles. She opens her menu as the mature lady at the next table tucks her long fringe behind her ear with a minuscule incline of her head towards us, her expression depicting 'tell me more'.

Caroline raises an eyebrow impishly. 'Can't get enough of me.' She shimmies her shoulders in the manner of a burlesque dancer and I can't help but give a little weak, laboured laugh. 'Anyway, you.' She taps me lightly with the drinks menu. 'You don't want him back, do you? So just let him get on with it. His loss.'

'But that's not the point, is it? You'd have thought that after five years he'd have the decency to at least have some remorse for what he's done. He should call me.' I push my fingers through my hair, 'Apologise. Explain!'

'The begging phone call?' Caroline smiles at me knowingly.

I shrug. I want him to call me, text me, leave messages on my voicemail begging me for a chance to explain. I can't bear this feeling of rejection crawling relentlessly through my veins. That he chose someone else over me.

I've played the scene out a dozen times in my head. Huge bouquets of flowers with deep, remorseful love notes arriving on my doorstep. I make the delivery guy wait while I read the attached card, then tear it up, shove it against his chest, and tell him to return them to the bastarding sender. But there's been nothing.

'You're going to have to talk to each other at some point,' Ola says as Caroline asks the waiter to give us a few more minutes. 'You've got to sort out your financial commitments if nothing else. Bills have no compassion.'

'Yes, I know, I know,' I say irritably. I drop my head into my hands, elbows on table. I don't want to lose my home but I've got to be realistic. I won't be able to live there on my own. Needless to say, I can't work at the restaurant anymore, even though Caroline has assured me that my job is safe if I want it. And my illustration business is only just starting to take off. It'll be a while before I'm earning enough to support myself. 'If I don't hear from him by the end of the week I'll give him a call,' I say, raking a hand through my hair. 'But only to sort out our finances.'

Ola nods in agreement, taking a sip of wine. 'That's my girl. So, what's happening with Isabella and her husband, then?' Ola turns to Caroline.

'I'm not sure.' Caroline replies, her eyes not leaving the menu. 'This chicken dish sounds nice.'

'Don't tell me she's back with Marc?' I ask in surprise. 'Have they destroyed my life and headed off into the sunset?'

'I told you, babe, Mas won't tell me anything.'

'What, and that's it? No interrogation? No post mortem?' Ola slams her menu shut. 'Come on, Caroline, I know Harry's your brother-in-law but Emma's our friend. We both know she's the innocent party here. OK, she flirted a bit with a young, hot guy. Who wouldn't, given the chance?' I feel a warm glow inside. Ola's always had my back. 'Even though he turned out to be a complete fucking wanker.' My lips twitch at the sound of Ola swearing. It sounds quite funny in her posh accent, particularly as she hardly ever swears. I cover my nervous smile with my fingertips. 'But there's no way anything else happened.' I throw my lovely friend an admiring glance.

'Yes, I know,' Caroline says through gritted teeth, taking a glug from her wine glass.

'I think you should demand an explanation from Mas,' Ola rants on. 'Hell, I'd want a blow by blow account if he were my husband.'

Caroline twitches at Ola like a free mason and Ola, taking the bait, sinks a little into her seat. Clearly she knows more than she's letting on but wants to spare my feelings.

'So, this creep Marc befriended you under false pretences on Facebook, did he?' Ola says, swiftly moving on.

'Yes, he tricked me.' I shake my head, feeling like a complete idiot.

'How?' Caroline asks, intrigued.

'Well.' I lean forward, crossing my arms over the table. 'He went under the name of Beryl Dolan and used a dog for his profile picture. A cute black and white Schnauzer.' I smile. 'I just assumed it was an indie author interested in my work.'

'Didn't you check to see if you had friends in common or anything?' Caroline goes on, craning her neck as a pretty, dark-haired waitress dashes past us with a lovely smelling dish. 'I always do.'

'No. I was a complete twat. I just accepted his request. Too trusting, I know.'

'I'm with Caroline on this one. I always check people's profiles first if I don't know them. If there's no info, no real photo, and we've nothing in common I just reject the request. Don't get me wrong, Facebook is great but it can be dangerous too. You've got to be careful. Lesson learnt, hey?'

'Yeah, well I'll be more prudent from now on, won't I?' I grumble, biting on my thumbnail.

'What are you doing about a proper website?' Caroline asks. 'I know you've got your blog, but is it adequate?' I tell her that it isn't, that my blog doesn't showcase my work to its full potential, but that I can't afford to pay a web developer for a professional one at the moment. Caroline frowns thoughtfully, then reaches into her bag for her phone. 'Vicky's sister-in-law is a web designer. She's doing mine now. I'm sure she can help you out. Her rates are really good. I've got her number somewhere.' She starts scrolling through her contacts on her phone. 'Ah, here it is. Audrey Fox. I'd call her for you now but I'm almost out of juice. I use Mas' mobile at home but he won't let me take it out. His phone goes on forever. And he's got unlimited everything. Bastard. Do you want the number, sweetie?'

'Sure. I'll give her a call when I'm a bit more settled.'

As Caroline calls out the number and I log it into my phone, I can't help wondering what Harry's doing. Is he sorry? Is he at home thinking of me? Does he want to call? Love can't just dissolve overnight like an effervescent tablet fizzing away in a glass of water, can it?

Chapter Twenty-Four

'There's plenty more fish in the sea,' Caroline says kindly, sensing that I'm thinking about Harry. Her intuition is second to none. She places her phone down next to mine on the table.

'I've had it with men,' I huff, glancing around the now heaving restaurant.

'Oh, enough about men.' Ola waves a hand dismissively. 'Screw the lot of them. We're here to have some fun and look to the future.'

I can almost see Caroline's muscles relax. I really ought to be grateful. Harry is her brother-in-law. At least she isn't taking sides. No doubt Mas has been pouring poison into her ear for the last two days; yet here she is having dinner with me, agreeing with me. Clearly, she values our friendship. I can't ask for more than that from her. And besides, filling me in with the gory details of Harry's affair isn't going to help, is it?

'So, what are you having, then?' Caroline muses. 'The chicken sounds scrummy.' She rubs her chin, 'I might have that.'

'Which one is that?' Ola opens her menu again and runs a long, slender finger down the 'mains' section. 'Oh, yes, mushroom sauce, sauté potatoes, and rocket salad. Hmm ... does sound nice, doesn't it? Emma?'

'I'm not hungry,' I say miserably as the waiter appears at my side, filling my empty glass. I've been dying for a drink for ages, so I'm glad he's serving me first. He must be psychic. Talking of which …

'How are you getting on with The Magic Touch, Caroline?' I need to stop thinking about Harry and get on with life, talk about other things. I take a small sip from my glass. The pale yellow liquid slides down my throat, giving me a small, upbeat kick. A few more of these and I'll be alright, I'm sure.

'It's doing quite well, actually. I've had almost three-hundred downloads and some brilliant five-star reviews.' She glances at the smiling waiter, nodding in gratitude as he fills her glass, her blue eyes sparkling. He stands to attention like a soldier as he scribbles down her order on his pad, repeating it word for word in a heavy French accent. He looks incredibly like Elvis Costello – black, thick-rimmed square glasses and short, dark hair – only a French version. 'How're you getting on with it?' she asks, as Ola discusses the chicken dish with the Elvis Costello lookalike.

'I deleted the app because it was acting weird, remember?' I glance at my iPhone as it bleeps with a Facebook alert. Probably a response to my recent status update:

Going out with friends tonight. Whoop whoop. Can't wait.

I left it in case Harry logged on. I don't want him thinking I'm sitting at home wallowing or anything.

Caroline nods. 'Oh yes, I remember now. Did you not download it again?'

I take a large gulp of wine as the waiter scurries off with our orders, menus under his arm. Ola ordered me the special too, despite my reservations. I won't eat it. I'm on a self-imposed starvation diet. I've been living off toast and coffee for the last two days. 'I was going to, but then all this kicked off with Harry,' I say. 'But I'll do it when I get home. I promise.'

'I'm sorry I haven't downloaded it, Caroline.' Ola rests a hand on Caroline's arm. 'I just haven't had the time. But I'm really glad it's doing well. What do your kids make of it all? I bet they're really proud.'

'Embarrassed more like,' Caroline groans. 'They've banned me from talking about it when they've got their mates round. Can you believe that? Banned from speaking in my own house. Pfft.'

Ola laughs. 'Teenagers, hey. Who'd have 'em?'

'Anyway, Emma,' Caroline says. 'The bugs have been fixed now.' She takes a small sip from her glass, then does a little joyful flinch. 'Oooh, that's a lovely Sauv blanc, very tangy. Don't you think so, Ola? Good job we took the waiter's advice and went for the Canadian over the Chilean, I've ...' The words die on her lips. She's staring into the distance towards the entrance of the restaurant, mouth agape, eyes wide as if in a trance.

'Are you OK, Caroline?' I touch her forearm.

'What's wrong?' Ola and I have spoken at the same time. I wonder if she's allergic to something in the wine. She looks like she's about to faint.

'Caroline? Is it the wine?' Ola lifts her hand in the air, summoning a waitress. 'I'll get you some water.' But Caroline grabs her arm and pulls it down quickly.

'No, it's OK.' She looks at me, her face ashen. 'He's here again, Em.'

'Who's here?' I furrow my brows tightly. Please don't tell me Marc has hunted me down again. I made sure I didn't put where I was going on Facebook or Twitter. I have unfriended and blocked him, of course, but computer geeks have a way of finding things out, don't they?

Ola and I follow Caroline's eyes and stare at the entrance in wide-eyed wonder.

'That neighbour of yours.' She swallows hard. 'Alistair,' she says with a smile, the colour returning to her cheeks.

Ola raises her eyebrows at me, eyes widening, which I reciprocate with a small, knowing smile.

'And don't you two give each other those looks behind my back as if I'm mad,' she retorts, waving her finger at us accusingly. 'He's here. I can see him. Well, not completely, of course.' She slants her head to the left and scrunches her nose. 'He's sort of transparent with a white, glowing outline. Weird, but quite lovely.' Caroline gazes at the empty space in the distance. The Elvis Costello lookalike walks past, stops, asks her if she needs anything. 'No.' She fidgets with the collar of her short-sleeved lime green sweater, 'I just thought I saw someone that I knew.' At which he nods, smiles at me and Ola, then dashes off.

Ola gives me a sly wink. 'So, what is Alistair saying?' she asks, elbow on table, chin in palm.

'I can't really make it out. I'm only grasping bits. He's holding his heart. Oooh, he's just popped into the seat next to you, Em.'

I stare darkly at the empty seat, then swish my hand up and down over the wooden chair. 'There's definitely no one there, Caroline.'

'Well, of course there isn't, dummy. He's a flipping spirit, isn't he?' She rolls her eyes, then shakes her head. 'Did he die of something chest-related?'

'Caroline! I told you he died of a heart attack, remember?' I glance around, making sure that no one is watching us having a conversation with a wooden chair.

Thankfully the diners within earshot are tucking into their meals.

'No, I don't think you did, sweetie,' she says with a hint of incredulity. But I'm certain I did. At the funeral parlour while we were waiting to go in. Caroline's memory is like a colander these days. She mentioned a few weeks ago that memory loss is a menopausal symptom.

Caroline's eyes light up. 'He wants me to tell you that he's fine. That he crossed over safely, and that he's with his wife. He's smiling, he's happy.' She grins at the chair. 'Oooh, ooooh, wait! He's saying something about a map now.' She grabs my arm tightly. 'He was harping on about that the other day too, wasn't he?'

I interlace my fingers, elbows on table, gently biting my bottom lip. 'Did you see your doctor about your menopausal symptoms or are you still taking those Chinese herb things?'

'Emma, symptoms of the menopause do not include seeing spirits,' she says bluntly.

'No, what I meant was ... those herbs you're taking might be ...'

'Shhhh ...' She raises her hand to silence me. 'I know what you meant but shut up for a second, will you? I'm trying to tune in.' Her face creases in concentration, eyes focused on the empty chair. 'It's like a frequency on a radio. There's all this crackling and hissing and a babble of voices. So strange.' She frowns, listening intently. 'Hostel? Oh, sorry,' she looks at us briefly. 'Motel,' she says loudly. 'I thought he said hostel. What motel, love? Emma and motel? I think he's saying you need a break, Em.' I take a deep breath as I throw Ola a worried glance. 'He wants you to get a map and find a motel in Charlotte,' she says finally, smiling at me smugly. 'That's in North America, isn't it?' She takes a swig from her glass.

Ola and I gawp at each other.

'So, you see dead people now?' Ola says, head slightly inclined.

'Yes, I do,' Caroline replies indignantly. 'I am psychic, in case you hadn't noticed. Stop shaking your head, Ola. You're quite happy for me to read your palm, so I don't know why you're being so cynical now.'

'Fair point.'

I say nodding, lips curved downwards. Only I'm not quite sure what she's talking about. A map and a motel in Charlotte make no sense at all. And besides, why would Alistair be telling me to go on a holiday? Surely he'd know that I can't afford it.

Ola twists her lips to one side thoughtfully. 'Actually, I've always been interested in the paranormal.' She whips her purple cardigan off and drapes it around her chair. 'Can you see my dad, Caroline?' she says hopefully, leaning in. 'Is he here?'

I know Caroline is gifted and I want to believe her, but Alistair hated mediums. And he especially warned me against Caroline, telling me she was a fake and to be careful. He wouldn't communicate through her. I know he wouldn't. He specifically said, 'No mediums. I'll find another way.'

'No, sorry, Ola. I can't see your dad, or anyone else for that matter. Oh, and now Alistair has gone too. Phew,' she says in a thrilled tone, hand on chest. 'I'm getting good at this, aren't I? Who'd have thought that I'd be able to communicate with the other side?' she says with glee. 'That's another skill to add to my CV.'

As Ola and Caroline discuss her new psychic skills a message trills through on my phone. They both stop mid-sentence and stare at my phone. I know what they're thinking because I'm secretly thinking it too.

'It's Tessa, my sister,' I announce half-heartedly

'Oh, I thought it might've been …' Ola's voice trails off as the waiter arrives with our food.

'She just wants to confirm our meet-up.' I lean back as the waiter places a plate in front of me, warning me that it's hot. I smile up at him in gratitude, then dodge him to get a clear view of Ola. 'To discuss the donation.'

'Donation …' Ola repeats, glancing briefly at the Elvis Costello lookalike with a smile.

'Yes, Ola, the kidney donation I told you about.'

'For her dad,' Caroline explains.

'Yes, I know what you mean,' Ola says, elbows on either side of her plate, fingers entwined. 'But I thought you were going to give it more thought before you took it further.'

'I was.' I pick up my knife and fork. 'I am …'

'And?' Ola cuts into a sauté potato. 'This is a serious operation, Emma.'

'She's right. You've got to consider the implication it'll have on your health.' Caroline sprinkles salt over her food. 'You really do need to speak to Ha …' she falters. 'I mean … you know … a medical professional, someone who knows about these things.'

'I've got an appointment to see Dr Shantikumar next week.' They both frown at me, chewing on their food. 'My GP,' I clarify, shuffling some rocket around on my plate. 'But I've googled kidney donations and I've found out all I need to know. The risks are minimal, something like only one in three thousand die on the operating table.'

They both stop chewing and gawp at me, cutlery in mid-air.

'But what about after the operation?' Caroline asks.

241

'Four to ten days in hospital while I recover, then about twelve weeks to recuperate. But it said on the website that most people are back on their feet within six.'

Caroline looks horrified. 'What if you get kidney failure?'

'Living with only one kidney will compromise your health, surely.' Ola frowns at me. 'You might have to give up running, and you won't be able to knock back as many of those.' She gesticulates at my wine glass with her knife.

I shake my head vigorously and tut. I can't believe they're being so ignorant. 'Don't be stupid. Lots of people only have one kidney. The report said that it won't affect the quality of my life whatsoever. I won't die, I won't get kidney failure. I can still do all the things I did before. Don't look at me like that. It's perfectly safe to live with one kidney, and I'd be at no greater risk of any future health problems than you two. Honestly! All I'll be doing is saving my dad's life.'

'Well,' Caroline says dubiously, twirling rocket around her fork like spaghetti. 'See what your GP tells you next week before you go shooting your mouth off to Tessa or your father. I know how impulsive you can be.'

'Yes,' Ola affirms, 'make sure you know all the facts first before you make such a huge commitment. Remember, you are a bit vulnerable at the moment. You don't want to do anything you'll regret.'

I slice a potato in half, then shuffle it around in the mushroom sauce. I wish they'd bloody well stop patronising me. I'm not going out on a limb here.

I've spent the last few days researching kidney donations online. I know all the facts and figures inside out. I want to help another person have a decent life. I want Tessa to be happy. I know how much this means to her. Is that really so bad? Family is important, after all. And I've been neglecting mine for years. It's about time I built some bridges.

'I *have* thought about it and I'm aware of all the facts,' I say firmly. 'And we're going to see Dad together tomorrow.' Tessa and I will be meeting up for a quick coffee first, just to recap, make sure we've got all our facts right.

'Tomorrow?' Ola and Caroline cry in stunned unison.

'Yes, tomorrow.' I place my cutlery together in the centre of my plate. 'To tell him the good news.' I push the plate away and look at them.

'But …' Ola falters.

'Good news?' Caroline says in a high-pitched voice.

'Yes, that's right, the good news. If I pass all the tests and examinations, *I* am going to be his donor.'

Chapter Twenty-Five

Tessa is waiting for me outside the main entrance at Camden Market; looking as glamorous as ever in a knee-length orange and white floral dress hugging her protruding tummy.

'Emma.' She throws her arms around me.

'I'm sorry I'm late, Tess,' I pant into her gorgeous-smelling soft blonde curls. I'm glad she hasn't worn a strong perfume today. She must've remembered that it gave me the sneezes the last time we met. She's thoughtful like that, my little sister.

'It's OK. I just got here myself, to be honest.' She holds me at arm's length by the shoulders. 'You look great.' I don't. In fact, I resemble an aging ginger troll. I moved on to a pub after dinner with the girls last night, and emerged from my bedroom this morning feeling like I'd drunk the brewery dry. I just about had time to brush my teeth, let alone put any make-up on. I haven't even combed my hair.

'I had a bit of an emergency this morning,' I lie. I don't want to tell her that instead of going straight to bed after I staggered home last night, I decided to have another glass of wine, then spent the next half hour gazing adoringly at photos of me and Harry on my iPhone. I finally passed out on the sofa in floods of tears, woken by the shrill of the telephone just an hour ago by my mother, demanding to know how I was and insisting that I go to convalesce with her in Stratford-upon-Avon.

With one hand covering her bump protectively, Tessa leads me by the hand as we snake through the crowds of the bustling market to a coffee stand, music pumping, tourists swarming around us. I feel as if I've been teleported to Thailand.

She grabs a table, I grab two cups of coffee and some freshly made doughnuts. I'm absolutely famished.

We sit opposite each other at a tiny hand-painted metal table for two, munching on our pastries to the delightful backdrop of zen music as she tells me all about her pregnancy. I'm transfixed. I listen with complete abandonment, my turmoil taking a back seat to Tessa's fortuity. It's been easier than when she was carrying Jamie, she says; no sickness at all, no headaches, and bags of energy. With only two weeks to go it feels as if she's about to drop her at any moment. She knows it's a girl this time, and I'm delighted. I've always wanted a lovely little niece to leave all my worldly goods to. Don't get me wrong, I adore my gorgeous nephew, but you can't go clothes shopping or paint your nails with boys, can you?

'I bet Tom's happy,' I say, licking sugar off my fingers. Tom, her husband of four years, wanted a girl from the outset.

'Yes. He threatened to divorce me if I had another boy.' She rolls her eyes to the clear blue sky in disdain, sweeping her thumb repeatedly over her sugary fingers. A waft of incense streams through the café as we giggle in our bubble of sibling harmony.

'What about Dad? I bet he can't wait to meet his first granddaughter.' I look at her properly for the first time today. She's looking radiant and more like Dad every time I see her, which isn't as often as I'd like. I'm not sure if it's the age gap between us or the fact that we didn't grow up together that's stopped us from having that sisterly bond.

It's more than likely that it's because we have different mothers, and she's much closer to Dad than I'll ever be, come what may. But seeing her now, knowing how supportive she's being, how loving she's been to me all these years despite my standoffishness at times, is giving me a warm, fuzzy feeling in my tummy. I can feel her love as we speak, as if it's penetrating my skin, streaming into my veins. Perhaps I've been missing out on family love by shutting her out of my life. But it isn't too late to make amends, is it? And that's exactly what I plan to do.

'Well, you know Dad. He's not really kid-friendly, is he?' She bites hungrily into her third doughnut. 'These are really good,' she enthuses, licking her lips. 'Fresh!'

'Talk of the devil.' I take a quick sip from my polystyrene coffee cup. It scolds my lips and I wince. 'What time is the old goat expecting us?'

Tessa finishes off the last piece of her doughnut then rubs her fingers together. The sugar crystals fall over the empty white paper bag like rainfall. I wait as she chews.

'Well?' I cradle my cup. I'm being impatient, I know, but I'm feeling quite nervous about today, which is probably why I sank copious glasses of wine down my throat last night. I haven't seen my dad in years. I don't know how I'm going to react. I might take one look at him and run a mile. I expect he'll be pleased to see me, given that I could quite possibly be about to save his life.

Tessa munches, shaking her hands as if to speed up the chewing process. She takes a swig of coffee, complains it's too hot, then waves her hand in front of her mouth. I can see she's stalling for time. She always does this when she wants to avoid a sore subject.

I narrow my eyes. 'He does know I'm going round today, right?'

She bites on her bottom lip, staring into the mass of shoppers in the distance. 'Well, the thing is, Em ...'

I slam my hand onto the garden table and it shakes. 'I *knew* it.'

Tessa's warm hand curls around mine, squeezing tightly. 'You know what he's like. Stubborn as ever. If I told him that I'd got in touch with you about this ...' she pauses, pinching the bridge of her nose, '... that ... that I'd told you all about his illness. Well, he'd have done his nut, wouldn't he?'

'Why? I'm his daughter, too. I have a right to know if my dad has a serious illness, don't I?'

'Yes, Emma.' She closes her eyes for a moment, one hand wrapped over mine, the other on her belly. Oh God, I hope the contractions haven't started. Not in the middle of Camden frigging Market. 'Of course you have every right, which is why I've told you,' she says coolly, as if she's talking to one of her dental patients. 'But because you haven't spoken to each other for so long I thought it might be best to go round unannounced. That way he won't have any time to think. You know how proud he can be.'

'Won't have time to refuse to see me, more like. So he hasn't changed much.' I suck my cheeks in, glance away, then look back at her again.

'He does want to see you, Emma. He's always asking after you. I've told you that before, many times.' She throws a hand up. 'I dunno, maybe I'm wrong but I just thought that because you've been estranged for so long he might look upon it as a pity visit, that's all.'

'Well, it is ... sort of. But what's wrong with that? Crises often reunite estranged families, don't they? I mean, showing your love at the required moment is what it's all about, isn't it?' I shake my head and stare into the crowd, angry warm tears blurring my vision. 'This was a mistake.'

I go to stand but Tessa grabs my arm and pulls me back down, causing a man in a flat cap to look up at us. She gives him a quick reflex grin, and he returns his attention to his iPad.

'Please Em, you may be his only chance.' Silence. 'Do it for me!' She looks at me pleadingly. But her big blue eyes aren't going to do it for her this time. She's gone too far.

I shake my head, covering my quivering lips with my fingers. Maybe Ola and Caroline were right. I'm upset. Fragile, even. I haven't thought this through properly. I grab my bag. I've got to get out of here. Go home, sort my life out. I don't need all this. I don't do families. What was I thinking? I take a lungful of warm, incensed air. 'I'm sorry, Tessa. I can't do this. I've got enough on my plate.'

'If not for me then do it for her.' She pulls my hand over her pregnant belly. 'She deserves to see her granddad, doesn't she?' Flat cap man gazes up at us again from his iPad.

Our eyes lock and I notice that she's getting those red blotches on her neck. The same ones I get when I'm feeling stressed or anxious. I sit back down, sighing heavily, and Tessa breathes a sigh of relief. I don't know if it's because I'm feeling so vulnerable but I'm suddenly overwhelmed by family obligation.

'Just say that you called me and wanted to see him, OK?' I rub my tired eyes, wordless. I want to see my dad. He is what he is, what's done is done, I don't hate him. I don't want him to die. 'OK?' she demands.

'OK, but one single criticism and I'll be out of there.'

Half an hour later we're sitting in Dad's flat. Surprisingly, he was delighted, albeit a tad stunned, to see me standing next to Tessa on the doorstep.

He makes a fresh pot of tea while Tessa and I sit on his worn brown sofa in front of the small TV, staring at barely-audible horse racing. Dad always watched the horse racing with the sound turned down; said that the commentator's gibbering got on his nerves. I could never understand that. Surely the running commentary jigs things up, adds to the thrill.

'I've got some biscuits somewhere,' he calls out from the tiny kitchen adjoining the living room. I gaze around his tired, musty-smelling room, taking in the smoke-stained walls, the grubby net curtains that probably haven't been cleaned for years. Harry and I do ours in the summer. Harry. One moment I hate him, the next I'm wondering what I did to drive him into the arms of another woman. I've got to stop thinking about him. He's no longer a part of my life.

'It's OK, Dad,' Tessa shouts. 'We've just had some doughnuts.' She winks at me.

'Really? Oh, wait, I know where they are.' After a racket of clashing saucepans and cabinet doors, Dad appears looking flustered, Jammie Dodgers in hand.

'These used to be your favourite when you were little.' He starts unwrapping the packet noisily, and for a moment I'm transported back to our three-bedroom terrace on Brecknock Road. We're sitting on a green and orange fabric sofa in front of the TV, munching on biscuits, Dad with his arm around Mum's shoulders, and Mum's arm around mine. An idyllic family.

I take a biscuit from the packet in his trembling hand. He looks older, worn. His thinning hair is now almost completely white, his leathered skin pale against his once vibrant blue eyes. My heart melts. This illness has really taken its toll.

We chat enthusiastically about the weather, holidays, and Tessa's baby for a good twenty minutes.

He asks me about Mum and I tell him she's settled in Stratford-upon-Avon with her new husband, that I only see her a few times a year but that we talk regularly on the phone. When we get on to the subject of my personal life, I don't disclose that Harry and I are estranged. Instead I hear myself waffling on about our lovely home, beautiful garden, his nursing career, and my growing business.

'I'm glad you've settled down, love,' Dad says, taking a slurp from his red KitKat mug, probably an Easter Egg gift from Tessa. She bought me one just like it. 'That Carl was a wrong'n.' He shakes his head with dry, pursed lips. It's a pity he didn't share the same sentiments when I was married to him. He prattles on about Carl, how I was too good for him, what a waste of space he was, and that I should've listened to his advice and not married him in the first place.

I wish Dad was always this lovely. If age has done anything, it's mellowed him, made him into a calmer, more caring person. It feels good being here with my dad and sister. Snug, safe, homely. As I lean back into the sofa I'm stabbed in the spine by a protruding loose spring. I carefully lean against the armrest, avoiding any further collision with the metal offender.

'Dad,' Tessa says, settling her mug onto the oval coffee table stained with glass rings and cigarette burns. I feel my muscles tense a little. I know what she's going to say. 'Emma and I have some great news.' She looks at me carefully.

'Oh yes?' He nods at us, smiling.

'I don't want you to get all worked up now,' she says smoothly.

Dad furrows his fraying white brows and leans forward, elbow resting on his knee, 'Go on.'

'I've told Emma about your illness and ...' she grins at me, 'she's agreed to have a donation test.' She clasps her hands together in excitement.

Dad's face darkens. There's a bang as he puts his mug down heavily onto the table, tea spilling over the rim. No wonder it's covered in stains. 'So, that's what all this is about?'

'Dad,' I begin, wriggling to the edge of my seat.

'I thought you just missed me,' he says petulantly. 'Wanted to see me.'

'Dad, calm down, will you?' Tessa says, throwing me an apologetic glance. 'We thought you'd be pleased.'

'I don't want your pity, girl,' he bellows and I flinch, my mind spiralling thirty-two years into the darkness of my subconscious.

'Dad, you're angry.' Tessa puts her hand out as if calming a wild animal. 'You're shocked ... I can see that.'

'Don't tell me what I'm feeling, girlie.' His voice makes her jump.

Tessa and I exchange glances. 'Dad, please,' I say. 'Hear me out. I ...'

'Emma's here to help, she's ...'

'Shush, the pair of you!' His voice slices through the air, silencing us. He gets to his feet, shoulders back, feet apart. Then he starts rolling up his yellowing shirt sleeve, staring at the ground thoughtfully as Tessa and I go on and on about how I could help him save his life, that he should give me a chance.

We're all shouting at once, talking over each other. There's banging on the wall from the flat next door. A loud voice calls out 'Shut the fuck up!' A dog starts barking manically in the background. Then the sound of a TV blares through the thin walls. But none of it deters us. Our voices only grow louder to drown out the noise.

'Please, Dad, let me help you. I …'

'Dad, stop being such a bloody idiot. Emma could save your life.'

'No,' he shouts, rolling up the other sleeve. 'It's a big operation. Anything could go wrong. I can't risk my own child's life over mine. Does your mother know about this?'

'No, I haven't had the chance to tell her yet, I …'

He laughs. 'I thought so.'

'Dad, please …'

'I said *no*. I'm on the donor list, anyway.' He starts pacing the tired blue carpet, rubbing his white stubbly chin, face red with fury.

'But that could take years,' Tessa exclaims. 'It might be too late.'

'I'll take my chances.'

'I can't believe this.' I stand up, Tessa looks at me, horrified. 'This was a mistake.'

'Emma, no, please. Wait. Dad!'

'Let her go, Tessa.' Dad stares out of the window, hands clasped behind his back, regimental style, chest puffed out heroically.

I grab my bag off the settee and flounce towards him. 'You'd rather die than let me help you, would you?' I spit. He doesn't answer. I shoulder my bag angrily. 'Do you really hate me that much?'

He looks round at me then, startled. 'I don't hate you, Emma. Why are you saying that?'

'You've never loved me.' Fresh tears swamp my eyes.

'What?' He looks genuinely surprised. 'Of course I have, you silly girl. I still do! I loved you, your mum. Those were the happiest days of my life. I didn't want a divorce.'

'Then let her help you, Dad.' Tessa is at my side, her face and neck covered in red blotches.

'No, Tessa,' I say. 'It's too late.' I turn to my dad, my heart in my mouth. 'You can't love anyone, not even yourself. You've always hated me. You're the reason I've never had any success with men.' Oh my goodness, did I just say that out loud? I read in a magazine the other day that you choose your partner based on your father, and it resonated with it instantly. But I shouldn't have said it to my dad, not now he's so fragile.

'No, no.' He covers his ears with his big hands, agitated. 'You and your mother never let me in.'

'What? I've always craved your approval but I was never good enough. I could never match up to Tessa.' I make for the door but then I feel his hand around my arm, pulling me back towards him. We're face to face.

'I've always loved you, Emma. I always will.' He glances at Tessa. 'It's just that your sister's always been more needy.'

'Needy?' Tessa pipes up, offended. '*Me*?'

'Yes, you've always needed more of my attention,' he snaps. 'You haven't got Emma's balls, never will.' This may sound strange, but I feel a rush of pride. Am I weird? 'I love you both equally, just in different ways. You girls mean the world to me, and I don't want you to leave here thinking otherwise. Not when I'm ...' Our eyes lock, and for the first time ever I see my big, strong, no-nonsense dad crying. My heart slowly melts.

'Look, Dad,' I say quietly, my bag sliding off my shoulder. 'At least let me have the test, then we can take it from there.'

'Yes, Emma's right,' Tessa says brightly, enthused by our sudden progress. 'She might be a match. Just think you could be ...'

'No.' His eyes don't leave mine.

'Oh, for heaven's sake, Dad.' Tessa throws her hands up in exasperation, giving me a look that says, 'I'm so sorry, you were right all along.'

'I won't let you do it.' His voice is soft, his chest is heaving.

'Dad, please, let me save your life.'

'No,' he says tearfully. 'No tests. You'll be wasting your time.' His eyes close briefly. 'I'm sorry, Emma. You can't be a match. You're not mine.'

Chapter Twenty-Six

I've always believed I was quite strong. Good at dealing with emotional stuff. That my experience at the hands of a monster years ago created an impenetrable protective layer around my heart, but I feel completely broken. In seventy-two hours I've lost everything.

Tessa was so distraught when Dad told us I wasn't his biological child I thought she'd drop the baby on his living room floor. Dad. The word feels so surreal now. Alien on my tongue. Because he's no longer my dad, is he? He's just David King. And who on earth am I? I'm certainly not Emma King anymore, am I?

I stare out of the window at passing traffic in a state of numbness as the bus trudges down the hill. My mind combs through every word he said. Mum was four months pregnant when he met her. They were both working at Keyes Motors, she a bright-eyed twenty-two year old typist and he a new apprentice mechanic.

'Bu … bu … but …' I stuttered, trying to form the sentence in my mouth like a toddler learning a new word. 'Ma … my …' I touched my hair.

'What can I say?' he'd said with a soft, sympathetic smile. 'Your mum had a thing for ginger blokes.'

Tessa and I sat in stunned silence, mouths agape, eyes fixed on him as he recalled how their love affair began. It was shortly after she joined the firm. It was love at first sight. Bewitched by her stunning good looks, her dark glossy hair, green eyes (like mine) offset against her milky white skin, he married her within weeks; agreeing to take on her child, which was a big ask in those days. On the day I was born he made Mum a solemn promise. I'd never know that I wasn't his. His name went on my birth certificate and that was the end of that. And he kept that promise – until today, that is.

'Don't be angry with her, love,' he went on. 'She was only trying to protect you. People weren't as forgiving in those days. She didn't want you to suffer, you know. Neighbours pointing their finger, kids calling you names at school. She didn't want any of that, and neither did I. And you felt like you were mine. All mine. I never loved you less than Tessa, so please don't think that. It's just that you and your mum always shut me out. I couldn't get into your cocoon, she wouldn't let me.' He combed his hand through his white hair. 'I was jealous. Jealous of your close relationship, of your real dad, even though I didn't even know who he was.'

I'm not quite sure how I managed to get out of his front door. It's still all a blur. I remember Tessa walking me to the bus stop, crying the entire time, giving me a heartfelt hug before I boarded the crowded bus, making me promise that things wouldn't change between us. That we were still sisters, no matter what. I then slipped to autopilot, my mind fizzing with questions the whole journey home.

I'm still in a daze as the bus pulls in at the stop. The doors open and I hobble off. A flood of students in red sweaters pepper the street like an army of ants. I walk along Albert Road making a mental to-do list as their screams and banter flood my ears like a swarm of wasps. I've got to ring Mum, find out what the hell happened. Who I really am. I need to know who my father is. Why he abandoned us. Why she kept this secret from me my entire life. How could she do

256

this to me? Things could've been different if I'd known. I love Tessa dearly but I can't help thinking that I might have real siblings somewhere out there. Brothers or sisters who bear an uncanny resemblance to me.

My heels click along the pavement as I imagine a scene out of *Long Lost Family*. Davina McCall arrives at my house, tells me she's found my real dad. He's a Parisian artist who's never stopped thinking of me, who can't wait to meet me. I'm not sure that many French men have red hair, but anyway. Davina tells me that he's written me a letter, then asks if I want to read it. I choke on the words and she has to finish the last sentence for me. Then in a later scene Nicky Campbell leads me by the hand to a café in Brighton (because he stayed in England in the hope of finding me one day), or somewhere else by the sea, because my father loves the sea as much as I do. Dad, I mean David, hated the seaside. I didn't have a foreign holiday until I was old enough to go with my friends. Then there's a tearful reunion when I'm face to face with the man who gave me life.

My reverie fades as I approach my house and see a figure bundled on my doorstep, a tiny suitcase between her legs. What's going on? I rush to my front door. 'Caroline?'

Caroline leaps to her feet in haste, missing the step and twisting her ankle. I catch her by the arm. Her face is red, her eyes raw. 'Emma,' she says tearfully, 'I've been here for hours. Where've you been? I tried your mobile, your house, I …'

I pull her into my arms to stop her jabbering. 'I'm so sorry. I had my phone on silent. I went to see my …' I swallow hard, 'my dad and sister. Remember?'

'Oh yes,' she sniffles, searching her pocket. 'The kidney transplant.' She pulls out a crumpled tissue and blows her nose. 'I forgot about that. How'd it go?'

'Caroline, what's happened?' I don't want to talk about my dad, and poor Caroline looks totally crushed. 'Is everything OK?'

'No, Emma, everything is *not* OK. Can we go inside, please? I'm bursting for a wee.'

I'm in the lounge, shuffling through the post. Bills, bills, and more bills, mostly final reminders. The one from the building society looks ominous. I tear it open, unfurl the letter, and gasp as the sound of the toilet flushes in the background.

I'm still staring at the letter, fingers pressed against my lips as Caroline limps back into the room. 'Sorry, Em. I was dying for a wee. I was sitting out there for an hour and forty-five minutes. I've got a sore arse and now a limp to go with it.' Her arm brushes mine. 'What's up?'

I show her the letter. 'We're in arrears. Oh God, Caroline, we might lose the house. Jesus, this is all I need.'

Caroline shakes her head, taking the letter from my hand. 'How did this happen?'

'Harry. That's how. Oh, come on. I think we both need a stiff drink.'

I march into the kitchen, yank the fridge door open, and pull out a bottle of white wine. 'So, come on, tell me what's happened?' I call out, grabbing two glasses from the cabinet. 'Are the kids alright? You're not ill, are you?'

She hobbles to the kitchen and takes the glasses by the stems. 'No, they're … we're all fine.'

'So, what is it?' I twist the screw cap and start pouring.

She downs her glass in one. 'Sorry, I needed that.' She looks up to the ceiling, taking a deep, courageous breath. 'It's Mas.'

'Oh no, has he had a heart attack?' I cry. She shakes her head tearfully. 'What then, a stroke?'

'No,' she blubs, pleating the edge of her cardigan nervously, 'It's much worse than that.'

'Oh God,' I press my hand against my chest as a feeling of dread washes over me. 'He's not dead, is he?'

'He's having a bloody affair!' Her blue eyes flush with fresh tears. Did I just hear right? Did she say Mas has been cheating on her? Mas is a devious little shit but his family means everything to him. He'd never risk everything for a quick shag.

'Are you certain?' I ask, arching my brow as I pour more wine into her empty glass.

She nods as tears roll down her red cheeks. She wipes them away with the back of her hands, sniffing. 'Definitely sure. I saw them together.'

I pull her into my arms and she sobs quietly into my chest.

'Shhh.' I can't think of anything to say. But sometimes silence is the best comfort of all. 'Bloody Georgiades brothers,' I say once the tears stop. 'They sure are cut from the same cloth, aren't they?'

Caroline pulls out of my embrace, her nails dig into my arm. 'No, no ...' She retrieves the crumbled tissue from her sleeve and blows her nose again. 'Harry's innocent.' She shakes her head vigorously. 'He was right to tell you nothing happened between him and Isabella. He's just been Mas' scapegoat.'

'What?' I feel as if the room has zoomed in on me, like a dramatic scene out of a film.

'It's Mas that has been seeing Isabella, not Harry. Harry was just covering for him, as per.'

'*What*?' Am I dreaming? This is completely mad.

'Mas confessed everything.'

I press my hand against my chest. 'But how?'

Caroline shuffles towards the patio doors, one hand in the pocket of her long, blue cardigan, the other holding her wine glass so tightly I was worried it might begin to crack. 'He met her via Harry one night at the pub, after-work drinks or something. She was having trouble with crazy Marc. The boys were consoling her, offering advice, help. I dunno.' She stares forlornly into the garden. 'Mas gave her a lift home and that's when it all started. Harry was the go-between. They'd make their arrangements through him. She couldn't text or call Mas because I use his phone most nights, he's got unlimited everything, you know.' I nod, telling her that she told me that the other night.

'But why would Harry do that?' I ask, hand on my chest. 'Risk everything for Mas? He's got so much love and respect for you, Caroline.'

'I know,' she says loudly, 'I can't believe he's let us down like this. I always thought he was a decent guy. But hey.' She shrugs. 'Family comes first, doesn't it? And you know Mas has this hold over him.'

I'm overwhelmed with the strangest feeling. Is it possible to feel delight and sadness at the same time?

An empty bottle of Sauvignon blanc later we're still on the sofa, having spent the last hour spilling our hearts out to each other. But it's her revelation about Alistair and how he helped her catch Mas in an uncompromising position that makes me reach for another bottle.

'Alistair's spirit had been bombarding me for days, gabbling on, talking gibberish as usual, not making any sense.' She says as I fill our glasses to the brim. 'Then this morning he shows up at the restaurant while I was helping Valentina with the moussaka. Poor love was so distraught when you didn't show up on Thursday. She was lagging behind because of your absence so I went in to give her a hand.'

'Yes, I know. She called me yesterday afternoon and I explained everything. She was almost as upset as I was.'

'She's such a lovely lady, isn't she? She can't cope on her own. Mas'll have to find her a replacement soon.' I nod, holding my neck. 'Going back to Alistair, he frightened the shit out of me, he did.' I stifle a giggle, Caroline is so funny, even in a crisis. 'Valentina thought I was bonkers when she saw me talking to the AGA stove. Anyway, he insisted that I go to a hotel in Fitzrovia immediately.'

'That's around the corner from your restaurant, isn't it?' I ask, scratching my hand.

She nods, taking a sip of wine. 'It's on Charlotte Street, a lovely boutique hotel. Do you know it?' As I shake my head the name suddenly bolts into my mind. The Charlotte Street Hotel. That was the name on the hotel receipt that Marc showed me. I close my eyes as Marc's angry voice rings in my ears. 'In the name of Mr Georgiades, arrival time 8 p.m., departure time 10.15 p.m.' I remember thinking it wasn't just a quick shag; that they'd spent two hours and fifteen minutes locked in a hotel room together.

'He even gave me the room number: thirty-six. Same number as our house.' She stares silently into the distance for a few moments as I try to digest everything. Alistair is actually making contact with Caroline? He's actually floating around somewhere, in another dimension? 'I slipped by reception, got into the lift, and found myself standing outside number thirty-six. I knocked on the door and called out "room service" in a funny voice, as per Alistair's protocol. And there he was. Jaw ajar with a white towel around his fat arse, and that bitch, butt naked behind him. Honestly, Emma, I almost threw up there and then.'

She knocks back the wine and grabs the bottle on the coffee table by the neck.

I stretch my arm out for a refill. 'I can't believe this, Caroline. I … I don't know what to say. I mean … you are *actually communicating* with Alistair?'

'Yeaaaah.' She puts the bottle down, plunges her hand into her bag and pulls out a piece of paper. 'He said he's been trying to contact you via The Magic Touch for ages but you weren't taking any notice of his predictions. Then, of course, you deleted it,' she sniffs. 'That's what he was harping on about the other night, remember? Hotel. Charlotte. Map? Only he was saying app but I couldn't understand him. I'm new to all this.' I gawp at Caroline, completely stunned. 'Don't look at me as if I'm some kind of nutter. Here.' She hands me the paper, 'He told me to give you this message. I hope you understand my writing. I jotted it all down quickly. He's got a habit of suddenly disappearing mid-sentence.'

The words dance before my eyes as if under bright spotlights – *BKDACODE. I did it for you.*

'Oh my God,' I gasp, taking off my glasses and glaring at Caroline. 'It's really him.' My body tingles with a mixture of delight and trepidation. Alistair is safe. There is life after death. I've always wanted to believe there was more to life than this, that another realm existed, but I just couldn't. It didn't seem feasible. I wanted concrete evidence. But now …

'Caroline! You're a bloody genius.'

Caroline smiles smugly. 'Well I did tell you, but you wouldn't believe me would you?'

I grab my phone excitedly. 'I'll download the app again now. I need to communicate with Alistair.' I open the App Store. 'He might be able to help me find my real father. I'm sure my mum won't have my father's details after all these years and … and …'

'Oh, too late,' she chirps, putting her wine glass onto Harry's *Doctor Who* coaster. 'I've knocked it on the head. It no longer exits.'

'Caroline!'

'I haven't got time for apps anymore.' She pushes her hair off her face, 'Not with my marriage crumbling around me. Besides, I've got a new skill now. I'm a spiritual medium.' I look at her, horrified. 'What? You can contact him through me.'

'I suppose,' I groan.

Caroline perches at the edge of her seat. 'Is it OK if I stay a few days? The kids are away. Andreas is in Oxford seeing some flats and Demi's gone to Cyprus with her grandparents for ten days.' She fishes into her handbag again, then pulls out a set of keys. 'I had the locks changed earlier today but Mas'll be hammering the door down drunk when he finds out, no doubt. He's already phoned me twenty times after our showdown this morning and left half a dozen voice messages. I haven't retrieved them. I don't want to hear his voice. Not yet, anyway. I really can't face seeing him, either.'

'Yes, of course,' I give her shoulder a light squeeze. 'Stay as long as you like. I'll make up the bed in the spare room for you.'

'Thanks, Emma,' I feel her cold tears on my face as she reaches out and gives me a kiss. 'And here, take these. Go to Harry. Sort it out. He needs to know the truth about you and Marc.'

I look at the keys in her hand as if they're a poisonous scorpion. 'What're these?'

'Keys to your future happiness.'

'Huh?'

'Keys to the in-laws, you numpty. I nicked them out of Mas' jacket earlier and used them to dump two bin bags of his stuff round there before I came here.'

'I can't just turn up,' I gulp. 'What if he doesn't want to see me?'

'Duh ...' She jingles the keys in my face.

'No.' I fold my arms and pinch my bottom lip between my thumb and index finger. 'Too much has happened. I ...'

'Emma, darling, listen – in life, you've got to take the rough with the smooth. Sometimes you've got to fight for your rights, for what you want. Other times you've just got to accept things for what they are and roll with the punches. The trick is knowing when to fight and when to roll. Now's your time to fight.'

'But I can't ...'

She covers my mouth with her hand. 'Just go.' She looks at her watch. 'He should be back from work soon. Go on.' She waves a hand, 'Shoo.'

Chapter Twenty-Seven

I ring the doorbell repeatedly then stand back, gazing up helplessly at the bedrooms. It's almost seven. He should've been home by now. I wonder if he's seen me and is hiding behind the curtains until I leave. Or maybe he's taking a shower or fallen asleep in front of the TV. He often does that when he comes home after a long shift. Fuelled by copious glasses of wine, I ring the doorbell again and again, hammering the knocker with my free hand at the same time. 'Harry!'

Next door's curtains twitch. Then the door opens.

'They're away, love.' Tina, Xenia and Spiros' neighbour of thirty-five years, is standing on her doorstep, fag in hand, in a pink, hooded onesie with a white snowflake design along the chest. On her feet are huge animal slippers. I think they're reindeer ones. I wonder if they're Christmas gifts from her grandchildren or whether she actually went out and bought them.

'Oh, hello, Tina.' I smile, folding my zip-up sweatshirt across my chest to block out the chill. 'Yes, I know they're in Cyprus but um, it was Harry I was after. He's um … house-sitting for them.' Alistair always commended me on my quick thinking.

'Yes, saw him earlier.' She blows smoke into the cold evening air. 'He's such a darling. Takes me bins out for me when he's around.' She takes a long drag from her cigarette. 'Much nicer than that narky brother of his. All I did was ask him to shove his car back a bit so I could park

265

mine outside me own front door, and he got the bleeding Engelbert.'

'I'm sorry, Tina, the what?'

'The Engelbert. You know, the singer? Engelbert Humperdinck? The hump.'

'Oh, I see,' I smile. I'm not up to speed with rhyming slang. 'Yes, it doesn't take much to rattle his cage, does it?'

She nods approvingly, does a little shiver, then looks up at the dark skies, zipping her onesie up to her neck. 'Looks like rain,' she groans. 'Do you want to come in and wait? I've just put the kettle on.'

'Nah, it's OK. But thanks, Tina. I'll just let myself in.' I jiggle the keys at her. 'I can wait for him inside.'

Satisfied, she smiles happily then closes the door behind her.

It's dark and still inside the house, but I daren't put the lights on. I don't want Harry to think they've been burgled. I'll just sit here quietly by the window, then I can open the door when I see him coming.

I look at the classic-style mahogany clock on the pine mantelpiece, which is lined with knick-knacks – icons, vases, a Virgin Mary tea light holder, and photos of the entire clan. I watch steadily as the long hand ticks away like a pulse. Every minute seems like an hour. I pull my phone out of my handbag and load my Facebook app. I know it's got me into a lot of trouble recently but I still love it. It's like a newspaper, only it's about people I know, people I care about.

As I scroll through my timeline I hear a babble of voices, followed immediately by the squeaking sound of the front gate. I look up. Shit. It's Harry with Mas in tow. Shit. Fuck!

I don't want to see Mas. I've got to get out of here. Fast. I dash into the kitchen and try the back door. Damn. It's locked. Of course it is, what was I thinking? I push my fingers through my hair manically and sprint back into the hall. I think I'm going to wee myself. There's a rattle at the door, a rumble of male voices. The key is in the lock. Oh bloody hell! In a moment of sheer madness I open the under stairs cupboard door. Unlike ours, which is heaving with rubbish, it's neat and tidy with only a few bottles of Metaxa brandy and Thisbe wine in the far corner. A watering can, a mop, and a broom sit in the centre. I grab the huge watering can; scramble inside, steering the broom handle out of the way and closing the door behind me.

I sit in silence, watering can on my lap, neck bent against the electric meter, broomstick pressing on my head as my eyes slowly adjust to the darkness. God knows how I'm going to get out of here. I hope they're planning on going upstairs or to the pub sometime soon.

The lights flick on, followed by heavy footsteps in the hallway.

'I can't believe it, man.' Mas' voice is heavy, angry. 'She's only gone and changed the fucking locks.' There's a kerfuffle of bags hitting the floor, the door closing, feet shuffling, the zing of a jacket being unzipped. 'I don't believe it,' he cries to the swish of plastic bags unfurling. 'She's just chucked all my stuff in bloody bin bags. Fuck, fuck, fuck!'

The lights go on in the lounge. I peer through the gap in the door at the two figures by the door. Harry walks in first, going straight for the sofa right in front of me. Result. I'll be able to see everything from here. I press my eye closer to the gap to get a clearer view, the electric meter clicking away in my left ear like a time bomb. Unlike our under stairs door, this one has about a half inch gap between the frame, which is very handy given the circumstances.

Mas swishes out of his leather jacket, tosses it onto the cushions, then collapses onto the sofa next to Harry with a loud sigh. I've got a fairly good view of both of them now and, fortunately, I've got excellent hearing. When I was a little girl, Dad used to tell me they'd put a bionic device in my ear when I was born, and I believed him for months, thinking I had a superpower. Until Mum put me right.

Harry slips off his brown tweed jacket. He looks tired, despondent. 'Well, what did you expect?' he asks with a long sigh. Mas doesn't answer.

Harry leans back on the sofa, tipping his head onto the headrest. 'Don't tell the girls, you said, not after what happened last time.' I furrow my brows. Last time? Has Mas done this before? 'One whiff of this and Caroline will put a stop to it all. Get the wrong idea, you said.' He pauses, looks at him. 'No, let's do this good deed together. Us brothers. Help out a young, defenceless girl who's in trouble.' Mas stares ahead silently. 'I told you to tell Caroline about Isabella and Marc from the beginning. I said she'd understand. But no, you knew best as always.'

'Yeah.' Mas squeezes his top lip between his fingers. 'OK, so I messed up. Shoot me.' He glances at Harry. 'Oh, quit with the evil looks, will you? It doesn't suit you.' Mas leans forward, his arms resting on his knees, legs wide apart. 'I didn't mean for this to happen, you know. It wasn't part of the plan.'

'So, you just fell into bed with her?' Harry says accusingly. Mas rubs his stubbly chin, wordless. 'I don't know how I let you talk me into this,' Harry goes on. 'Have you any idea what trouble you've caused?' Mas anxiously combs his hand through his hair. I've never seen him lost for words. Harry presses back his index finger. 'Firstly, you've made me lie to Caroline, whom I care for dearly, by the way. I don't know how I'm ever going to be able to face her again.' He pushes back another finger. 'My relationship with Emma is in tatters because of you. Do you know how hard it was for me to take the blame for that hotel receipt Marc fucking Poirot discovered? And for what? So you could have a quick shag in a hotel?' He shakes his head. 'I shouldn't have let you blackmail me.' Blackmail? I furrow my brow. 'I should've come clean earlier. Told Emma the truth.'

'Blackmail?' Mas says incredulously. 'That's a bit harsh, isn't it?'

'Harsh?' Harry repeats indignantly. 'You said you wanted your fifty grand back, remember? Threatened to sack Emma and me from the restaurant if I didn't keep my trap shut? You had me by the balls, man. We'd have lost our home. Our lives would have been in shreds. I had no choice but to go along with your deceit.'

'Yeah, well, I was desperate, wasn't I? I couldn't risk Caroline and the kids finding out.'

Harry shakes his head. 'You do know that Isabella is thinking of taking Marc back, don't you? Gah, those two are just as bad as each other.' He throws his hands up. 'What a bloody mess.'

Mas pinches the bridge of his nose. 'Well, maybe it's for the best. It's not as if he beats her up, is it? He's just a bit possessive.' I can't believe he's actually said that. That's how these bullies start. I swallow hard, watching him closely through the gap. He rubs his lips, staring into the distance. 'And besides, she can give as good as she gets.' So, Marc was right about her being quite fiery, then. 'Look, it was just a bit of fun, that's all. I'd never have left my wife and kids for her, for fuck's sake. She knew that from the start.'

'Well, I hope you're going to try to get Caroline back. You're mad if you lose her. She's by far the best thing that's ever happened to you.' I've never seen Harry this mad at Mas.

'Yeah, whatever,' Mas says, biting on a fingernail. 'Right now she doesn't want to hear my voice, let alone have me back. What I can't understand is how the hell she found out we were at the hotel in the first place.' He rubs the back of his neck. 'She must've followed me there. She must've been suspicious for weeks.' He twists his body towards Harry. 'Are you sure you didn't tell Emma about Isabella and me?'

'Of course I didn't,' Harry retorts. 'You said it was just a few times, remember. How was I to know you were screwing her in a hotel room on a regular basis?'

Mas drops his head into his hands and covers his ears as if to ward off Harry's words.

'It was a moment of weakness. She's so bloody gorgeous.' He looks up at Harry. 'And what a body.' Silence. 'What was I supposed to do? A young, sexy woman, half my age, throws herself at me.' Goodness, is that the best he can do? Caroline won't be swayed by that line, for sure. 'And anyway,' he goes on, 'it was great for our marriage. An aphrodisiac, you know. That Isabella ...' He nudges Harry's arm and lets out a low whistle. 'Just thinking about her gave me a – '

Too much information, too much information! I cover my ears. Lalalalalalala.

'What are you talking about?' Harry's voice belts through the room. 'Caroline is a beautiful woman.'

'Yeah, I know, I know.' Mas rakes a hand through his greasy, messy hair. 'It's just that she's let herself go a bit, hasn't she?'

Harry gets to his feet. 'I don't want to hear it.' He walks out of sight, returning moments later with a bottle of Grey Goose vodka and two tumblers. 'Dad called this morning,

270

said the valuation on the land is six-hundred grand. He's leaving it to us in his will – fifty-fifty.' They knock back their drinks in quick synchronisation. Harry unscrews the bottle and re-fills their empty tumblers. 'Have you got that number of that Wills and Probate solicitor? I need to sort out my share of the assets.'

Mas reaches into his inside pocket and pulls out a bundle of cards. 'I suppose you'll want Demi and Andreas' full names. Have you got a pen handy? I'll …'

'No,' Harry cuts in. 'I'm leaving it all to Emma.' As I jerk back in haste I sit on something long and hard. I let out a tiny shriek in surprise, and whatever I sat on bounces against the back wall of the cupboard, hitting the back of my legs as it falls.

'What was that?' Harry asks.

Shit. I keep completely still. My heart in my mouth.

'What was that?'

'Shhh. That noise. It sounded like a knock.'

'Must be a bit of house movement, happens at ours sometimes when it's all quiet.'

'Yeah, probably,' Harry says carefully, looking into the hallway. I slowly reach down and retrieve the item. I don't think I've ever been so happy to see a torch. I switch it on and my tiny shelter is dimly lit with a ray of soft, orange light.

'Anyway, as I was saying,' Harry continues. I let out a little sigh of relief then feel something crawling on my hand. 'I need to draw up a will to make sure Emma is secure.' Oh bloody hell, it's a spider. I'm no good with creepy-crawlies. Harry always captures them then sets them free in the garden for me.

'What?' Mas huffs. 'After what that ginger bitch did to you?' The bastard. I knew he'd badmouth me to Harry. I shake the spider off my hand furiously.

'Don't you dare speak about her like that,' Harry bellows. I hug the watering can, smiling. You tell him, Harry. 'Because if that's how you feel you can …'

'OK, OK, keep your hair on.' There's a brief silence and then, 'Ginger minge did fuck Issy's husband behind your back, though. I'd never put up with that.' Double standards; why am I not surprised?

'Emma has done nothing wrong,' Harry says through gritted teeth. 'Marc rang me the next day, explained everything. Nothing happened between them.' Phew, I *am* glad to hear that. I bite my bottom lip, listening intently.

'If you say so.' I hate that patronising turn of phrase. It gives me the creeps, like fingernails scratching a chalkboard.

'And even if she had, I wouldn't have blamed her, not after the way I've been treating her lately.'

'What, because of the sex?' Ah, so he confided in Mas about our sex life. This should be interesting. I press my eye closer to the gap.

'No, it's not just about the bloody sex, for crying out loud. Try thinking with your brain for once instead of your dick. Did you know that Isabella told Marc about my problem?' Mas shakes his head. 'I thought I could trust her. She really has let me down.' Problem? What problem?

'That's women for you, can't keep their mouths shut,' Mas complains.

Harry sighs loudly, leaning back into his seat, out of view. 'Isabella said she had to tell him. Had to convince Marc that she and I weren't having an affair.'

'Did he believe her?'

'After finding the hotel receipt? What do you think?' He downs the rest of his drink then refills both glasses. I press my legs together. I'm getting cramp in my right calf. And I need a wee. When are they going to leave? 'I don't know if she'll ever forgive me,' Harry whispers.

'Forgive *you*?' Mas sounds surprised. What a complete twat.

'Yes Mas, *me*.' Harry taps his chest with his fingers. 'I'm the one who's been a miserable sod for weeks. I'm the one who's been feeding her lie after lie about you, Isabella, Caroline.'

Mas shakes his head. 'Your funeral. No pun intended. Oh, come on man, lighten up. What's wrong with you?' He rubs the back of Harry's neck, playful but hard. Harry shrugs him off.

'I'm quitting the restaurant.'

There's a bolt of silence. 'What?' Mas' voice echoes through the room. Tina will be banging on the walls before too long. He's on the edge of his seat. I can see the back of his big, square head.

'Look, I've paid you back some of what I owe you.' Ah, so that's why we're in mortgage arrears. Brilliant. 'I'll give you the rest once I've spoken to Emma and we've sorted something out.'

'No, man, come on. You don't have to do that. I …'

'Look,' Harry cuts across him. 'You're my brother and I love you but I can't work with you anymore. I need to sort my life out. See if Emma will have me back.' I close my eyes, feeling the warmth of the torch on my face. I want to leap out of the cupboard and run into his arms. 'Spend whatever time we have left together.' I open my eyes wide and position my eye against the gap. What's that supposed to mean?

Mas lays a protective hand on Harry's back. 'When do you go for the scan?' What scan? Has he had a cycling injury again? I draw the watering can close to my chest. My hand tightens around the rubber torch.

'Monday.' Harry knocks back his drink. 'I'm just a bit worried, you know, 'cos of Dad.' He gives a little depleted laugh. Dad? What does he mean? My heart is thundering against the watering can. I want to scream.

'Is the nut one hereditary?'

'Yeah, the testicular type is.'

'So? It doesn't mean you've got cancer, too,' Mas says reassuringly. At the sound of cancer I let out an involuntary little yelp.

'Did you hear that?' Harry asks, moving to the edge of his seat. 'It sounded like a rat.'

'Hear what?' They both look round. 'Are you sure you don't need a hearing test as well?' Mas cackles, taking a gulp of vodka.

Tears flood my eyes. I press my lips together, stifling a scream that has ballooned inside my mouth.

'There it is again.' Harry jerks forward, positioning his ear towards the door.

'It's probably just cats outside.' Mas whirls the vodka in his glass, knocks back the last dregs and winces. 'Where're you going?'

He's walking towards the under stairs cupboard. I gulp. Oh God! Oh no! The door opens. I look up at him, eyes full of terror, watering can in lap, torch shining in my face.

He looks at me in horror. 'Emma! What the hell are you doing?'

Chapter Twenty-Eight

I knock back the shot of vodka in one. Even though I had several glasses of wine at home with Caroline, Harry's news sobered me up within seconds.

Harry sweeps my hair tenderly off my face. 'Are you OK?' I nod as I put the glass down onto the coffee table in front of me, hand shaking, giving Mas an indiscreet glare. He stares back at me through cold, hard eyes. Then for a moment I imagine getting to my feet, picking up the bottle of Grey Goose, strutting over to where he's sitting on the armchair opposite us and pouring the entire contents of it all over his head. 'How did you get in, Emma?' Harry's voice. 'How did you get here?' He glances at the window. 'I didn't see our car outside.'

'I got a taxi,' I sniff. 'I had a few drinks with ...' I falter, wiping my clammy hands on my jeans. 'Ola popped round to see me and we opened a bottle of wine.' I can feel Mas' eyes on me, scrutinising me, waiting for me to slip up. But I'm one step ahead of him. 'I went round to see Caroline earlier today and got the spare keys off her.'

At the mention of Caroline's name, Mas sits bolt upright, legs apart, hands gripping his knees firmly. With his eyes closed, he stretches his neck from side to side until it clicks, takes a long, deep breath, then fixes me with a hard stare. 'Did she tell you what happened?' His voice is tight, angry. I nod. 'Don't you go badmouthing me to her, Emma,' he says, pointing his finger at me. 'I love my wife. It was one stupid mistake. I'm going to do everything I can to make things right. She'll come round in the end, she always does.'

This man is so full of himself it turns my stomach. I glower at him. 'There's nothing I can say that'll make her loathe you more than she already does.' Did I just say that out loud?

'What did she say?' he demands. 'She can't kick me out of my own fucking house. I've got rights.'

I don't answer. Instead I look at Harry, worriedly. I care about Caroline deeply, but right now my priorities are with Harry. What's wrong with him? What's happening?

'Harry …' I begin.

'I asked you a question,' Mas spits, standing up and walking towards me furiously.

Harry gets to his feet, his arm outstretched. 'Back off, Mas,' he warns. 'Sort out your own damned mess and leave my wi …' The word dies on his lips and my heart cracks a little more.

'Your what?' Mas sneers, curling his lip in disdain, hands loosely on his hips. 'She won't even marry you.' He leans forward, his face close enough for me to smell the tobacco on his breath. 'Reckons she's too good for the Georgiades family, does she? King by name, king by nature.' Harry sits back down heavily, one arm around me protectively, the other against Mas' chest.

'No,' I protest, putting a hand out, palm up. 'That's not how it is. Trust me, I …'

'Trust you?' He snorts, taking a step back. 'After what you did to my brother with that arsehole? After you broke into our house and sat there,' he points at the cupboard, 'spying on us? I don't think so.' He bends down. 'I'd rather choke on my vomit than trust you,' he whispers, face almost touching mine. I wince, jerking my head to one side.

'That's enough.' Harry leaps to his feet again, fists clenched by his side. 'Emma is as good a wife to me as any woman could be. We don't need a piece of paper to prove anything. Just get out of my sight, Mas, before I do something I might regret.' Mas opens his mouth to speak. 'Now!' Harry roars.

'Why should I go? This is my home, too! Tell that bitch to get out.'

Harry pushes his chest towards Mas. 'Don't make me choose, Mas.'

They glare at each other for a few moments.

'Pffft,' Mas huffs, face deadpan. He sweeps his hair back and gives me a daggered look. 'I'm going out for some air.' He snatches his jacket from behind me angrily, catching wisps of my hair. 'Leave you two love birds to make up.'

As the front door slams I turn to Harry urgently. 'Harry,' I cup my hand over his cheek. 'What's happening? What's wrong with you?'

Harry stares down at his feet and my hand drops heavily into my lap. 'I found a lump,' he says quietly. 'Down there.'

'A lump?' I repeat, my voice barely audible.

'Yes, a lump. I'm not sure what it is yet. It might be nothing. But …'

'But it might be cancer? Is that what you're saying?'

He nods. 'Maybe. I don't know.' He takes a deep, heartfelt breath.

A tear spills from my eye and runs down my cheek. I wipe it away with my fingers. 'How long have you had it?'

'A few weeks.'

'*Weeks*?' I say, almost leaping out of my seat. 'How many?'

'I can't remember exactly … three, maybe four.'

I start calculating quickly. That was about the time I initiated sex in the kitchen, when he pushed me away, said he was on call. 'And you're only getting it checked out now?' I cry in horror. 'God, Harry, you're a nurse. You work in a flipping hospital.'

'So?' He closes his eyes, pinching the bridge of his nose. 'It doesn't mean I'm not frightened, Emma.'

We sit in silence for a few moments listening to the swishing traffic outside, the muffled sound of Tina's TV through the walls, the clank of a car door. I can't believe what Harry's saying. Surely this is a dream?

'When I first found it I thought it was nothing. That it'd just go away, then when it didn't I …' He pauses, moves to the edge of his seat, arms on knees, fingers entwined. 'By the time I got an appointment with Dr Shantikumar a couple of weeks had passed. Then I had to wait two weeks for a referral. Just because I work for the NHS doesn't mean I can jump the queue, you know. I've got to wait my turn.'

I take a deep breath in. 'Is that why we haven't been having sex? Why you've been rejecting me? Pushing me away?'

'Partly, yes, although I have been feeling exhausted these last few months, which isn't a good sign.' He draws his lips in and rubs his chin. 'Look, I didn't want to frighten you. I thought I could handle it. I thought …' He presses his hands together, staring at his black trainers.

'I had a right to know, Harry. What were you thinking? You should have told me.' I choke on my words as tears build up in my throat. 'Instead you chose to tell Isabella, Mas …' Fresh tears spill from my eyes. I wipe them quickly away on my grey marl sweatshirt.

'I almost told you.' He glances at me briefly. 'Twice, in fact. Remember the night when Alistair had the heart attack?' I nod, picturing that tragic scene in my mind's eye. Harry's bike on the pavement, the ambulance, lights flashing, sirens blaring, traffic heaving. 'But when I saw how hysterical you were, when you thought it was me lying on that stretcher, I lost my nerve.'

'Oh, Harry.' I lay a hand on his shoulder and he gives it a fleeting look.

'Then on the day of Alistair's funeral, before Marc turned up, when I said I was going out for a bottle of wine? I was going to tell you about it then. I'd stopped panicking by then, had it all worked out in my mind.'

My mind rewinds. We've just got back from the funeral. I'm on the sofa reading a text from Marc. Harry is telling me we need to talk about us, my dad...

'Yes,' I say in a muffled voice. 'I remember.' My eyes feel sore. I wipe my snotty nose on my sleeve. Harry reaches behind me and plucks a few tissues from the box on the sideboard, then starts dabbing my face softly.

'But Marc put a stop to all that,' he says gently.

I take the tissue from his hand and blow my nose. 'It's OK.' I dab my eyes. I've got to stop all this crying. I need to stay strong, focused. 'What's done is done. Let's concentrate on now.' I scrunch the sodden tissue and push it into the pocket of my jeans. 'A lump doesn't mean cancer. It could be anything. But whatever it is, we'll deal with it. Together. Right?'

He nods, taking a lungful of air, his eyes full of hope.

'When are you having the scan done?'

'I'm seeing the specialist on Monday morning. I'll be having the ultrasound on the same day.'

'And when will you get the results?'

'Right away.'

'OK,' I say, shoulders back, feeling like Joan of Arc at the stake. 'I'm coming with you.'

279

The doors slide open and Harry and I step inside the humid, crowded box. Then, just as the doors are about to close, a thirty-something couple with a toddler sucking on a Slush Puppie rush inside, wheeling their designer pram in front of them. Harry and I take a few steps back to accommodate the bustling trio.

As the couple shuffle around to make room for the closing doors, the man – tall, dark, with glasses – opens a packet of Worcester sauce crisps and shoves several into his mouth, filling the humid air with a nauseating stench. I squeeze Harry's hand reassuringly and he smiles.

'Stand there, sweetie,' the mother says to the child, her long, dark curls covering most of her face.

'But Daddy, where are *my* crisps?' the boy asks as the lift starts ascending. The man mumbles something to his son then shoves several more crisps into his mouth, crunching in my ears. Loudly. Harry and I exchange glances in the mirror opposite. I wonder what he's thinking. If he's frightened, anxious? He always puts on such a brave face. I wish I could aspirate his fear and flush it away.

'You OK?' he asks. I nod. Typical Harry, always putting others before himself. 'This is us,' Harry says as the doors slide open.

We're in the waiting area of Clinic 4b. I place my hand over Harry's reassuringly, 'Don't worry,' I say softly. He nods, squeezing my hand, and I smile. 'It's all going to be fine, you'll see.' I'm not sure who I'm trying to convince, him or me.

I stare around idly at the waiting area. I'm not entirely sure how I got through the weekend, to be honest. Harry put me in a taxi and sent me home on Friday night, saying he'd better stay put for the weekend, make sure Mas was OK, and that I should get back to Caroline.

Saturday and Sunday were a bit of a blur. Caroline ended up ringing Mas, mainly because she was concerned about Harry and wanted to make sure he wasn't stressing him out. I kept in contact with Harry throughout with texts and phone calls, and it was his insistence that made me call Mum to find out why she'd lied to me about my real father.

As expected, Mum was furious to begin with, cursing David for going back on his word, forcing me to give her his number so that she could call him and give him a piece of her mind.

'I don't care if he's ill, Emma,' she screamed down the phone. 'This is unforgivable. He should've consulted me first.'

After a few tearful, angry exchanges she told me the whole story. How she'd had a holiday fling with a lad in Poole. See, I knew my dad loved the ocean. That she didn't know she was pregnant until she'd missed three periods and by then it was too late. Charming.

'We didn't have the internet in those days, Emma. I couldn't find him. And to be honest I didn't even bother to look. I met your father ...' she faltered, 'David ... shortly after and we got married. And that was the end of that. You were his daughter. No one knew otherwise.'

'But Mum ...' I protested. 'You should've told me. Didn't you ever think that I had a right to know?'

'I'm sorry, Emma.' Her voice was quiet, remorseful, not like Mum at all. 'I meant to, believe me, I did. Once or twice I came very close to it but lost my nerve. Then as the years went on, the harder it became. I was only a young thing myself. In those days things were different, people were more judgemental. I didn't want them pointing at you,

281

bullying you, treating you differently. I did my best for you, didn't I? You're my world, you know that.'

She was right. I couldn't have asked for a better, more loving mother and, given the circumstances, I could understand her plight. I wanted to know more about my real father but I was too upset about Harry to go into details over the phone. So we ended the call agreeing to meet up to discuss it all properly once everything with Harry was sorted. However, she did give me a name. James Sumner.

I look at the clock above the nurses' station. 'What time is your appointment again?'

'Ten-thirty,' Harry sighs. I know he's nervous. And who could blame him? 'We're fifteen minutes early.' I nod, telling him that it's better to be early than late, as a message buzzes through on my iPhone. It's Caroline asking if we're OK; how it's all going.

I smile as I punch in my reply.

Just arrived. Don't worry. Harry will triumph!

I've got to stay strong and positive, for Harry's sake.

I slip my phone back into my handbag, then stare at the orange and green vinyl floor, and can't help but eavesdrop on the conversation between the two young girls in the seats in front of us.

'She was with Jason, wasn't she?' one of the girls asks, scratching her face with a long, decorative black and white fingernail.

'Yeah, but she dumped him,' the other girl replies, mobile phone in hand. 'And now she wants him back, but he's married with two kids.'

'Emma,' Harry whispers as a nurse walks past holding a cup of coffee. 'Once this is all over, whatever the outcome ...' he pauses, a phone goes off in the background, the sound of a smartphone game chimes. 'I think we should take a holiday. I know we're broke but we can …' I cover his lips with my hand to silence him.

I swallow hard. I've been rehearsing this all weekend in front of a mirror. It isn't going to be easy but I've got to say it, tell him exactly how I feel. There's no point in lying, not anymore. This last week has shaken me, put everything into perspective. 'Harry,' I begin, then a large lady appears in a pink tracksuit, hair piled on top of her head. She gestures at a vacant seat in the corner. Harry stands up and I swing my legs round, making room for her to pass.

'Yes, you were saying?' Harry asks, once the lady has sat down with a copy of *Heat*.

'I was going to say …' The door opens and a doctor appears holding a brown file. Tall, slim, in her mid-forties. I wonder if this is Harry's consultant. I'm not sure he'll be happy with it being a woman. As she turns her head I notice that her light brown hair is pulled back off her tanned face and secured with a green scrunchie, which I find quite odd given that the rest of her attire is very business-like.

'Mrs Campbell?' she calls out. The lady with the tracksuit in the adjacent seat stands up. She smiles and thanks me as I swing my legs to the side to let her pass. The doctor smiles at her, holding the door open as Mrs Campbell pads in.

Harry lets out a loud sigh. 'I thought that was me.' He pauses. 'Anyway, go on.'

I'm losing my nerve. Maybe I should wait until after the ultrasound. I don't want to stress him out any more than he already is. I bite the inside of my lip as I focus on a tear in the green chair in front of me, the interior foam protruding from the split like tanned lips.

I look at the clock again. It's almost ten-thirty. I glance around at the busy clinic cluttered with machines, weighing scales, oxygen tanks, desks, chairs. My heart is picking up speed. I can't bear it. I've got to tell him now. He has a right to know. I've been plagued by these thoughts all weekend. I can't go on living a lie.

'Look, these last two weeks, well, they've made me think,' I hear myself saying. 'So much has happened, things have just ...' I scratch my forehead nervously. 'Well, they've changed, haven't they? *I've* changed.' Harry is looking at me carefully, hand pressed against his lips. 'What I mean is, life is so short ...' I waver. I'm not making a very good job of this. Maybe now is not the time. Oh, bloody hell.

'What is it, Emma? You've gone pale.' Harry takes my hand. 'Are you OK? Shall we go out for some air?'

'No, no, I'm fine,' I insist, squeezing his hand. 'Look, I want to tell you something and I want you to promise me you'll stay calm.'

Harry frowns at me. 'Go on.' I focus on a small cut on his chin, a shaving abrasion. I imagine how anxious he must've been this morning.

'Harry,' I gulp. 'I love you with every part of me and I probably always will ...'

'But ...' he goads, eyes full of apprehension.

'Well, you know I said that I wanted things to just go back to how they were before?' I take a deep breath.

'Yes, and I told you that's what I want too.' His eyes search mine anxiously, hand curled gently around my wrist. 'I love you, Emma, more than ever.' The two girls in front of us have stopped talking.

'The thing is ...' I take another deep breath, closing my eyes.

'What is it, Emma?' One of the girls looks round at me then turns back quickly, whispering something to her friend. 'Just tell me, will you? You're scaring me.'

'Harry, I've thought this through and I can't be your girlfriend ... not anymore, not after everything that's happened.'

He looks at me, mortified. 'What? You're dumping me?'

'Oh God, no! Ohhwah, this isn't coming out right.' I shake my hands in front of me as if drying varnished nails. 'What I mean is ... Harry, will you marry me?' My eyes search his. He's staring at me, wordless, jaw slightly ajar. The two girls have now twisted around in their seats and are blatantly staring at us, eyes wide, mouths agape. We all fall silent and I'm suddenly aware of fingers tapping away on a keyboard, a phone ringing, papers shuffling. 'Well?' I quiver, swallowing hard. 'Say something.'

'Mr Georgiades?' a male voice calls out.

Chapter Twenty-Nine

Something old, something new, something borrowed, something blue.

'Where do you want it, love?'

'Just bring it through here, please.' I hover over the two burly removal men. 'Be careful,' I cry as they twist the piece of furniture and back into the lounge. 'We've only just decorated.' The last thing I want is marks and scratches. House buyers notice these things when they're viewing, don't they?

'Here OK, love?' the older man asks, face red, cap pushed back on his sweaty head. Must be a father and son outfit.

I'm about to answer when Harry charges down the stairs and springs into the lounge, cleanly shaved, hair gelled back and smelling gorgeous. 'Come on, Emma, are you ready?' He stops dead in his tracks. 'I thought I heard voices.' He twiddles with his left cufflink. 'What's all this?'

'Delivery from next door, mate.' The man and his young assistant bend down to release the heavy sideboard, the elder of the two revealing a rather unsightly builder's bum. I always imagine pushing a coin into that gap whenever I pass a builder on the street.

'OK ...' Harry looks at me, confused, as he straightens his sleeve.

'It's Alistair's sideboard. I always loved it.' I look at him imploringly. 'He left it to me in his will.' I flap the

brown padded envelope in my hand. 'The keys are in here.'
Something old.

The two men dust themselves down. I think they're waiting for a tip but we can barely afford to feed ourselves these days, let alone offer gratuities.

Our beloved house went up for sale last week. We're looking for something smaller, more affordable. Despite a lot of begging from Mas, Harry stuck to his guns and quit his job at the restaurant. We're going to pay Mas back what we owe him as soon as the house is sold, and be out of his clutches for good. Thankfully, the new clients I took on recently paid off and we're out of arrears but we're still up to our necks in it.

But I don't care about money. I had the best news I could ever have wished for seven weeks ago. The ultrasound showed that Harry's growth was benign. He had it drained there and then. I can't begin to tell you how ecstatic we were when we heard the news. It felt as if we were given a new lease of life. Another chance. A new beginning. Once we were outside the hospital I collapsed into a heap by the revolving doors and cried and cried while Harry tried to hold me up. A few people stopped and asked Harry if I was OK, offered their commiserations. But they were tears of joy. I felt euphoric. I've never known anything like it.

Harry searches inside his trouser pocket and pulls out a couple of coins, handing them to the younger man as a tip. 'Sorry, mate. It's all the change I've got.' I smile sadly. That man of mine is generous to a fault.

'S'alright,' the boy mumbles, slipping the coins into the pocket of his red checked shirt as he pads behind his dad to the front door. I suppose they're used to paper tips these days.

Harry stands in front of the marble oak sideboard, hands in pockets. 'It is lovely, Em, but you do know we'll never be able to fit it into a one-bedroom flat, don't you?' He creases his nose at me sadly.

I go over to him, slip my arm under his jacket, and wrap it around his trim waist. 'No matter.' I lean into him and he slings his arm around my shoulders. 'We've got each other, that's all that matters now.' I gaze around me. 'I don't care about all this.' I stare out of the patio doors into the garden. I managed to do a lot of work on it this summer. It's still looking quite gorgeous, despite it being autumn. The white, yellow, and purple hedge shrubs, which I planted to secure the fence, are still going strong. And my orange dahlias, sternbergias, and snowdrops are all in full bloom. I take a deep breath as I gaze at the thick green leaves of my ice cream tulips adjacent to the plum tree. They've taken nicely but I won't get to see them blossom because they only flower in mid-late spring. I was so looking forward to seeing the delicate white flower nestling within the dark pink petals.

Harry pulls me closer, tucking my head under his chin. 'I promise you,' he sighs, stroking my hair, as if he could read my mind, feel my disappointment, 'I'll do everything I can to get us a house again, one with a massive two-hundred foot garden.' He stretches his arm out for effect. 'You can have that greenhouse you've always wanted, a garden study room. You know, like the one we saw on that house programme last week.'

'We could have a gym too,' I muse, 'if it's big enough. Or get a house with a basement and renovate that.'

'Yeah.' Harry's brown eyes sparkle with anticipation. 'And a double garage and drive for our fleet of cars.' We both giggle. We both know that's never going to happen. 'You've got to dream, don't you?'

I walk towards the sideboard. 'We could sell it.' I stroke the smooth surface. 'It might be worth a few quid, you know.'

'Might be.' He nods, hands loosely on hips. 'What time did Caroline say she'd be here?'

'Two o'clock. What time is it now?'

He glances at his watch. 'Ten to. We'd better get a wiggle on. She'll be here soon.' He starts knotting his black bow tie in front of the mirror above the fireplace.

'Mas isn't coming here, is he?' I smooth down my dress, then grab my earrings from the coffee table. They're ivory rose studs. Harry bought them for me as a wedding gift from one of his colleagues whose daughter has just started up a jewellery making business. They're only costume, but they're handmade and look stunning. *Something new.*

'You did make sure he'd meet us at the registry office, didn't you? I don't want him turning up unexpectedly while she's here with that Richard Adams bloke.'

Richard Adams is a hot Channel 4 TV producer. He headhunted Caroline while she was doing one of her psychic demonstrations at the local church hall a few weeks ago. She started off with a handful of people but when word got around of how good she was, she had them queuing around the corner. Richard Adams was so taken by her ambiance that he offered her a guest appearance on a celebrity psychic's show with the possibility of her own show in the future. She *is* gifted, there's no doubting that, but I think he secretly fancies her, too.

'Don't worry.' Harry straightens his tie. 'Mas will be meeting us there with Mum and Dad. But he won't be happy seeing Caroline with another bloke. You know that, don't you?'

I secure my left earring, then step into my new stiletto heels, leaning on the sofa for support. I don't know why I let Ola talk me into buying these five inch heels. I don't know how the hell I'm going to get through the next half hour in them, let alone the entire day. 'Yes well, we did say she could bring a friend, and I hope Mas doesn't get drunk and kick off.'

Harry raises his eyebrows at me in the mirror and I shake my head at him knowingly.

Mas went to pieces when Caroline filed for divorce. His business is going down the pan, his kids aren't talking to him, and even Harry won't work with him. Still, at least he's got his parents. They've been a tower of strength for him.

Caroline refused point blank to give Mas another chance. On a night out with the girls, a week after their bust-up, she confessed to me, Ola, and Vicky that this wasn't the first time Mas had cheated on her. That she'd forgiven him twice before when the children were little, but enough was enough – their marriage was dead.

'Sometimes you can change things,' she told us over a bottle of Prosecco at Café Martinez in Highgate. 'But sometimes you can't, because it is what it is and you are what you are. And he's a philandering little shit. Anyway, we've agreed to sell the house, and I want my half of the business too, otherwise Customs and Excise might get an anonymous tip off.'

As annoying as Mas is, and trust me he can try the patience of a saint, I do feel a bit sorry for him. The last I heard was that Isabella and Marc had moved to Reading and were trying to make a go of things, a fresh start, so it was all in vain. I think that Mas is looking forward to seeing Caroline today, hoping that he might get a chance to talk to her, put things right. But that's not going to happen.

When Caroline makes up her mind, that's it, there's no changing it.

Car doors clank in the background. Harry yanks back the net curtains and lets out a low whistle. 'They're here.'

'I hope she's not upstaging the bride,' I say, taking a peek over his shoulder.

Caroline promised me she'd lose two stone when I asked her if she'd give me away six weeks ago. And she's stuck to her word. Ola devised an exercise programme and healthy eating plan for her and the pounds melted away. I gaze at her dotingly. She looks slim and elegant in a long, crimson dress. 'Ooooh, I think she has,' I enthuse as I secure the falling strap on my long, cream silk dress, a loan from Ola. I didn't have anything in cream or white, and couldn't afford to splash out on a new dress at such short notice. *Something borrowed.*

'She'll freeze her arse off in that,' Harry moans. Men have no concept of women's fashion at all. 'I think someone should remind her that it's the 9th of November, not August.'

'She'll be alright. Look, she's got that lovely silk shawl, that'll keep her warm.' I wave a hand. 'And once she's got a few drinks inside her ...'

Harry accepted my marriage proposal seven weeks ago to the jeer of the two girls in the waiting area of Clinic 4b. They even stood up and gave me a high-five before reaching over and giving us both bear hugs.

I've been flapping about like a lunatic ever since, trying to get everything organised quickly. Thankfully, I've had my troop of lovely girls at hand. Ola and Caroline took control of all the catering. They were both here until the early hours of the morning setting everything up. Tessa and Demi were in charge of the decorations. Our lounge looks like something out of a fairy tale. Thick pale pink and white ribbons adorn the fireplace and door frames. Heart-shaped fairy lights line the windowsills and the painting above the fireplace. Our table is covered in a crisp white table cloth and scattered with heart confetti. A dozen three-tier cake stands, which will be filled with homemade finger food on our return, sit beautifully in the centre, framed by crystal champagne flutes and tumblers, gleaming in the autumn sunshine. Tall vases of white calla lilies, silver plated cutlery, and gold coloured plates complete the setting. Perfect.

Thankfully, Richard Adams was kind enough to offer his brand new navy Audi A8 as transportation. *Something blue*.

So, we're practically all set. The only people who will be missing are Mum and Mike.

Mum called David straight after talking to me that Saturday and they had the fallout from hell. Tessa called me in floods of tears afterwards. In fact, I'm sure that's what made baby Emma (I know, so sweet of her) arrive two weeks early. I was beyond thrilled. Harry and I can't wait to be her godparents.

When I told Mum I'd be inviting David to our wedding, she refused point blank to come.

'It's me or him, Emma,' she said crossly, I could almost feel her squeezing the phone in protest. 'You choose. And just remember, I'm your mother, the one who's always been there for you through thick and thin. Who carried you for nine months and gave birth to you in agony.'

But how could I choose? I just invited them both.

Caroline wraps her cold arms around me and we hug excitedly as Harry and Richard exchange alpha male handshakes.

'Doesn't she look absolutely gorgeous?' Caroline squeals, doing a little jumpy dance on the spot.

'She certainly does.' Richard, dressed in a swanky three-piece, pale blue shirt, and a gold tie, reaches over and gives me a light peck on the cheek, his designer auburn stubble tickling my face. I don't miss his hand on the small of Caroline's back. I guess they're officially official!

'All set?' Harry rubs his hands excitedly. I gaze at him adoringly. He looks like he's just stepped out of a James Bond movie in that black tuxedo. I could quite easily tear all his clothes off right now and have my wicked way with him. And yes, sex has been explosive since he got the all clear. We've more than made up for it, I can assure you.

'Andreas and Demi are meeting us there, right?' I ask. Andreas is going to be Harry's best man. I stood my ground when he suggested asking Mas.

'Yes, they should be on their way now. Demi was just finishing her make-up when I left.' Caroline smiles at Richard as he secures her cream shawl, which has slid off her right shoulder. 'Will Ola be coming here first, Em?' Ola is going to be my maid of honour. I was going to ask Tessa, but Ola was so excited when I told her Harry and I were finally tying the knot I just felt it was the right thing to do, especially as I didn't ask her the first time round. Tessa will be my bridesmaid, along with Demi.

'No,' I reply, 'John had to pick Ben up from a sleepover last night so they're going straight to the registry office, too.'

'So shall we make a move, people?' Harry puts his hand on my back, ushering me towards the door.

'Your carriage awaits.' Richard's deep blue eyes sparkle as he gesticulates towards the door and the waiting car outside. Then, as Harry steps outside, Richard shouts out. 'Wow. What's that?'

We all stop at the door and look round. Richard is still in the lounge, hovering over the sideboard.

'I thought you two were broke?' Caroline says, walking towards the unit.

'A gift from Alistair,' Harry says, following her back inside, hands in pockets. 'You haven't heard from him again, have you?'

Caroline shakes her head. 'Nah, he told me his work was done here. The old sod's buggered off. I miss him a bit, to be honest.' She furrows her brows, stroking the top admiringly. 'It's a lovely piece of furniture. What's it like inside?'

I don't need asking twice. I snatch the brown envelope from the coffee table as Harry rolls his eyes and complains that we're going to be late, that we can check out the damned furniture when we get back.

'It'll only take a moment, babe.' I push the key in the lock and we all gasp at the beauty of the interior. The doors inside are fitted with mirrors and three immaculate shelves.

Richard crouches down. 'I'm a bit of an antique enthusiast,' he says, examining the inside closely. 'I reckon this could fetch around one to two grand.' He runs a hand along the side of the inside panel. 'It's in pretty good nick too. I could ask around if you want to sell it. I know a few dealers.'

Harry and I beam at each other. 'That'll pay for a honeymoon.' He smiles. 'That's if there is one. Come on, we're going to be late.'

'Room for two little ones?' A familiar voice calls out.

I spin round on my heel, almost toppling over. 'Mum!' I rush to her and fall into her arms. 'Oh God, don't … my make-up.' I dab at my eyes. 'Harry, did you know anything about this?' Harry shakes his head as he dashes forward to greet them.

'You really thought I'd miss my beautiful daughter's wedding?'

'You look gorgeous, Julie.' Harry gives Mum a kiss on both cheeks.

'Er, I think it's about time you started calling me Mum.' Mum strokes Harry's cheek.

'You look gorgeous, *Mum*.' Harry grins, cupping her hand warmly.

'And darling.' Mum takes a deep, heartfelt breath, eyes brimming with tears. 'You look simply stunning. Doesn't she, Mike?'

'Dazzling,' Mike says, reaching over to kiss me.

My bridal party is now complete. Yippee! Thank you, God.

As we all make for the front door, Richard pulls something out from the lower shelf. 'Hey, it's a violin.' He opens the box as Harry starts pulling at his shirt collar, agitated. 'There's a letter in here addressed to you, I think. Miss E. King?'

'Not for long, if I can help it. Come on, Em,' Harry whines impatiently. 'You can read that when we get back. If we leave it any longer ...' I can still hear the sound of his voice but I'm no longer listening.

I'm at Richard's side. 'Alistair left me a letter?' My heart dances with joy. I tear it open and read it quickly, a smile dancing on my lips. I read the last sentence again and again until it becomes a blur. My hand shoots to my mouth. 'Oh my God,' I cry, 'How could he?'

'Emma?' Caroline says, concerned.

'Is everything OK, darling?' Mum asks, touching my arm gently.

'What is it, Em? I told you to read it later.' Harry snatches the letter from my trembling hand. 'Oh, Jesus Christ.' He cups his hand over his mouth.

'Is someone going to tell us what it says?' Caroline asks worriedly, eyes wide with concern. 'Is it bad news?'

Harry and I still have our hands clamped over our mouths, gawping at each other in disbelief. Unable to speak, he hands the note to Richard.

Richard clears his throat:

Dear Emma,

If you're reading this you've either broken into my house and unlocked the sideboard, or I've popped my clogs. I'm guessing, as you're a woman of great integrity, that it's the latter. You know you were like a daughter to me and I want you to know that I appreciated all you did for me – for making my garden beautiful, for being my chaperone on hospital visits when my own family were too busy to help out their old dad and granddad, for the endless trips to the cemetery to visit my Olive. For doing my shopping, for playing Scrabble with me, and for being my friend. Anyway, as a thank you for all your love and support I wish to leave you a little something to remember me by. My executor has obviously contacted you, which is why you now have the key to the lock. So, without further ado, I leave you this beautiful piece of furniture, which I know you admired from afar. The valuation for the sideboard, attached, is £3700. I also bequeath to you my beloved violin, which I know you ridiculed, but I'll have you know it is one of 450 made. The valuation for my Stradivarius violin, attached, is £1.4 million. You may do with both as you wish. Enjoy your life.

Love always. Alistair. X

Á

Proudly published by Accent Press

www.accentpress.co.uk